JUNK
MILES

www.totallyrandombooks.co.uk

Other titles in the Brenna Blixen series

Double Clutch
Slow Twitch

Also by Liz Reinhardt

Fall Guy

JUNK MILES

LIZ REINHARDT

Definitions

JUNK MILES
A DEFINITIONS BOOK 978 1 782 95137 7

First published in Great Britain by RHCP Digital,
an imprint of Random House Children's Publishers UK
A Random House Group Company

CreateSpace Independent Publishing Platform edition published 2012
RHCP Digital edition published 2013
Definitions edition published 2014

1 3 5 7 9 10 8 6 4 2

The Random House Group Limited supports the Forest Stewardship
Council® (FSC®), the leading international forest-certification organisation.
Our books carrying the FSC label are printed on FSC®-certified paper. FSC is
the only forest-certification scheme supported by the leading environmental
organisations, including Greenpeace. Our paper procurement policy can
be found at www.randomhouse.co.uk/environment

Set in Palatino

Definitions are published by Random House Children's Publishers UK
61–63 Uxbridge Road, London W5 5SA

www.**randomhousechildrens**.co.uk
www.**totallyrandombooks**.co.uk
www.**randomhouse**.co.uk

Addresses for companies within The Random House Group Limited can be
found at: www.randomhouse.co.uk/offices.htm

THE RANDOM HOUSE GROUP Limited Reg. No. 954009

A CIP catalogue record for this book is available from the British Library.

Printed and bound in Great Britain by Clays Ltd, St Ives plc

*To my far, Sonny Hansen. You raised me to value
hard work, gave me access to the big, beautiful world
outside my safe bubble, and showed me, without a doubt,
that a father's love always perseveres — even through
those crazy teen years. Jeg elsker dig.*

Junk Miles: *many miles run at a slow pace – a training strategy used by runners who confuse high mileage counts with improvement.*

Chapter 1

My mother is one of the most thoughtful, loving, caring women in the world. That doesn't mean that she's dumb, and it doesn't mean that she's nice.

I should add that I have no respect for nice mothers, at least not if you use the common teenage definition of 'nice'. My mom doesn't look the other way when I do something she doesn't like. She doesn't try to fit in with friends she doesn't approve of, or with any of my friends at all, for that matter. My mom has high expectations of me, and she drives me with a huge mixture of love, neurotic pressure and guilt.

A whole lot of guilt.

All this ran through my mind Christmas morning, while my head was still bent, my eyes fixed on the open box on my lap. I had a split second to come up with the appropriate face for my mom and Thorsten, my stepfather, and I knew that my initial feelings of shock and disappointment were in no way appropriate. My mother had done exactly what she was best at.

She had rocked my world with her generosity and cunning.

I hope that I can one day be that good.

I made my eyes wide, opened my mouth, and shook my head. 'Paris? Paris!' I grasped the ticket in my hand and jumped up. 'Thank you, thank you, thank you.' I hugged her tight. And I was thankful and genuinely excited.

Mom smiled and kissed me hard. I could feel her triumph. Because this gift wasn't exactly what it seemed.

Mom had plotted this out with all the intelligence of a military tactician, and that was why there was no chance of moping or sulking. I had always wanted to go to Paris, and there was no one in the world I wanted to go with more than Mom.

But there was more to it than just that. I had told Mom and Thorsten about my super-sexy, super-awesome boyfriend, Jake, several weeks back, and they had handled it really well: no yelling, no threats, no unreasonable restrictions. They had even included him in things. Jake went out with us for my birthday, they gave him a gift on his, invited him over for Thanksgiving, and he was coming over later that afternoon for Christmas dinner. I didn't take advantage of their willingness to be nice about Jake. I am, after all, my mother's daughter, and I knew that I had to keep Jake distanced from them or they would start to find things about him that weren't 'good enough' for me. Well, *Mom* would start to find things. Because Jake isn't exactly what she wants for me, and my mother does not even consider second best when it comes to me.

I understand where she's coming from, but it's still constricting. And since I wanted to stay with Jake, I limited the time I spent with him, even though my body physically ached with the need to be near him sometimes. Cheesy as it might sound, that's the best way I can explain it. I thought I had done a pretty good job of disguising just how obsessed I was with him and how deliciously he had taken over my life.

But Mom started watching me, in exactly the way I knew she would. She looked for anything that would provide evidence that Jake was breaking my heart, making me sad, keeping me up too late, stopping me from pursuing my interests, hogging my company, keeping me away from other friends, or any other trumped-up charge. In her mind, she filed any shred of evidence away to digest later.

If I woke up with dark circles under my eyes

because Jake and I had had an amazing conversation on the phone the night before, Mom narrowed her own eyes and made a mental check. If I arranged to go out with Kelsie and she cancelled, and I went out with Jake instead, Mom noted it and frowned. Little details grew and compounded until Mom had, in her mind, a real reason to orchestrate a campaign against Jake, or at least against me being so wrapped up in him.

Mom was a huge proponent of 'dating lots of different people', 'keeping your options open', and 'focusing on yourself'. All sound good in theory. Until you meet someone like Jake Kelly and have to think about living without hearing his sweet laugh or smelling his clean, minty smell or feeling his arms tight around you. Thinking about him made my heart skip and surge. This was love.

And my mom was no fool. She wasn't about to drive a wedge between us by harping on about Jake or voicing her neurotic concerns. My mother was too brilliant for that kind of novice work.

'It's part of a program with my college, honey.' Mom took out a pamphlet and handed it to me eagerly. 'They want to give the tutors a chance to scout prospective study-abroad locations before they choose them, so we're allowed to bring family members and check out the museums, local universities . . . Oh, sweetie, it's going to be so incredible.' She hugged me again, and I took a deep breath.

'Mom, this sounds so great.' I swallowed hard and prepared for the worst. 'So, when do we go?'

'We leave the day after tomorrow! We'll be gone for a full week, just past your winter break. I've already cleared it at your schools if you need some jet-lag recovery time on the way back, so don't worry about that.' She put an arm around me and squeezed me close.

'Mom?' I dug deep and tried to find the courage to argue on Jake's behalf. She looked at me and the look was new-knife sharp. I swallowed back my arguments like the weak coward I often was around her. 'I have to pack right now. What's Paris like in December?'

'Chilly.' The flinty light was gone from her eyes. She took both my hands in hers. 'Go ahead and get packing, honey.'

'Thank you, Mom. So much.' I modulated my voice carefully to keep it happy, and I hugged her again. 'This will be amazing.'

And I hoped that by saying it, I would force myself to mean it. Because as I walked quickly to my recently redecorated room, I felt the itchy pain of tears pricking behind my eyes. I tried not to think too hard about the fact that I would miss New Year's Eve with Jake. It would have been my first-ever romantic New Year's kiss.

In my room, with its duck-egg-blue walls and poppy-covered bed linen, the Chagall and Cassatt posters hanging in wooden frames, the softly glowing paper lamps, and the books piled everywhere, I popped my iPod onto its dock and put on some happy packing music, even though I wanted to scroll through my specially made teen-angst mix and let it all envelop me in something suitably dreary. I started to put piles of clothes here and there and took out my brand-new pink leather traveling bag, the one I had unwrapped this morning and hugged Thorsten for. I didn't feel any ill will towards Fa. He was a puppet in Mom's very capable hands, no doubt about that.

I didn't feel any ill will at all, not really. I picked up the picture of me and Mom in front of the big tree in Rockefeller Square. We were both rosy-cheeked and pink-nosed with cute hats on, our arms around each other. I knew that what my mom was feeling stemmed from a lot of really deep emotions and events that all proved the one thing I've known my entire life; my mom loves me so fiercely, it's scary.

Mom had me when she was barely out of high school. The guy, my father, had left her high and dry when she got pregnant. He was her boyfriend, and as far as I can tell, she had believed this guy was the love of her life. I knew that she assumed what Jake and I had was very similar to what she thought she'd had with my biological father. It took her a long time to get her life back on track after him. I knew it was the ghost of that experience that made her uber-protective.

Mom never told me much about the whole thing with my father, but I knew she felt a lot of resentment toward my grandparents. She felt like they should have been looking out for her more, making sure she was on the right track, that she had the right backup.

It was what she was doing for me right now, or at least what she thought she was doing for me. So I shouldn't be upset.

But I was.

And I had to do the one thing that I really, really didn't want to do. Especially on Christmas Day, knowing the kinds of Christmases Jake had experienced every year before. But every second that I moped and put off packing, every second that I chickened out about calling him was one second that I took away from our time together, and I couldn't do that.

I was always a good packer. Thorsten, Mom and I traveled a lot, so I knew how to roll my clothes, how to pick things that will layer well and that will move from casual to fancy easily. I knew how to make a little bag of accessories that would dress everything up. I had a special tiny cross-over purse with a wide zippered strap to keep my passport and anything else important in. Once I'd laid out what I wanted to take on my bed, pared down the pile and removed what I knew I didn't really want to take, I rolled the clothes up and put them in the suitcase. I picked up the phone and turned my music up a little bit. I'd packed so fast that I had time to call Jake and give him a little bit of a heads-up before he got here.

'Merry Christmas, Brenna.' His voice was silky and deep on the phone, and I felt my mouth go dry at the sound of it. I loved that voice.

'Merry Christmas, Jake.' I smiled despite the bad news I was about to deliver.

'Did Santa leave you some good stuff?' Jake asked. He sounded happy, inexplicably.

I had been to his house early on Christmas Eve, before the candlelight service and Christmas caroling at our church. His father bought a small, dry turkey with two wilted vegetable sides and mashed potatoes – a veritable feast as far as the Kellys were concerned. We sat on the couch and ate off plates balanced on our laps while we watched *It's a Wonderful Life*. Jake's father barely spoke to me. He didn't seem mean, just socially uncomfortable and nervous. When the movie was over, he got up and announced that he was going out bowling. Jake and I had a few hours before I had to go home, so we snuggled in his room and talked and laughed under the blankets. His dad kept the house at twenty degrees in the winter, so snuggling was pretty much a necessity.

'I got a lot of great stuff.' I pawed through my bras and underwear one more time, making sure I picked out the nicest ones. This was a trip to Paris, after all. 'Thorsten got me an awesome new design program for the computer. Um, did you get anything good?'

He laughed like I'd made a joke. 'I got my socks, flashlight and a fifty. I told you, babe, it's what I get every year.'

'Well, I got you some good stuff.' I tried very hard not to get aggravated at Jake's dad on the most peaceful day of the year. How could he be so cheap with his own son? And I didn't mean cheap monetarily, although that was true, too. Jake was this vibrant, amazing guy, but his dad put no effort whatsoever into making things good or nice for him. It was just basic necessities as far as Jake's dad was concerned, and he didn't even stretch his imagination much there.

'I can't wait to see what you got me. I'm still trying to get over my birthday gift.'

I had custom-made him a motocross jersey. Jake

was really into dirt bikes, and when he raced during his last big amateur competition, I had taken a bunch of action shots of him. I transferred them to the computer, played with the images, and made them into really high-quality iron-ons. I'd had the shirt ordered and put his last name and the images on it – it was pretty professional looking.

'It wasn't a big deal.' I sat on my bed and unknotted a tangle of necklaces from my jewelry box. 'It was just a shirt.'

'And the rest of the outfit to match, and a helmet that you custom-designed. And the decals for my bike.' He sighed a happy, adorable sigh. 'Don't downplay it, Bren. It was awesome.'

'Well, it all had to match.' I moved on to my bracelets. 'And it was cool that that big dirt-bike magazine was at Dingmans when you won that race.'

'I can't believe I got a spread.' Jake laughed. 'It was your design. It was good luck.'

'I know I'm pretty great, but don't you think it had something to do with the fact that you won the race?' I smiled at the memory, a little girly pride pricking me nicely. 'Like by a mile.'

'By a couple yards,' he corrected humbly. Typical Jake. 'Yeah, I guess. You just—' He stopped. 'All right, I didn't want to get all mushy on you, but what the hell? I never had someone care about me the way you do. It makes me feel like I could do anything. Like you give me the confidence to do whatever I want. You don't know how incredible it's been for me to have you in my life.'

And now my heart felt like it was singing and tearing apart at the same time. How could I help but fall in love with a guy like this? Jake was the whole package, no question.

We had plans for winter break. Since Jake turned seventeen this November, he'd been cutting some of his hours at Zinga's, the farm where he worked. He'd been a full-time employee when he needed to keep a farmer's license, which was a special permit that let younger drivers have more driving freedom if they worked on a farm, but since he'd gotten his regular license, he was able to scale back and spend more time with me. This break was supposed to be a chance for us to hang out together as much as humanly possible. How was I going to tell him that we were going to have no time together at all?

'Jake, you don't need me around to do all of that,' I pointed out. 'You're too hard on yourself. You've always had the talent and the drive. You just need to believe in your potential.'

It was an old speech on my part, and one I didn't

love making. I've never been great at pep talks in general, and I hated when people didn't just admit it when they're good at something. But in Jake's case, I always made an exception because I got the feeling that he honestly didn't understand his potential. So I tried to reassure him without rolling my eyes too much.

'You can have whatever theory you want.' I could hear his goofy grin over the phone. 'I know that it's all Brenna Blixen magic. I'm just glad you had some sort of mental breakdown and decided to date me.'

'Jake.' I giggled. It was easy to dismiss all of his humble talk when he had such a good sense of humor about the whole thing.

'So, what's up with tonight? It's gonna be dressy like Thanksgiving was, right?'

He had worn his blue button-down shirt to Thanksgiving . . . and my birthday dinner . . . and every other occasion he'd come to my house for. Jake's wardrobe was depressingly limited, but I had remedied that.

'Look under your bed.' I bounced up and down on my springy mattress, excited despite the impending bad news that I knew I had to tell him.

'What?' I heard him put the phone down and move around in his bland, boring little room. He picked the phone back up. 'Bren, what is all this? How did you get it here?'

'I sneaked them into your room in my big purse. You know the one. You make fun of it all the time.' I smiled with pride. 'Open your presents up.'

I heard him tearing wrapping paper. 'Wow! Um, these are from Banana Republic. That's just a stupid amount of money to spend on clothes for me.'

'Jake. I love you in blue, but if I'd had to look at that button-down one more time, I was going to have to rip it off you.'

I jumped up and ran my hand over the many, many gorgeous outfits hanging in my closet, and it was such a deeply satisfying feeling. I was well aware Jake probably didn't feel it in quite the same way, but there had to be some sense of happiness when he looked at his new clothes.

'Uh, you did. The last three times I wore it. I thought you were ripping it off me because of how good I looked in it.'

'Shut up.' But I smiled from ear to ear. I loved that I found him so irresistible. 'Do you like them? I kept the receipts, so you can take them back if you want.'

'No way. You have the better judgment in clothes and stuff. If you think I'm gonna look hot in this stuff, I'm wearing it. Not that you need any encouragement.'

'Ha ha.' I rolled my eyes. 'At least you dropped the whole humble-guy thing.'

'Well, I think you exaggerate about how smart and great I am. But as far as my hotness goes? There's no debating that.' I heard him opening another package. 'Seriously, you just quadrupled my wardrobe.'

'Well, considering you had less than ten pieces of clothing in total, that wasn't very hard to do.'

I took a few pair of shoes out and assessed them. Shoes were always big space-takers in luggage. But as much as I loved going through my awesome clothes, I knew I needed to come clean and tell Jake about Paris. But our conversation was so fun and sweet, I was greedy for a few more minutes.

'You spent a lot of money.' Now his voice had an edge of grumpiness to it.

'I made a killing at the last two Folly shows,' I said, trying to sound casual.

I designed shirts for a local band, Folly, and got a cut of the profits they made from the sales. It was only a small amount per shirt, but it added up. Especially now their fan base had been growing in the last few months after a couple of incredible shows.

'You should be saving that money. Aren't you going to Ireland this summer?' he reminded me. 'You're going to need it, Brenna.'

I sighed. A study trip in Ireland was looming, and I was upbeat about my chances of getting into the program, but not positive. Mom and Jake, on the other hand, had no doubts and talked about it as if it were already set in stone. 'It's not for sure.' I fell back on my bed, pushing my case to one side with my elbow. 'Rotary still has two rounds of interviews. I can't be sure about it until the end of next month.'

'Yeah, like there's any way they're going to reject you,' he scoffed.

And that was why Jake was so amazing and so frustrating at the same time. He really did believe that I was pretty perfect. If I told him that I was going to quit school to be a model or a racing driver or an astronaut, he would not have one negative thing to say. He would be supportive and wonderful and ... Jake.

'So, speaking of Europe—' I started.

And stopped.

'Yeah?' I heard his steady breathing, the happiness in his voice, and I didn't want Paris. I wanted Jake! I wanted Jake all winter break. I wanted to drive around in his big blue truck with no particular place to go. I wanted him to take me ice-skating. I wanted to eat out at our favorite Japanese place and go see late movies and talk on the phone all night. And if I worked on him long and hard, I knew I could get him to sneak over, climb in my window and sleep with me, spooned around me all night and into the gray morning.

'Jake, I got another big present today.' I sat up and pushed the fringe off my forehead. He waited. 'I got a ticket to Paris.'

'France?' Jake's voice rang with more genuine enthusiasm than I'd been able to muster.

'Yes.' I was about to spill the details, but his excitement for me eclipsed my attempts.

'That's perfect, babe. You've wanted to go there for ever.' Jake knew how much I wanted to see Paris. 'You and Mom going?' It was weird to hear him call her 'Mom', but also kind of cute. He didn't do it to her face. When he talked to her it was always strictly 'Mrs Blixen'. He just referred to her as 'Mom' with me.

'Yes.' I dragged the word out slowly.

'Cool.' He seemed actually cool with it. 'When?'

'Day after tomorrow.' I rushed the words out – like ripping a Band-Aid off in one shot – and winced. In the second of silence Jake took to collect his thoughts or quietly freak out or hang up on me, I added the clincher that was sure to break his heart. And mine. 'And I'll stay all winter break.'

Jake let out a long sigh. I knew what he felt. I pictured a big, bright, shiny balloon suddenly punctured by a sharp needle. 'It's so good for you and Mom to do this together. I'll be able to pick up more work at Zinga's. Can I call you?' There was an almost unnoticeable shake to his words, but leave it to Jake to put the best possible spin on the situation.

'Jake, you can be a little less perfect about this.' I fell back on my bed with relief. I'd prepared myself for a tantrum because that is what I would have done. But Jake was on a different level when it came to cool and calm. He was like a saint. Or Buddha.

'I'm not gonna lie.' His voice sounded thick, like he was talking around a lump in his throat. 'I'm gonna miss you so much. I was really excited about seeing a lot of you. A lot of you,' he repeated. His voice went husky, and my body screamed for him.

Why? Why did the choice have to be between Paris and Jake? How evil could life be? Correction: how evil could *Mom* be? God, her love hurt.

'I'll miss you so much.' I closed my eyes and let the hot tears fill right up to my lashes and drip out the sides of my eyes. 'I almost don't want to go.'

'Are you kidding?' he practically screamed. 'You can't ever not do something because of me, OK? Your mom already thinks that I'm going to drag you down. If you didn't do this, she would assume I'd told you not to, or that you didn't go because of me. And

I want you to go as much as she does. Maybe more.'

And I had nothing at all to say. Because Jake was dead on.

Mom had already come out and said that Jake wasn't headed in the same direction that I was. She peppered that lecture with lots of nice compliments about Jake's good manners, his work ethic, his good looks, his kindness, his careful driving. But the message had been that all of that didn't make up for what he didn't have: the right upbringing and a solid drive for education. She would use any excuse to point out how Jake was 'holding me back'.

I felt like Jake had so much potential, there was no box to put him in. Mom felt people couldn't escape their fates or what they were born to do. Mom said that I was too young to understand, that I was too idealistic. It made me feel like arguing, but what could I say? I *was* too young. And I guess too idealistic.

But I didn't want to be some hard-hearted gold-digger with a checklist and an unwarranted sense of superiority. What was so wrong with loving someone good and kind and different? What was so wrong with believing that someone can be more than they seem? It just wasn't an argument I could have with my mom. We couldn't see eye to eye on this one, but I was trying really hard not to be an average asshole teenager and take her opinion seriously.

'It's not so long.' Jake's voice was calm in my ears, smoothing out all the wild thoughts clawing around and tearing at my brain. 'Don't be upset. And we get to see each other tonight, right?'

'Yes,' I pouted.

'What time did you say?' I heard the springs on Jake's bed creak as he stood up.

'Four.'

'Three?' he repeated. 'Let's just say I misheard.'

I smiled a tiny smile. 'I love you, Jake.' I sighed. 'You can get a phone card. Or I can get international calling on my cell this month.'

'Can you do that?' His voice bubbled with hope. I'd let him down so hard, but he was still happy with the little I offered.

'To be able to talk to you? You know I'll do whatever.' I wiped my cheeks dry with my fingers.

'You're the best. Go pack. I'll be over before you know it, all right? I love you, Bren.'

'I love you.' We clicked off, and I felt like a lifeline had broken. Without Jake I was lost.

But I put a big smile on my face and went out to the kitchen. Mom had wrestled the huge turkey into the oven early that morning. She was now peeling the

19

potatoes over the sink. I went to a drawer and took out the extra peeler, the old metal one that dug into the skin on your hands when you used it.

'Hey, sweetie,' Mom said. She was already dressed to the nines in her red cashmere sweater, a present from Thorsten, and a black pencil skirt. She had on black high heels and the gold Virgin Mary necklace I'd seen her admire in Macy's a few weeks earlier and had picked up for her Christmas gift. I knew she'd love it. Her light brown hair was curled, and it was already almost down to her shoulders, grown out since her last haircut. So pretty. She was just so pretty. She gave me a kiss. 'You don't need to do this. Go pack.'

'I did!' I cringed when I realized how cheesy and bright it sounded. It sounded artificial. 'I think I'm all done.'

'I'm really glad we're doing this.' Mom put a wet, potato-flecked hand on my arm. Her voice was getting that lecture quality to it, and I wanted to dodge it.

'Me too.' I picked up a hot potato and popped it from one hand to the other to cool it before I gouged and scraped. I hated peeling potatoes. I hated lectures, but my forced enthusiasm made Mom suspicious.

'I know you and Jake probably made plans. But this is a once-in-a-lifetime opportunity. The time to travel is now and for the next few years. You have to live your life, sweetheart. You can't do everything based around a high-school relationship.' Her peeler hung idle in her fingers as she talked.

I had to bite my lips and peel harder. If I answered, I was going to say something she'd disagree with. If I was quiet, maybe whatever deity there was would have mercy on me and make the lecture stop. But then Mom surprised me.

Her voice got very low and a little watery. 'Your biological father was a guy who seemed so perfect. Nice and kind and really smart. I felt lucky to have him around. But when it came down to it, he wasn't the right guy for me, sweetie. Or for you. He didn't have what it took, and if I'd been more independent, I wouldn't have fallen apart like I did.'

I held the cooling potato, peeled to a nub, in one hand and stayed still. Now I was hoping that the deity would ignore my former prayer and just let her continue. Who was he? Who was this dad of mine? She was so quiet I didn't know for sure if she would continue.

'He kept right on going, after us.' Her voice was tissue-paper soft. I could see her gray-blue eyes, dewy with tears. Her lips made a wobbly line and her small hands shook a little around the brown potato skin. 'And I hated him for it. I hated him so much. But in the end, I learned from him. I learned that it's important to have your own thing, your own life. I'm not saying he was a good person. He had a lot to learn about compassion and respect and love.' Her voice was wet with sadness. 'But he knew all about being selfish. It's something we have to learn a bit about.'

And I didn't say, *But Jake and I aren't you and my father*. And I didn't say, *This is a totally different situation*. And I didn't say, *Tell me more about what happened*. Because I knew that every one of those things would ruin this weird spell she was casting with her velvety soft voice. And I didn't know how much I believed any of those things or how much more I really wanted to know.

'Because it's hard to balance compassion and love for others with selfishness,' Mom continued. 'I think, just by nature, you've got the loving thing down. So now I need to teach you to be selfish. And I need to see you experience a whole range of things, so you have a choice. We tend to get too comfortable too quickly, honey, and that's no way to make any big decision.' Her eyes lightened like a soft blue sky after a summer storm. She smiled and took my potato-caked hand in hers. 'Get dressed. I bet Jake will show up a little early. You two can have a nice dinner.'

Mom kissed my cheek and I knew I had the imprint

of her lipstick on my skin. I floated to the bathroom, rinsed my hands, and peered at my reflection, marked by my mother's lips. I needed to do what my mom asked me. I needed to listen to her, no matter how much I wanted to ignore what she was saying. I needed to prove to her that I wasn't her from that time. I wasn't the same teenager she had been, and I wasn't my father; she had raised me better than that.

I realized that my mom was scared about this. She was afraid for me, and I had to show her that I would be fine. Jake wasn't like my father, but the only way Mom would understand that was if I went with her and proved it. If Jake and I both proved it. We could do this. No words would change her mind. She had to see it for herself.

Proving that I wasn't just like my mom would be harder. How could I deny that I loved being in love with Jake? And I would probably fall apart a little without him. Wasn't that normal? And we had been spending a lot of time together, but that was because we wanted to, not because I couldn't hang out on my own. Wasn't it?

Well, at least I knew that Jake was just as loving as I was. He was not selfish. He wasn't. Was he? My mom's lectures tended to do this to me. They took a perfectly rational, reasonable situation and turned it on its head. Was she right? Was I too comfortable?

I pushed that all out of my head for right now. I had an afternoon with Jake to look forward to.

And, on the bright side, it was a trip to Paris! I loved to travel, no matter how much leaving home would make me ache this time. It was a trip to Paris with my mom, and it would be wonderful. When I got home, I could fall right back into Jake's arms, and Mom could be less worried and less critical.

At least I hoped that would happen.

Chapter 2

I went to my room and took out my dress, a scarlet red
silk wraparound with cap sleeves. I loved it, and it was
kind of my first adult Christmas dress. I had black
stockings with a line sewn up the back like the old-
fashioned silk style, and a pair of really cute black
strappy heels, which were uncomfortable enough that
I was glad I would only be wearing them around the
house. I had just cut my fringe, so it was right above
my eyebrows, where I liked it. I put on a black silk
hairband and the rest of my hair up into a carefully
messy bun, which is deceptively hard to do. A
thousand bobby pins later, and it looked really good,
in a windblown way.

I put my make-up on and a little jewelry, including
the silver 'B' necklace Jake had given me for my birthday and the pearl-drop earrings Mom and Thorsten
gave me for Christmas. I also had a new watch with a
wide leather strap. I loved watches, but hardly anyone

wore them anymore. Most people my age just used their cell phones to tell the time. But I loved them no matter how old-fashioned they were. I had at least a dozen, and wore them all the time.

The minute I finished, I heard the doorbell ring, and felt a leap of joy. When I looked down at my watch, I saw that it was only two-thirty. I knew Jake had to be more upset than he was pretending about my leaving because he was usually really careful about respecting Mom's timetables. Mom was already at the door, being unusually nice and kissing Jake's cheek. I realized then that she felt a little guilty about this whole thing, too. I shook my head. How could Paris cause so much upset? Paris!

Jake looked incredibly hot. And it actually had very little to do with my excellent taste in clothes. Jake was the kind of guy who would look hot in just about anything, since he was tall, with delectably chiseled muscles and a face that set girls drooling wherever we went. But today he was wearing his gray dress pants and a black crewneck sweater. It was cashmere, which I'm sure he didn't notice or care about, but it made me happy that he had something other than threadbare cotton or denim. His boots were new, too, a birthday gift from his ever-practical father. Dress shoes weren't part of Jake's mindset, and I knew that buying them would just be a waste of my efforts. He was handing my mother a wrapped package.

I hadn't realized he would get her a gift. Part of me was shocked that he hadn't asked for my help with it at all. I wondered what he had got her.

'Oh, Jake!' she cried. It was a pair of bright purple leather gloves. They were almost funny, but in a way that was just plain adorable.

'I know they're kind of a weird color.' Jake shifted his weight from one foot to the other and stuffed his hands in his pockets. 'But I just thought that if anyone could pull them off, it would be you, Mrs Blixen.'

Mom's eyes glistened again. 'How thoughtful. I love them.' My mother moved in for a hug.

'And now your hands will be warm in Paris.' Jake put his arms around her in an awkward reciprocation of her offered hug.

'Brenna told you?' Mom asked, surprised.

'She called right away. She was really excited. I am, too. I mean, for you two. It's so great that Brenna gets to travel so much, and I know how much she's been missing you since you moved back to the States and you got your job and life just got crazy.' He was rambling now, but I could see Mom get emotional, and I felt the dangerous burn in my own eyes. I had to sternly remind myself of just how crazy I would look with my new Bad Girl mascara running down my cheeks, and held the tears back. 'I hope you two have a blast.'

Mom hugged him again, murmuring kind Christmassy things. My heart swelled a little. I walked up to them, and Jake looked over at me. His eyes went wide.

'Wow!' He licked his lips quickly, like he was nervous. 'Bren, you look incredible.'

And now Mom was eating out of his hand. All you really had to do to get my mom to like you was be super complimentary to me, and Jake was a natural at that.

'You look pretty good, yourself, Kelly.' I walked around him. He turned to watch me as I circled him, like he couldn't stand to take his eyes off of me. Oh, Jake!

'Thank you.' He turned back to Mom. 'Brenna got me some new clothes. I guess she was tired of my five T-shirts.'

'Well, if I'd seen that blue shirt one more time, I was going to take you shopping myself.' Mom laughed. 'I mean, you're a handsome young man. Take Brenna's advice, and you'll have to beat the girls away.' I saw through her weird comments the kind of tough love that she usually restricted to me alone.

'No worries there.' Jake was completely oblivious to my mother's motives. 'I've already got the best girl there is.'

Mom just smiled. 'Bren, why don't you and Jake grab a cup of cocoa from the stove and sit by the fire? I'm almost done in the kitchen.'

I got two mugs and hurried to the living room with Jake, thankful for Mom's thoughtfulness despite her odd 'date other people' messages.

Our fireplace was set in a big stone-covered wall that went around to the kitchen, so Jake and I were able to sit on the other side in semi-privacy. We sat on the couch, and he put our mugs down and took me in his arms. Our nearly silent kisses were so ravenous, I was instantly turned on.

'You're so beautiful.' He pulled his mouth away and held my upper arms hard in his hands. 'You look like Christmas.'

I laughed and kissed him really softly and silently, since Mom and Thorsten were just around the corner. 'Thanks. I got you other stuff. Do you want to see it?'

'I don't want you spending all of your money on me.' He looked really serious, his gray eyes wide and his mouth set in a line. He was so hot, it was hard to breathe steadily around him.

'I didn't. I mean, I made some of it. Anyway, it's

Christmas, so stop arguing about it.' I went under the tree and found some silver-wrapped packages. In our crazy Christmas-centered house, each person got assigned a different colored wrapping paper. Mom was red, Thorsten was green, I got gold, and Jake got silver. Mom always went a little crazy with Christmas decorations.

Jake laughed. 'Man, your house is like a magazine.' He craned his neck and took it all in. 'Christmas music, cocoa, a fire, that big-ass tree, all the dinner smells. I'm glad I get to do Christmas here.'

I thought about this morning – how depressing it must have been for him in comparison to my morning. It made me too sad to think about it for long, so I didn't.

'I'm glad you're doing your Christmas here, too.' I carried his shiny presents over. 'Open them.'

He undid the paper so carefully it was ridiculous. A full minute into the first one, I lost my cool. 'Jake! It's just paper! We're not saving it, so rip it open!'

He smiled. 'Fine, bossy pants.' He ripped it with exaggerated relish. 'Hey, a watch!' He took it out and put it on right away. I normally hated it when people bought gifts that were things they liked, but I thought my watch obsession had a lot of merit. 'Thanks.' He pulled me over for a long kiss.

I also got him a new sketch pad and some really good pencils, and the rest of my English reading on CD. Jake liked to keep up with me, but his dyslexia made it impossible. I liked to be able to talk to him about the books I was reading, so he listened along.

'Some of them look so awful,' I apologized. 'Oh, and this one is super hard, so I recorded it for you to make up for it.'

'Like, you read it?' He turned over the CD case with its obviously homemade insert.

'Yeah. I have a program on my computer.' The truth is, I have every program on my computer. Thorsten got me a laptop so jacked, I don't think secret government agents have the kind of programming I have. 'Anyway, it's pretty short, but *Ethan Frome* is just plain torture, so I hope the fact that I'm reading it makes it a little easier to swallow.'

Jake crunched me in a bear hug. 'Thank you,' he said, his voice a little husky. Jake never had anyone really care about him or think about him, so this kind of gift-receiving was a little emotional for him. 'I left your stuff on the porch. I'll be right back.' He ran out the door, my mom glancing at him curiously. He came back with a big bag.

Jake got me a bottle of the perfume I'd tried when we were out shopping one time and loved, every Jane

Austen movie made on DVD, a sketch book with a bright blue cover and little brown birds flying on it, and finally, right at the bottom of the bag was one tiny box. Jake sat on the floor in front of me on the couch. When he fished that box out, he was on his knees and my heart leaped. I felt like I might faint and wanted to tell him 'no' right then.

'Jake, what is that?' My voice shook hard.

He seemed oblivious to my nervous dread.

'I just thought of you when I saw it.' His ears burned a little red. He pushed the box into my hands, but I dropped it twice because they were shaking so much. Finally, he just plucked it from me and opened it himself. He popped the top of the box off, and there was a ring.

I felt myself freaking out. This was a lot. This was too much. Mom and Thorsten would freak. I wasn't ready. I didn't want to look at it.

But it didn't have a stone or anything, and I felt a hot flush of relief about that.

'Jake . . .' I began, but he cut me off.

'It's called a posey ring. People who were . . . in love exchanged them, like, a long time ago. It says, *Here is my heart, guard it well*, in French. Weird, right? I didn't even know you were going to Paris.' His laugh was nervous. He looked up into my face.

'Don't freak, Bren. It's not like an engagement ring.'

I laughed a little breathily. 'Duh. I mean, of course. We're still in high school!' My voice sounded on the verge of hysterical.

I picked the ring out of the box carefully. It was shiny gold, the words etched around the outside: *A Vila Mon Coeur, Gardi Li Mo.* I traced my finger over the metal, loving the feel of the bumps and grooves despite my general unease about it being a ring.

I looked at it for a long time before I slipped it on the tip of my right index finger, and Jake took my hand and pushed it on all the way.

'I shouldn't have bought that one, huh?' He held my fingertips and didn't look up from the ring on my hand. His ring on my hand. It sent a little shiver down my neck, even as I told myself that it was silly to think that way. It was just a piece of jewelry! No big deal! No hidden meanings!

Right?

And when I looked at his face, crestfallen with worry that he'd given me the wrong gift, I stuffed all of my crazy neuroses aside and let him know that I loved how much he loved me and the way he showed me. Even if it was overwhelming sometimes.

'It's so beautiful.' I cupped his face and kissed his gorgeous model-perfect mouth. 'I love it.'

'Good.' He nodded, relieved. 'I'm not great at picking out gifts.'

'Are you crazy? These are perfect. Thank you.' I waited a moment. 'So, how did you pick the wording on it?'

'They had all different ones. The girl behind the counter told me what they meant. Like, *I am yours, you are mine*. Or, *All I desire*. They all made sense. This one just made the best sense. I feel like I can trust you with my heart. I guess.' He ducked his head shyly. 'Jesus, Brenna, you make me say the sappiest crap.'

'You love it.' I wanted to say whatever would break the awkward energy in the air. I was about to kiss him again.

Mom and Thorsten came out just then. Jake quickly broke away from me and started picking up wrapping paper and putting it in the bag that he'd packed the gifts in. He held out a box to Thorsten, who opened it and got all excited over a little pouch of tobacco.

'My dad picked it up for me,' Jake explained. 'It's a special blend. Something they still pick by hand. Brenna told me you smoke a pipe, so I thought you might like it.'

Thorsten slapped him on the back and smiled happily. He and Mom looked at the gifts, and Mom didn't even make a big deal out of the ring, though I caught her looking at it a few times with her mouth twisted disapprovingly. They gave Jake a new pair of riding gloves. It was the only part of his bike gear I hadn't given him for his birthday.

'These are great.' Jake turned them over admiringly. I had been with them when they bought them, so I knew they were amazing. You can buy a whole spectrum of gloves for dirt biking, and, of course, Mom and Thorsten had gone to the top of the range for them. He hugged Mom tightly, then bypassed Thorsten's hand and hugged him, too.

I felt a little choked up, and I think my parents did, too. We all sat in silence for a long minute before Mom said, 'Oh! Dinner!'

We went to the dining room, laughing. We all walked back and forth to the table with food, way too much food. Thorsten got us together and took pictures, snapping a few himself, then setting up the camera so we could all get in one together. Jake took over and made the three of us squeeze up for a family shot.

I tried to stretch the dinner out as long as I could. Jake ate so much that even Thorsten, who is a bottom-less pit, was impressed. We made conversation and laughed. Mom and Thorsten drank wine and she relaxed a little, then a lot. We laughed more, and then

Mom brought out apple pie for dessert. It was delicious and cozy and wonderful.

Jake and I offered to clear up and Mom and Thorsten went to the living room to watch an old movie on AMC.

'Wash or dry?' Jake picked up the sponge in one hand and the tea towel in the other.

'Normally I'd pick dry.' I rubbed my chin as if I had to give this a lot of thought. 'But I don't know if I can trust you to wash the way my mom would approve of.'

'You doubt my abilities?' Jake teased.

'Definitely.' I turned on the water and started to soap everything up. I had one of my mom's crazy aprons on, a red plaid one with a Santa head on it.

'You look really pretty.' Jake leaned one hip on the counter and took the first dish I handed him, his eyes on me the entire time.

'You just like to see me slaving over a hot sink in a crazy apron.' I stuck my tongue out at him.

'I'm gonna miss you a lot.' Jake dried the plate with his eyes cast down.

'I wish the timing was different.' I looked down at the food-encrusted plates in the bubbly water.

He put a hand on my shoulder and squeezed gently. 'No matter when it was, I would be sad you were going. But you have to go. Every time. You can't put this stuff off.'

Sometimes I was scared Jake wasn't going to be into what I was into. Sometimes I was really scared that I was going to outgrow him. I couldn't really imagine anything worse than growing away from Jake, but the reality was that he and I didn't have remotely similar goals when it came to things like travel and education. I cringed.

Was Mom right?

'Maybe next year we could go somewhere together.' I willed Jake to home in on my get-independent plans. Did it still count as his goal if I suggested going? Was it independent if Jake came along? Was it weird to think we could pull off a European trip together? Like my mother wouldn't freak out too much over that.

Jake looked at me for a long time. I could tell he was wrestling between the desire to do something new and all the fear that went along with doing just that. 'How much money would I need?'

I shook my head. 'I've never really paid for it when I traveled.' I felt a little embarrassed admitting that.

'Of course not.' Jake pulled his eyebrows together. 'How do I get a passport? I need one, right?'

'You do.' I scrubbed the gravy boat, rinsed it, and

handed it to him. 'There's an application online you can download. You have to get it notarized and get your picture put on it.'

'It doesn't sound any harder than a driver's license.' He made neat stacks of the dishes as he dried. 'So, where are we going, Bren?'

'Where do you want to go?' I squirted more soap into the water.

'How about Australia?' His eyes were bright as, I imagined, kangaroos and wallabies jumped through his head.

I honestly hated to shoot his wallabies but... 'That's, like, a twenty-hour flight.'

'You're kidding.' He stopped drying, and I could almost see his brain visualizing where Australia was in relation to the States.

'It's on the other side of the world, Jake. Not that we can't go. Maybe we should just think closer. Like Europe.' I closed my eyes and focused on the first amazing, beautiful image that popped into my head. It was Venice. 'I've always wanted to see Italy.'

'That would be incredible.'

The kangaroos hopped away, and I imagined Jake thinking of marble statues, cobblestoned streets, and the Colosseum. 'Wow! Italy. OK, Italy next year. It's a deal.' He stuck his hand out, I took mine out of the soapsuds, and we shook.

Next year. I'd be a junior plus and Jake would be a senior. I hoped we would still be dating, but just thinking like that made me scared to death I would jinx something. Would my mom and Thorsten ever agree to it? Right now it was just fun to think about. There was no way I was going to let the whole plan get bogged down with possible problems.

Jake rubbed his thumb over the gold posey ring on my finger. 'What are you going to see in Paris?'

I shrugged. 'Mom and I have barely had time to talk about it. But the flight is long, so I'm sure she'll fill me in.'

'You'll take pictures?' Jake asked. He let my hand go reluctantly, and I went back to scrubbing the dishes.

'Of course.' I imagined the two of us looking through my pictures together when I got back. 'Will you take pictures?'

'Of Sussex County?' He shook his head. 'Why?'

'I don't know. I'll miss almost two weeks of Sussex County in the winter. You can document it for me. Like a fortnight in the life of Jake Kelly.' I slid my eyes over to him. 'Or you don't have to. It was just a thought.'

'No.' He smiled from behind the cabinet door as he stacked clean, dry dishes in it. 'I'll do it. You can look at them when you're having trouble sleeping.'

'You're not that boring.' I finished the final pot and came to help him finish drying and putting away.

'You're delusional. My life is painfully dull.' He took a pan out of my hands and pulled me in for a kiss. 'And soon I'll have photographic proof.'

We finished the dishes in good-natured quiet, then Jake got more pie and we settled in the living room. It was nice having Jake around. I had grown up an only child, and Christmas tended to be pretty quiet at my house. This was the first Christmas I had someone my own age around, and it was nice even beyond the fact that it was Jake and he was my boyfriend. It was fun to have someone to talk to and be with. Mom and Thorsten were watching *White Christmas* with Bing Crosby and Rosemary Clooney, and Jake soaked it in with wide eyes.

I slipped my heels off and tucked my feet under me, checking him out for a few minutes. I leaned close. 'You like musicals?' I took a deep breath of his clean, crisp smell.

'I guess so.' His index finger ran along my fingers gently. 'I've never seen this movie.'

'*It's a Wonderful Life* isn't the only Christmas movie in the world.' I weaved my fingers with his and held on tight.

He clicked his tongue at me. 'I know. I've seen *The Grinch* and *Rudolph the Red-Nosed Reindeer*.' He paused. 'And *Frosty the Snowman*.'

'What about *Elf*?' He shook his head. 'What about *Emmett Otter's Jug-Band Christmas*?' He looked at me like I was crazy. 'Oh, man, we have some catching up to do.'

So for the next few hours we laughed through Christmas movies. Jake had seen *A Christmas Story*, but had never heard of *A Child's Christmas in Wales*, my all-time favorite.

'Figures your favorite would be a weird poem story.' He pulled me over and kissed me on the temple.

'Dylan Thomas is not weird.' I defended one of my favorite poets. 'You're the most unexposed person I've ever met in my life.'

Jake tweaked my nose, which I thought was completely adorable and lovable of him, even if he hadn't taken my seriously made comment very seriously at all. Thorsten and Mom had more coffee and dessert, and Jake joined them. When they were done, he stood up, thanked my parents, and told them that he had to get home. One thing Jake was really good at was not overstaying his welcome.

Everyone wished him a merry Christmas and Mom

handed me my coat and shooed me outside with him. There was no snow. Except for a freak storm in September, we hadn't had a single flake. But the ground was hard and cold under our shoes and the sky had a crisp, clean smell that meant snow was near.

'Maybe I can see you tomorrow.' He wrapped me in his arms.

I put my head on his chest and breathed in the sharp smell of aftershave wafting from his neck. 'Maybe. I'll work on my mom.'

'I had a really nice Christmas.' He rubbed his hands over my arms. 'This might be the nicest Christmas I've ever had. I mean, since my mom died and all.'

I went really still. I heard about Jake's mom about as much as I heard about my dad. I waited and, just like Mom earlier, Jake lifted the mysterious curtain and let me take a brief peek.

'She was really into Christmas.' He held me tighter as he spoke. 'I remember being in the car with her. She took me all over town to random houses so we could look at the Christmas lights. And we just parked. She let me sit in her lap, and we just looked at this really big house with all of these lights on it. I don't remember much, you know. I was pretty young when she died. But she did really like Christmas.'

'I'm sorry you didn't get that many with her.' I felt the prick of tears in my eyes. No mother? I couldn't imagine a sadder fate. I had a hard time breathing without letting my tears run.

'Don't cry, Bren.' Jake kissed me. 'I never tell you about this stuff because you get too upset. It's OK, really. I miss her, but it's OK.'

I hugged him tight, so tight my arms hurt. Jake had so little. Jake needed so much. It was intimidating. It was a lot to feel responsible for. But I loved Jake – loved him, loved him, loved him. I would guard his heart, no matter what.

'I love you,' I whispered right in his ear, and suddenly I was pressed up against the house, his hands knocking bobby pins out of my hair, his mouth hard on mine. He had my coat spread open at the sides and I could feel his body crushed to me, hot through my silky dress. 'Come back tonight.' I didn't care that I was begging shamelessly.

'I can't, Brenna. Your parents will kill me if they catch me.' He kissed my mouth and down my neck.

'Please, Jake. They drank that whole bottle of wine. They'll never know. I don't have long with you. Please, Jake. Please.' I wrapped my arms around him and kissed him gently on his earlobes and under his jaw, where I knew he was most sensitive. 'Please.'

'OK.' He dragged his hands out of my hair, down my neck and along the front of my body. He closed his gray eyes, and I wanted to yell at him to open them up again. I wanted to feel his hands on me for a little while more, but he pulled away before I had my fill. 'I'll come back at midnight. I'll call when I'm at the window.'

I kissed him. 'Thank you.'

I didn't watch him pull out of our driveway. I ran back in, and I knew I looked pink and flushed and bright-eyed. I knew that Mom felt validated about whisking me off to Paris. I couldn't stop the love for him from brimming out of me, and it was so intense it was dangerous. I knew that, and she knew it.

Chapter 3

I forced myself to sit at the table and sip cocoa and chatter happily. Thorsten pretended to cry about Mom and me leaving him for a week and a half, but I knew he would be happy to walk around in his underwear and smoke his pipe on the porch. Mom was very giggly and Thorsten was pretty silly himself. I was fairly sure that they were at least toasted enough to turn in early, and I wound up being right. They wobbled off to bed after they kissed and hugged me goodnight, and I sat on the couch and looked at our bright, pretty Christmas tree for a while. Then I took the DVDs Jake bought for me and headed to my room.

I peeled off my stockings and dress and put on my pajama pants and top. I made sure they were cute, since Jake would be over soon. I flipped through the movies until I found the one I wanted, even though I didn't really want to watch.

It was my absolute favorite, *Sense and Sensibility*, the

one with Kate Winslet as Marianne. I put it on and started watching. And, even though I didn't want to, I felt a wave of sadness when Willoughby rode up and saved Marianne, holding her in his arms with such outright chivalry. The scene is really romantic, but it's also tragic because Willoughby isn't going to be Marianne's true love. He's going to spurn her in favor of a rich heiress so that he can keep his lifestyle. And he winds up leaving Marianne crushed. I know this story by heart. I've thought about it a thousand times. Because someone got it in my head and now I can't get it back out.

That someone was Saxon Maclean. Earlier in the year I'd thought I might fall in love (or lust) with Saxon. Then I'd thought I would hate him forever. Then he told me something about Jake that changed everything, and since then, I haven't been able to get Saxon out of my head.

On my birthday he left a book on my windowsill. It was *Sense and Sensibility*, and before I'd had a chance to read it and make my own judgments about it, I'd read his inscription in it to me. Which basically said that I was Marianne and he was Willoughby, that our love was true, but ultimately wouldn't work. That Austen was smart for sticking me with Colonel Brandon (Jake? Not really a great fit), and that I should be smart enough to stick with my fated role.

He had fallen off of the radar just before my birthday. For a while, he didn't even show up at school. We were supposed to spend the day together as a reward for winning a class competition for a government assignment, but he didn't show and I wound up going with a girl who'd won third place. He was gone for almost three weeks, then suddenly he was back and no one knew where he'd gone or why. He hardly looked my way, didn't talk to me, and closed his Facebook account. He left me the book on my birthday, and other than that, it was just a look once in a while that let me know he was working really hard at keeping his distance.

The problem was that I couldn't keep myself from thinking about him. He and Jake used to be friends, but there was bad blood between them, and he had almost split me and Jake up. Then he had backed off. He took the heat when Jake could have been mad at me, and then he told me something that shook me to my core: he and Jake had the same father, a fact Jake was still in the dark about. Saxon also told me that he didn't want Jake to know, didn't want to disappoint him as a brother in addition to disappointing him as a friend. He told me that if Jake wasn't with me, he'd fight for me. And then he'd vanished.

I never told Jake. Beyond the whole problem of Saxon liking me, Jake and Saxon had grown up close, and Saxon had exposed Jake to a lot of vices. When Jake had finally had enough of that crazy lifestyle, he'd cut Saxon completely out of his life, and he hadn't had any dealings with him again until I came into the picture. It would make sense for me to stay as far away from Saxon as I could.

There was just one problem.

I could never quite wriggle out of Saxon's grasp, no matter how hard I tried. And something in me didn't want to. There was something about him that drew me in, whether I liked it or not. I wanted to talk to him more, specifically about the whole Jake thing, but he just avoided me or flat-out ignored me. It sucked, but there was nothing I could do about it.

I cried a little at the scene where Marianne sees Willoughby at the ball and he brushes her off. It wasn't that I wanted Saxon to want me or fight for me; it was just that if he felt that way and was open about it, we couldn't even be friends. But then Jake hated him so much that being friends wasn't even an option. It was a lost cause.

Before I knew it, my phone rang. Jake. I slid my window up and helped him in.

Jake had sneaked in before, but he didn't like to

make a habit of it. Especially since he'd met my parents. He knew they didn't completely approve of him, and doing anything to make that sense stronger didn't work for him at all.

But there was the undeniable attraction between us that always managed to skew his judgment and force him to bend his rules. Which worked for me.

I had never been much of a rebel, but Mom's new tactics were teaching me something I don't think she expected; I was learning that I had to do what I needed to do without worrying about who I was hurting. I had to be a little selfish.

I knew Mom would have freaked out if she knew that was how I interpreted her speech.

Jake shed everything down to his boxers and slid the neat pile under my bed. He wiggled in between the covers and snuggled up to me. His clothes and skin were still icy cold from running in the night air, across the fields and through the woods. He didn't park close because he was afraid someone would recognize the truck. I put my hands on his body, ran them up and down his back and along the muscles of his shoulders and arms. He pulled a long piece of my hair and brought it to his nose.

'Your hair smells like cinnamon.' He breathed it in and hummed with contentment low in his throat.

'It's my holiday shampoo,' I whispered.

He laughed quietly. 'Holiday shampoo. You're a weird girl.'

'Just because you don't celebrate at all doesn't mean that I never want to.' I poked him in the ribs under the blankets.

'I'm sorry.' He brushed his fingertips over my face. 'Next year I'll get candy cane deodorant and mistletoe aftershave.'

'I think mistletoe is poisonous.' I giggled.

'I'm willing to sacrifice to get into the holiday spirit. I want to be a hardcore Christmasser like you.' He kissed me softly. 'Maybe you can snag me one of the pictures Thorsten took of you today.'

'It was a great dress, wasn't it?' I sighed.

'I guess.' He kissed me again. 'I just think you looked amazing. I don't know if you realize how pretty you are.'

'Oh, I do.' I put my hands on either side of his face. 'I totally use it against you. Bat an eyelash, get you to carry my lunch tray. Toss my hair, you run over to my house and jump in my window.'

He chuckled. 'Yeah, I'm just your little monkey on a string.'

'You've got that right,' I said.

And then we were kissing again, and then the

kisses got deeper and Jake's hands were all over me. I relaxed back into the mattress and closed my eyes in the dark. I loved the cool, scratchy feel of his skin on mine. He touched me where I was softest and where I was most sensitive, and I loved it. It was like he had an instinct about how to make me feel incredible. I touched back, and soon the world had narrowed in exactly the way I loved it to. It was just me and Jake in my bed, all roving hands and kisses.

And then, in the middle of it all, I heard someone in the kitchen.

Jake snatched back from me like I'd burned him. I straightened my pajamas and pushed at him.

'Under the bed,' I whispered.

He was off the bed and scurried under in a few silent seconds. I could hear him breathing, and I was positive it was the loudest sound in the world, but I couldn't tell him to stop.

My heart hammered, and I tried to relax my own breathing, but in the midst of pure, palpitating panic, I couldn't remember how people breathed when they slept. Trying to breathe too slow made me need to gulp bigger breaths. I suddenly had an itch on my nose that I didn't want to scratch, but I realized I must scratch my nose in my sleep sometimes. I felt like the seconds stretched out forever, as I lay on my bed, breathing erratically and trying not to scratch what had become the most unbearably itchy nostril in the world.

I imagined getting caught. I imagined my mother's extreme disappointment. I imagined what it would be like if she made me dump Jake. How the house would light up on this otherwise peaceful night and be full of arguments and accusations, disappointment and crushed trust. My stomach clenched, and I felt sweat break out under my armpits. I bit the inside of my lip and willed this whole thing to be over.

Minutes of shuffling in the hall later, and my door cracked open. I relaxed my muscles and kept my eyes closed.

My mother's bare feet padded across the room, and stopped inches away from where Jake lay under my bed. I couldn't hear a sound from him, but I was nervous he was holding his breath. What if he let it out in one long rush and my mother heard?

The mattress creaked under her weight as she sat on the side of it. It was pure, agonizing torture to keep my eyes closed and not sit up and just confess to end all of the nervous anxiety of the moment. I felt Mom's hand smoothing my hair, then she leaned over and kissed my forehead.

She stayed less than a minute, then stood up and

headed back out of my room, closing the door behind her quietly.

Jake stayed under the bed for a long time. Finally I had to call him out.

'Jake, are you still there?' I felt guilty. I had convinced him to come over. This would probably be the last time.

He spoke softly from under my bed. 'I'm here, Bren.'

'Sorry.'

'It's not your fault.' His voice was flat.

'I shouldn't have convinced you to come.' I chewed on my lip nervously. Jake didn't say anything. 'Tell me what you're thinking.'

'I'm thinking that I'm so glad we weren't sound asleep.' He pulled out from under the bed. He'd managed to get his clothes on, and he knelt on the floor, not daring, I was sure, to climb back in next to me.

'You're leaving now, aren't you?' My voice had that wobble I despised.

'You can't really want me to stay. What if Mom is having indigestion? She could be back every hour. Let me go. You get a good night's sleep, and work on getting out for a few hours tomorrow. I'll call in sick for work so I'm ready if you need me.'

Jake never, ever skived from work. I knew he was

offering me an olive branch so I didn't freak out. And I knew it was completely ridiculous of me to even contemplate freaking out. He was right, he was reasonable; I was being selfish.

Maybe Mom had underestimated my capacity for selfishness.

'OK, go.' But I wasn't ready for him to leave, and I wasn't happy he was going.

He pulled me close and kissed me, a long, thorough kiss that had only the barest hint of his desperation to be gone.

After a few more moments of my pulling him to me and his pulling away, he vanished back into the goose-bump inducing black. From my window I watched him run across the fields and back to his truck, somewhere in the dark, cold night. Now the bed would feel even larger and emptier. The night stretched longer and lonelier than it ever had before. I couldn't help the tears that fell. The frigid air outside made me feel better, and soon I was cold and shivering. I closed the window, got back under the covers and dreamed about Jake and Saxon, racing around the school track, me in a snow globe watching them, pounding on the thick, clear glass. I woke up with a start in the early dawn, then fell back into a restless sleep until long after sunrise.

Mom knocked lightly on my door. I was already awake, but not up. My first thought was that she knew what I had done last night, and she was coming to give me a long, long lecture. I felt panic sweep through me.

'Sweetheart? Did you get a chance to finish packing?' She waited outside my door, but I sensed part of her wanted to barge right in while another part of her thought staying outside was a better idea.

It occurred to me that Mom was just unsure how much space and privacy to give me. 'Come in, Mom.'

She poked her head round the door and I patted the bed, just like she would do for me. 'I finished packing yesterday.'

'What did you pack for a jacket?' she quizzed.

'My blue wool trench coat.'

'Good. And for nights out?'

'I have the red silk from last night, with stockings and my black mohair sweater.' I stretched my arms over my head. 'What coat are you taking?'

'I thought my new plaid. The one with the orange in it.'

'Ooh, that one is so pretty.' I had definitely inherited my love of gorgeous clothes from my mother. 'I love the lining. It's too bad no one ever gets to see it.'

'You're right, with that gorgeous Japanese floral

and bird thing going on. Well, I'll be sure to fold it inside out whenever I hold it.'

'And I'll appreciate it every time I see it.' There was nothing like an amazing, hidden lining. 'So, what's on the itinerary for Paris?'

'The usual museums and churches, but we'll have a lot of free time, down time. And the other tutors will be bringing their families, so there will be kids your age.' She smiled. 'A bunch of nerdy professors' kids.'

I grinned. 'Yeah, right. You, a nerdy professor? Thorsten and I had to wait half an hour last time we came to pick you up from college. There were so many hot young guys drooling over you I could barely see you.'

Mom laughed, and I remembered all over again how much I loved that sound. A desperate need to see Jake crashed over me. I didn't want to tear this moment apart, but I knew she and I would have lots of time together in the next few days. Just as I was about to open my mouth . . .

'Brenna, if you want to go out with Jake today, you should. You won't see him for a while, and I'll be busy getting everything in order here.'

'Thanks, Mom.' I looked at her face, but she didn't meet my eyes. I could sense my mom's intentions warring with her guilt. Instead of trying to figure it all out, I kissed her cheek and got up. 'I'll give him a call so we can go out early. What time is our flight?'

'We'll need to be at the airport at three. Our flight is five in the morning. Bright and early.' She smiled apologetically.

Yuck. Our five in the morning was Paris's eleven. If the plane flight took eight hours, we'd land right around seven at night, Paris time. 'I'll be ready,' I promised. Mom kissed my forehead and left me.

I got up and picked through my many watches. I selected my old pink leopard-print watch and set it to Paris time. I liked to get myself thinking ahead so I didn't get severe jet lag. Then I called Jake.

'Hey, Bren.' His voice was adorably sleepy. 'How is it in the Blixen house?'

'Getting ready for travel.' I twirled my watch on my wrist. 'How about you and me spending the whole day together?'

'Your wish is my command.' He sounded much more awake.

'Do you need to go back to bed?' I didn't want to dwell on the night before. It was just so far from what I had wanted. It wound up being rushed and guilt-filled and completely unromantic.

'Why are you always so obsessed with getting me into bed?' he teased. 'I am not tired.'

I heard him get up out of bed, and, if I closed my eyes, I could picture it – his long, muscled body with only a pair of boxers hanging low on his hips, his hair cutely messy, the phone at his ear and, especially, that great smile with its chipped front tooth and twisted eye tooth. 'I want to see you soon. How ready are you?' His voice was awake now.

'I'll be ready in twenty minutes.' I hopped off the bed, ran to my closet, and pulled out some clothes.

'Good, because I'll be there in twenty minutes, and I'm taking you captive as soon as I get there. Go get ready.'

We hung up and I got in the shower. I was as quick as I could be, but I felt like I had to shave, and I always felt like it was a waste of good conditioner if I didn't leave it in for a full five minutes. It was just a theory of mine, but I didn't think the possibility of frizzy hair was worth cutting conditioning time short, even if I was trying to rush it. When I got out, I dried my hair quickly and put on some make-up as fast as I could. I threw on black knit leggings and this great bright blue tunic sweater. I pulled on a pair of high boots with fur tops. They seemed kind of silly, but I loved them at the same time. I slung a wide belt over my hips, took it off, then put it on again. I tied on my 'B' necklace and selected a pair of dangling silver earrings Thorsten had bought me in Sweden when we visited. Since Jake still hadn't arrived, I applied more eye make-up and slid on a hairband that I took off again right away. Just when I was feeling certifiably stir crazy, I heard Jake's tires crunch on our gravel.

Right there, in the middle of my room, I did a little happy, hopping dance since no one was there to see me and I felt, in that moment, so perfectly, burstingly happy that I could have burst. This wave of sublime bliss washed over me, and I was buoyed like I was full of golden light.

Then Jake was in my doorway.

'Jake!' I wasn't dancing anymore, but the only times he'd ever been in my room were when he'd sneaked over at night or while Mom was teaching and Thorsten was at work.

'Mom told me to come and tell you I was here. She was in the garage getting out a big, big suitcase.' He leaned against my doorframe, his hands in his pockets and a huge grin on his face.

'Did you help her?' My mother was fiercely independent, to the point where she'd rather fall off a ladder backwards than ask for a hand.

He rolled his eyes. 'No. I love to see crazy moms struggling with their arms full of luggage.' He strode into my very feminine room, filling it up with his big, beautiful guyish being. He picked me up and swung me around, and it felt as good as I always imagined it would. 'After I helped her with the case, I came to find you. I kind of hoped you would still be in your towel.'

I popped a hard kiss on his mouth. 'When did you become such a pervert?'

'I guess you're rubbing off on me. I made you something.' He pulled a CD case out of his jacket pocket. It was a new, thick, warm Carhartt jacket. Mom and Thorsten had picked it up for his birthday along with new gloves and a hat. I thought he would be offended, but Thorsten got all puffed up about how 'working men need working clothes', and Jake had accepted them happily. I loved Thorsten so much sometimes.

'Did you make me a playlist?' I hopped from foot to foot again. What can I say? Jake Kelly awakened my inner dancer.

'Yeah.' He put his hands on my hips and held tight. 'No screaming, and just enough whiny boys to keep you happy.'

'Thank you, Jake.' I kissed him. 'I'll listen to it on the way to Paris.' I noticed he was wearing the new watch I bought him. 'Let me see that.' I pointed.

He gave me the watch, and I spun the knobs expertly. I loved the tiny mechanisms on watches, and

I loved the rapid spin of the hands around the face when you changed the time.

'Um, you're like six hours off.' Jake glanced at the watch face.

'Paris is six hours off,' I clarified. 'Six hours ahead of us.'

'Oh.' He looked at it again. 'It's weird that we'll be in totally different time zones. Like, you'll be right in the middle of your day when I'm waking up.'

It sounded very melancholy, whether Jake meant it that way or not. 'It's not for a long time.'

'I was just making a time-based observation.' He took the watch out of my hand and wrapped it around his wrist. 'I want you to do this. You need to get some more traveling under your belt so you'll be ready for Italy. I'm not going to be any help.'

I loved that he was taking the idea of Italy so seriously. 'OK. Maybe we should take Italian next year.' Jake had discussed doing Share Time, meaning he'd go half the day to the academic high school and half the day to technical school, like I did. He was currently enrolled full time in the tech school we both went to, but it wasn't very academically challenging.

'Ooh, la la.' He nuzzled my neck.

I laughed. 'That's French, Jake.'

'I'm trying.' He grinned.

I ran my hands over him, along his wide back and up his neck and through his surprisingly silky hair. I felt his soft cheek, newly shaved and nicked right at the jaw, and pulled on his ear lobes. He licked at my mouth, and I melted into him willingly. This was heaven.

Jake pulled away suddenly. 'Sorry, babe,' he said shakily. 'Much more, and your parents will have good reason to shoot me. You want to head out?'

So we said our goodbyes and got into his big blue truck, and it was just me and Jake, driving all over Sussex County. I felt a crushing sadness that this was the end of our winter break together instead of the beginning, but I tried to push all of those thoughts aside.

'I think there are a few things you need to do before you leave American soil.' Jake busted me out of my sad thinking. We pulled into the Hampton Diner. 'You need to eat at a good, greasy diner.'

'Mmm. Perfect.' I loved this diner. It was the place where Jake and I had celebrated our newly minted relationship with apple pie à la mode the day he asked me to be his girlfriend.

Not only did Jake order way too much delicious food, he stopped the waitress from getting too oogly over him by asking her to take our picture in front of said delicious food.

'What's the picture for?' I turned the camera so I could see our smiling faces over the whipped-cream covered desserts we were working through.

'Your photo project.' He lifted a forkful of lemon meringue pie to my lips, and I took a bite. 'I've decided to do Sussex County before and after Brenna Blixen. So there will be life with you, then life without you.'

'Sounds awesome.' I scooped up a forkful of cheesecake with strawberries and whipped cream and offered it to Jake. 'Any layout ideas?'

'Before will be really dynamic, full color and beautiful.' He dipped into the chocolate crème pie and held it out to me. 'After will be a flat format in black and white, washed out, sad. What do you think?'

'I think you're kind of adorable.' I sipped his Coke instead of my own milkshake just because I wanted to drink out of his cup and not because I was at all thirsty for soda.

'I think you're kind of gorgeous.' Suddenly his gray eyes raked over me, hot and hungry. He took my hand and rubbed his thumb over the bump of my ring, then pulled me across the table and kissed me. 'Food won't be as delicious without you,' he said solemnly.

I held up a fork loaded with flaky apple pie. 'Maybe some food will lose its taste. Not this food. Never.'

Jake shrugged. 'Maybe my taste buds will just go dead without you.'

'I hope not!' I put a hand to my heart.

'Don't worry about me—' he began.

'I'm not worried about you,' I interrupted. 'If your taste buds die from longing, mine will be obliged to die, too. And what fun will Paris be if I can't taste all the delicious food?'

'You're a caring girl, Bren.' He scooped a dab of whipped cream on his finger and swiped it onto my nose. 'All right. I'll let half of my taste buds go dead.'

'Like flying a flag at half mast?' I stuck my tongue out and attempted to lick the whipped cream off my nose.

'That's right. But I'll taste all the good stuff, in your honor.'

'Consider me honored.' I gave up on getting the whipped cream off with my tongue and swiped at my nose with a napkin. Jake laughed. It was a good, deep sound and it made me feel warm and happy.

Once we'd finished at the diner we went to both of our schools and snapped obligatory pictures while I complained. 'Being near school the day after Christmas seems so wrong!' I wrapped my arms around my chest as the wind whistled hard and cold.

'Shut up and pose!' he called from behind the camera.

I struck a studious pose as he snapped away. Then we went to the overlook where we had skipped school, the bar where Folly had their first concert, the movie theater where we'd had our first real date, the Chinese restaurant where we'd shared our first meal. Jake made me stand and sit and smile and frown until he had enough pictures to wallpaper his room.

'OK,' he said, finally. 'Just one more place that will miss you.'

'Where's that?' I stepped close to him, and he wrapped me in a tight hug.

'My room.' His voice was a little sad despite all our fun.

We headed to his drab little house. It had a wreath on the door, but no lights around it. There was a tree inside decorated only with glass baubles. There were no sentimental ornaments with school pictures of Jake or popsicle creations with too much glitter. It looked like a tree they had stolen from a dreary bank lobby.

Jake's room was minimally improved from when I'd first seen it. There were now pictures and drawings and notes taped or tacked neatly over most of the wall behind his bed. He had more stuff around too. There were framed photos of us, random items from our dating life. He had a pair of clean chopsticks from our first Chinese food date on his desk next to the piles of books on tape I'd been giving him for weeks. Some of my barrettes were scattered around, along with a couple of bangles that I'd forgotten. He never wanted me to take them when I left, so I let them live on his desk and imagined him looking at them once in a while and thinking about me.

'Sit on my bed,' he instructed.

I sat cross-legged on his bed and smiled. He snapped the picture. 'How does it look?'

'Perfect.'

That was the last thing he said for a long time.

He kissed and held me so gently it made me feel a little sad. He smelled my hair and nuzzled my neck and ran his hands over my face and my body softly, like I was delicate and would break if he was too rough. We reached and touched and rolled over one another, twining together like we would never see each other again.

He ran his finger over the gold poesy ring. 'Was it too much?'

'It was perfect. I'm sorry I got a little freaked out. It just felt ... official.' I looked down at the shiny band of gold on my finger.

'It will be official someday.' He tilted my face with

his fingers and looked into my eyes. 'Because I'm never letting you go.' He wrapped his arms around me and nestled his nose in my neck. 'Never.' His voice was muffled by my skin.

I knew what he was saying. It was a sweet thing for a guy to say to the girl he loved. And I liked it. I really did. But I also had the sudden urge to yank the ring off of my finger.

Why?

'You'll have to let me go sometimes.' I didn't mean for my voice to sound as panicked as it did. I wriggled a tiny bit against his hold. 'Like, what about when you go to college?'

'I don't think that's anything to worry about.' He unclamped his arms and flopped back on the bed, his eyes fixed on the ceiling.

'You're going to college. You have to go to college.' It was a no-brainer for me. What else was there to do if you didn't go to college? How would you learn what you needed to learn about life and yourself? What would you do?

'I'll be happy for you when you go.' He shrugged his shoulders like it didn't matter to him whether he went or not.

I sat up and pulled my knees to my chest. 'Jake, you have to go. Are you seriously thinking that you're not going?' A little bubble of panic swelled in me and threatened to burst wide open.

He looked at me, his eyes a little sad, his mouth fixed in a set smile. 'You have a lot of opportunities that other people don't get, Bren. And that's cool. That's what I want for you. But that doesn't mean everybody has all those advantages. I don't, but it's all right, and I'm gonna be there for you when you need me. OK?'

He meant it to be sweet. I knew he did, but it made me so furious, I felt like I'd swallowed something cloying and spicy. My skin burned and I couldn't think straight all of a sudden. 'No. Not OK. I know things are really good for me. I know that. But you can't just give up on wanting more! There are people who can help you. You can take other classes. You can apply for loans. Don't you want to see more? Don't you want to experience things?' I looked at him, but his gray eyes were calm and serene.

He reached out and took my hand. 'Being with you has made so much in my life better. I don't need to do all the same stuff you do. I'm a simple guy, Bren. I know you need more than Sussex County, and I'd never stop you from doing what you have to. And if you need me, I'll follow you. And if you're doing your own thing, I'll be here waiting. And I'll be fine.'

I wanted to argue. I really wanted to argue badly. But I had a feeling my arguments would go right over his head. How could I explain wanting some intangible 'more' to someone so content with what little he'd been given?

And then, just as quickly as it flared up, all of my anger melted away, and I decided not to go crazy about the whole issue of Jake's future. Because he was destined for better; I was sure about that. It might take him longer to realize it, but he wouldn't just stay in Sussex County for ever. He'd start to realize there was more out there.

'Hey.' He pulled me down next to him. 'What are you all worried for? I'm the one who should be worried. You're jetting off to the most romantic city in the world, all hot and fine like you are. And I'm here chopping trees into firewood.' When he smiled at me, it was shaky with worry.

'All the more reason for you to brush up on your Italian for our big trip.' It wasn't college, but it was travel, and he said he wanted it, so I knew it meant he dreamed about more than our current tiny life. Or did he want it because I wanted him to want it? I swallowed the lump that jumped up in my throat.

'Bren, promise me something,' Jake said when I was pinned under him.

'OK,' I answered, nervous at what he might ask.

'Don't fall in love with some slick French dude.' He rubbed my nose with his.

'I think French guys are really short.' I grabbed his shirt in both hands and pulled him back to me for a kiss, and I made it hard and hungry, to push away the doubts that swirled around in my head.

'I heard they're ugly, too,' Jake said between kisses. 'And weenies.'

'And smelly.' I arched my neck so he had better access. 'And womanizers.'

Jake shook his head and buried his face in my hair. 'All right, now I'm relieved. I thought I might have something to worry about.'

'Never,' I promised. And at that moment, I meant it with my whole heart.

Finally, too soon, it was time for Jake to take me home. He didn't want to come in. He crushed me in his arms for a long time under the bright, clear stars. When he let me go, the cold was so jarring my teeth clattered.

'I love you, Brenna. Come home quick. Life is so damn boring without you.'

'I love you. I'll be home before you know it.'

And then he was gone. I felt like the entire world dimmed, like it rotated more slowly on its axis because

I wouldn't see Jake for more days than I really wanted to count.

But there was Paris. Mom had already gone to bed when I got home, even though it was early. Mom had strong theories about jet lag, and she had devised a sleep system that made no sense to me.

I got ready for bed and turned in without bothering to call Jake. I wanted to, but it was too sad. I felt like I wanted to remember him the way he had left. The next time I called him, I'd be in France and excited and have happy things to tell him. That would make being away from him a little more bearable.

Chapter 4

I slept really well, but then, I never really tossed or turned much. We had to be out of the house by two in the morning to get to the airport in time for check-in and security, and it all felt unreal.

Mom and I hugged and kissed Thorsten in the chilly gray air outside the industrial, energetic airport. I loved the bustle and potential in an airport. It always made me feel connected to something bigger to melt into in the middle of all that movement and promise. We checked in and went to stand in the short security check line. Soon we were making our way to our gate and preparing to sit on the hard-backed chairs for longer than necessary, since Mom had us checked in and ready way before we really needed to be.

Mom immediately saw some faculty friends and went to talk to them, pointing to me and bragging with embarrassingly exaggerated tales of my brilliance. I tried to smile nicely and bury my face in my book.

I couldn't believe Dawes was giving us so long to read *Ethan Frome*. I had started on our next novel, which was, unfortunately, *Crime and Punishment*. Dostoevsky is not exactly airport reading.

I was slightly caught up in the story of poor Raskolnikov and his murderous urges when a faintly familiar scent assaulted my nostrils. I knew exactly what it was, but I just couldn't fathom that it was part of my actual reality. That smell belonged to one person and one person only – Saxon Maclean.

I forced myself to look over the edge of my book, and there he stood, larger than life. Saxon in the flesh. What was he doing here? Why was he suddenly right in the middle of my Paris adventure?

'Saxon?'

He looked at me, a long hard look that gave absolutely no clue about what he was feeling or thinking. His black eyes were completely dark, his mouth set in a firm line. He held himself stiffly, uncomfortable in the middle of this group of people, who he obviously considered alien and offensive. I felt myself tense under his dark glare, daring him to keep looking so openly. But Saxon being Saxon didn't have the good sense to look away from my angry gaze. He stared straight at me, moved right up to me like he was a ship lost at sea and I was the bright blink of a lighthouse.

'Blixen.' He fell into the seat next to me. But I was looking past him at a fabulously beautiful woman with long dark hair and bright, laughing eyes, the same color as Saxon's, but with none of his sardonic nastiness. She was slight and bubbly, confident and lovely. She gravitated to my mother and kissed her on both cheeks, like some chic European woman. 'I see you noticed my mother.'

'You never told me your mother was a tutor.' My wide eyes followed her as she flitted around the sterile airport lounge like some kind of dazzling little sprite.

'You never asked.' Saxon's lazy voice dripped and oozed sexily. How did he do that? How did he take the most commonplace words in the English language and turn them into something undeniably sexy? I hated him for it, and hated him more because I felt like rubbing up against that thought. My brain didn't even have the power to link him to Paris, but it bubbled around that possibility, and it was as powerfully delectable as it was toxic.

'You're going to Paris?' I asked, even though the answer stared me in the face.

'Looks that way.' He flicked his eyes over my face.

I hated that I felt relieved to have put make-up on this morning. What did I care what he saw, what he approved of? Saxon and I had no business even attempting any type of relationship with each other. We were gunpowder and one hell of a spark, and I wasn't about to test our combustibility.

'I can't believe this,' I muttered, and I knew myself enough to admit that I hoped he heard me mutter it and would respond. He did.

'Can't believe what? That I'm crashing your Mommy-and-me Paris trip? Trust me, it wasn't my choice.' He slumped lower in the molded plastic chair and pressed his fingers to his temples.

I tried hard not to notice how good he looked in his slightly wrinkled button-down and fraying jeans. His hair was a little too long. One piece needed to be pushed back from his eyes. Not that I was about to do it. It just needed to be done. It was just an observation. That's all.

'What would your choice have been?' I closed my thick Russian book over my finger and tucked my legs up under me.

'To be between Sara Olsen's legs.' His mouth curved into a wicked smile. He wanted to shock me, but I refused to let him. My facial muscles didn't budge. 'But *mi madre* said it was Paris or rehab. And I'm not living for two weeks without a cigarette or a decent meal. So Paris it is.'

'Rehab for what?' I asked, even though I didn't want to ask. What did I care what he'd been smoking/snorting/inhaling/shooting up? I didn't. But I asked anyway.

'Rehab for drugs and drinking.' Saxon looked right at my breasts. I crossed my arms over them. 'She's cool with rock 'n' roll. And a little sex, just as long as it's safe.'

'I wish you'd gone to rehab,' I griped. I clutched my novel until my knuckles went white and told myself that throwing it at his handsome head would get me kicked out of the airport. I was not about to miss Paris because Saxon was acting like the ass I always knew he was.

'Don't lie, Brenna.' His voice was velvet rubbing along my neck and against my ears. 'It doesn't suit you.'

'You really think I'm happy you're here?' Screw the repercussions; smacking him upside the head with four hundred pages of Russian tragedy would be worth any price.

'I know you wanted Jakey, but maybe you'll accept my sloppy seconds.' He looked down at Jake's ring on my finger. 'Let me guess. *Autre ne veuil? C'est tout mon deuil?*'

I ignored how Saxon's French snaked around his

76

tongue and spilled into my ears like warm honey. '*A vila mon coeur, gardi li mo,*' I snapped.

'Well, well.' Saxon's smile was hard. 'So you're Jake's heart now? Or am I misreading the sentiment? Keep guard, Blix. I would hate to see my baby brother hurt.'

'Fuck off, Saxon,' I hissed. 'You don't give one damn about Jake, and I know it.'

'Yep.' He flipped his words out so they would seem casual, but underneath that I thought I could hear hurt in his voice. Maybe he did care after all? 'I bet a spoiled little brat knows exactly what it's like to have a sibling you can't talk to because a girl got in the fucking way. Spare me the lecture.'

'Spare me your conversation in general, you asshole. I don't want to talk to you again.' I felt my blood actually boiling in my body.

'Done,' he snapped and sat up with an irritated jerk of his long limbs. 'And likewise. I would really appreciate it if you could keep the hell away from me.'

'Take your own advice.' I picked up my carryon bag, ready to storm away from his idiotic company. 'I want nothing to do with you.'

Just then, I noticed Saxon's mother standing over us. 'Hello, Brenna.' Her face looked ageless and remarkably lovely. She smiled at me like a real-life

Renaissance angel. 'I'm Lylee, and I've heard so much about you from Suzanne.'

'I'm sorry if my mom was a little crazy,' I apologized. 'She doesn't realize that not everyone on earth wants to talk about me all the time.' I returned her smile, despite the fact that she was Saxon's mom. Or maybe because of it. There was something undeniably attractive about her.

'Not at all.' She looked me up and down, and there was naked approval in her black eyes. I was sure of it; I had seen the exact same thing in her son's eyes often enough. 'Everything she tells me meshes with all the things my son has said. And hasn't said.' She winked at Saxon.

He rolled his eyes. 'Very deep, Mom. How long until we board?'

'Don't be a jackass, Saxon,' his mother advised cheerfully. 'You're not seriously going to be upset about a vacation to Europe, are you? I mean, I know teen angst is cool with guys, too, but that would be a little extreme, wouldn't it? We are, after all, going to Paris. Try to keep that at the forefront of your thoughts, little man.' She made a move to brush that errant piece of hair back, but he ducked her touch.

'Thanks, Mom,' Saxon ground out.

'So nice to meet you, Brenna.' She floated back in my mother's direction.

'Oh shit.' Saxon let his elbows fall forward onto his knees and hung his head.

'What?' I felt particularly snarly and nasty.

'She likes you.' He rubbed his temples like that fact gave him an instant headache.

'How could you possibly know that? She only talked to me for a few minutes.'

'I could tell by the way she looked at you.' His voice was so low I could hardly hear it. 'She looked at you the way I do. Like she wants to eat you alive.' He slouched back in his seat, a general air of belligerence cocooning him from any more of my questions.

So Saxon looked at me like he wanted to eat me and was fine admitting it? I wanted to feel offended, but I didn't. If I was totally honest, I felt completely thrilled by his confession. I wanted to know what it would feel like to have Saxon devour me. Even as that thought crossed my mind, I rubbed my thumb over the ring Jake put on my finger the day before yesterday.

Jake, back home, tucked up safe in Sussex County. Jake, who was planning his future around me and only me. I felt a hot prickle all over my skin, like I wanted to shake off a weight I wasn't strong enough to carry. One wrong move, one slip-up on my end, and I could ruin Jake's world. He had so much riding on me, so much he needed my help to figure out, and here I was, flirting with Saxon Maclean while I wore the ring Jake had given me to remind me how much he loved me.

The ring that said I was his heart. Oh, Jake, forgive me!

I tried to focus on the book I was supposed to be reading, but Raskolnikov's story was just giving me ideas. For example, if I'd had a hatchet, I might have gone after Saxon's skull with happy determination. What was wrong with me? One minute I'm thrilled at the prospect of Saxon devouring me, and the next I want to kill him! I guess that stupid saying about love and hate being opposite sides of the same coin gets quoted a million times for a reason.

I plowed on through the dense mazes of guilt-laden sentences and refused to lift my eyes to see what Saxon was doing. I didn't care if he looked my way. I didn't care if he got up and left to hunt down perky little Sara Olsen either. I hoped he would, actually. Paris would be better without him. Much less complicated.

But my ranting was just that; ranting. Because I realized that Paris was just going to have to be about Saxon for me. And whether I felt badly about that or not, I wanted to talk to him. About Jake. About life. About us. I didn't want to admit it, but it was the truth.

I wondered what he would say about Jake's reluctance to go to college or dream bigger. And, at the same time, I wondered what Saxon dreamed about. What did he want, other than life as a demi-god in Sussex County? Had the two of them ever made plans that involved more than a couple of cans and some hard-partying girls with over-heated sex drives?

They finally called for us to board. Mom and Lylee were bonded at the hip, tittering and giggling like girls. I was glad, because Mom didn't have many friends, and I felt like it was good for her to have someone to talk to.

'Brenna,' Lylee said. 'You don't mind if I steal your mom for the flight, do you? I definitely need to brush up on my Impressionists before we hit Paris. Plus, my son is being a bear, and I have a feeling you'll be a much better animal tamer than me.'

She smiled so beautifully, I found myself nodding before I knew what I was doing. Mom looked like she wanted to say something, but Lylee swept her away before she had a chance. They were seated just in front of Saxon and me.

It occurred to me that the last place on earth Saxon

and I should be was next to each other on a plane. There was something strangely intimate about the dim cabin. It was like everyone on planes was part of a big nomad group, traveling together in a precarious metal cylinder and bonded by the innate scariness of the trip.

'So we're seat-mates,' Saxon grumbled as he sat heavily next to me. I could smell his cologne and the pungent aroma of cigarettes on his hair and clothes, and deeper than both of those, I could smell the scent that was completely and only Saxon. 'Think you can keep your hands off me?' It was no warning; it was a clear challenge.

I stuffed my bag under the seat in front of me with more aggression than was really necessary. 'Why don't you switch with someone else? There have to be some easy, brain-dead girls on this plane.'

He shrugged. 'I like a challenge. Want to meet in the front bathroom after the first lame movie?' He smiled at my growl. 'Can't fault a guy for trying.'

The flight attendants passed out bottles of water and went over safety procedures. Saxon shut his eyes and leaned back while they demonstrated proper plane exit procedure for a crash in the open ocean. He opened one eye a slit and looked over at me, sitting upright, listening intently to the directions.

'If this plane hits open water, we die on impact or freeze to death in the north Atlantic before anyone realizes we're missing.' He flicked the glossy laminated tri-fold sheet that showed animated people calmly exiting the crashed plane on a slide into the ocean.

'If you want to nap through the directions, go ahead. What do you care if I pay attention? I didn't wake you up to listen.' I kept my eyes glued to the brightly colored cartoon catastrophe.

'You seem kind of grumpy. Maybe you should take a nap with me. I'll try to spoon you.' He nudged me with his shoulder.

'Can you let me contemplate my possible icy death in peace?' I begged, and a teeny bit of my naked worry seeped out with the words.

'Are you nervous?' His voice had gone soft. I glanced at him and saw his eyes were warmer. The flecks of gold stood out, the way they did when he was interested.

'No,' I lied. I partially lied. I wasn't nearly as nervous about the possibility of death in the cold northern waters as I was about spending almost eight hours practically on Saxon's lap. 'I just like to play out all possible outcomes in my head, even the bad ones. That way I won't be overwhelmed by shock if the plane does go down, and I'll be able to concentrate on saving myself.'

He looked at me for a long time and a grin tugged at the corners of his mouth. 'In a ridiculous way, that makes sense.'

'I know. That's why I do it.' And I ignored the ludicrous surge of happiness that went through me when I realized that Saxon looked at me with grudging respect. He sat up and watched the rest of the safety presentation.

'All right.' He turned to me. 'I've pictured the whole gory scene. If we go down, I'm ready.'

'Me too.' I nodded and exhaled the breath I'd been holding in one long stream. 'Good luck. In case it happens.'

'Good luck to you.' Then he shook his head and laughed to himself.

'What's so funny?' I should have backed off, should have let him sit and laugh to himself without digging for information that was sure to disappoint me.

'I swear to God, I try to hate you, Brenna. I try to wrap my head around any other girl, and trust me, there's a lot of willing girls. But there's something about you that I can't deny. You drive me nuts, but I love it.' He looked at me, and his eyes were warm and crinkled at the corners from a rare real smile.

I felt like a hot rash prickled over my skin. 'I guess you're just a glutton for punishment.'

We sat next to each other in uncertain quiet for a few minutes. The pilot came over the intercom to announce that we would soon be taking off. I'm generally a good flyer. I've never minded it much, unless we were dealing with some serious turbulence. But takeoff was different. It gave me a weird feeling; hurtling through the air that sucked the breath from my lungs like an elevator rising too fast. Anyway, it was never a time I wanted to get into any deep or serious conversations.

It was right at the zenith of our ascent when Saxon turned to me again.

'Bren.' He used my name, which was kind of weird. Usually he kept me at arm's length and used Blix, an abbreviation of my last name. 'We've tried hating each other for a few weeks now. I think we really put in a good effort. And, let's face it, it's not working. And I have a feeling you're not open to experimenting with letting me in your pants.'

'Saxon, can you wait just a second to have this conversation?' I closed my eyes and leaned back, my hands gripping the armrests until we leveled out. I opened my eyes slowly, then turned to look at him. 'So you don't want to hate me, and you don't want to piss me off by trying to seduce me?'

'Yeah.' He smiled a little. 'Look, I wasn't excited to come to Paris until I found out you were going. Then, I have to admit, the whole thing seemed a lot cooler. So let's call an International Truce, OK?'

'So we'll be friends overseas?' I said, loving that we would have our own strange agreement, just between the two of us.

'That's it. We'll be friends, but I won't put the moves on you. Unless you want me to.' He smiled that wide, wolfish smile that set my heart thumping.

'No, I don't want you to,' I said too adamantly. I didn't want to think about that one too much.

'Deal, then.' He stuck his big, warm hand out.

We shook, and if he held my hand a little too long, it wasn't by much. By now the flight was going smoothly, and Saxon seemed much more relaxed. But, somehow, Saxon relaxed felt more dangerous than angry, on-edge Saxon.

'So what's this whole friendship plan have in store for me?' I asked, my suspicions still pretty intense.

'You don't trust me,' Saxon announced, his black eyes glinting. 'I'm not going to say that I don't want you, Brenna.' When my name slipped from his lips, it made me shiver. 'I do. But if the only way I can have you is by playing the good boy, then I'll be the best.'

'I think that's easier said than done for you.' I could

feel the excitement of a challenge radiating off him.

'I think it's going to be harder for you than you think.' He leaned towards my face, and our lips would have touched if we leaned in one more inch.

'Harder for me to what?' My voice sounded like it strangled to get out of my throat.

'To keep your hands off me.' His voice was like a hypnotic purr.

I rolled my eyes at him and backed away from the heat of his skin. 'I have nothing to worry about. You're so busy being in love with yourself, I don't know if you could make room for anyone else in that cold little heart.'

'I'd make room for you.' He ran one finger down my arm, and I jumped at his touch. 'Now I'm going to close my eyes and dream all the bad-boy things I want to do to you but can't . . . Yet.'

If it was possible for my skin to catch on fire, it would have done at that moment. He looked me up and down, slowly, then shut his eyes, a smug smile on his way-too-attractive face. There was nothing I could say to him. My loss for words was aggravating on so many levels.

I put my earphones in, pointedly ignoring the fact that his muscled forearm was lying on the armrest and his hand was draped over it, his fingers inches from me. Even in sleep, I realized Saxon would never touch me. It was all another game.

I sighed a little. It was already exhausting me to think through his next few moves. But, even as that thought went through my head, my heart thrilled to accept his challenge. I wanted him close, partly because he was dangerous, but also for other reasons I wasn't ready to look at too closely. He definitely ignited something in me. The furious anger we had been lashing at each other was like a summer storm, hugely powerful and almost frightening, but always followed by a refreshing break in the tension. I liked the idea of us as friends. Hating him was too extreme a feeling. It was too close to the only other thing that I felt so absolutely, which was love. Love for Jake.

I stared out of the tiny window at the blankets of clouds and thought about the fact that Jake had never been in an airplane. If we wound up traveling to Italy together, I would be with him on his first flight. It made me feel good that there were things I would introduce him to. Jake'd had a pretty wild past with girls, and he had made a name for himself as something of a ladies' man before we met. Since I had almost no experience with boys, I always felt like the younger, more immature person in our relationship. Even though I had a lot of life experience in aspects that Jake knew nothing at all about.

The last conversation he and I had replayed in my head. I thought about how easily he'd brushed off the idea of his future being exciting or amazing. Jake was satisfied with things the way they were. Or maybe he was just enjoying what he had? Jake tended to be tight-lipped about what he'd gone through, what he knew about the world in general. I felt like I was always trying to share, trying to make him see things my way, and he was trying to protect me from all the big bad evils he'd already encountered and dealt with. And, a lot of the time, it was just the two of us butting heads over and over again.

I was thinking about Jake and all of our crazy issues when my head fell back on the seat, and, as uncomfortable as it was, it was a relief to rest. The next thing I knew, Saxon was shaking my shoulder to wake me up.

'Food.' He pressed me back and lowered the tray on the seat in front of me, his arm warm and solid next to my body.

The trays had too-tiny foods, all individually wrapped and sealed. I had something like grilled chicken and vegetables. Saxon got up and flirted with the stewardess for a minute, then came back with a bottle of water for me.

'Can't have you thirsty.' He eyed my almost empty bottle from earlier in the flight.

'Thanks.' I uncapped the bottle and took a long sip. 'I could have gotten it myself.'

'But that's what friends are for.' Saxon's sugary sweet voice was offset by his wicked eyes.

'Thanks,' I repeated.

'This little tray doesn't look like enough for you, Blix.' He poked the edge of my tray.

I felt a little catch of relief that he was using his nickname for me again. It was less intimate, which made it easier for me to keep up with him and not get lost in his game. 'It's all right. Mom packed me snacks, and I ate a big breakfast.'

'Porridge?' he checked.

'Yep. Did you get your Cocoa Puffs in?'

'Nah. I haven't done anything healthy like eat breakfast in months. I had a cigarette and some Tic Tacs.' He slid a hand into his pocket and shook the little container of orange candies.

'Technically, the Tic Tacs are food, so you did have some breakfast.' I hoped I sounded more heartless than I felt. I wasn't about to get caught stressing about Saxon's eating habits, even if my natural inclination was to be worried about him. He was healthy as a horse and more than capable of taking care of himself.

'That's my hard-hearted girl.' He tore into his bread roll. It must have been as stale as mine.

'You decide what you eat,' I said calmly. 'If you don't want to take care of yourself, that's fine, but don't expect my pity over it.'

'That's pretty harsh, pal.' His voice was suddenly tight. 'I wasn't asking for your pity, anyway. I just answered your question. The one that you asked.'

He had a point. 'Call it tough love. And from here on in, I'll make sure I take less interest in you. Shouldn't be too hard, since that's kind of what I've been doing the last few weeks.'

And it should have been a zinger. Sure, a slightly mean zinger, but one he would appreciate nonetheless. But something about my words changed from slightly mean to very mean when they hit Saxon's ears, and the look he gave me was a kind of panicked upset, like he didn't want to be as affected as he was by them.

Then it hit me: his hints about rehab, the fights he'd been getting in, the missed school, the self-destructive things he was doing had all started when we'd cut off all contact.

Was I making something out of nothing? I looked at Saxon, but it was as if he'd never heard my last words. He didn't look upset or happy or otherwise. He was chewing. His face was bland.

But I sensed that he was hurt. By my not caring. And if my gut was right, and I had a pretty dead-on gut, then he was acting up to get my attention, trying to get me to care about him.

And I had to know then, because mulling something like that over would give me an ulcer. I chose my words as carefully as I could. 'I could care as your friend. About you. If you want.'

Saxon chewed for so long, I was fairly sure he was going to ignore my words, and I could decide he was basically the same old jerk and get over my strange new guilt.

'Considering how much you fawn over Jake, I guess it wouldn't kill you to throw me a crumb now and then,' Saxon said in a low voice, his mouth thin and bitter.

'Jake is my boyfriend,' I reminded him.

His eyes were a little wild when he looked at me. 'That first day of school,' he said slowly, forcing me to remember back to that day, 'you met me first, right?'

'Yes.' I made sure my voice was pointed and deliberate. I had to keep my footing. Saxon's logic could get winding, and I didn't need to get lost in it.

'You and I felt something for each other, didn't we?' He pushed his food aside and looked hard at me. I felt that same can't-put-my-finger-on-it something that I felt the minute I first saw him.

'You also felt something for Kelsie.' I tried to dismantle the whole thing as quickly as I could. It was too close, too confusing to talk about so openly. 'You were going on a date with her.'

'One date, Brenna,' he protested, his voice a growl. 'One innocent date, and God it pisses me off to even have to say that, like you need some damn evidence. You and I could have had something that day, but you thought I was with someone else.' He rushed on before I could dive in and argue. 'No. That's not even accurate. You and I *had* something together that day, and we still do. You and Jake are together over a technicality of time.'

'That's not true.' I wrung my hands frantically and kept my voice hushed. I wished this conversation had never started because there was no escaping it. We were in a tiny plane high over the Atlantic. 'I knew Jake was the one. I knew it from the minute I met him.'

Saxon's face contorted a dozen different ways before he settled on a resigned grimace. 'You knew the minute you met Jake that he was the safe one. He was the one who wouldn't challenge you or test you.'

'That's not true. Anyway, I don't want to be challenged. I want to be loved,' I said unsteadily.

In the cool, dry air of that interior, Saxon leaned over until he was so close to my body we should have been touching, but we weren't. He kept that fractional amount of separation between us with total concentration. 'You deserve to be challenged *and* loved. I would do that for you. And then you could care about me.' His words were torn and harsh, pulled from somewhere deep and hurt.

Our lips were so close, they could have brushed. I thought about what it would have been like, to kiss him. To kiss Saxon's mouth. I had done it before, months before, but since that first time, I had always stopped myself. Because of Jake.

Jake. I loved him and I would never hurt him. But something about Saxon tugged at me. I wanted to be closer to him, to know who he was under the façade we both kept up. I wanted both of us to relax and let down our shields. I wanted to know who he really was, without all of the complications.

And I wanted to reach out and make whatever was hurting him disappear. I wanted to be the amazing, awesome healing power he imagined me to be. But I felt cornered and manipulated and confused, so I turned my head away. 'I'm going to sleep, Saxon,' I said abruptly over my shoulder, forcing the whole taxing conversation to grind to a halt. 'I don't feel like talking about this anymore.'

I could feel his eyes on me, feel the tense clench of his muscles as he held himself so close to me but not as close as we both wanted, no matter how stupid it was to want it. He didn't want this to end. He knew he had me thinking things, considering things, and he wanted to keep weaving his spell, but I couldn't let him. He'd already sapped me of so much energy, and I'd only been near him for a few short hours. Finally, he pulled away and leaned back in his seat, and after a long, long time, he fell asleep. I felt shaky and angry, but eventually I was able to sleep, too.

Chapter 5

And then we woke up over France, and there was enough going on that I could keep my mind away from Saxon for a while. We landed, and it was nice to have to worry about finding my bags, load into a van with Mom and the other parents and kids, get settled in the rooms they had us set up in. We were spread over the city, but most of us were in dorm-type university rooms that the students had vacated over the winter break. In our block there were lots of cool, bright common areas with little kitchenettes and sitting rooms, and small single rooms, each set up with a narrow single bed, a desk and a little closet. It would have been a little dreary, except for the fact that there was Paris, right outside my window.

And even though Jake and Saxon were still always warring somewhere in the back of my head, I got caught up in the reality of being there, in Paris. It was night when we landed, and everyone felt kind of jittery and chattery. A bunch of people wanted to go out and eat, but Mom had a really strict anti-jet-lag system and she was sticking to it.

'You go if you want, sweetie,' she said around a yawn. 'Just stay close to the group.'

'No.' I shook my head. 'I'd rather get some rest and be ready for tomorrow.' I didn't even acknowledge whether or not Saxon was going. My life was always simplest when I was far away from him, and that included in my head. Especially considering thoughts of kissing him flipped stubbornly through my mind, no matter how hard I had tried to push them away for the remainder of our flight.

'This is going to be so much fun,' Mom said, and I could hear that little twinge of weird guilt in her voice. I liked her mean and in command best. I didn't know how to handle my mom when she wasn't being controlling.

I just wanted to get away from all that was unknown and warped. I felt so off-balance it was making my stomach queasy. I squeezed her hand. 'It already is, Mom. This is amazing. Once we sleep off this jet lag, it's going to be fantastic.' I gave a little fake yawn that turned into a real one just like I hoped it would.

Mom kissed me hard and went to her room.

Even though the rooms were only about seven feet wide and a little claustrophobic, they each had one huge window at their far end, and they were private. That made them perfect. I went to my bag and zipped it open, then pulled out my phone. It was still fully charged, and I had updated it for international calling. I hadn't asked Mom and Thorsten if I could. I just needed to be able to contact Jake, and I didn't want an argument or a lecture. And the time difference was enough that I would always be able to call him in as much privacy as there was available.

The phone rang a few times, and I had a sinking feeling that I had messed up and wouldn't be able to talk to Jake at all while I was gone. Then I heard the connection click through.

'Brenna!' His voice rang out so good and happy it was like sinking into a hot bath; I relaxed instantly.

'Hey, Jake.' I took out my clothes and started hanging them on the hangers someone had (wonderfully) left in the closet. 'It's really good to hear your voice.'

'Same here.' I could hear yells and an engine in the background.

'Where are you?' I asked.

'Leaving work. It is really cold here. How about there?'

'Not Jersey cold, but it's chilly.' I didn't really want to call Jake and talk about the weather. It aggravated me the same way Saxon's intensely gripping talk had. I didn't want intense or boring conversation.

'I don't want to talk about the weather with you,' he said, and I smiled sadly at his perfection as a boyfriend and my inability to appreciate him. 'It's a little weird for me that you're in Paris, and I'm back here in Sussex County. But I do want you to do this . . . I just feel left out. I'm not whining,' he rushed to add.

'You are whining a little.' I plopped down on the bed's thin mattress. 'But I forgive you. I'm feeling a little whiny, too.'

'Is it jet lag?' His sympathy made me feel loved and safe.

And I realized that I had to tell him. I couldn't spend nearly two weeks in Paris with his once-best-friend-and-now-arch-enemy without saying something about it. But I didn't really want to. I rationalized that if Jake was in my situation, I would want to know. That didn't really help. But I knew from experience with Jake that any lie I told or truth I withheld would just get bigger and bigger until it buried me under an avalanche of my own guilt.

'No. Jake, I have to tell you something. This trip isn't

just for me and my mother. It was for all of the college tutors and any family they wanted to bring, so—'

'Oh shit,' Jake interrupted. 'Saxon is there.' His tone was flat and harsh.

'How did you know?' Shock had me sitting straight up on the bed.

'I didn't know for sure, but Lylee is a college tutor, and what else would you be so nervous about telling me?' Jake cleared his throat. 'Saxon's traveled a lot. They used to do these trips when we were younger, back when we were friends.'

'Oh.' Jake only seemed reasonably upset about this, not freaking-out upset, and I felt a little relief that it wasn't going to be a big deal.

'Did he bother you at all?' Jake said each word carefully.

Now it was time to lie a little. I needed to lie the kind of lie that doesn't hurt the other person and makes life easier all around. It's not quite a white lie. Maybe it would be safest to call it a gray lie.

'No,' I said simply. And I said the most comforting thing I could think to say. 'There are a lot of other kids on the trip, so I'll probably hardly see him.'

'Good.' Jake sounded decisive, like he was determined to make the situation 'good' even if it kind of sucked. He wasn't a complete angel, and I didn't really expect it. From his perspective, Saxon was all bad. Jake tended to be much more black-and-white about things than I was, and Saxon was definitely all black in his book.

'I'm excited to explore tomorrow.' I got off the bed and went to my window so I could peer at the sloped tin roofs and the cobblestoned streets below.

'Hey, I have a surprise for you.' Jake sounded excited. 'Can you log onto your Facebook page?'

'I can.' Jake's enthusiasm spread to me. I plugged my adapter into the wall and flipped my laptop on. The dorms had Wi-Fi, so logging on was quick. 'OK, what now?'

'Check out my page, under the pictures.'

He had changed his profile picture from one of him standing against his dirt bike to one of the two of us that my friend Kelsie had taken at a Folly gig. I liked that he was advertising our togetherness. Jake's shady past with girls coupled with his seeming irresistibility to the female gender made him really susceptible to flirting, especially cyber flirting. His entire comment section was clogged with girls sending him ridiculous glittery lips and cyber kisses and sexy e-cards and bumper stickers. It made me cringe whenever I went on his page.

I ignored the new kiss invites and 'Just thinking of

u!' messages surrounded by blinking hearts from his many relentless admirers and clicked on his picture link.

There was an album entitled 'Brenna Is Gone ☹!'

I laughed. 'I like your little sad face.'

'Don't toy with my emotions, woman.' I could hear his smile.

I saw the first picture. It was the sun rising over the lake behind his house, the black branches of the trees dripping with rain.

'I like the first picture.' It was very dreary and damp looking, but that was the reality of winter in New Jersey.

'It's like everything's crying because you're gone,' he explained.

'I get it.' It was so adorably metaphoric, I couldn't keep the giggle down. 'Even sadder than your little sad face.'

'Are you mocking me, evil girl? I put a lot of thought into this. I guess I'm going to have to throw out your home-made valentine card and the love poems I wrote.'

'Did you really make that stuff?' Even though it was cheesy, I was dying with curiosity to see what Jake would make and write for me.

'No. But I might have done, if you hadn't teased my

attempts,' he pouted cutely. After a second, he added, 'And I still might.'

The second picture was my bike, leaned against the garage.

'Oh no! I forgot to put it in!' I imagined my poor bike rusting away as Thorsten lounged in his underwear, oblivious of my oversight.

'I put it in. I stopped by to drop off some apple tarts to Thorsten and saw it sitting there.'

'Well, now that I know the whole story, that picture doesn't make me sad.' I sighed with relief, happy that I could depend on Jake, even across the ocean. 'And it's sweet that you took over apple tarts. If we ever broke up, Thorsten would never talk to me again.'

'Better keep me around, then.' His voice had a tinge of worry in it, but I ignored that.

I clicked on the third picture. It was Thorsten, smiling with a box of apple tarts in his hand.

I laughed out loud. 'That's excellent! Mom will love it. Jake, this is really awesome. I didn't even know you like to take pictures.'

'I wanted to keep in touch with you, but I'm not a really good writer, so I thought I'd take some pictures. Like, to show how I'm missing you.' He laughed self-consciously.

'I love it.' I did. It was the perfect gesture. 'I'll put

some of Paris up for you tomorrow. Remember, I'm in a different time zone.'

'I have my watch set.' He sighed. 'And it's late in Paris. You should probably get some rest.'

'I guess.' My heart sank a little. I just didn't want to be alone, and I didn't want to get off the phone with Jake. 'I love you.'

'I love you, too. And I miss you already.' His voice fell by a few octaves. 'I can't wait until you get home.'

'Bye, Jake.'

'*Buona notte.*' It sounded for a minute like he had put his Italian cousin on the phone.

'Jake!' Would this boy ever cease to amaze me?

'I got a good Italian CD set out of the library.' He sounded very pleased with himself.

'You go to the library?' There was so much about Jake I didn't know.

'I'm a man of great mystery. Get some rest, Bren.'

We clicked off, and I found myself still shocked that he started learning Italian on his own. He really was full of surprises.

I logged out of Facebook and was listening to the mix Jake made me when I saw a piece of paper poke under the door of my room. I opened the door and Saxon was bent over, his face turned up in surprise.

'I thought you were sleeping.' The look on his face

told me he was glad that I wasn't. Saxon didn't bother to stand up. He balanced on the balls of his feet like he had meant for me to see him crouched over when I opened the door. I crossed my arms and leaned against the doorway, refusing to ask him in.

'I thought about it, but I guess I got my second wind. I was just putting my stuff away.'

'Let me help,' he offered.

'Help me put away my clothes?' I raised my eyebrow. 'Why would I need help with that?'

'Your bras and panties might need organizing. Friend.' His smile was infectious.

'No thanks.' I stepped back.

'The moon is almost full tonight.' Saxon stuck his hand out as I tried to close the door. 'Let's go roam Paris.'

'It's probably freezing.' I looked over my shoulder through the window at the bleak, gray sky, getting darker by the minute. I could already see the almost-round moon shining palely.

He narrowed his eyes at me. 'It's cold,' he allowed. 'But I never pegged you for a wuss, Blix.'

I looked down at him and considered pushing him over and shutting the door in his face. 'Because I don't want to run around a city in the dead of night with some doofus?'

'You want to.' He rolled from the balls of his feet to his knees and grabbed at the edge of my shirt. 'C'mon. You'll love it.'

'I don't know . . .' I glanced nervously at Mom's door.

'We'll leave a note. We'll take our cell phones. I'll buy you something to eat.' He grabbed my hand and pulled at me, begging shamelessly.

It made me laugh. It was so unlike the Saxon I knew back home, it didn't even seem like it could be the same guy. And he was promising me food. How could I say no? 'OK. Let me write a note to Mom.' I was a little nervous, but Mom would understand. She and Thorsten had always encouraged me to go and explore on my own in Denmark. They felt like Europe was this really safe, fun place. It was probably kind of naïve on Mom's part, but we'd lived near New York City for so long, I guess Paris seemed quaint by comparison. We'd also left right on the heels of another mall shooting tragedy somewhere in the Midwest, so I think Mom felt like we were taking a break from the violence of America for magical Europe, where things seemed so much calmer. I tried to rationalize that they would actually *want* me to go out with Saxon.

Alone. At night. In a city we didn't know.

He jumped up and stood close, and I closed my

eyes against the tingly feeling of need that reverberated through me. Thoughts of kissing him went through my head again, no matter how hard I tried to push them away. He dipped his head so close, we might have kissed. I might have let him kiss me, but he was the one who pulled back.

'Grab a jacket.' He sounded completely relaxed, but his hands were clamped in tight fists at his side.

My breath ripped in and out of my lungs too fast, and I felt the clash of guilt, desire, confusion and worry echoing in my brain. Part of me wanted to tell him that I'd changed my mind, but that would be like confessing that there was something wrong. It would mean facing the awful, strangling feelings that tangled through me, and I was all for denial instead.

'No problem.' I shrugged like my heart wasn't a train wreck. 'Let me grab one.' I groped through my clothes for longer than necessary, trying to get my equilibrium back.

We crept down the stairs quietly, sneaked out the door and were outside in the cold city air. My heart pounded in my chest as we walked away from the dorm. I grabbed Saxon's arm without really thinking. He draped it over my shoulders casually, and we walked down the wide sidewalk with our bodies pressed close together. I knew what a mistake it was, knew it was pushing my already shaky limits, but something in me couldn't stop it. I needed to prove to myself that I was in control of all of this.

Saxon was the kind of guy who never, ever looked like he was lost or late or rushed. He always gave this impression that he was exactly where he wanted to be, when he wanted to be, because that was the only place on earth that held any appeal to him. We walked along the street and he was so confident, I followed him without a second thought. I didn't even pay attention to signs and landmarks the way I usually would. If he didn't know where he was going, he was doing such a good job of faking it that I didn't question him.

He finally led me to a tiny table outside a noisy, dimly lit café and left to go inside to the counter. Through the window, I could see Saxon leaned over, and the pretty girl behind the bar giggled and nodded, and when he pointed to our table she nodded again.

He walked back across the patio like he owned the place and sat down too close to me. 'I ordered you a bunch of stuff. I figure the way to your heart is definitely through your stomach.'

'Are you looking for a way to my heart?' I was surprised that he would be that emotional.

'That among other things.' His eyes roved over my body suggestively. 'I think the heart might be a little overrated.'

'Maybe if you used yours once in a while, you'd develop more affection for it.'

'I've used it now and then. It seems like a lot more trouble than it's worth.' He took a pack of cigarettes out of his pocket and packed them, a habit that always annoyed me. 'Now there are a few other body parts that I've used with much more enjoyment.' He put a cigarette in his mouth, and I did not watch when he half closed his eyes and lit it, even if it was disturbingly sexy. Or maybe because it was.

'I've heard the rumors.' I rolled my eyes.

'You're not interested at all to see if they're true?' He took a deep drag and smiled through the smoke.

'Well, the rumor is that you always get what you want. As for your partner, I hear it's a little bit of a gamble,' I said boldly, even though I was quaking a little inside. I didn't completely know where I was going with this, and it didn't really work well with the idea of mutual friendship. Then again, I was turning Saxon down. That had to be a plus.

Saxon exhaled, rolled rings of smoke off of his tongue with ease and chuckled. 'I guarantee you, I don't leave my partners unsatisfied. I'm a sure thing,

Brenna.' Leaning back, his shirt tight against the muscles of his chest and arms, his black eyes hungry, cigarette hanging out of his mouth, I didn't doubt it at all. But I wasn't about to let Saxon know that I felt his pull.

I crossed my legs and brushed my hair back over my shoulder. 'I've *got* a sure thing, and I think the first sign of it is that he doesn't advertise it all over.'

Saxon's mouth hardened. 'You don't really have any idea what the hell you have,' he said, a little meanly. He crushed his cigarette in the ashtray on the table, blotting it out with more force than was really necessary.

It was a sore spot for me. As far as anything sexual went, I was in way over my head compared to Jake and Saxon. Not that that was necessarily a bad thing; it just put me at a disadvantage when it came to any bragging rights or arguments. I could be shut down pretty easily just by referencing my lack of experience. It was irritating when Saxon did it because he was so cocky, and that arrogance made me see red.

'Well, I know it's not all blow jobs in public bathrooms and quickies in your car's backseat, but there are some aspects that are really nice,' I said acidly. And then I was on my feet. 'I'm not going to argue about this with you.'

Saxon grabbed my wrist in a flash of movement. 'C'mon, I'm sorry. I was being a jackass. I know you and Jake are together, but you don't have to rub my face in it.'

I shook my head. 'Don't do that. *You* started this.' I jabbed a finger at his chest.

Saxon laughed. 'Don't get so serious. Jesus, it's just a little flirting. Between pals. Come on, sit. I have crêpes coming. You're going to leave before you get your crêpes?'

I did love crêpes. I sat down heavily.

'You look pissed off.' He leaned forward and studied me so sincerely, with such concern in his eyes, it was intoxicating. When Saxon paid attention, it was like having the strength of the entire sun shining directly on me. His mouth was so close to mine. I knew the taste of him, all smoke and guy and orange Tic Tac. For a minute, I leaned closer. Part of me wanted that taste again, and was tired of thinking about it. At the moment when I would have let it all go, stupidly forgotten Jake and his sweet pictures and his music mixes and his pure love for me, the waitress came over with steaming cups of coffee and a plate piled high with crêpes, pots of jellies and butter. I was narrowly saved by the delicious food of Paris.

I backed away from Saxon, my heart racing, and

decided that I was going to ignore my momentary lapse in judgment. It was better if I forgot that I'd even had the urge to kiss him. I took a deep breath, enjoying the delicious aromas of the food in front of me.

I dug in, drinking the strong, sweet coffee and eating as if I hadn't had a meal in weeks. Saxon leaned back and watched me, but I didn't mind. If he wanted to look while I stuffed my face, that was his thing. I felt no need to pretty up my manners for him. He began to light another cigarette.

'Don't.' I put my hand on his.

'Why?' he asked, his lighter in midair.

'I don't want to breathe your smoke while I eat.' I pushed his hand back down. 'It ruins the taste of the food.'

'Are you kidding? Look around this place. There's more smoke than actual air out here.' He shook his head. 'If it bugs you, I won't.'

'Thanks.' I smiled around a forkful of dense, perfect crêpes.

Without his prop, Saxon didn't seem to know what to do with himself. He drummed on the tabletop, fidgeted with the knives and forks, made a big production of fixing the cup of coffee he drank in a few gulps. He tapped his feet, then drummed his fingers again. After a few minutes of his rotating distractions, I gave up.

'Smoke, then!' I finally said. 'Just let me eat in peace!'

He grinned. 'You make me edgy.'

'Nicotine makes you edgy. Don't blame me for your bad habits.'

'You're the worst of my habits by far,' he muttered.

I ignored him, finished my meal, and felt disgustingly stuffed. The smoky air was difficult to breathe, and it made me feel a little nauseous. 'Do you want to head back?' I asked.

'All right.'

I put up the hood on my sweatshirt and zipped my jacket. It was cool and a little damp under the café awning. The clean, cold air felt good in my lungs, and I had to push down the urge to run. Saxon was still inside, taking care of the bill. I was glad he'd brought money with him; I had nothing at all on me. When he came out of the café, I realized how much I liked the way he looked – a little wild and a little like he had a really bad idea he was going to try to convince me to go along with.

'There's a park there.' He pointed. 'If we walk along the outer loop, we'll take the long way back to the dorms. Will you walk with me?'

He asked to be polite. He knew I would follow him.

We walked in silence, the huge, black trees making a dark tunnel around us. The moon was only visible once in a while through the long, gnarled branches that stretched over our heads.

'I want to smoke.' His voice punctured through the quiet.

'I don't want you to.' I didn't expect it to make any difference to him at all.

'I won't if you'll hold my hand,' he said stiffly, waiting for me to shoot him down.

I wanted to. But what kind of deal was that? He shouldn't smoke anyway. Why was I contemplating bartering with him at all? I could see the dark silhouette of his face, could see the hazy puff of his warm breath in the cold air, and I knew that he was nervous.

I reached my hand out and my fingers grazed his. He reached out and caught my fingers at the tips. He pulled me closer, ran our hands palm to palm, then opened his fingers, pressing them between mine. His hand was big enough that it stretched mine a little to hold on to his.

'I thought I'd be able to move out of your orbit for a while, Blix,' Saxon said into the cool night. 'I tried to get you out of my system. I really wish I managed it.'

'You keep saying that.' He squeezed my hand. I squeezed back. 'I'm really happy with Jake.'

'That's what makes this particularly fucked up.' Saxon moved his thumb along the skin on the back of my hand. 'I want you and Jake to be together. I want you to work. I feel like giving you up is the only way I can make things even.'

'That's crazy and you know it. Your father is the one to blame.'

A few months before, Saxon had told me a secret that made sense of all his infuriating actions: he and Jake shared a father. Jake had no idea. In fact, Jake lived with a man who he assumed was his dad, and they barely talked at all, let alone about family issues. There was a good chance Jake was the only one who didn't know the truth. I left it up to Saxon to tell him. Or not.

'My father isn't here.' Saxon ground the words out bitterly. 'But I am. And I screwed Jake so many ways, it should make me cringe. Yet here I am, finding a new way to screw him.'

'Jake knows you're here. He's not worried.' It was a stretch, and neither one of us believed it.

'I know I shouldn't do this. Shouldn't be holding your hand and taking you out and flirting with you. But whether I do it or not, I want it and so do you. So what's the difference?'

His voice was silky, convincing. I had to stay above it.

'There's a huge difference. Everyone has urges, but you can't just act on all of them. Acting on them is what separates good people from bad.' I was sure I was right.

'Not acting on them is what separates the martyrs from the plain old humans, Brenna.'

We stopped in the middle of the path. There was no one else around, just Saxon and me and the fog of our breath mingling between us in the barely moonlit night.

'I'm not a martyr.'

I looked at his shadowed face.

'Yes, you are.'

He took a step closer, overshadowing me. 'You're in high school. Why do you feel like you have to cling to Jake so damn hard? Don't you want to be a little more sure before you promise yourself to someone when you might have feelings for someone else?'

'I don't want to be with you.' My voice was faint in the dark.

'Yeah? 'Cos that's where you are right now.' He took my other hand, and held both hard. 'When you started dating Jake, you kept telling me you weren't his girl. You said you were your own person. But that wasn't true, was it?'

'It was. It is,' I countered.

'It's not. Because something in you is attracted to me. But something about Jake keeps you away. Don't disagree with me. I'm right.' His voice was firm and soft.

'You aren't.' I tried to jerk my hands away, but he held tight. 'I want to stay away from you because you make me nervous.'

'I make you nervous because I make you feel something strong. And you don't think you should feel so much for two guys at once.' He was telling me what I was thinking, and I felt like he was right, but I knew that I wasn't thinking clearly.

'I agreed to be friends,' I said in my defense. 'I spent the night out here with you. How scared could I be?'

'I don't really want to see how scared you are.' Saxon pulled me so that I was pressed against him. 'I want to see how brave you are, Blix. How far are you willing to take this?'

'I can't.' I shook my head to clear my thoughts.

'You have to,' Saxon growled. 'If you don't, you'll stay faithful to Jake, but you'll always wonder. That's no way to be.'

'I don't wonder with him. Stop this now.' I looked around for someone, something to break this spell. How could we be in the middle of one of the most populated cities in the world, but be so completely alone?

'You lie.' His mouth was so close to mine, our breath mixed.

'Let me go.' I twisted my hands, but he held tight.

'Coward.' Saxon said it like it was a fact. It wasn't the first time he'd called me that, and I knew that even if it had a ring of truth, it also had a strong line of conniving challenge to it.

Abruptly, I broke away and started back on the path. Saxon followed. We kept walking, and we didn't hold hands this time. My hand felt cold without his. Soon we were back at the dorms.

'Hurry in,' he said flippantly.

'I had a nice time.' I raised an eyebrow. 'You're a pretty moody friend, Saxon. You're as much trouble as a boyfriend.'

'If I'm going to be that much trouble, shouldn't you at least reap some of the boyfriend benefits?' he said in a low voice.

My back was pressed on the door of my room and he had me caged in with his arms. I lifted my face and kissed him on his cheek, just a fraction of an inch to the side of his mouth, very softly. He closed his eyes and pressed into me. He pushed off the door and smiled at me, then shrugged. 'It's a beginning,' he said ominously.

He turned down the long hallway and was gone. I

went into my room, where the full moon shone directly through my window. I changed into my pajamas and fell onto my firm mattress.

Then I got back up and paced in the cool blue light, my feet chilly against the scuffed wood floors. I checked the clock. It was almost two in the morning. That was eight at night at home. I could call Jake. It would clear my head.

I picked up my phone, but threw it back onto my bed without dialing. Why didn't I want to call him? He would help things make sense again. It would be simple.

Maybe that's what I was afraid of.

Because this wasn't simple. A few hours ago I had been so happy in Jake's arms, Saxon didn't even enter my head. Now, one night later, I couldn't get Saxon out of my mind. What did that mean? I chewed on my bottom lip until it felt sore, and reached for the phone again.

I picked it up and squeezed hard.

Had I rushed things with Jake?

Was it fair if I swore I was in love with him, but spent all of my time in Paris imagining what it would be like to kiss Saxon? Was Saxon right about the fact that I would always wonder?

I sat on the bed heavily and held my pounding

head in my hands. I rubbed my temples in an attempt to stop the full-blown migraine that was creeping up on me. I wanted this to be easy. I wanted to know for sure who I loved and why. I wanted to be in love without a hint of doubt.

But I realized that I could want as much as I liked; the reality was that I was in this way over my head, and this was day one with Saxon. My brain felt scrambled, my heart thumped heavily in my chest, and I had a panicked feeling that I wasn't going to be able to maneuver my way through this without screwing up big time.

I took a deep breath and yanked the sheets back. I snuggled down obstinately, intent on getting good sleep and rethinking this in the morning with a clear head. Maybe it would all make sense then. My eyes closed slowly, and my last thought was that the moon was pouring too much light into my room.

Chapter 6

The next morning, it was Mom who woke me up. I was so happy to see her face smiling over me in the sun-bright room. The ghosts of the previous night's worries tried to rear their ugly heads, but I slammed them into the back of my mind and resolved to focus exclusively on exploring Paris with my mother.

'Morning, Bren.' She smoothed my hair back. 'We're going to the Museum of Modern Art this morning. Are you ready for some Fauves?'

'Yes.' I sat up and rubbed the sleep out of my eyes. 'Just keep me away from the Dada. I'm in no mood for all that nonsense.'

'I love a kid who can swipe a whole artistic movement away with one grumpy morning proclamation. Come down to the kitchen. Lylee picked up fresh croissants and I've got hot chocolate on the stove.' She smiled and kissed my forehead.

She wore her emerald-green sweater and a

herringbone wool skirt with a pink scarf. She looked like she belonged in Paris, and it made me feel a weird, warm pride. I got up and jumped in the shower down the hall, which had terrible water pressure, then wrapped myself in my towel and ran back to my room. I shivered as I toweled off and dressed.

I wore my gray shirt dress and red leggings with my new gray Converse. I pulled my hair back in a high ponytail and tied on a red scarf as a headband. I made my make-up heavy and sprayed on some of the perfume Jake had gotten me, something sweet and citrusy that I had loved when I'd tested it at a mall counter. He had remembered, and, typical Jake, made sure I had it for Christmas. I grabbed my coat and headed to the kitchen.

Lylee looked chic and pretty in a black dress with giraffe print flats. 'Good morning, Brenna. You look adorable. My son will probably spend the entire day mooning over you.' She smiled, and I saw Mom grimace a little.

'Saxon will be fine.' I glanced in Mom's direction, but she was stirring the hot chocolate with quiet intensity. 'There will be a lot of stuff more interesting than me to check out at the museum.'

'You assume my son is as highbrow as you are.' Lylee sighed. 'With any luck, you might rub off on him.'

'Talking behind my back again, Mom?' Saxon appeared out of thin air. His hair was shiny and damp, hanging a little in his black eyes. He had on a tight Killers T-shirt with a thermal under it and dark jeans. He was wearing Converse, too.

'Doesn't Brenna look so pretty today, Saxon?' Lylee raised her steaming mug in my direction.

It was pretty unsubtle and I knew it made Mom more than a little uncomfortable, but Lylee was oblivious.

He looked me up and down, and I felt extra irritation race through my veins.

'She always looks pretty,' he said finally, somehow drawing anything nice out of the words entirely with his flat, bored tone. 'Mom says we're heading to the Modern Art Museum.'

I tried to ignore it when Lylee rolled her eyes a little at Saxon. I had that feeling you get when someone who's sure she's cooler than you is making fun of you for being so square. I bristled a little.

Mom brought me a cup of hot chocolate and I thanked her. 'I'm so excited,' she gushed. 'Some of Brenna's favorite Matisses are there. I can't wait to see them with her.'

'You two are so adorable,' Lylee said in a voice that was slightly condescending.

'Mom is a really great teacher.' My voice sounded defensive to my own ears. 'She got me into art when I was really young.'

Lylee just smiled. I was always respectful to adults, always. But Saxon's mother was starting to grate on me. I found myself glaring at her a little, and I had to glance away before I embarrassed myself and Mom with my bad manners. Lylee chuckled when I did, like she knew just what I was thinking, and I felt my dislike curl up and out.

Saxon kept his eyes on me, but I stuck to Mom like glue. Her good mood was easy to catch, and I caught it hard. We went to the big white museum with the famous tube stairway, and she dragged me from painting to sculpture to installation piece like a kid in a candy store.

Art had been a huge part of our life growing up. I credit my own interest in color and design to Mom's love of art. When I was just a baby, she'd sit me on her lap with art history books, and we'd look at the colors and the pictures. I counted stars in Van Gogh's sky, learned my ABCs with Cézanne's fruits and Monet's flowers, and drew colors out of Raphael's cloaks and wings and Titian's ladies dresses. Mom and I went gaga over the Warhols and Duchamps. I'd only seen them in books before, and now, there they were, right in front of us. After a few hours, the tutors went to have a meeting in a little antechamber that had been set up for them, and the kids were allowed some free time.

I was staring at the colors in a Modigliani when I smelled the sexy, smoky scent of Saxon next to me.

'Nice painting.' He nodded to the Modigliani with his chin like he was giving his approval.

'I like it,' I muttered back and walked away. He followed.

'There's a roof terrace here. We can go on it. You can see Paris for miles.' He caught my sleeve between two fingers and turned me toward him.

'I don't really feel like going to the roof alone with you.' I moved on to look at some Expressionist paintings I didn't know well. He followed.

'Is this about me calling you a coward?' He maneuvered so he was in my way no matter which direction I tried to take. 'Because I meant it, but I also didn't mean it. If that makes any sense.'

'As much sense as you ever make.' I stopped trying to move around him and looked into his eyes. 'Look, I'm not in Paris to spend my time wrapped up in you.'

'That's not how you felt last night.' His voice was a little angrier now that I hadn't gone along with him unquestioningly.

'It was. You can't seem to hear it when I say "no".' I plopped down on a bench and turned my back to him.

'You didn't say "no"!' he snarled back. I whipped my head up and looked at his face. 'You can say whatever you want.' He calmed his voice down. 'The truth is, you feel something.'

'Fine. You win. Let's go to the roof.' I was ready to fight with him for real, but I wasn't willing to do it in front of dozens of milling patrons of fine art. I didn't know what had come over me. Maybe it was my lack of decent sleep. Maybe it was all the confusion that had been bubbling in the back of my head all day, threatening to boil over every second that I didn't clamp a lid on it. Maybe it was just that I was unsure and overwhelmed, and I had no clear answer to the problem I didn't even want to face. I wasn't sure what it was, but something had flipped like a switch, and I felt like I couldn't even anticipate my own next move.

All of the uncertainties from the past few months were swirling through me, and Saxon had managed to stir the proverbial shit. Now I was feeling so unlike myself, I didn't know who I was exactly. I wasn't usually edgy. I wasn't usually angry. I wasn't usually melancholy. But I felt all those things, and confused and excited and unsure at the same time.

Holy shit. Maybe I was having a long overdue mental breakdown.

Once we stepped onto the roof, I tried to use the benefit of the biting wind to clear my mind, but it was no use. I felt tipsy and dizzy, and the only good thing was that I was feeling it with no one but Saxon as a witness. The roof was probably more popular when the weather wasn't freezing with a stinging wind.

He lit a cigarette and looked at me to see if I'd say anything. I didn't.

'Pretty up here.' He looked at me wolfishly.

'Yeah.' I sighed, tired of all the beating around the bush and mind games. So I said what I thinking, the way I knew Saxon wanted to but didn't have the guts to. 'You are really good looking. And attractive in a lot of other ways. I don't like to admit that I feel that way about you, but I do.

'He raised his eyebrows. 'Thanks?'

'No thanks needed. I'm just tired of games.' And then I said the words that had been alive in me since September, hibernating somewhere every happy second I spent in Jake's arms. I said the words that might crush every good thing I had. I said them because I couldn't feel right caring about Jake so much, but living some private Saxon fantasy in my head. I said it out of desperation and out of hope. I said it hoping the whole thing would blow up in my face, and at the same time hoping it would work out better than I had ever imagined.

I said, 'Let's do this.'

'Do what?' His black eyes were alive with tiny gold flames, and I knew that his question had more to do with wanting to hear my answer than actually needing to know.

And then I made a proposition to Saxon that I wasn't sure I could live with. But I honestly felt like I had no choice. Or maybe I felt like it was my only choice.

I grabbed him by the lapels of his jacket and pulled him close to me, the aggressive jerk to his system bringing a surprised smile to his mouth through the cloud of cigarette smoke that curled around his head. 'Let's see what there is between us, if anything. Just you and me, just between us. And if we just go with it, maybe it will relieve some of this tension. OK?'

'How far are you willing to go?' Saxon asked, the cigarette now dropped and smoking from the cool ground of the roof.

'As far as I want to, but no farther. No cowardice.'

He looked at me and shook his head, not able to process what I proposed. It broke my heart to do it, but I lifted my hand and pulled my posey ring off. I dropped it in my pocket and looked up at him. Thoughts of my vow to guard Jake's heart flashed painfully through my head, but I pushed them back.

'I'm no one's girl but my own.' I forced the words out, my voice shaky. 'Just me. Just Brenna. And I'll do what I want.'

He reached up and grabbed my shoulders. 'You want to kiss me.'

'Are you sure it's not just your wishful thinking?' I shot back. Because a kiss was real. That went beyond words or even gestures. A kiss was a kiss, and it couldn't be taken back.

'Ask yourself,' he threw back. 'If you're not too much of a coward.'

So I grabbed him again by the lapels of his coat, and I was satisfied that I shocked him silent this time. I reached my face up and kissed him, my lips firm and hot on his. He was taken aback by it, almost pulled his head back, but I kissed harder, then opened my mouth a little. He relaxed and pressed into me. I balled my hands round his coat and screwed my eyes shut and kissed him hard. He wrapped his arms around me and lifted me up, closer to him, and kissed deeper.

Finally I pulled away, breathing hard.

I had broken everything. I had smashed what I had with Jake.

I felt like throwing up. I felt like punching Saxon in

the face. I didn't feel like kissing him again.

'Was it good for you?' I asked, my voice as nasty as I felt.

'Brenna.' Saxon's voice was a ragged edge, but he didn't say anything else.

'So now we'll do whatever I want whenever I want. Seduce me, Saxon. Do your worst! How long have you been telling me that you wanted me out of your system?' I yelled into the cold air over Paris. 'Let's do it, then! I'll get you out of my system, you get me out of yours! And I bet it will be so damn cool and fun!' I was gasping for air.

'Brenna.' He went to put his arms around me again. His voice was calming, and I could see in his eyes that I was freaking him out a little. Good. I was freaking myself out a little.

What had I done?

'Get the hell away from me.' I put both hands on his chest and pushed hard. He stumbled back. 'I don't want to see you. And it has nothing to do with Jake. I fucked that up, didn't I? Now go! Go!'

Saxon looked like he was thinking about what to do next. But he couldn't come up with anything. So he left, looking over his shoulder at me as he went.

I had beaten him at his own game. I gripped the railing around the roof hard. I had beaten him, and I felt like curling into a ball and putting the covers over my head and just not coming out. What was I supposed to tell Jake? What was I going to do now?

I stuck my head into the wind, leaned over the railing and drew the air deep in and blew it back out. From the pit of my stomach, I screamed loud and long until the poisonous feeling that was pouring through me left, and I felt empty.

If anyone thought it was weird that some random girl was hanging over a railing screaming her head off, no one stopped me or checked on me. Saxon didn't come back.

Coward!

I felt like I shrank and grew in those few minutes. My heart, at least what my heart was, shriveled a little and hardened. And my ego and anger grew. It grew so much that it even encompassed Jake. I tried to hold onto it as hard as I could, because I knew I would need it that night, when we talked.

If we talked.

I took my camera out and hung over the railing, pointed it down and focused on the street. My own hair got caught in the frame, and I thought that was a good thing. It was a little piece of me falling down farther than was safe. I snapped the picture.

I went back into the museum and found a wild,

colorful Fauve painting that was so bright it looked furious. I snapped a picture, not caring if I was supposed to or not.

Mom found me, was worried, and I hugged her hard, breathing in the smell of her perfume on her bright-green sweater, but I didn't explain anything. I ate a sandwich and an apple with her in the cafeteria. I took a butter knife from our serving set and plunged it into the fruit, then snapped a picture.

'Bren?' Mom eyed the oozing fruit. 'Are you OK? You've been a little quiet.'

I felt like I was buzzing, like there was some kind of electrical current running through me, like I was filled with neon.

'Did you ever want something that wasn't good for you?' I asked forcefully. 'Like, did you ever want a piece of chocolate cake when you were on a diet?'

'I don't diet, sweetie.' Mom narrowed her eyes at me. 'You are gorgeous. I knew moving back to America was going to be bad for your self-image.'

'It's not that, Mom,' I assured her. 'I'm just saying, did you ever indulge in something you shouldn't have and ruin something else you had that was good?'

She looked at me for a long time. 'When you were a little girl,' she began, 'you had a really beautiful picture book. Your grandfather gave it to you. It had this really scary story about a witch and two children in it. You loved it.'

'The one where the witch had red eyes and it looked like her hair was a thorn bush?' In my mind's eye, I could see the image as clear as if it were hanging in front of me on the museum wall.

'That's the one.' Mom took a sip of her coffee and eyed me a little sadly. 'It was your favorite thing in the world. Then you got a set of coloring-in pens.'

'Uh-oh.' I had a feeling I knew where this was going.

'Yep.' She laughed. 'You loved those pens as much as you loved the book. Anyway, I wasn't paying attention one day and you went a little crazy, adding all these squiggles and pretend words and drawings. I was so upset with you! I felt like you ruined that book, and that was before you could just get online and order a new one. I had never seen that book before, and I've never seen it since.'

'Was I upset?' I palmed the pierced, juicing apple in my hand.

'No.' She shook her head. 'That was the thing. You loved the book even more. I guess you'd somehow made it your own. Anyway, not only did you have me read the story the way it was, you had your own story added in. So I would read the page and then you would read me your version.' She leaned her cheek on her hand, her eyes far away. 'It was so creative and wonderful. I wound up realizing how artistic it really was, and since you didn't mind, I didn't.'

'Do we still have the book?' I wanted to see this amazing mess I made as a kid.

'Probably in the attic somewhere. It's one of my favorite art pieces from your youth. It was like you were doing early-found art.' She preened. 'Anyway, I have no idea what's wrong, but whenever you've decided to indulge, you've always made something wonderful come out of it.' She took my hand across the table, now slightly sticky from the sweet, seeping apple juice. 'Brenna, we women need to learn to stop denying ourselves. Indulge.' She squeezed hard.

'Thanks, Mom.' Though I was pretty sure if she knew the details of my problem, she wouldn't have been so pro-indulging.

We went back to the museum and looked around some more. I didn't see Saxon, and I really, really didn't care. I heard some of the other kids, kids a little older than me, talking about going dancing.

'Are you guys going out tonight?' I felt a little weird barging in on their conversation, but dancing sounded perfect.

'We are,' said a pretty red-haired girl with blonde eyebrows. 'You're Professor Blixen's daughter? Brenna, right? I'm Caroline. This is Lydia and Brian.'

'Nice to meet you.' Lydia had dark, short hair and a sullen look. Brian was a little pudgy with light brown hair and a nice smile.

'Do you want us to come and get you? Is eight OK?' Caroline asked.

'I have to check with my mom, but it should be cool. Thanks.'

Mom was overjoyed, of course, so I told them yes and gave them my room number.

And then I saw Saxon. He looked at me from across the gallery, where he was surrounded by downlit paintings and blank white wall space. He looked possibly nervous, but also definitely happy to see me. That look on his face made me feel a confusing mix of power and guilt.

'Some kids invited me to go dancing,' I said, going over to him. 'Come with me.'

'Are you asking me on a date?' He stuck his hands in his pockets.

'I'm telling you that if you want to do this, you'll come with me and dance.' I borrowed his usual arrogant tone. 'Be at my room at seven thirty.'

I turned on my heel and walked away, and Saxon whistled as I left. That made several guys turn and check me out appreciatively. I didn't even turn to glare, and I didn't care if he was disappointed that I wasn't reacting.

Soon we were ready to leave, but Mom and I got dropped off a few streets down from our hotel. She wanted to get me something to go dancing in. 'Something sexy.' Her eyes trained on a storefront window too far for any other human's eyes. 'Something like that.'

And there was a shimmery purple dress, which I tried on and thought was way too short. Mom said I was being a prude, and finally managed to convince me to live a little. So we bought the gorgeous, sexy dress. She also talked me into silver heels and big, dangling silver disc earrings.

We ran back to the hotel, giggling over our purchases. Mom went to her room to nap, and I went to my room to untangle the knot I had tied around my love life.

I checked my watch. It was five thirty Paris time. That meant it was still the middle of the day at home. I needed to call Jake.

My stomach clenched. I felt the buzz in my veins from before, but now the good energy from it felt worn out and I just felt a dull, draining ache, like I had been exposed to something too strong and very toxic.

I dialed the number and when he said my name, I felt a little queasy. 'Jake?' I said dully.

'What's wrong?' He picked up on my bad vibe immediately.

The silence ticked between us.

'Brenna.' His voice was heavy. 'Just tell me.'

'I . . .' How could I start? What could I say?

'That bad, huh?' I could hear his voice strain. 'You can tell me.' He sounded so resigned.

'I kissed Saxon,' I said robotically.

He swallowed hard. I could actually hear it over the phone line. 'Did he pressure you?'

I felt a little offended, inexplicably. 'I kissed Saxon,' I repeated.

'Do you, um, have feelings for him?'

'No.' I pressed my hand to my temples. 'Some. Feelings. But not the way he thought. Not the way I thought. I feel . . . I feel like I messed some things up. And I feel like I had to. Does this make sense?'

'Well, you're talking to the king of messing shit up, Bren.' Jake sounded hollowed out. 'We had a decent run, right?'

'Jake, don't—'

'Don't what? I'm not the one sticking my tongue down someone else's throat.' His voice sounded strangely barbed. Not strangely considering the situation. Just strangely considering that Jake had always been so gentle with me. 'It's a little bit of a shock, but I always did feel like you were out of my league.'

My face was already wet with tears. I sniffled and felt pathetic for doing it. 'That's not it. I felt something for him when we first met, and it's never gone away. I don't know what it is, but I feel like I needed to know before you and I—'

'There is no more you and I,' Jake cut in coldly. I felt like I was drowning, like I couldn't breathe. It was all my fault and there was nothing I could do to stop it or put it back the way it was. 'Do you seriously expect me to wait here for you while you screw Saxon?'

I was desperate to explain, but every way I turned the words, they still sounded shallow and terrible. I was still breaking the heart of the only guy I'd ever loved. And I was a little defensive when I realized Jake thought I'd jump into bed with someone so casually. 'I'm not screwing anyone. You don't have to have sex with every person you're mildly interested in, Jake.'

'OK.' His voice sliced across the line. 'Just have a little respect for me when I tell you that I'm not at all cool with your little experiment.'

'I understand that.' Tears slid down my face, and if I could have shaken myself by my own shoulders I would have. What had I done? And why had I done it?

'I guess I'll be going.' The voice on the other end of the phone might have been coming from Jake's mouth, but it wasn't Jake. My Jake was dead and gone in a split second, so fast I didn't even have time to catch one last sweet word to hold on to.

'Um, OK?' I took his ring out of my pocket and put it on the scratched desk in front of me. I felt like my heart was cracking into pieces in my chest. And what about his? What about the heart I promised I'd guard? I'd promised, just days ago, and now I couldn't hold myself to it. I felt sick to my stomach. 'I just want you to know that I love you. I still do. I have to do this for myself, but I love you.'

'I hope you're happy with this, Brenna.' His voice was warmer than I would have expected. 'Wow. Today was going really well until this. Whatever. Take care of yourself. I guess I'll see you around.'

'Jake . . .' I said, but there was nothing left to say. I was just afraid to hear the click of our final disconnection. It was all spiraling out of control way too fast. I wanted to stop time, rewind, fix this, solve this, but it was too late! I was left in the ruins without knowing for sure how completely I'd made it all tumble down.

'Goodbye, Brenna,' he said quietly.

And he clicked off.

Chapter 7

I lay on the bed and shook, sobbing into my pillow. What had I expected? Jake had been surprisingly cool and calm about the whole thing. I had been unfair to him. I hadn't given him any warning, hadn't told him enough, and hadn't been as honest as I should have been. I shouldn't have done this over the phone. I should have had the respect to tell him what I felt to his face.

What did I hope to gain from this? Did I really think Saxon and I would be boyfriend and girlfriend? Did I even want that? What would happen in a week when I was back home, sitting across from Jake for half the day every day? I knew from the sick clamp in my gut that I had made a huge mistake, one that I couldn't come back from. I had screwed up with Jake, and he wasn't going to understand.

I thought about the book from my childhood, the evil witch and those scary red eyes. What had I written in my childish scrawl? How had I changed the story? In my childhood I had understood all of my intentions and changes, but if I looked at it now, what would it be? Just a big mess, I was sure.

Jake and Saxon weren't a book and a pack of pens. I couldn't just rewrite their stories any way I saw fit. And I was scared that maybe I was the evil witch with the red eyes. Maybe I was the villain and there was no way to change it, no way to stop what I'd so stupidly started. This wasn't going to end well. I wanted to stay in my bed and let the gaping hole in my chest close up. But I had started this whole thing rolling, and I had to see it out.

I fished in my bag and found the curling tongs I packed. Forty minutes later I had on way too much make-up, my hair was big and sexy and my dress was gorgeous and too tight and short. I lay on my bed and rolled Jake's ring between my fingers.

He wasn't mine anymore.

He wasn't thinking of me.

He didn't care about me.

We were done.

It felt too final. My throat felt clawed at, raw and painful. Dozens of images of me and Jake went through my head, all his love and kindness. But I knew that behind every good time, there was my feeling that maybe this wasn't it. Maybe he wasn't the one. There was the sneaky nagging reminder that my heart leaped when I saw Saxon. And I wanted to know why that happened.

So now I was free to know why. Had I expected it to be pleasant? It hurt. How else could it have worked?

Before I knew it, there was a knock on my door.

I opened it and Saxon was there, wearing a gray shirt with the sleeves rolled up to his elbows and dark jeans. He looked really sexy. He smelled really sexy. But my heart wasn't in it.

'Have you been crying?' He ducked his head to study my face and, I'm sure, my red-rimmed eyes.

'No. Come in.' I wiped at my eyes with the back of my hand.

My room was right next to my mother's, and if it had been any other day, I would have never invited Saxon in. But it wasn't any other day, and not only did I pull him into the room, I pulled him directly over to the bed. I sat down on it, and he sat next to me. I put my mouth on his. He tasted good, the way I remembered him tasting. He kissed me back, pulled me to him, but after a few seconds, he pulled away.

'Brenna, what's wrong?' He cupped my cheek with his hand and rubbed his thumb along my cheekbone.

'I told Jake.' My voice was watery. It was such a relief to talk about it with someone else.

'And?' He held my hand gently.

'We broke up.' My voice shook hard.

'Are you sure?' Saxon looked a little like he was laughing at me.

'Yes!' I hated his condescending chuckles. 'Why are you asking like that?'

Saxon shook his head and grinned. 'Brenna, I don't think you understand how . . . crazy Jake's past is. Do you plan to sleep with me?'

'No,' I said flatly. I was in no position to even think about that. I knew for sure that no matter how much I was attracted to Saxon, what I felt for him wasn't love, at least not yet. And that was my only real prerequisite for sex.

'Jake might be pissed off. But he hates me, and he's going to blame this on me, not you. When this is all over, if you want to kick me to the curb and take Jake back, you'll be able to convince him.' He rubbed his hands up and down my arms.

'How can you say that?' I demanded, my voice high and warbling.

'Because I've known Jake his whole life. And I know how he feels about you. I don't want to build a case for him, but he's completely crazy about you.

And you don't understand the power you have over guys.' He looked me up and down. 'I can't believe you look the way you do, and I'm sitting here holding your hand while you cry to me about Jake Kelly.'

'What's that supposed to mean?' I pulled my hand away.

He caught it again and brought it up to his lips. 'Don't, Brenna.' He kissed my palm softly. 'I know you're sad about Jake. But trust me, it isn't over if you don't want it to be. Can I ask, now that you've gone this far anyway, if you'll at least consider taking me seriously? Forget all of our past bullshit, OK? I've got less than a handful of days to convince you that I'm not a complete douche bag, and I want a fair shot. Give it to me.'

His eyes had so much gold in them they looked almost brown. He looked so handsome, so sincere, that this time when I kissed him, I really felt it and really meant it. He pressed me to him, kissed me lightly on my jaw and my ears.

He whispered things to me that made me feel shaky. That I was beautiful. That he thought about me all the time. That he loved the way I smelled. That he had never felt happier than he did now.

And since I was already in deep, I let myself get lost in his words. I wound my arms around his neck and opened my mouth and filled myself with the smoky, dangerous taste of Saxon. Before I knew it, he had me back on the bed and was trying to move the straps on my dress down. I could see that crazy, fevered look in his eyes, but I stopped him.

'Enough.' It was crazy how different this was from what I had with Jake. With him, I was always the one pressing for more, but I was too muddled and Saxon was too eager. It wasn't comfortable for me.

Saxon backed off, his hands up in the air in an 'innocent' gesture. Just then there was a knock at the door.

Caroline was there in a slinky black dress. Lydia scowled in tight jeans and a red halter and Brian looked less dorky in a plain shirt and jeans with some gel in his hair.

'Hey, Brenna.' Caroline eyed my dress with one blonde eyebrow raised. She smiled appreciatively at Saxon. 'Hey, Saxon.'

'Caroline.' He nodded.

Something flashed between them, and once again I felt like the idiot innocent in the middle. Saxon's past was just as shady as Jake's, but Saxon didn't have any of the regrets Jake had, at least on the surface.

Caroline introduced everyone, then the parents came out to take our pictures and warn us to be careful. Mom looked worried, but happy, even if I was dressed in a tiny dress and killer heels and we were going to a large, popular dance club.

'Be good.' She took my hand and twirled me round, then kissed me.

And we were off, released into the cold air of Paris, jostling and laughing. Saxon took my hand without asking, and we walked slightly behind the others.

'Do you know Caroline?' I tried not to be jealous. I had no right to be, of course.

'She and I made out when we were in middle school. One of these trips, but it was England.' He shook my hand back and forth. 'There's nothing for you to worry about.'

'I'm not worried.' My hand was limp in his. 'At all.'

'Really? 'Cos you seem a little huffy, Blix.' My heel got caught on a loose cobblestone, and he caught me under the elbow when I tottered.

I regained my balance and pulled my arm away from him. He grabbed my hand.

'Look, I know you have a man-whore history, so I won't even be shocked if you've pawed every girl we meet for the next two weeks.'

'What's with you anyway, Bren? You've got some bad taste in guys.' He dropped my hand and threw his arm around my shoulders. 'Jake Kelly and now me.

Two of the worst, Blix. What's wrong with a nice straightedge from one of your AP classes?'

'You are in my AP classes,' I pointed out.

What was strangest about this whole night was that once Saxon and I decided to go beyond just friends, he became friendlier than he'd ever been to me. And now that I was preoccupied thinking about Jake and what he was doing and thinking, I had no interest in trying to outthink Saxon. It was liberating, in a way.

By the time we got to the club, I was ready to stop thinking. About Jake and the catastrophic phone call, about Saxon, about everything. The music was way too loud and it was all French, which was actually great. I didn't want to hear anything that would remind me of home.

Saxon checked our coats and went to the bar. I don't know how he got them, but he managed to get two shots.

'Here, Blix.' He held the glass out to me. 'It's not going to get you plastered or anything. Bottoms up?'

I took the tiny glass and we clinked together. I felt bonded to him, the way doing anything secretly bad makes you an instant accomplice. I threw the liquor down my throat in one fiery liquid ball that tasted no worse than Listerine. Saxon grinned and led me to the edge of the dancers. The others in our group were already on the dance floor, but Saxon was clearly not interested in hunting them down.

The music was infectious, and that one shot coursed through my untried system with a lot of strength. I felt good moving, and my muscles relaxed as I sank into the music. Saxon wound up being as great a dancer as his sexiness promised. He was attentive and funny, and when he moved, I didn't want to take my eyes off him.

We danced to show off at first, throwing in a crazy move here and there, making each other laugh, and it was the laughter that closed the gap between us. Soon, we were dancing closer, and Saxon would reach out to touch my waist or I would balance myself with a hand on his shoulder. The music got louder and more intense and we laughed harder. Soon Saxon's hand didn't move from my waist and then both of his hands were on me. Then we were dancing so close our hips ground together, and I had a flashback to our *Dirty Dancing* group date a few months back, when his finger on my ankle had irritated me.

Suddenly that perfect day rushed back, and Jake rushed back with it. I realized that I still had the picture of him from the movie theater on my cell phone, and I wanted to see it. Maybe it was just torturing myself, but I needed to see Jake again, however I could. I told Saxon I had to go to the bathroom. He watched me head out. I had stuffed my cell phone in the cup of my bra so that I would have it to hand no matter what.

The bathroom was quiet compared to the noise outside, cool and white tiled. There were a few girls in the stalls, two of them throwing up loudly, but I just ignored them and closed myself into my own tiny space. I turned the phone on and went through my picture menu. There was the image of Jake, his great smile and chipped tooth and sexy gray eyes. I felt a rush of remorse. What was I doing? How had things changed so quickly?

But there was also the feeling that I had been hurtling toward this since the day I met Saxon, a full half-day before Jake. I chalked it up to bad fate that I had to meet the two of them at once. But it was my fate, and now I had to follow it.

I came out of the stall and wiped some of my runny mascara from under my eyes. I didn't feel like going back out, but I knew I would. A text appeared on my phone suddenly, and I felt a thrill, thinking it might be Jake.

It was Saxon.

Outside, it said.

I left the bathroom and headed out. Saxon was

waiting, my coat over his arm, a cigarette hanging out of his mouth. He held my coat open, and I slid my arms in appreciatively, I was cold in my skimpy dress.

'You done dancing?' He ran a hand down my arm.

I nodded, then made a face at his cigarette.

'You ever try one?' He took the smoldering stick out of his mouth and held it out to me. I shook my head.

'You broke up with your perfect boyfriend, made out with the biggest asshole you know, drank a shot, dressed up all sexy, dirty danced, and now you're going to turn your nose up at one little cigarette? You're going to get enough damn second-hand smoke hanging out with me anyway. Why not give up and smoke one?'

I smiled at him. 'You think I look sexy?'

'Hell, yeah.' He held me at arm's length and his eyes dropped to my feet. 'With the sexiest shoes. Man, those are fuck-me shoes.'

'That is not the message I'm trying to send with them.' I turned my heel and looked at my shoe from the side. Saxon shrugged and held the cigarette out again. I laughed a little, then took the cigarette from his hand and eyed it quizzically. I held it the way he did, low between his index and middle fingers, pulled a drag into my lungs, felt it burn and blew it back out.

Saxon cracked up. 'You need to hold it higher up. That low look only works for guys, OK?'

I adjusted it so it was higher between my fingers and tried again, pulling the smoke in smoothly and blowing it back out. 'Nah. Not for me. But I realize why you do it now.'

'Why's that?' He took it back and took another a deep drag.

'Because of how it feels. And looks. It really is just a prop.' He started to walk, and I walked with him.

'You're implying that I'm insecure?' Smoke clouded around his face.

'Oh, I'm not implying. I'm coming out and saying that you're insecure. The cigarette is just a cool toy . . . That will kill you and makes you stink.' We listened to the sound of his footsteps and the click of my heels as he contemplated my words.

He studied the cigarette. 'It might have started as a lame security blanket. But I get edgy if I don't have one now.'

I raised my eyebrows at him. 'Obviously, Saxon. They're addictive.'

He smiled at me and switched gears so quickly and uncharacteristically, it made my head spin. 'I like it when you say my name.' His voice was sweet and sexy twined together. He took my hand, and I let him.

'How come?'

''Cos it makes me feel like you're my girl instead of some random hot girl I'm lusting after. When you use my name, I feel like you might really want to be talking to me because I'm the one person you want to be around most.' His smile was so adorable it made my heart seize up.

'Do you want that?' I looked into his eyes, now so warmly gold they were practically glowing. 'You want us to be together? Like, beyond this trip?'

'Yeah.' He stepped closer to me. 'That's the goal.'

'And you plan to just date me? If we got together?' My hands shook.

'Yeah.' He ran the back of his fingers along my cheek and I closed my eyes. 'I never really had this urge before. To be with one girl. I feel like I wouldn't get tired of you.'

And I instantly felt a rush of nervousness. Like what if I couldn't keep Saxon entertained? How many boring nights before he turned his attention somewhere else? Would he pay attention when I was upset? Could it ever work?

We walked until we were back in front of the dorms.

'Do you want to just chill for a little while?' Saxon asked.

'Sure.' I nodded to the cozy group of chairs grouped in the warm foyer. 'Do you want to sit in the lobby?'

'My room is at the end of the hall,' he suggested, his voice low.

I thought about it for a minute. 'OK,' I said, my voice expressing so much more certainty than I actually felt. I followed him down the corridor, and he opened the door and led me in.

His room was exactly the same as mine, but it was smoky, dark clothes were thrown all over along with his packs of cigarettes and lighters, his iPod and laptop, his racing magazine and a copy of *Brave New World* by Aldous Huxley. I walked over and picked it up, then sat on his bed and kicked my heels off. I flipped through the pages.

'What are you reading this for?' I held it up for him to see.

'Junior Honors. Dystopia unit. Ever read it?' He emptied his pockets, tossing his cell phone, lighter, cigarettes and change on the desk.

I nodded. 'I love it.'

'Yeah, me too.' He took off his shirt. He was wearing a tight black vest top underneath. I saw he had a tattoo on each shoulder, some kind of matching, snaking dragons. He sat on the desk, his booted feet on the chair, popped the window open and lit another cigarette. 'It's kind of sick, but I love the world they live in. The one we're supposed to hate.'

'I kind of do, too.' I flicked through the pages and skimmed words that were familiar and delicious. 'I like the machines that give you the scented powder. And the crazy porn movies!'

'Yeah, *Hamlet* on a bearskin rug.' He laughed through the cigarette smoke. 'And I think it would be cool to see whole groups of identical people, dressed in their own particular color.'

'I always think that I would be an Alpha. Don't you?' I held my hair up off of my neck and let the cool night air breeze over my over-warm skin, but as soon as the sweat dried, a sudden, sharp chill bit through me.

'Oh, yeah.' He flicked ash out the window. 'I think every person who has half a brain assumes they'd be an Alpha. You cold?'

'Yeah.' I held my coat closed tight and folded my bare legs up under me.

I thought he'd close the window, but he jumped down and rummaged through his stuff, then tossed me a clean, but smoky, thermal top and sweatpants. I pulled the pants on under my dress, shed my coat, put the thermal over.

'I kind of thought I'd get a show.' He bumped his head back against the wall and blew smoke out the window.

'Tough. You didn't.' I looked at him, so hot and muscled in the moonlight. 'I never realized you had tattoos.'

'They're recent. Maybe two months old.' He looked at them with obvious pride. 'Five hours total. They're not completely colored in yet. Then he pulled his shirt off by the neck. I sucked my breath in at his caramel-skinned six-pack and bulging shoulder muscles. He had two swooping birds on his pecs and when he turned so I could see his back, there were two mermaids with long, flowing hair swimming up his shoulder blades in addition to the dragons that I had seen partially snaking his shoulders.

'That's a lot of ink.' I was proud when my voice didn't wobble. 'All pairs?'

'It just felt right to get two of each thing done.' He jumped back on the desk and hunched over, his back muscles bulging as he hung his head. The end of his cigarette glowed orange in the room. 'You like them?'

'Yes.' They were very sexy. I wondered if Jake had ever contemplated tattoos, then put that thought out of my head. Jake wasn't my boyfriend anymore – just like that. I had broken Jake's trust, and I knew that Saxon was wrong about the possibility of me winning him back.

Jake once told me about how easy it was to slide into doing something that you didn't really want to do, but I never believed him. I thought that he was weak or immature because he'd had sex with so many girls. And maybe that was true. But I'd been throwing some big stones from the front door of a glass mansion. In one day I had broken so many of my hard-and-fast rules, it was daunting to think about it.

'You're not even considering me as a boyfriend, are you?' Saxon asked suddenly, taking another long drag. His dark eyes glinted in the night.

'I don't know.' I tried to make out his features in the dim room. 'Jake won't want to date me now.'

'I don't want to be your damn rebound,' Saxon snarled. He ran his hands through his hair and left it standing up at crazy angles. 'Jesus, Brenna. Just don't date anyone if you don't think you can get over it.'

'It's *not* just anyone.' I took a deep breath and pulled his thermal closer around me. 'It was you, that first day. When I found out you were going out with Kelsie, I was a little crushed. There's so much about you that I'm attracted to. But there's also so much that freaks me out.'

He jumped off the desk again and came over to me, his figure lean and powerful in the dimness. I felt my blood thrum in my veins. He sat on the bed next to me, his skin smelling like soap and smoke and Saxon.

'I'm fucked up,' he admitted. 'But I could be better than I am. With you, I know I could be. Give me half a chance,' he pleaded.

'I don't know if you really want this.' My hands itched for his skin, but I was already scared. 'Once it's real, and the chase is over, it's not going to be exciting all the time. I think you'll get bored.'

'You never bore me.' He took my face in his hands and kissed me, then leaned me back on the bed and kissed me more. And just when I thought I should stop things before they went too far, he pulled me into his arms and just held me. I was nervous that he'd fallen asleep when I heard his voice, low and quiet in the dark. 'There are things I want, too. Things I want to change. I'm tired of only being there for a good time, Brenna. I'm tired of being a corrupter of the people I love. No one wants to be the perpetual fuck-up.'

I relaxed against him, against the warm body of someone who screwed up a lot. I liked holding our mistakes up against each other, for comparison's sake, even if it was completely awful of me. It made me come out looking better than I was. It made my own failures feel like they could be overcome. 'I know how you feel. I get overwhelmed by it all, too.'

He snorted. 'Overwhelmed,' he mocked. 'That's one way to look at it.'

I sat up from him. 'You don't think I have similar experiences to you?'

'I think you think you do,' he said carefully. 'I like you because we're the same, Blix. But I want you because we're different.'

'What does that even mean?' My gut already hated whatever it was he was about to say.

'It's the virgin/whore thing.' He shrugged. 'Don't get all offended when I explain what I'm talking about,' he warned.

'You don't need to explain anything to me.' Of course I was offended. I couldn't fathom any other way to feel considering the crap that just oozed out of his mouth. 'Do you really think I don't know about the whole virgin/whore idea? And how exactly am I supposed to keep from being offended by it?'

'You represent the best possible kind of girl.' Saxon ran a hand down my arm, and I batted it away. 'C'mon, Bren, don't be a prude about this.'

I stood up, hating that I was wearing his clothes.

'I'm not being a prude. Maybe it's just a little freaky that this isn't really about me at all. It's about what I *represent*.'

'It's about what you think versus how you are.' He turned me by the shoulder, but I shook his hand off again. 'You have the ability to see it all, to think it all, but you haven't done it all. That's what I like. You and I *think* alike, but you haven't *done* the things I have.'

My face burned hot. It made no sense to be ashamed that I had less experience whoring and drugging, but I felt like Saxon held it over my head that I wasn't as knowledgeable as he was, or something like that.

I scooted back up the bed, out of his immediate reach, and leaned my head back on the wall. 'So you like me because I can think like a rebel, but I act like a good girl?'

'Pretty much,' he agreed. 'Of course, when you say it that way, it makes me sound like a dick.'

'Maybe you sound like a dick because you *are* a dick,' I suggested.

'Don't get all high and mighty with me.' He moved off the bed, went to his window, and lit another cigarette. 'It's the same reason you get all hot for Jake, just in reverse.'

'That's *not* why I like Jake,' I insisted fiercely.

'Yes it is.' Saxon pointed his cigarette at me. 'And it's because you feel bad about it that you're here, in my room right now.'

'What do you mean?' My words were cold, but I was curious. Like it or not, Saxon said what other people didn't. That didn't mean he was right or true. Just worth listening to.

'Jake did all the bad, and in his head, he's good. Kind of worked the devil out physically, so he can be an angel in his head.' He laughed and took a drag. 'That's why you two never made sense. He did all the bad you've only imagined, and you know he thinks he can protect you from doing any bad yourself.'

'But you think bad and do bad.' The crazy logic of it all made my head spin. 'If I do what Jake is warning me against, I'll be just like you. Based on your stupid theory.'

'Yep.' He took another long drag.

'Then your fascination with me will probably go away.' As much as I felt a twinge of regret at that thought, I felt relief too, and that made me feel a little more sane.

'I doubt it.' He narrowed his eyes at me. 'Then I'll just feel less guilty being with you. I won't be the dirty older pervert who ruined you.' He blew a long stream of smoke out. 'We'll be partners in crime.'

I shook my head, which had just started to pound. 'Yeah, we'll be just like Bonnie and Clyde,' I said sarcastically. 'It won't work, anyway. In order to do the bad things, I'd have to do them with you, so you'd be like my rebel mentor. And since you'd have the upper hand, we couldn't be partners.'

'That's where you're thinking too much like Jake's girlfriend.' Saxon gave a careless, one-shouldered shrug. 'I'm willing to keep our relationship open.'

'What does that mean?' I didn't bother to point out that we weren't in a relationship, because Saxon would just laugh at that. I was deep enough in this to know that he wasn't going to get tripped up with technicalities.

'It means that in theory I'm happy to just be with you, but if you need to do some experimenting without me, I'm not going to preach you a sermon about it.' There was no light except for the moon coming through the window. It highlighted the planes of his face and glinted off of his eyes, making him look like a ghost. 'I'm not saying I won't beat the crap out of a few guys to work out my jealousy. I'm just saying that I'm not going to expect you to be on some leash.'

'Like a pet,' I snapped.

He didn't seem upset at all. He seemed amused, and that only made me more upset. 'No, not like a pet.

A pet is something you keep on a leash, Bren. Or in a cage. Or right by your side. You would be free. With me. No checking in, no rules.'

'You can't have this both ways, Saxon.' The feeling that went through me was mostly sadness. 'You can't have us united and let me do what I want while you do what you want.'

'Why not?' he demanded. Now he seemed a little irritated.

'Because you have to give things up to be in a relationship.' I spoke with all the wisdom of someone who had dated one guy for four months. It wasn't much, but it was more experience than Saxon had. I finally had the ability to trump him in something!

'I disagree.' He got up and put his hands on my waist. 'I think you can be yourself completely and let the person you're with do the same thing,' he said slowly, his voice falling as he bent his head. 'And I think you can enjoy each other without all of the complications of being monogamous.' He put his lips on mine, and there was the burn I had felt before, the excitement, but it was dampened.

This wasn't what I'd wanted. Even given my low expectations as far as a relationship with him went, this was not at all what I had expected.

I pulled my lips from his. 'You want me all to

yourself sometimes, but sometimes you're happy to think about me with other guys? It makes no sense. You make no sense.'

'No one makes any sense. That's my point.' He kissed my neck slowly, flicking his tongue on my skin. 'I'm just honest. Sometimes I want you alone, sometimes I'm willing to acknowledge I can't do it all for you. Not that I'm happy about that one, by the way.' He kissed all along the underside of my jaw, and it felt so incredibly good I could almost forget the idiot things he was blabbering about. 'I just feel like we would both like being flexible together.' He laughed at his own dirty pun.

I pulled away. 'I'm going to bed.' My neck was painted with the cooling moisture of his tongue, my mouth still puffy from our hard kissing.

'Coward,' he said affectionately.

'Take a look at yourself,' I said, so bone tired, I could only think about my bed.

I made my way down the hall, still in Saxon's clothes, the acrid smell of smoke so overwhelming I considered a shower, but decided I was too exhausted. I stopped outside of Mom's door. Part of me wanted to crawl into bed with her, not to tell her any of this crap I had managed to wade deep into, but just to be near her. But I knew she'd get wound up about the smell of smoke on me. Mom worried a lot about that kind of thing. Good thing she didn't know the other less than desirable activities I'd been participating in lately. Things that would make a few cigarettes look like nothing.

Chapter 8

Once I got to my room, I expected to pass out from weariness, but even though my body was heavy and beaten, my mind raced at a hundred miles an hour. I tossed and turned, something that was completely out of my norm, then pulled out my laptop and logged on to Facebook.

Jake hadn't unfriended me. My heart leaped a little when I saw that the picture of the two of us was still the one he had up.

I wondered why this had happened in the first place. Now, groggy, miserable, and disillusioned by Saxon's cowardly hard-ass approach to dating, I wondered why I hadn't grabbed on to Jake and never let go. I wondered why I had ever let my mind wander to anyone or anything else.

I clicked his picture section. My album had been renamed. Now it just said 'Gone'. I opened it, though I knew that wasn't the best idea considering how much I already had crammed and crashing in my head. There were four new pictures.

The first one was actually two pictures side by side. On the left was a color photo of me, smiling in the diner, a forkful of waffle held out to the camera. On the right was a black-and-white close-up of a waffle, cut up with two butter knives stuck in it and a cigarette smashed in the center. My breath caught in my throat. It was such a weirdly ugly, jarring image. And very similar to the one of the apple with the knife through it that I had taken earlier.

Each picture after was done in the same format. On the left side was a color picture of me, on the right a black-and-white of whatever had been in the picture with me, but undone. There was a picture of me in front of the school, then a close-up of the school mascot, toilet papered and graffitied. There was the picture of the overlook where we had skipped school, me smiling brightly, then a black-and-white of the same backdrop, deserted, a dusky light making it look ominous. And the last was me sitting on Jake's bed, grinning like an idiot. The black-and-white on the other side showed his blankets rumpled and disheveled, and a wrapper on the sheets.

A condom wrapper?

I felt my throat tighten. I wasn't sure. I'd never had

a reason to use a condom, but Jake had some. I had found them deep in his closet when I was spying. He told me he had bought them while he was still living crazily.

I swallowed hard. Was I being melodramatic? But Jake was a precise artist. He was methodical. If there was a wrapper in the middle of that picture, it was there to send me a message. He knew I'd check it. He knew it would make me crazy.

I realized then how dangerous it was to get so close to someone. Only Jake could know exactly how to punish me so perfectly.

I simultaneously realized that I deserved every second of agony. I thought about him smiling his slow, slightly crooked smile at someone else. I imagined him laying her down and taking his time, being gentle. Or had he gone back to the way he was before? Drunk and uncaring?

How had it happened so fast? It was winter break. All of the lowlifes in the Sussex County area would be throwing parties, getting plastered and humping each other with jolly abandon. If Jake wanted, he could pick up a different girl, or even two, every night of the week, and it could happen in no time at all. In just one day, with just a few stupid decisions, he and I had probably smashed everything good and real we spent the last few months building together. And I started the whole ball rolling.

I wished I had never opened my laptop, but I also embraced the awful feelings that made me want to sob. I deserved to be hurt. I had hurt him so badly. I deserved to feel awful.

I lay on my bed and every crazy, terrible, wonderful thing that had happened in the last week swirled though my head, dizzying, and, finally, sleep inducing.

I slept a sleep so miserable it felt like a complete waste of time and woke up feeling drained and weary. I knew what I needed. It was still so early, barely dawn, but I forced myself out of bed and took a hot, weak-watered shower, scrubbing off the caked-on make-up from the night before and the clinging smell of Saxon. I hurried back to my room and tore through my closet, taking out my one crazy, luxury item.

I had learned to pack sensibly from my mother, and I knew every inch counted. But something had pressed me to bring my running shoes, a gift from Thorsten. They were fancy, made to cushion and support, and just be generally great. And they were super-cute. I put on a pair of sweats and a hoodie and tied my shoes tight, just the way I liked them. I taped a note for Mom to her door, and left the dorms.

The air was cold and biting. I started to run on the almost empty sidewalks. I ran past an old couple walking their dog, past a baker filling up her display case with hot pastries. I ran past buildings that were dove-gray and so lovely, they looked almost feminine. I ran past empty parks with empty black benches and noisily splashing fountains. I passed a young couple bickering in a language that didn't sound French while they put fruit out in their market stall. I ran past newspaper stands, movie advertisement posters, beggars, surprised-looking men in suits and women in smart trenchcoats that flapped open when they walked. I was in Paris, France. There was more to life than the two boys from Sussex County who had turned my world upside down. I double clutched, two breaths in and one out, two in and one out.

Thoughts in my head bounced like so many ping-pong balls, ricocheting. I didn't push Jake's pictures out of my head. I let them bob there, right with all of the other images, and tried to accept that they were part of the whole collage of my romantic life. I could see the tip of the Eiffel Tower, and wondered if Mom and I would go to the top. I knew we would if I asked. Mom. I loved Mom. I didn't want to keep lying and moping.

I was breathing hard and my lungs felt a little torn,

but also like they were stretching to accommodate all of the new air I drew in. I liked the feeling. Just like I'd felt my heart shrivel and harden on the museum roof after kissing Saxon, my lungs seemed to expand as I ran on the pavement.

Less room to feel, more to breathe. I would make do with that.

The sun was coming up bright and warm, and my stomach growled and turned on itself. I looped back to the dorms, following the line of cheese stores, grocers and bakers I had committed to memory like a bread-crumb trail. When I got back to the dorm, Mom stuck her head out of her door and hugged me.

'Did you have fun last night, sweetie?' She pulled off the towel that she had wrapped around her head and her damp hair fell in light, wet waves around her shoulders.

I nodded, my body feeling incredibly hot now that I wasn't racing through the cutting air outside. 'Yes. It was good to dance. I'm getting soft.' I gasped for breath.

She rubbed my back with one gentle hand. 'You look all flushed. Go get dressed. We're going to the Louvre today!'

I hugged her hard because I was really excited. Things with Jake and Saxon would be whatever they would be. In the meantime, I would go and see the Louvre with my mother, and I would sincerely, adamantly love it. I had to give my slightly shriveled heart something to expand around, and boys were just too treacherous right now.

Mom and I met for breakfast.

'So how was the dance? Details, please.' She sipped her steaming hot coffee.

'It was OK.' I buttered a roll, paying a lot of attention to the process. She had already asked me in a cursory way, but she obviously wanted more information, and if I didn't give it to her, she would keep digging. 'The music was all French, but everyone danced. I danced until my feet ached.'

'I'm glad you went out.' Mom ran a finger around the rim of her cup. 'I was always self-conscious about that kind of thing when I was young.' She rolled her eyes. 'It's so stupid to be that way. You think everyone else is watching you, that they think you look like a fool, but that's ridiculous. You miss out on the fun of dancing, and the only one who knows if you danced or not is you.'

It was one of her tried and true sayings. 'It was really fun.'

'Those are real travel moments.' Mom dipped a piece of croissant in her cup and took a bite. 'More important than museums and tours are the things you do with the regular French people.'

Another of Mom's favorite topics. She thought our time in Denmark was my most valuable experience because it was so normal: going to the post office, going to the bank, seeing a movie, watching television, taking walks. It was just everyday stuff, but she thought that was the best way to understand a country.

'I'm glad I went.' I wished I could work up more excitement, but it was difficult to push the time in Saxon's room away from my memory.

There was a long silence, then Mom looked up, her blue eyes appearing more gray, probably because she had a great gray cardigan on over her Swiss dot blouse.

'Did you have fun with Saxon?'

I realized that Mom was nervous, and I realized that she saw more than I thought, more than I wanted.

'He's a good dancer.' It was the most neutral thing I could think to say about him.

'He's taken an interest in you,' Mom said pointedly. 'Is that something you want?'

I wanted to tell her everything, starting with the first day of school. I had my mouth open to do it, but something in her eyes stopped me. I knew it would feel good in the moment, but I would wind up regretting it. Mom's love for me was so strong it would override respect for my privacy or my need to work things through on my own. Asking for her help by listening meant that I was inviting her to comment and take action.

And as messed up as things were, they were my own controlled chaos.

'Saxon takes an interest in lots of girls,' I said lightly and shrugged. 'He's fun to go to a dance with. He's just a friend.'

'Good.' Mom took a tiny sip of coffee and made a purposefully bright face. 'So how's Jake?'

My heart fell. 'He's great.' I forced enthusiasm on my words. 'He delivered some apple tarts to Thorsten.'

'He really is a sweet guy,' she said reluctantly.

I felt my heart pounding so loud I could hear the blood sloshing in my ears.

'Yeah,' I said, as evenly as I could. 'He really is.'

If I was unusually quiet for the rest of the morning, Mom didn't seem to notice. She was busy gushing admiration and love for art like blood from a ripped open artery. I was able to fairly effectively turn off my brain to all things boy related and soak in the beauty of the art. I walked the wide marble floors and listened to Mom chat with animation about how certain paintings had changed this or that movement or started a riot or been commissioned by royalty. I looked at dark faces that I would never know and dramatic landscapes that didn't exist any more and wondered about the people who had painted them, wanted them, looked at them every day in homes and churches and offices for hundreds of years before they landed in this museum-to-end-all-museums.

I had snapped discreet pictures all morning. I wasn't insane enough to think I could take any definitive pictures of such great art. But I did want to catch some of what Paris was really like. I got one of a man and woman kissing on the steps outside the museum. I snapped one of two young kids running through the museum halls, unchaperoned. Another of a display box full of pens with a sliding Mona Lisa in the liquid-filled interior; a man tying his shoe next to a group of melting, molding Rodin statues. I clicked whenever I saw a 'real' moment. Jake might never want to see them, but I took a lot of them with him in mind, imagining how we could look at the pictures and invent stories behind them.

It had been one of our favorite things to do: watch people and make up stories about why they were where they were, what they were planning, thinking, doing. Jake always had a knack for making the stories completely wild and making me laugh. I felt a whole new pang over losing him.

Then we were moving down a long, wide corridor with Leonardos on both sides, moving closer and closer to the group of ogling tourists snapping pictures at the end.

'That's the *Mona Lisa*?' I looked at the biggest group of people in the whole, wide museum full of amazing sights.

'Yes,' Mom said, her brow wrinkled. 'You'd think they would give a second of attention to the other paintings. I know she's famous, but come on.'

It was strange, how everyone gravitated to this one painting, agreeing that it was something special, something worth all of the hysteria, even if they had no idea why. It was in that gallery that we saw Lylee and Saxon. When Lylee saw my mother, she walked to her with purpose.

'Suzanne, where were you? I thought we were coming here together?' She sounded annoyed.

Mom gave her an incredibly intimidating stare-down. Even Lylee backed off. 'My daughter was up early, and I decided to take her with me before the rest of the group. You shouldn't count on me to always be right there, Lylee. I'm really here for Brenna.'

Mom's words were icy, and I was so proud, I could have crowed. I felt embarrassed that I had ever been charmed by Lylee, and thought it was weird how completely my opinion of her had changed. Now every time I was around her, she gave off a vain, shallow vibe that just didn't sit well with me. But I didn't tell my mother, because I didn't like to discourage Mom from having friends.

Lylee looked suitably chastized, but there was something about that look I didn't trust one hundred percent.

'How nice that the two of you had time together.' She smiled as indulgently as if she had been the one to give us permission. 'Should we stroll over and see what all the fuss is about?'

Mom put her arm around my shoulders, and we all headed down to the painting. We had to wait in the middle of a big, jostling crowd. It was definitely the most densely populated few square feet in the museum. Maybe it got some competition from the gift shop and the cafeteria, at least at lunchtime, but otherwise this was where you would find most of the museum's patrons.

Mom and Lylee struck up a pseudo-friendly conversation, and Saxon came to stand behind me.

'Morning, pal,' he said softly.

'Hey, Saxon,' I answered, not taking my eyes off the painting. It was hard to see, since it was behind a scratched, slightly blurry piece of Plexiglass.

'Do you want to talk a minute?' He was wearing a faded Quiet Riot T-shirt and a pair of brown suit pants. He looked shower-damp and so handsome, it made my throat tighten.

'Mom, Saxon and I are going to look at the statue of Nike. She's over here, right?' I pointed into the next room.

Mom tossed me an absent-minded smile and nodded, then went back to what was quickly turning into a heated debate with her 'friend' about the relevance of pop culture in art. I knew it could be a while.

Saxon and I walked into the open, cool foyer where Nike stood between two huge staircases that met in the middle. We both stared at the enormous, marble, headless winged goddess.

'I wanted to say that I'm sorry about some of the stuff I said last night.' Saxon's voice sounded the opposite of sorry.

'Like you're sorry because you were wrong, or you're sorry because you don't want me to be pissed?' I sat down on the first step of the left staircase, and the statue shadowed us.

'I guess it makes a difference to you?' He sat too close to me.

'Yes, Saxon. It makes a difference whether your apology is sincere or bullshit.' He took my hand, and even though it felt good, I knew I was mostly just putting up with it.

'Have you talked to Jake?' His voice brushed softly against my ears.

'Not in words.' I felt twitchy when I thought about the photos.

'Smoke signals?' he teased.

'Pictures. On Facebook.' And I briefed Saxon on our photo project, and on the first pictures, then on the second set, and by the time I was done, my head was on his shoulder and he rubbed a hand over my hair roughly.

'He sounds pissed off,' Saxon observed.

'He should be,' I returned, and my voice quavered embarrassingly.

'He's an understanding guy,' Saxon assured me. 'You don't have any reason to be nervous.'

I pressed my face to his T-shirt to hold back the tears that threatened to pour out. 'You're so full of crap, it's hard to believe one word that comes out of your mouth.'

'I can tell you what I'm sorry about from last night.'

Saxon kissed my head. I closed my eyes and leaned into him. 'I'm sorry for pretending I would be cool with you being corrupted, because all of that really was crap. I just think it would be the only way for me to go after you without feeling like you were getting a totally raw deal.'

'I figured that. What about the virgin/whore thing?'

'That stands,' he said firmly. 'Sorry. I know it bucks your whole feminist view of yourself, but it's what makes guys fall all over you.'

I sighed. 'I don't want anyone falling over me.'

He shook his head. 'Did you just steal my bullshit crown? You're so full of it, it's sickening. Something in you takes sick pleasure in seeing guys on their knees for you.' He pulled away and faced me. 'Admit it.'

'It's not true,' I said, though there was, as always, an uncomfortable ring of truth in everything he said, even when he claimed it was mostly crap. And then I kissed him, because he was being so understanding. Because he was so handsome it made my eyes ache to look at him. Because I wanted to. Because Jake's pictures made me lonely and miserable, and I didn't really enjoy feeling punished, even if that's exactly what I deserved.

I wrapped my arms around Saxon's neck and kissed without holding back. He put his hands on my hips and held me to him, kissing back. The goddess of victory towered over us and the cool, damp museum smell surrounded us. I could hear the silky chatter of French museum-goers and the tread of their feet as they passed by us. I pressed harder, and Saxon was the only thing I thought about.

Saxon.

Complicated, understanding, infuriating Saxon.

When I finally pulled away, he smiled and looked happy.

'We only have a few days left here.' He tucked my hair behind my ears. 'Let's be exclusive, you and me, all right? International dating buddies. And when you get home, you go back where you belong.'

'It's not going to work like that, Saxon.' It was annoying that he was trying to plan my life out, despite his obvious good intentions. 'Anyway, I thought you were working on not being someone to have fun with.'

'This isn't fun.' He held my face in his hands. 'You're not giving up the goods and it's gonna be uncomfortable as hell when we get back to good ol' Jersey. This is just pure indulgence.'

It was that word that did it for me. Maybe my childhood desire to scribble over a perfectly good fairy tale had just morphed into my teen life. Because I'd had all of the elements of a fairy tale with Jake, and here I was, scribbling hard with every crazy, relationship-ending color I could find.

'It sounds like a really stupid idea,' I said, then kissed him softly. 'I'm in.'

He took my hand and stood me up. 'You know they had to move this in World War Two?' He looked at the colossal Nike.

'Why?'

'Hitler was an art lover. Kind of. He stole famous art from all over Europe and holed it up for future display in some planned master museum. Anyway, the Germans were marching on Paris, and the museum director got scared, so they moved it.'

'How?' I liked this storytelling side of Saxon. I liked thinking about historical facts instead of emotional intricacies. This was good.

'They put up all kinds of ropes and pulleys and just pulled her down the stairs and out the door.' He chuckled, something in him loving the idea of a Classical statue being dragged down a marble staircase by frantic Frenchmen with Nazis hot on their tail.

It made my eyes pop just to imagine the effort that

must have gone into getting it down. 'Could you imagine if they broke her?' My voice was hushed with the horror of it.

He laughed, the sound echoing off the big cave of a room. 'Brenna, she's got no head! How much more could they do?'

I looked at the huge, intimidating marble goddess, who was strangely headless in that way so much ancient art is, that I just kind of imagine great sculpture purposefully limbless and beheaded. 'Well, there's the wings,' I said indignantly, but when he kept laughing, I gave up and joined him.

Mom found us standing on the stairs, our arms loosely around each other, laughing hard and leaning on each other for support.

'What's so funny?' Mom asked.

'That she has no head,' I gasped and Saxon leaned his head back and howled.

Mom narrowed her eyes at me a little. The idea of mocking an ancient, headless marble statue was practically sacrilege to my mother, and she crossed her arms and glared our laughs dead.

'If you two jokers are done, we have a lot more to see.'

I left Saxon's embrace swiftly and put my arm around Mom's waist.

'It wasn't really that she was headless that was so funny,' I said soberly, willing Mom to feel less disappointed in my disrespect of the arts. 'It was the Nazis trying to steal her . . .' Yeah, there was no way to explain it that didn't make us sound like idiot teenage American tourists.

'The Nazi occupation of Paris was a real hoot.' Mom clicked her tongue. '*Tsk*. Brenna, they have an amazing Dutch landscape section. Would you like to see it? If clouds and dikes aren't too hilarious for you.'

Saxon choked a little, and I tried to stifle a laugh behind my hand. Mom rolled her eyes, but she smiled. A little.

We went through the rest of the massive, cool museum and looked at the clouds and dikes with perfectly respectful appreciation, though Saxon did pinch my arm and wink behind Mom's back. Lylee joined us, and I found her innuendo and fawning irritating. It seemed like Saxon did, too. Finally everyone's eyes except Mom's were glazed over from fine-art overload.

'Should we go examine the Rococo display again? I don't think I really had time to drink that Fragonard in.' Mom clasped her hands over her heart like she was a lovesick teenager.

I could see Lylee and Saxon suppressing groans.

'Maybe we should get something to eat first, Mom,' I suggested.

'Oh! Yes, good idea.' Then Mom wrinkled her nose. 'I just can't eat at the Louvre cafeteria. Let's go and grab something outside . . . there's a great little place a few blocks away.'

Lylee seized the opportunity and drew Mom away by the arm. They chattered over each other about sexual suggestiveness in French Rococo paintings. Saxon grabbed my hand.

'Hey. Sorry if I offended your mother with my headless art and Nazi humor.'

'Mom is serious about art.' I offered him a titbit of advice with my smile. 'Excepting a racial slur or something less than complimentary about me, I don't know if there's anything that would have offended her more.'

He watched her walk in front of us and nodded. 'I like her passion. She doesn't care if she's cool or not, and that's pretty damn awesome on its own.'

'Of course she doesn't care if she's cool.' I put my hands up. 'She's my *mom*.'

'Being a mom doesn't give you automatic self-esteem.' Saxon's eyes switched focus to his mom's back, her long, silky black hair swishing around her firm little butt.

'Your mom seems to have good self-esteem.' I followed his gaze.

'My mom has a big mouth and lots of opinions. That's different.' His face hardened a little.

'Do you two get along?' Before this trip, I felt like Saxon must have just sprung to life, fully formed. Or hatched from a giant egg. The idea of him having parents seemed impossible.

'No.' The word fell out of his mouth bluntly. 'My mother likes me, but I don't really feel any pressing need to be around her much.'

'Why not? She's so smart and pretty.' I didn't like Lylee myself, but it seemed kind of terrible to not like your own mother.

'Jake's told you all about how we were when we were younger, right? How I was the bad guy who introduced him to all the crazy stuff he did?' He grabbed my hand tighter.

'He mentioned it.' I didn't add that he mentioned it often and angrily.

'Well, Jake had the option to get rid of me, and good for him, you know? I'm not being bitter. It's the reason I can't tell him that we're brothers. For a friend to drop you on your head, that's one thing. For a brother to do it? That's not as cut and dried.'

'What does this have to do with Lylee?'

185

'Lylee was my teacher of the dark arts.' He smiled sardonically. 'She didn't want to be burdened with a kid, especially when my dad left. Once I was remotely old enough to be a little party prop, that's what I became. And her friends were such liberal intellectuals, they didn't think there was anything wrong with a ten-year-old sipping beers and smoking cigarettes.' He ran a hand through his hair. 'For the most part, I liked it, you know? It gave me the freedom to do what I wanted to do. But it also means that I'm not great at following rules.'

'You could try a little harder to follow them,' I suggested. He dropped my hand and wrapped his arm around my waist, pulling me out of the way of the busy, crowding pedestrians on the narrow sidewalk.

'You say that like it's just some switch I can flip.' He shook his head and pulled me closer. 'Remember last night you got pissed off when I compared you to a pet?'

'Yes. I was upset because it was a moronic thing to say.' I was prepared to stand my ground on that one.

'You were upset because I was calling you a pet.' He smiled at me. 'But we're all pets. Kids, I mean. Our parents keep us and feed us and make choices for us. We're just pets until we're old enough to be our own keepers.'

'So, I'm just like a hamster to my parents?'

'No.' He swept a quick kiss on my hair. 'Nothing as mindless and disposable as a hamster. You're like a thoroughbred, like some magnificent creature they're going to care for and set in the right direction, and bet all of their fortunes on. And probably win.'

'Weird, but OK.' I thought about it for a minute. 'What kind of pet are you, then?'

'Something no one's supposed to have as a pet, but they have it because it's cool. Like an anaconda. I'm like a show-off kind of animal, but I'm not going to show you affection or love.'

'That's a stupid comparison, Saxon. You're not uncaring. You're just . . . misguided.' I looked over at him, and his face made my throat feel scratched and dry. His mouth was crimped into something like a smile, but his eyes were definitely sad.

'What am I then?'

'Maybe you're like a wolf cub,' I suggested. 'Maybe you're half domestic and half wild.'

'You're holding out hope for me?' His hand tightened on my hip.

'Always,' I promised. 'So if you think of yourself as a wolf cub and not a snake, isn't there real hope that you could give in to your domestic side?'

'Yeah.' He kissed my head again. 'But shit, Brenna,

even domesticated dogs go crazy and maul their owners sometimes. Who the hell would trust a wolf?'

He's right. A wolf. It's something that I've associated with him since I first met him. He's savage and frightening, loyal and fearless, dangerous and beautiful.

'Maybe you need to find other half-wolves,' I suggested.

He snorted. 'I've been hanging with misfits and lowlifes my whole life. It hasn't done anything good for me yet.'

Ahead of us, Mom and Lylee walked into a café. Saxon stopped me before the entrance.

'Thanks,' he said, and kissed me softly.

'For what?'

'For voluntarily wading through my bullshit. For being willing to see something good in me, even if I don't give you much reason to.' He looked at me, and his look was definitely adoring, and definitely made my heart thud a little. 'Let's eat. You look a little faint. It's been, what, four hours since your last meal? I'm shocked starvation hasn't set in yet.'

'Well, I'm finding you really attractive, so my defenses are obviously down right now. I'm sure how good you look to me has a direct link to how low my blood sugar is.'

'You find me attractive because you're a red-blooded woman.' He smiled a self-assured smile.

We went in and sat with Mom and Lylee. He pulled my chair out for me, which I didn't expect, but liked.

'Saxon,' Mom asked over her menu. 'How has your junior year been? I guess you're coming close to choosing a college.'

'My mom has her heart set on Drew.' Saxon reached for his cigarettes, but caught my eye and decided against them. 'But I'm looking at taking a year off.'

'Do you want to travel?' my mother asked, reaching for the one and only reasonable alternative to going on to higher education right away.

'No.' Saxon moved the silverware around on the table in a jerky circle, his hands jittering for something to do. 'Just want to take a year to relax a little. I'm thinking of going to Alaska, working in a cannery.'

Lylee chuckled indulgently. 'Why would you want to head somewhere where the ratio of men to women is five hundred to one?'

'Maybe I want to get away from women for a while.' He glared at her.

'Saxon, you should just embrace who you are. You can't just bury yourself in Alaska and think that will make you some introspective monk.' She stirred her creamy coffee and took a sip, pursing her lips so cutely I thought she must have practiced it.

'I think some honest labor would do me good,' he snapped.

'Why? We don't need any more money, God knows that.' She shuddered delicately, like she was talking about more leprosy or more tornadoes.

'It's not *my* money.' Saxon's face colored. I had never watched people fight so intimately and openly in front of other people before. I looked at Mom across the table, and she wore the exact open-mouthed stare I was sure was plastered on my own face.

'It's family money, Saxon. That makes it yours. Don't quibble over the fine print.' Lylee sighed. Then she looked over at Mom and me like she had just remembered we were there. 'It's so rude of us to have a family argument in front of the two of you.'

What was there to say? Mom and I looked at each other, but we couldn't come up with a single thing between the two of us.

'Where are you planning to apply, Brenna?' Lylee asked, but it was clear that she wasn't all that interested.

I shrugged. 'I'm still a sophomore. I haven't really narrowed anything down yet.'

'Brenna is going to study at Trinity College, Dublin this summer,' Mom bragged. 'Thorsten and I would be so happy if she went to college overseas.' She reached out and patted my hand. 'We would miss her so much, but you have to take these opportunities when you're young and unattached.'

'Or just never get attached. That's how I manage.' Lylee laughed, a tinkling sound that was ugly in my ears.

Wasn't motherhood the ultimate attachment?

Saxon gritted his teeth, then looked over at me. 'So, Ireland this summer?' He smiled. 'Maybe I should look into the program.'

'Maybe you shouldn't,' I said, and wanted to bite my tongue. Saxon and I had such a natural back and forth that I forgot to speak normally to him when we were around other people. His mother, of course, thought it was beyond funny. Mine frowned.

'There are several good programs, Saxon,' my mother said firmly. I'm sure she hated seeing Lylee put her own son down. It just didn't mesh with Mom's idea of good family. 'There's one in Egypt. Archeology,' Mom said brightly. I suppressed a sigh. That was the one she'd deemed 'way too unsafe for Brenna'. I guess it was good enough for Saxon.

The food arrived and we were all glad for the distraction. Conversation was actually getting painful, and I was really hoping we didn't get stuck going out in our little quad too often.

We tried a few more seemingly mundane topics, but it didn't get any better, so we hurried through our meal, and prepared to leave.

'I'm going to head back to the dorm, sweetie. I promised Thorsten I'd call before he left for work, and I want to make some notes on ideas for a Louvre trip the college wants to finalize for their new study trip this summer. Are you going to stay out?' Mom put on her coat and slung her purse over her shoulder.

Saxon put a hand at the small of my back.

'I think so,' I said. 'I think Saxon and I will roam around a little.'

She gave Saxon a wary look. 'Take care of your-selves.' She kissed me on the cheek.

Lylee and Saxon didn't talk. She just flipped him a wave and followed Mom. I could tell Mom wasn't thrilled.

'Your mom is badass.' Saxon watched the two women walk away and pulled out his cigarettes the minute they were out of sight.

'Sorry. She's a little scary, right?' I was used to my mother freaking people out.

'She loves you. She thinks you're awesome. And she obviously doesn't put up with any bullshit. Isn't that pretty much a perfect mom?' He pulled me close and kissed me. My head felt light and wonderful.

'She is pretty perfect.'

'Lucky,' he gritted out.

Chapter 9

We started out in the cool Parisian air. Behind the crisp
wind was the smell of coffee wafting from the open
door of the shop next door.

'Not really. It's good. It's really good to have Mom
and Thorsten. But there's a lot of pressure.'

'Why?' He looked at me like I had twelve heads
and took my arm to walk me around a man wrestling
with several baskets of baguettes, so fresh and hot we
could see the steam rising off them. 'You could do
whatever, and they would obviously still worship at
your shrine.'

'That's just it.' I knotted my scarf tightly around my
neck. 'I really like them. They're totally fair and
ridiculously supportive. So if I screw up, they don't
get mad. They just get disappointed, and I wind up
feeling like crap. If they were assholes, I could scream
at them, throw tantrums, rebel. But how much of a
creep would I be if I did that to them?'

'Good point.' Saxon put a cigarette to his lips and lit it. 'My mom and I have had our share of tantrums. It gets pretty old pretty quick.'

'Are you serious about the cannery thing?' I watched him take a drag out of the corner of my eye as we crossed the street. He snatched a small apple from a fruit vendor's cart, then quickly replaced it when I shook my head.

He smiled a wicked smile. 'It does incite fury in all reasonable adults. I guess that's a big part of the appeal. Other than that, I just want to get away from all of this bullshit. Sometimes I feel like I'm in the middle of a shitstorm that I created, and I just want out.'

I took his hand. I think he did create his own horrible, shitty world to live in, but, knowing more about Saxon's home life, I realized that he was somewhat a product of his own crappy upbringing.

And I knew exactly what he was feeling when he talked about creating his own shitstorm. I decided I'd better stop judging the guys in my life for all the crazy things they'd done. It seemed like the harsher I judged them, the worse I felt when I made the exact same mistakes. The smartest thing I could do was just accept that the two of them had done a lot more than I had, and that I was going to make my own crazy mistakes the more experience I gained, whether I liked it or not.

'Why not just study abroad or something?' I took a look around at the gorgeous balconied apartments and wrought-iron gates that we were passing. Living here for a year would be amazing. 'Isn't that Notre Dame? There?' I pointed and he followed my finger, nodded, and grabbed me by the arm.

We hurried down the street and then we were standing there, mouths open, dwarfed by the imposing white cathedral with its bursts of colored-glass windows. It was like I could feel the ghosts of Napoleon and Joan of Arc, the hunchbacks and parishioners, saints and sinners all crushed in this one space. There was nothing quite like this in America. Nothing so full of history that spanned so many hundreds of years.

'Do you feel that?' I ask Saxon, but he's definitely laughing at me. 'How can you laugh? How could you not want to live here? You could do a Rotary program, hang out for a year, eat baguettes, drink coffee, smoke all day . . . it sounds like your own version of heaven.'

He shrugged. 'Seems kind of goody-goody, even with the smokes, doesn't it? Unless they have an exchange program with Amsterdam. That might fit.'

I refused to let Saxon's attitude destroy the magic of Paris. We left the cathedral without going in and walked along the banks of the Seine, crossing one of the elegant bridges until we came to a quieter part of the city, hidden like a buried treasure.

We walked to a huge French garden, obviously a lot less charming in the dead of winter, but still really nice. We walked through trees and past bubbling fountains and then to a small manmade cave. He stopped me in the middle of the dark, private enclosure.

'C'mon, Blix. Seriously? A cozy little cave in a garden in the middle of Paris? I know I'm not the most romantic guy, but give me a little credit.' He pulled me over, and for a few minutes the world revolved solidly around the two of us. He had been fairly considerate of my prudishness, but the cocooning dark made him bolder. One warm hand slid under the hem of my shirt, then another. He pushed up along my ribs. It was different than the way Jake touched me. Saxon was smoother, slower and more controlled. When Jake touched me, it was like our minds turned off and our bodies jumped at each other. But Saxon seemed to know exactly what he was doing. He moved his hands around to my back, and slid them down until they popped out and down over my pants and held my butt hard, then squeezed and kissed harder as he did it.

I felt a rush of warmth as I relaxed in his arms. He nibbled along my jaw, kissed at my ears and sucked gently on my neck. He walked me backwards to the wall of the cave and lifted me up, so I was trapped between him and the wall and he pressed into me, wanting me to feel that he was hard.

'It could be a lot better than this, Blix.' He kissed me again. I knew now that when he called me Blix it could mean any number of things, but it always meant that he was trying to lure me into doing something bad.

'No.' I kissed him again. 'This is enough.'

'I don't mean sex. I could do things for you, to you . . .' He trailed off suggestively and rubbed against me harder.

The one thing I expected from the Saxon experiment was undivided lust, but now that I was in his arms, I didn't feel comfortable with it. Flirting around lust was one thing, but acting on it was the ultimate vulnerability, and Saxon didn't inspire the kind of comfort that made it OK to reveal what was vulnerable.

'No.' I shook my head.

He pulled away and let me plop to my feet with a thud. 'Whoa. Shot down by super-virgin.'

It was mean, and it was meant to be. That was so typical of Saxon, and so completely irritating. He had let himself get close to me, which he loved and hated, but any form of rejection, even completely reasonable rejection, set him off snapping. I stalked out of the dark little space.

'Wait!' he called, but not very loudly or adamantly. He knew he'd been an asshole, and he didn't want a confrontation that would basically end with him admitting that fact. Again.

I jogged, then ran through the park, enjoying the way the pigeons burst up and flew out of my way when I came close. I liked listening to the tiny kids swinging off of jungle gyms, calling out in their perfect babyish French. I liked the dark immigrants with coolers bungee-corded around their backs, selling semi-cool sodas for a fraction of the official refreshment-stand price. I liked the gypsies begging and dancing and singing just outside of the doors of the major attractions.

I raced past stone steps being swept by elderly women, past churches with steeples that grazed the brooding clouds, past department stores with bored shop-girls leaning on the counters, flipping through magazines, and grocery stores with fluorescent lights that looked too cold and sterile for Paris. I ran across the streets when there weren't too many treacherously driven cars and made it right down to the river, where

199

the earth was muddy and sucked at my sneakers. I came back up off the river bank and ran around a garden, brown and shriveled in the cold except for some evergreen bushes. I ran across the streets again, playing with my life as I dodged cars that seemed to speed up when they saw me, and finally wound up back on the gravelly walk of a park that was familiar. I ran in and out of every twist and corner turn until there wasn't a corner I hadn't chased.

Then there was a hand on my shoulder, and I screamed.

'Whoa, it's me, Bren. It's just me.' Saxon was doubled over, his breathing labored and wheezy.

'How do you keep up on the soccer field?' I put my hands on my hips and watched him choke and hack.

'I don't have to chase the ball five miles straight,' he gasped.

I clicked my tongue. '*Tsk*. That was not five miles. Maybe two.' I smiled at his physical weakness. 'You need to stop smoking.'

'You need to listen when you run.' He breathed hard. 'I called to you.'

'I decided to tune out irritating noise.' I pushed at his shoulder so he wobbled over.

'I'm running after you like a lunatic to ... apologize,' he said finally.

I looked at him critically, tilted my head and looked again. He was so hot. Ten times hotter than when I first met him, since I now knew what he looked like with no shirt on and when he was actually being sweet and when he was hard with lust.

But he was also a pain in the ass. I hadn't appreciated how easy Jake was to be around until I decided to blow him off for someone with so much drama he should have his own acting company.

'Um, I don't think this is working,' I said, unsure I was actually saying what I thought I was saying.

'Are you dumping me, Blix?' He was still gasping for breath a little. Wow, this was low of me. I could at least let him catch his breath, but I was still mad at him. 'We're not even completely dating.'

'Then I guess I'm not completely dumping you.' I rubbed his neck. 'I just don't want to play your game anymore, Saxon. It's hard and boring and frustrating. And you're so hot and smart, I thought you might be worth the stress, but this is just ridiculous.'

He gave me a sour look, and I think he must have mulled over ten different things to say, but finally he just shook his head and walked back the way he had come.

So I had successfully fallen in love, dated and dumped two incredibly hot, incredibly sought-after guys in less than five months. Where would I go after this?

I went back to the dorm. I changed into a cute dress, white with little yellow polka dots and a wide red belt, and Mom and I had a nice dinner in a quiet restaurant with candles on the table and waiting staff in stiff black uniforms.

'You've been down, Bren.' She saw straight through me, and I knew she never missed much. No matter how many secrets I kept from her, she would always know when something was wrong.

I looked at her closely. I thought about the moment Jake had given her the gloves, the way I knew she was conflicted about how sweet the gift was in comparison to how much she didn't want to acknowledge Jake's natural sweetness. I thought about standing in front of the stove with her and talking about my father. It hurt her to talk about it, but I had a sudden nasty streak and didn't care who was hurt while my own heart was so shredded.

'Who is my real father?' I kept my voice respectful. I had been raised better than to be a total asshole.

Mom went rigid and put down her fork. 'Thorsten is your father, Brenna. He puts food on your table. He covers your health insurance and remembers your birthday and makes sure you have everything you could possibly need or want.' She blinked several times, and when she spoke again, her voice was tight. 'Thorsten Blixen is your real father.'

'If I could have chosen my father,' I said carefully, 'I would have chosen Thorsten. He's the best. I love him completely. And I'm not about to go searching for some guy who never cared about me. But I deserve to know a little about him.'

'Why?' Mom demanded. 'What possible reason could there be to know more about him?'

I put my hands over my face and just sat, pressing the cool skin to my hot eyes. I was so hot, in my head, in my heart, over Saxon, over my mother never treating me like anything but a child. 'There are plenty of reasons,' I say, my voice sharper than I mean it to be.

'Brenna, I love you, but lose the tone. There are some things you're just not ready to know about and—'

'Mom, stop!'

Her jaw dropped and I shook my head, so many thoughts racing through, I didn't know what to do with them all. So I just babbled. 'I'm just . . . I'm sick of being treated like a little girl! I'm not. You can talk to me, you know that. You don't need to keep things some big secret. I think I've earned that! I've earned . . . trust. A little faith? Maybe. I need to . . . I can't breathe here!' I got up, my hands clumsy on my chair, and rushed to find the bathroom, but I made a wrong turn and ended up out the door, crossing my arms in the stinging air.

I took a few long, deep breaths.

Mom burst outside after me. 'Brenna!' She was scolding me. Like she didn't listen at all. 'Listen to me. If you have something to say, fine, say it, but I am not going to put up with you behaving like that in public when—'

'Stop!' I cried. She did, her eyes wide. We stared at each other, shivering in the frosty air. 'Listen to what you're saying! You tell me that if I have something to say, I should say it. Well, I do! I say it and say and say it again, but I feel like you only hear what you want to hear! I'm sorry I'm yelling, I'm sorry I'm losing my cool, but Mom . . . I need you to respect that sometimes I'm going to think things that aren't what you think.'

She opened and closed her mouth. 'Well. Of course. I know that.' She sighed heavily.

'Do you?' I blinked tears back. 'I feel like if I don't agree with you . . . if I don't do things exactly the way you think I should, you're not happy!'

'I'm happy if you are, sweetie,' she said, trying to take my hand, but I shook it away so she'd listen.

'No! You aren't listening now, Mom! *Listen* to me, please.' My voice rose up until it was caught by a gust. My mother nodded tightly. 'I know you don't always agree with what I do, but I do care about what you and Fa think. I never want to disappoint you.'

She blinked hard. 'You never could, Brenna. Never.'

I took a huge breath and dove in. 'I want to be able to ask you things and have you treat me like I'm a teenager, not a little girl. That's what I want.'

She pressed her lips together. 'Well, that's fair. I'm sorry if I've been . . . overprotective. It's out of love, sweetie. You know that?' I nodded and she continued, 'Maybe it's just hard for me to watch you make decisions because I'm afraid you'll get hurt.' Her voice broke on the words.

'Mom, I'm going to get hurt,' I said with a teary laugh. 'But that's OK. I'm strong. Like you.'

She nodded, wiping back tears with her fingers. 'OK. How about we get out of the cold and start again. And, I promise, I will listen to you and I will respect you enough to know you can handle the truth.'

I hugged her tight for a few long seconds before we rushed back in, rubbing our hands to warm them at the table. When we sat, Mom folded her hands, waiting for me to talk. So I did, nervously at first, but then with more confidence.

'I think you treat me . . . a certain way.' I stopped. 'When it comes to my, um, dating. I think you're scared I'll fall for a guy like my father. And the reality is, I might. If I don't know about him.' I saw her blink again, and felt like a beast. 'I'm not doing this to make you upset. I know you want what's best for me.'

'I do,' she said, weepily. So I knew she was feeling guilt, but I wasn't sure what for yet.

'Tell me, then.' I slid my hand across the table and took hers in mine.

'He was so smart.' Her voice was shaky. 'And really confident. I didn't have his confidence, and I didn't think I was nearly as smart.' She shook her head. 'His name is Robert Byron.'

'Like the poet?' *Robert Byron*. It was amazing how just knowing his name gave him more substance in my mind.

'Yes. No relation that I know of.' She went on. 'His family disapproved of me. They expected him to marry a girl whose family they knew, someone who went to their church, who could map her lineage back to their family's ancestral village and knew all their traditions. Some crazy nonsense like that. I think that made him even more determined that we should date. He never showed me off. Never took me out openly. We went to prom together, but as part of a group, and

206

his date was a friend, or so he said. Looking back, I was just so naive. If only I'd had some experience.'

'That's what you want for me?' I asked. 'Experience?'

'Yes.' She wiped under her eyes quickly. 'Is that so wrong of me? Did something happen with Jake?'

I wanted to tell her, but there was too much liability in sharing. 'He and I are taking a break. My idea.'

'I'm sorry, honey,' she said in a voice that wasn't completely sorry.

'Did my father try to contact me? Or you?' I asked.

'He was engaged by the time I was eight months pregnant with you. Robert Byron married Marcia Jellet when you were just about six months old.' She looked at me, blinking hard. 'I could deal with him rejecting me, Brenna. But *no one* rejects you.' Her eye had that lovingly maniacal gleam that always takes the angry wind out of my sails.

I couldn't be mad. Even if Mom had tried to make this all happen, had taken me from Jake and brought me here in the middle of winter break, she didn't call him and end it. She didn't push me into Saxon's arms. She didn't say or do anything on the level of what I said and did.

In the end, I had to learn that, as good as my

parents' intentions might be, I was still the one living my own life. And I had to be big enough to admit my own mistakes.

'Thank you, Mom.' I took a deep, shuddery breath. 'I know it sucked to talk about him. I just needed to know some basics. Trust me, I have no desire to meet this guy.'

Mom smiled and picked up her fork again.

We ate and made small talk, and back at the dorm, I felt such a strong pull to call Jake that I couldn't keep my hands off of my phone. But every time I picked it up to call, I felt like an ass.

What was I supposed to say? *I messed up, Saxon's more trouble than he's worth, wanna date again?* Any way I spun this, I was the jerk, and Jake had no business being with me.

But complete inactivity wasn't my thing either, so I went online and stalked him a little. His Facebook picture was just him next to his dirt bike again. I felt my throat close up. What had I expected?

There were no more installments of the 'Gone' photo album. That was a bit of a relief. I deserved to have it thrown in my face. Oh, I totally deserved it and much worse. But that didn't mean I wanted to see it.

* * *

The next day we toured the Impressionist Museum and hit the Salvador Dali Museum. I stayed far away from Saxon, who tried to corner me and talk to me at every turn. I kept my camera clicking and avoided him as best I could. But things slowed down after that. A week in Paris isn't remotely enough time to see anything. The day after was New Year's Eve. Paris was closed down, and so were we. The tutors had stocked up on food and drink and we were planning our own big bash. We would be leaving for America on the second of January. Mom and I cooked all day, napped, and I made a good dent in *Crime and Punishment*. Nice and depressing.

When it was almost time for the party, I changed into my scarlet silk dress, even though the last time I had worn it was on Christmas Day with Jake, and so it felt nostalgic and made me unhappy. I put on my heels and twisted my hair up. Mom and I gathered our food and headed to the large student lounge. Someone had already turned on the television, and MTV France was broadcasting, with bands and cheering people wearing shiny hats and jumping around, cold and happy.

Last year I had been in Denmark with Mom and Thorsten at New Year. I'd spent most of the night reading a collection of short stories by Karen Blixen, a famous Danish author Thorsten absolutely claimed as a relative. When it got close to midnight, we'd bundled up, gone on to the porch, lit sparklers, and drunk champagne. I'd only had one glass, but Thorsten and Mom had finished the bottle and spent the rest of the night dancing, wrapped around each other.

'Why the long face, Blix?' Saxon sidled right next to me, looking so good.

'I just broke up with this really big jerk.' I smiled sadly. 'Oh, and I broke up with this really nice guy, too.'

'So, you're single?' His eyes crinkled with his smile. 'You look smoking hot.'

'You, too.' There was music on, over the blare of the television. Frank Sinatra crooned, and Saxon held his hand out.

'Dance with me. Now that you're a sexy single woman.'

I let him pull me over to him. Saxon, strangely, could dance like Fred Astaire. I was pretty far from Ginger Rogers, but I was on a par with a fairly good *Dancing with the Stars* contestant. Since Saxon led, I could suck up his excellent moves and pretend they were my own.

'You've got skills.' I smiled when Saxon dipped me.

'Lylee put me in classes when I was a kid.'

I laughed when I imagined little Saxon ballroom dancing. He twirled me around and pulled me back neatly into his arms. 'Not bad, Blix. You're good at following my lead.'

'I'm supposed to. This is ballroom dancing,' I pointed out.

'Don't make excuses.' He whirled me around dizzily. 'You just like following a big strong man.'

'If there was a guy like that around, I might follow him.'

We smiled. I laid my head on his chest as we swayed back and forth. 'Talk to Jake recently?'

'No.' That one single word vibrated with emotion.

'Maybe you want to hook back up with me?'

'Saxon, I was able to stand you for two days. That's it. I don't think it's going to work.' I looked at him, and he smiled his wide, cocky smile.

'I don't really feel like this little experiment helped get you out of my system. Maybe we need to do a little more experimenting?' His voice slipped over my ears.

'I thought about that.' I looked up into his devastatingly handsome face.

'And?' he pressed eagerly.

'And I think we're never going to get out of each

other's systems. Being attracted to you is like having lead poisoning.'

He pulled me closer. 'Your flattery kills me. So you're blaming me for poisoning you?'

'Exactly. Once you ingest lead, it's never gone from your system. Remember all those Roman Caesars who went crazy? Lead poisoning. Incurable.' I leaned my head on his shoulder again. My personal poison.

'So I'm in there forever.' He pressed one large, warm hand to my heart.

I moved his hand down to just over my liver. 'I think you're actually here.' Then I raised his hand to my head. 'And here. And the damage is permanent.'

'So your crazy will never go away?'

'No, thanks to you,' I grumbled.

'So what do we do about it?' He put his nose close to my neck and breathed in deeply.

I didn't really know the answer to that one. 'I think we just stop trying so hard. And keep ourselves open.'

'Are you going to set up rules for us?' Saxon pulled me to him again.

'Nope. Remember, you're half wild. Rules just make you crazier.'

'So you're just going to exist in my world and try to resist me at every turn?' His black hair was so shiny I felt like I should be able to see my reflection in it. His black eyes glinted at the new challenge.

'It's so typical that you would think of it as your world,' I said, but I didn't feel any particular anger at him. I was just glad that he and I could be in a room and dance without anything crazy happening.

We spent the rest of the night eating, dancing, playing a really funny game of charades, eating some more, and before we knew it, the old year was almost gone. The adults cracked into bottles of champagne and were giddy and red-cheeked. Soon the countdown was on, and we were screaming the numbers, some of us in French, some in English. Then the ball dropped and everyone cheered and screamed and music played. Mom smacked a happy kiss on my lips, then moved on to kiss the cheeks of all of her coworkers. Once she moved away, Saxon was right there.

'Ring in the New Year with me,' he said. 'Brenna.'

I nodded and he led me to a door labeled with a notice that I couldn't read, but probably said 'no entry'. I could tell we were doing something we weren't supposed to by the look of pure joy on Saxon's face. We climbed up two flights of stairs, and he swung open the door at the top and propped it with a brick. We were looking at the Eiffel Tower, lit up with explosions of fireworks in pinks, golds and bright reds.

'It's a little cheesy, right? Paris, New Year, the Eiffel Tower?' His voice was soft against my ear.

I shook my head, my eyes locked on the spectacle of shimmering light illuminating the sky. The subtle tinge of smoke snaked through the night air, and the happy cheers and shouts of the crowds made my heart leap.

'Not cheesy at all,' I whispered. 'It's perfect. It's so amazing. I can't believe I'm here . . . I can't believe I'm here, in Paris, watching New Year's fireworks over the Eiffel Tower with you, Saxon.'

'Is it a good thing?' The black of his eyes reflected every burst of color and light in the sky, and, it was funny, but I decided watching the fireworks in his eyes was more beautiful.

'Yes.' There was more to say, but I didn't need to say it, because it crackled in the air between us and we could feel it, as sure as we felt the pop of the fireworks and the buzzing excitement from the crowd's shouts.

He pulled me close to him, his hands sliding along the silk of my dress. He drew me into his arms and put his lips on mine. And for a moment I felt them tremble with his uncertainty. That was sexier by far than any of his aggression or cocky assuredness. If he was always like that . . . well, I should be glad he wasn't, because it would just complicate everything all over again. We kissed, softly, fully. I heard him make a noise between a grunt and a moan deep in his throat.

'Brenna,' he said again, then pulled away and smiled. He looked like he wanted to say something, but didn't know if he should or not. He opened his mouth again. 'Happy New Year, Blix.'

I was positive that wasn't what he wanted to say.

I wrapped my arms around his neck. 'Happy New Year, Saxon. Shall we dance?'

We danced on the little private section of roof above the still-cheering, laughing, kissing crowds, just two screw-ups, arms entwined, moving to a music no one else seemed to hear.

Chapter 10

New Year's Day was a holiday, so we didn't really have much on our schedules. The entire floor was silent, everyone sleeping in after a late New Year's Eve, and for some, sleeping off the inevitable hangover from too much celebrating. I was the lone exception to either scenario.

France is six hours ahead of New Jersey. Which meant that at six in the morning, Jake would be ringing in his New Year. In a few short days I had managed to unravel everything good between the two of us, but I had learned some things, too. I wanted . . . I wanted him to know. Maybe I just wanted to hear his voice. I told myself over and over that he wasn't going to just forgive me and ask me back, but a big part of me was hoping for exactly that.

At five thirty I was up, my eyes open and staring at the white, cracked ceiling above my bed. My stomach churned noisily, a combination of my intestines processing the cheese and champagne from last night and true, fretful nerves. The worst he could do was hang up on me. I tried to tell myself that it wouldn't be that bad if he did, but I had an awful feeling that I would be crying in a little while.

I only had a few minutes to psych myself up. I wanted to call him before the official ball drop, just in case he had plans. To kiss. Someone else.

I sternly reminded myself that that was exactly what I had done the night before. I had no reason to play the hurt innocent. He could do whatever he wanted now. We were not a couple.

Because of me.

I dialed, and another, worse possibility came to mind. What if he just never picked up? I was so desperate to talk to him that I was ten times more prepared for a confrontation than just nothing.

But he did pick up.

My voice stuck hard in my throat.

'Jake?' I finally burst out.

'Brenna.' He said my name evenly, his low, deep voice so good in my ears.

'I was calling to wish you a happy New Year.' My voice wobbled.

He blew out a long breath. 'So you called to dump me a few days ago, and now you're calling to wish me a happy New Year? There are a few choice things I'd like to say to you, but I'll stop myself.'

'Don't,' I rushed. 'I deserve it, Jake. I deserve to hear whatever it is you have to say. Tell me.'

He sighed. 'There's no point, Bren. You and I are done. What is there to say?'

'Do you, um, regret that we broke up?' My nerves made my tongue thick and clumsy.

'How can I regret it, Bren? It wasn't my decision.' He sounded irritated, and his prickly tone was so unexpected, I felt my eyes well up again. I hated that he was talking to me that way. He used to choose his tone so carefully when he said something to me. 'How's Saxon?' he asked, his voice thick with accusation.

'He's all right.' I swallowed a wave of tears. 'We're not a couple.'

'Did you really think that would work out for you?' he sneered. 'I can't believe that. I know for a fact that you're brilliant. That's why this whole thing is so frigging confusing.'

I grabbed on to the one little compliment, the one glimmer that he was still interested in having me in his life. Plus being confused was good. It meant he didn't know. It meant he was thinking with a big 'maybe' in his mind. 'I'm coming home tomorrow.'

My statement hung in the air between us.

'I hope you have a safe flight.' His voice was perfectly serious because Jake was a perfect gentleman, and he would never, ever be nasty or vindictive the way so many guys would be. 'I hope you had a nice New Year.' His voice was so cold I almost believed he could see my kiss with Saxon. 'Bren, I have to go.'

I heard a voice in the background. Distinctly feminine.

Oh no.

'OK. Goodbye, Jake.'

He paused and covered the phone while he answered whoever it was. Then he breathed into the receiver. 'Happy New Year, Brenna.'

The connection was broken and my mind went racing, reading into every little thing Jake said and left unsaid. He said I was brilliant, he said he wanted me to have a safe flight and a happy New Year's. And I know he meant those things.

But he hadn't said that he missed me. He hadn't said that he wanted us to get back together. He had acted a little bit like my call was annoying him.

And that was fair. I was, in fact, just an ex-girlfriend calling for no real reason. He might even have had a date for New Year. I thought about the condom-wrapper picture. Could Jake have already hooked up

219

with someone as more than just revenge sex? Could he have another girlfriend?

That question was ridiculous. Jake was so gorgeous and sweet and a little bad, there was no reason to wonder whether girls would be lining up for a mile. I knew without a doubt that the ball was completely in his court. If he wanted a girlfriend, he could have his pick.

I paced the room a little, and realized that my body was telling me what my mind didn't have a handle on: I needed to run. It was only a little after six, no one would be up for hours. I put on my running clothes and shoes, left a note for my mother, and set off, my pace so crazy it would have made my cross-country coach turn cartwheels. I ran past the rivers and parks and buildings of one of the most beautiful cities in the world, but all my eyes wanted to see was a gray-eyed boy with a crooked smile.

As I ran, I cried and didn't bother to wipe away the tears or the gross amounts of snot that poured out along with those tears. I ran because if I didn't expend some energy fast, I was going to go crazy.

My sad little heart thumped happily, pumping blood through my body in mad, crashing waves. My lungs worked like a bellows, and I got lightheaded from all the air I gulped in too fast. Coach Dunn had taught me all the techniques to maximize my energy and breathing and control my heart rate, and I knew I should double clutch now, before I lost it entirely, but I couldn't care less. I just wanted to run this aggression off. I made a wild circuit, and when I felt like I was running out of steam, I looked for the giant trees in the park Saxon and I had walked through holding hands on our first night in Paris.

I just made it to a bench when I felt my muscles bunch and my breath slice in and out of my lungs, and I had to stop and double over. I couldn't catch my breath.

I started when I felt a large hand on my back. 'There, there, Blix.' Saxon rubbed my back comfortingly despite the cheerfully mocking tone of his words. 'You'll be OK. Here, have some.'

It was bottled water. I chugged it, then looked at him with my puffy, red eyes and snot still under my nose and chapped lips. 'How did you know I'd be here?'

'Because at six this morning it was New Year in New Jersey. Plus, this is the only park in Paris you know, so I figured your run would bring you through here eventually.' He wore dark aviator sunglasses, so I couldn't see his eyes, but would've bet they were laughing at me, even if his mouth was serious. Saxon sat next to me and stretched his arm behind my back. 'You call him?'

I nodded and felt very close to tears again.

'Blix, I told you he would take you back,' he snapped. 'Stop looking so damn weepy. It's a shitty look for you.'

His callous reaction was actually exactly what I needed. I laughed and punched his arm playfully. 'Fuck you, Saxon.'

'Nice if you would,' he drawled, then helped me up. He took the sleeve of his hoodie and pulled it down, long and loose, then wiped at my face gently, sopping up the tears and even the snot. It was one of the most intimately kind things anyone had ever done for me. 'It will all be different when we get back. Trust me.'

I put my arm around his waist and he put his around my shoulders, and I realized that as much as I hated having Jake out of my life, I loved the freedom to be with Saxon, however I needed to, without feeling any guilt. I leaned my head on his shoulder as we walked back, matching my breathing and eventually my heart rate to his. He had been there when I needed him, and that gave my mind a chance for real peace.

The rest of the day rushed by. It was mostly filled

with Mom lamenting all the things we hadn't been able to do and see, including the Eiffel Tower and Notre Dame. I was relieved that we had a reason to come back. Much as I had loved being here, I wanted the chance to experience Paris without the drama of Jake and Saxon looming over my head. And it would be great to see Paris in the spring or summer, when things were in bloom. When I pointed that out to Mom, she calmed down and we had a fairly peaceful night.

Mom turned in early, to better ready herself for a long flight and to take extreme precaution against jet lag. I was ready to be home, much as I dreaded what I might have to face when I got there. I was done packing, had my travel outfit ready and was about to crack into Raskolnikov's story again, when I heard a light knock. I looked at the shut door for a moment, considering. I knew it was Saxon, but I wondered what he wanted.

There was no way I could just wonder for long.

'Come in!' I called.

He stepped into my room and looked around. I know they're just dorms, but mine definitely had something his lacked. First of all, mine didn't stink of smoke. It was neat and bright, the windows opened, the bed was nicely made, my possessions contained. He dropped on the mattress next to me.

'You don't hate me, Blix, do you? I mean, after all of this drama, we're still cool, right?' His voice was low and uncaring, but I knew that he was covering.

I took his hand in mine. 'I don't hate you, Saxon. I thought I could, once, but it didn't really work. No matter how much of an asshole you are, there's something likeable about you.'

He tucked a piece of hair behind my ear. 'I thought I could do it,' he said quietly.

'What?' I turned my face up and looked into his.

He swallowed and I watched the tendons in his throat constrict. 'I thought I could make you fall in love with me. I thought being in Paris with me, and Jake so far away, it would all just fall into place. Man, I was wrong, huh?'

'I did kind of fall for you, Saxon,' I said, our eyes and our hands locked together. 'But you wouldn't want me as a girlfriend anyway.'

He smiled. 'If I'd had any chance of ever having a girlfriend, it would have been you, Brenna.'

'So you're doomed to be permanently alone?' I felt the pressure of his hand as he squeezed mine.

'Maybe. Lose the long face. I'm going to have so much mind-blowing casual sex, it will be unbelievable.'

He kissed my cheek, then pulled back and took a deep breath. 'But that's not what I'm here for.'

'What do you want then?' Fear mingled with anticipation when I imagined what he might ask for and how I would possibly be able to say no to him.

'I want to help you,' he said, then fell back on the bed, his arms splayed out, his tattoos slightly visible where his shirt sleeves rode up.

I turned and looked at his long, supine figure. 'I don't need any help from you.'

'Yes, you do.' He shut his eyes. 'I drove you to this whole thing. I know you never wanted it.'

That irritated me. It was pretty much the reaction Jake'd had when I'd told him about me and Saxon. Why was it so inconceivable that I could make a decision to change something in my own life by myself? Why did every decision I made get taken from me as if I were some infant who could only react to what others did?

I was the one who had pulled Saxon in on the roof, and demanded we do something! I was the one who had initiated the whole thing! Part of me wanted to chicken out and hide behind Saxon again, but I was getting tired of living according to other people's rules and expectations, no matter how good their intentions for me were. And no matter how huge and messy my own mistakes were.

'I did what *I* wanted.'

'Yeah, I know, you're your own person, blah, blah, blah.'

'So, what big help are you offering me?' I asked through gritted teeth.

'I'm going to get you back with Jake.' He clapped his hands together like a genie granting a wish.

I felt my heart leap a little. 'Jake?' I said. Just his name felt so good. 'Saxon, what Jake and I had is gone. No more. Even if he agreed to date me again, it wouldn't work out.' Plus I didn't like the idea of Saxon involved with any plan to do with Jake.

'That's because he doesn't know the whole story.' Saxon looked up at me from under long, long eyelashes.

'What are you talking about?' I narrowed my eyes at what I felt in my bones was going to be a colossally bad idea.

'I'm going to make a story that works.' He shrugged like it was the easiest, most obvious idea in the world.

'What do you mean "works"?' Real dread poured over me.

'The truth is so fucking lame it's not even worth

telling. I'm going to figure something out that will make Jake blame me.'

'How many times do you think that will actually work, Saxon? Jake's not an idiot.'

'When it comes to you, that's exactly what he is.' He put a hand on my knee and ran it up to my inner thigh. I smacked at him and he did it again. 'You're so easy to piss off.'

'Only when I'm around you,' I snapped. 'I told you we'd bring out the worst in each other.'

'Speak for yourself.' He drummed his fingers on my knee. 'This is the best behaved I've been in a long time.'

'Are you kidding me?' I snorted. 'You've been a complete jerk-off.'

He frowned. 'Blix, there were several times I was pretty much a gentleman.'

'Really? Like when?'

'Like when you were in my room the other night, and I could have gotten you all hot and wet, but I didn't,' he said, and he was only half joking. 'I could have pressed the issue, and I bet you and I would have had a lot more fun than we wound up having.'

'Nothing with you has been fun.' I couldn't help feeling a twinge of sadness because that was the truth. When I had been unobtainable, he had been enticing but nerve-racking. And once I fell into his arms, he was high maintenance and unpredictable. I just thought the whole thing'd had so much more promise for . . . I don't really know what I expected.

Maybe it was like when people heard I had lived in Denmark for a year. They just couldn't help but imagine this sophisticated European experience, when in reality it was just fifteen lonely months on an old chicken farm. Not that it hadn't had its moments, but it wasn't all baguettes and berets.

Was I getting my European metaphors mixed up?

'What's wrong?' he demanded, like he knew I was thinking something uncharitable about him.

'I was just thinking that I thought it would be more fun. Between us.'

He smiled a little. 'If it had worked out, would you have been thinking about Jake so much?'

I took a few deep breaths and tried to phrase it correctly. Then I just gave up and said what I felt, no matter how much of a hussy it made me look. 'I don't know. I didn't really anticipate a certain outcome. I just needed to do it, so I would know. And now I do.'

'Know part of it,' Saxon corrected.

'I gave it a fair chance,' I argued.

'You pined for Jake.' Saxon rolled on his elbow and looked at me. 'I don't think you realize how much you like him, Brenna. I think it's ridiculous and irritating, especially considering what you could have right here, but I'm not judging.'

'Listen, it doesn't matter what I think or want. Jake isn't going to go along with this or any other stupid scheme you come up with, so drop it.' I pulled my knees up under my chin and held my legs tight to my chest.

'Can't.' Saxon flicked my foot. 'If you won't have me, then it's my mission to throw you into the arms of my half-brother. I like to keep it in the family.'

I ignored the more obvious attempt to aggravate me. 'Why don't you tell him that you're brothers?'

'Why don't you beat a dead horse? You're good at that.' His tone was clipped again. 'Drop it, Bren.'

'Take your own advice, Saxon.' I poked him with my toe. 'Let me figure it out myself, OK? Thanks, anyway.'

'Fine.' He smiled so wide his teeth gleamed.

Saxon finally got up and left the room, which felt much bigger without his overwhelming presence. It would be the last time we were together in this little semi-permanent room of mine. I snapped a few pictures, to help remember. And possibly, maybe, to help tell Jake the whole story. Someday. It was weird to think about going back to the States, where life was going to be basically the same as when we left. Oh, except that I no longer had my adoring/adorable boyfriend.

I thought about him on the flight, and it seemed like every mile we got closer to home, I wanted him more and regretted what I had done. More and more, Saxon's scheme seemed like a good idea.

There was just one problem, and it weighed on me just as much as the initial problem of my attraction to Saxon: why had I ever even considered leaving Jake?

He was perfect in so many ways. Jake was kind and attentive. He believed in me and respected me. I was totally physically attracted to him. Sure, Mom didn't approve, but she was basically fanatical when it came to anything that had to do with me. I couldn't imagine a single guy who would meet her criteria. So what had happened? How had I been begging Jake to stay overnight and two days later been pressing myself against Saxon? My head started to pound.

I thought back to all the times Jake had made me cringe a little, and I was filled with deep, relentless guilt. I hated that he couldn't read and understand things as quickly as me. I hadn't even considered emailing him while I was gone, because I knew it would be frustrating for him to write back. And I hated the culture he had grown up in, the girls who had liked him and the things he had done with them, too young and too much.

What was weird is that I didn't hate Saxon as much for that. Maybe because Saxon wore his past like an ironic badge? Maybe because it wasn't really Saxon's birthright. Saxon was a college tutor's son, smart and athletic and socially something closer to me.

My face burned red just thinking what I was thinking. Jake was the best. Better than I deserved.

I could insist that was truly all I wanted. But the truth was, I had a superiority complex when it came to Jake. That was a seriously bad thing in a relationship.

And then it dawned on me that maybe our breaking up was right. If I couldn't respect Jake one hundred percent for who he was, maybe I was never the right person to be with him.

My chest felt like it was being crushed by a vise, and I had to squeeze my eyes shut really tight because I didn't want to cry in front of my mom, even if she was zonked out. Mom had a weird knack for knowing any time I was upset, and I was miserable at hiding it from her. I hadn't had to sit with Saxon on the ride back. Lylee had been annoying enough that even my polite mother had brushed her off completely. Anyway, Mom's anti-jet-lag plan involved an eye cover, ear plugs and total sleep on the plane. I couldn't imagine that Lylee would have paid any attention to Mom's desire to sleep. The Macleans were as annoying as they were charming.

The plane landed late, but there was Thorsten, a big smile on his face and his arms held out. Mom and I hugged him.

'We missed you, Fa,' I said, using my particular pet name for him.

'I missed you girls. A man only needs so much underwear time. I'm ready to put some clothes on and have my ladies back!'

Mom tucked herself into the crook of Thorsten's shoulder and nuzzled against him. My heart bucked. Thorsten and Mom went to gather our luggage on a cart to leave, and just then I felt a familiar presence.

'It'll work out, Blix,' Saxon whispered in my ear. 'I'm on it.'

'That's not reassuring.'

He took my hand and kissed it softly. 'I know I'm kind of a dick, but I really like you.' His black eyes glowed gold. 'It puts a halt to my natural assholeishness and makes me a sometimes-nice guy.'

I put a hand to his cheek and brushed the soft skin with my thumb. 'So you're saying you're half the ass you usually are just for my benefit?'

But Saxon was serious. 'I'm saying that I care about you. Even if I do some fucked-up stuff, I would never want to see you hurt. That's all I'm saying.'

My laugh caught in my throat. This was the other part of the complication with Jake. Jake hated Saxon. He wouldn't approve of my spending any time with him. I didn't want to irritate Jake. But I wanted to be near Saxon.

As much as I was whining about ruining things with Jake, there was a part of me that felt free. I was glad that I could let Saxon kiss my hand and tell me he cared about me without feeling that obligatory stab of guilt that I felt when I was Jake's girlfriend. Maybe being someone's girlfriend just wasn't the right thing for me.

'I care about you, too,' I said, and I meant it with my whole heart. 'And I think you should keep your distance from Jake when we get back. I can't force you to do anything. It's just advice.'

Mom and Thorsten looked over at me, and I wanted to just get home and collapse. I put my arms around Saxon and hugged him hard. 'Thanks for Paris, Saxon.'

He buried his face in my hair and sighed. 'God, I wish you were thanking me for so much more.'

Then I went to Mom and Thorsten, and Saxon went

to do who knows what. He had probably driven himself to the airport. Lylee could be flitting off anywhere. He said he liked his freedom, but at that moment, the cocoon of love from my parents was feeling really good.

Chapter 11

In the car Mom and Thorsten chatted and caught up with each other's news, and I was able to close my eyes and try to make peace with my crazy life. I wanted to run. So many hours on the plane left me feeling cagey, and so many thoughts in my head made me feel a little like puking.

Finally, we pulled into our street, and I felt so happy and peaceful. I looked at the familiar trees passing by the window, and when we came to our driveway, I felt so good, I almost couldn't contain it. I ran through the door and it just smelled right. It smelled like home, and it was the best smell I could have imagined.

'You look tired, sweetheart,' Mom said. 'Do you want to go and lie down?'

I told her I did. I hugged and kissed them both twice and opened the door to my room. Oh, my room! I loved the one blue wall, the bright poppy bedding, the paper lamps, and glass-fronted bookshelves! I loved it all!

I was feeling so great, it didn't seem like anything could ruin it. Until I saw my bangles, laid out carefully on my desk. They were the bangles I'd left at Jake's house because he wanted them as a little reminder of me even when I wasn't there. I felt my throat clamp tight. They were a sign. We were over and he'd wanted to make it unquestioningly clear to me.

I lay on my soft down bedcover and felt the tears run hot and quick down my face. I burrowed deep under the sheets and imagined I could smell Jake on them. I turned my head into my pillow and cried, long and hard. I muffled my sobs and let my body shake until I felt tattered and worn out, until there wasn't one more hiccup or hot tear left. Then I slept, and it was a cold, dark, silent sleep.

I woke up late the next morning. Thorsten had come home from work the day before especially to pick us up, but he was going into the city today to make up for lost hours. Mom wanted to head to the college. She had a notebook full of neatly written lists and time-tables, and I could see her itching to show them to her boss. Her passion for everything always made me smile.

236

'You look awful, Bren.' Mom pressed a hand to my forehead. She put a bowl of hot porridge in front of me. 'Did you get any sleep?'

I shook my head. 'I should have slept on the plane. I think I messed myself up.'

'You should go back to bed for a bit. Or do you want me to stay here?' Her eyes were bright with worry.

'Mom, it's just jet lag. I need to get back on schedule, that's all. You worry too much.' I gave her a weak smile.

She didn't look reassured. 'I'll be right at the college.'

'I'll probably just zonk out.' I spooned the porridge obediently into my mouth. 'But, you know, I might take a run or a bike ride. I don't really want to throw my body clock off too much. I have school tomorrow.' We had missed all of winter break, but would start back with everyone else the next day, Monday.

'Baby, if you need to take a day, take it.' Mom's face was lined with worry. 'You push yourself too hard, Bren. Indulge, right? Didn't we talk about that?'

I suppressed the urge to groan. If only she knew how I had taken her well-meant advice.

'Maybe I will,' I said, noncommittally. 'Maybe I'll ride over to Kelsie's in a little bit.'

'It would be fun for you to see her.' Mom grabbed her purse and keys. 'Well, I'm off. Keep your cell on you. And be careful, sweetie.' She frowned and kissed my head, then she was gone and I was all alone in my big, empty house.

The last day of winter break. When I had looked forward to it, before I knew about Paris, I'd imagined all of the things Jake and I would do together. I'd imagined this last day filled with cuddling and more, goofing off and laughing about all we had done that week. I washed my bowl out in the sink and wondered at how it had all gone so wrong.

I was literally shaky from everything running through my head. I wanted . . . closure or peace or some kind of reassurance. I took a shower and got dressed in a super soft pink sweater and gray jeans. I was going for soft and pretty and maybe a little innocent. I put on a little make-up and did my hair and looked super cute. I got my bike out and remembered that this last day of break wouldn't have been filled with cuddling anyway. Jake always had work on Sunday. He would be at Zinga's.

It wasn't far from my house at all. In fact, Zinga's was closer than Frankford High. I headed there without letting myself think about it too much. And when my bike tires crunched on the gravel, I parked and went to look around without letting myself analyze what I was doing.

Then I saw him, and my throat closed up. Maybe it had all been physical for me. Maybe I was just ruled by my traitorous, hussilicious body. Jake wore his typical winter uniform: baseball cap with a skull cap over it, Carhartt jacket, faded jeans, beat-up work boots. His body was long and lean, but defined by muscle. I knew every muscle, every jutting bone and every smooth and hairy plane of skin. I felt like it was mine, no matter what I had done to ruin our bond.

He didn't see me. I could see his face. He was smiling, his gray eyes crinkled, his eyetooth crooked and perfect. My heart swelled, until he caught sight of me.

It was like an eclipse. All of the warmth and laughter and general happiness was gone. He yelled that he was taking a break and stalked over to me so aggressively, I felt a little nervous. I knew nothing at all about angry Jake. He had never shown me any-thing but love and kindness. I didn't know what to expect from him, but whatever it was, I deserved it. I had brought it on myself.

He came so close we would have been in each other's arms if he had put his around me. He didn't.

He stopped just short of smashing into me, but I

could tell it took all of his effort to stop. He licked his lips nervously and looked at me for a few seconds, his eyes filled with a combination of fury and longing.

'Why are you here?' he demanded.

'I'll leave.' My chicken heart showed its true self. I turned to go and his hand grabbed mine.

It was just like I remembered, big and rough and cold around my softer, smaller, smoother hand.

'Don't go,' he said in a ragged voice, yanking me back to him. 'I asked why you were here. You didn't call me. I didn't even know you were back.'

'Well, I'm back. Last night. I thought you'd made it clear you didn't want me to call,' I added, my voice little more than a squeak.

He raised one eyebrow. 'So you came in person instead?'

'I needed some apple tarts,' I lied. 'For Thorsten.'

'And you decided to ogle the help on the way to the store?' His voice was cold and a little distant, but still a tiny bit flirty. Things hadn't snapped back to the way they were. What had I expected anyway?

'I can't help you're good-looking.' I tried hard to play along.

His mouth tightened. 'Yeah. I guess I have *some* good traits.' I knew what he was saying: he was voicing my exact thought when I had first seen him a few minutes before. He was implying that all I ever liked about him was the physical.

'Look, I'm . . . sorry.' I cringed before I said 'sorry' because it was a lame thing to say. 'I'm glad to see you. I know things are weird. I missed you.'

He still had my hand. Without answering me, he dragged me to a greenhouse. It might have been the same one he dragged me into months ago, where he kissed me so happily. Looking at him now, it didn't seem possible that moment had ever existed. His eyes were steely and cold.

'What are you doing?' His voice was angry and accusing. 'You broke up with me, remember? You wanted Saxon. And I stepped back. Why are you torturing me now?' His voice was raw.

'I'm not,' I stuttered, shocked by his dark look. 'I do miss you. I've been confused.'

He pushed me against the door, his body blocking me in. 'You're a smart girl. Maybe the smartest I've ever known. It's hard for me to believe you're so easily confused.'

'I am,' I repeated. 'I love you.'

'Don't say that.' His voice was tight and furious. 'You're a liar.'

'I'm not.' I breathed hard. 'I love you. But I cared about Saxon. I still care about him, and I didn't know how much or why. I didn't want to be with you and think about him.' It felt good to say it.

'Well, thanks.' He spat the words out sarcastically. 'I hope you two had fun. Just one big genius bullshit party, right?' He pushed off the wall, but I grabbed his arm.

'It wasn't!' I cried. 'It wasn't, Jake. We ... fought a lot. We didn't get along. Not like me and you.'

'You didn't see that coming?' Jake sneered. 'He's a user. I've told you that a million times. But you didn't want to see that about him. Hey, I can't blame you for getting pulled in. He had me good once, too. But I never hurt someone else for him.' He started to walk away, but I grabbed him by his jacket and pulled him back.

'That I'm sorry for!' I said. He looked at me, his face contorted with what could have just as easily been anger or sadness. 'I never wanted to hurt you! I swear, I never wanted to make you upset, Jake.'

He pulled me to him then, crushed me hard to his chest and breathed in my hair. He tightened his arms around me, and I felt the air swoop out of my lungs. In that moment, my shriveled little heart filled and expanded until I was sure it was going to break through the bones that held it back. Then his mouth was on mine, hungry and persistent. His big, hard hands were all over, and I felt like my skin could ignite where he touched me. I pressed into him and kissed back, hard and fierce and sorry. I felt a regret I never imagined was possible and a fragile bubble of hope.

Then he pulled away suddenly, his eyes wild.

'Go home, Bren,' he ordered.

My eyes went wide, and I felt a shaky nervousness. 'Jake, I think we should—'

'Go the hell home!' he snapped. He looked furious. 'Go home now, Brenna!'

I ran out of the greenhouse, and it felt a little like my heart was cracking apart. That delicate bubble of hope burst and was replaced with despair. I got on my bike, my legs jelly-shaky, and pedaled away. I wasn't going towards home, and I wasn't going towards school, the only two places I really knew the way to. I just pedaled blindly, flying past houses I vaguely knew and going down roads I didn't know at all. Finally the sun was high, I shook with cold, and I had no idea where I was. I bit my lip to stop myself from crying. I would not cry!

I slid my cell phone out of my pocket, already hating the idea of calling my mother. She wasn't a fan of me riding my bike anyway. This call would be handing her a free pass to complain and nag every time she thought it wouldn't be safe for me to go out.

Which would be every time I wanted to go out. I scrolled through my contacts and stopped at the one that was so obvious, but also still unexpected.

'Hey,' Saxon said on the fifth ring. He sounded like he was sleeping.

'I . . . uh,' I began, and then I was crying.

'Brenna!' He sounded fully awake. I wanted to curl up and fade away. This was getting ludicrous. 'What's wrong?'

'I'm lost,' I gulped out.

He was silent for a minute, then he laughed. 'I was a Boy Scout for like three weeks. I'll come and find you. Anything nearby?'

'I passed that big mansion off Plains.' I breathed in and out steadily to keep my voice from shaking. 'I went past the emu farm, the one with the dead chickens always in the road. Now I can see the back of the mansion and there's a brick ranch with an old car on concrete blocks.'

'Is it a Mustang?'

'Saxon, how the hell would I know . . . wait, it has a running horse on it.' I peered at the silver emblem on the front of the car.

He laughed. 'How did you get behind the Garbage Castle?'

'Is that it?' I looked at the turreted monstrosity that

I had seen so many times. 'You know where I am?'

'Yeah. That's Roger Benson's house. His dad's had that Mustang since the 70s. It's incredible.' His voice got dreamy.

'It doesn't even have wheels,' I said, my teeth chattering. 'And it looks like one of the doors is rusting off.'

'You have to look at the inner beauty, Blix. The potential.' He was quiet a minute. 'Are you shivering?'

'It *is* January.' I tried not to be too ungrateful. He was, after all, willing to help.

'I'll be there in eight minutes.' He clicked off.

I didn't know where Saxon lived, but eight minutes was probably the amount of time it took if he broke every imaginable traffic law known to man on the way over.

I checked my watch, just for fun. It was twelve forty-seven.

At twelve fifty-four, I heard the rumble of his engine. He pulled up way too close to me, popped the passenger door open and came to get my bike. I got in the car and put my hands to the heat vents, blowing a full stream of hot air.

He got in next to me and grinned. 'So, I guess I'm gonna be your knight in shining armor whether you like it or not.'

'I'm not usually so dumb,' I apologized.

'What brings a lovely, sexually tempting young thing like you to a nearly deserted country road at lunchtime?' He fired up the ignition, held the wheel with one hand and leaned back as comfortably as if he were in a recliner. I loved the way he looked when he drove. I felt a lot of warm feelings towards Saxon when I compared his recent behavior to Jake's.

'I just got lost.' My words rang false in the hot interior of his car.

'Don't bullshit me, Blix.' He popped his cigarette pack out of his pocket and pulled one out with his lips. He took out his lighter and tried to light it, but the bumps in the road didn't make it easy. Neither did the fact that he was doing just under sixty-five. I grabbed the lighter and lit the cigarette. 'Thanks, friend.' He took a long drag. 'Now, what's up?'

'I went to see Jake.' I couldn't say any more. The whole thing was so melodramatic and horrifying.

Saxon rolled his window down and blew smoke out of it. 'I guess it wasn't all wine and roses?'

I shook my head miserably. 'He was pretty pissed off. He told me to go home. He was so mad. I've never seen him that mad.'

'Did you expect a parade? You broke up with him

after he gave you his fucking "protect my heart" ring. He went out on a limb for you.'

Leave it to Saxon to put the truest version of my behavior out in the cold light of day. His lack of sympathy, although right, was upsetting.

'He didn't go on any limb,' I said softly. 'Giving me that ring was just the next logical step for him.'

'Well, yeah.' Saxon flicked ash out the window. 'I told you, he's had his fun. He's not worried about screwing anyone else—'

'I'm not thinking about that!' I interrupted, feeling the burn of a lie, even though I really wasn't thinking about that. Was I?

He chuckled. 'You may not admit it, but I can see you salivating when we're in a room together. Your pheromones are practically choking me.'

'I'm not thinking about sex with anyone,' I repeated. 'Like I need any more complications in my life right now.'

'Your life has been one big complication since you came back from your Danish romp,' he scoffed. 'And you've loved every damn minute, so stop lying to yourself.'

Then the car stopped. We were in front of an enormous, white modern house. 'This is your house?'

'Nope.' He pushed his door open with his shoulder. 'We're breaking in.'

I was about to talk him out of it, calmly, to hide my panic, but then he shook his keys at me with a smirk and waved me to the door. We entered the cavernous house legally, and I hid my sigh of relief.

The front foyer had a fountain. A real fountain like they have in Chinese food restaurants. It was tiled in something dark and incredibly shiny with little shell-like fossils in it.

The living room had whatever would be beyond a cathedral ceiling. Hanging from the middle was a colossal chandelier made of swirling metal and colored glass. There was a big furry carpet over a super-shiny dark wood floor and several weird-shaped red sofas and chairs. Outside the enormous windows there was a massive pool, covered for the winter.

'Holy shit.' I gaped and my voice echoed off the walls. 'Saxon, your house is . . .'

'Incredibly ugly.' He looked around with cold eyes. 'Yeah, I know. Notice there's no Christmas tree? Lylee finds them "too quaint". It's like living in a really pretentious museum.'

It was weird to see someone look so ill at ease in his own home, especially one as incredible as this one.

Saxon led me to a huge white-tiled kitchen with stainless steel counters and cabinets. He opened the fridge, which had two doors.

'Hungry?'

'I am.' I peeked over his shoulder. 'Wow.'

'I'll make us sandwiches.'

The interior of his fridge was so enormous that someone could have easily lived in it. Maybe even an entire small family.

Saxon got out plates and condiments and meats and cheese and bread. It was so normal and felt so unlike Saxon, it was a little disconcerting to watch.

'So.' I pulled up a stool. 'Where's Lylee?'

Saxon put mayo on both sandwiches without asking me if I wanted it. I did.

'She is in Greece.' He spun the cap back on the mayo jar.

'What? We just got back!'

'From France. She wanted to go to Greece. I think she has some man-whore in Crete.' He shrugged. 'Whatever makes her happy.' His voice was flat and bland.

'I'm sorry.' I took the meat-stuffed sandwich he held out.

'Don't be.' He bundled up all the food and stuffed it back in the fridge. 'Life is a lot easier when she's not around. Lylee is hard to live with when she's totally happy, and that's not often. C'mon, we'll eat in my room.' He got up and grabbed two sodas, and I followed him with the plates of sandwiches down a hallway lined with modern art in thick metal frames.

His room was the one place that looked like what I'd expected. It looked like a dirty teenage boy's room was supposed to look like, just bigger. And possibly messier. He popped a window open. 'Sorry. It smells like gym socks, right?'

He looked so handsome and boyish, and that was at odds with the way I typically thought of him. Saxon always struck me as something wild, like some feral creature that slept in a tree at night. When we had talked about him as a pet in Paris, the image of him as a huge, coiling snake or ravenous wolf made sense.

'It does. You could clean it,' I suggested.

He looked around without much interest. 'No point. It would look like this again in no time. I have to try to be here when Carmella comes over, or she cleans it even though I say not to. She doesn't make nearly enough to deal with this crap.'

'You have a maid?' I asked.

'You think Lylee does housework?' he returned.

'I guess she doesn't seem that domestic.'

His room was so unlike Jake's it was crazy. We

were sitting on small couches, set up on one side like a little sitting room with a chipped but expensive-looking coffee table between them. There were thick rugs over the hardwood, littered with Dorito crumbs and spilled who-knows-what. The unmade bed was at least a queen, maybe bigger. It had gray sheets, and you could just tell from the way they bunched and piled so beautifully that they were something expensive. Maybe silk? The walls had framed art, mostly post-modern stuff, nothing I really knew. And there were band posters, the kind they use to advertise shows. I didn't know many of them either. There was a desk with enough computer equipment to fill a NASA control room. Clothes were everywhere, and there were old plates, empty soda cans, and what looked like a condom wrapper on the floor. What was it with the boys I cared about and suggestively placed condom wrappers?

'Maybe you should just give Carmella a bonus and let her in here.'

'It's freaking you out, isn't it?' He looked around, and I imagined he was trying to see it through my eyes.

'It is.' I squirmed a little, equally fascinated and horrified. 'Your dirtiest private dirt is crawling over everything in here. I can smell you. I can see evidence of you. It's like looking at you under a microscope.'

'So this room is like my nasty little personal Petri dish?' He seemed unaccountably happy with the idea.

'Yes. You are one huge, gross science experiment.'

'You crack me up.' He laughed and his eyes got a glint I didn't completely trust. 'I don't have many people in my life who make me laugh. I guess I don't have that many friends in general. I've fucked it up with a lot of my guy friends, and no girl wants me for anything but what I can give her in bed.'

I rolled my eyes, but it was mostly to stay my panic. 'If I have to hear about how good you are in bed one more time, I'm going to scream,' I joked. Though the delivery would have been smoother if my voice hadn't wobbled. My attempts at levity were lost on Saxon. His black eyes were homed in on me, and I knew for a fact I was trapped.

He moved across the space between us with all the feline grace of a jungle cat and then he was next to me. His body was warm and his skin emitted that amazing smell that was only Saxon's and made me crazy. I tried breathing through my mouth, but I was no good at denying myself things. It just went against my nature.

'You think I'm exaggerating about how good I am?' His voice dripped with sex. 'I'm not. I want to show you. I've thought about what I would do to you if

I got you in my bed from the first minute I saw you.'

It felt like there was something crushing my lungs. I knew what he was saying wasn't even just cheesy romance talk. I could see sometimes, when he looked over at me, that he was thinking things no normal human would entertain in public, even in his head.

'I kissed Jake when I saw him,' I confessed, desperate to derail this before it started, whatever it was. 'Or I kissed him back. He kissed me first.'

'I don't like it.' Saxon shrugged. 'But you aren't mine. Oh, wait. You're nobody's girl, right, Blix?' His eyes were bright with mockery. 'You're your own girl.'

'I am,' I insisted.

'Then stop pussyfooting around. Come to bed with me,' he lured.

'No.' I shook my head. Jake hadn't wanted full sex. Every time we were together, I knew he was going to talk me out of it. And that was a good thing. I wasn't good at talking other people out of things. Especially things I could potentially like.

'Did he want you? Did he tell you to wait for him?' Saxon's voice was so melodic it just couldn't be sinister. Could it? My brain was fogging.

'No.'

'You want him back?' Saxon asked.

'Yes.' I did. Badly.

'But you like me?'

'Yes.' I struggled to break through his hypnosis. 'And you and I tried in Paris. We didn't work. Remember?'

'Too much pressure,' Saxon argued.

God, he was handsome. I loved the angles of his face, his hard jaw and black eyes. Who had black eyes, anyway? When his lips moved toward mine, I tried to pull up an image of Jake, but all I could see clearly was him screaming at me to leave.

Fine.

He wanted me to leave? I was gone.

Saxon brushed his lips against mine, and I kissed him back. He put his hands on my back and dragged me closer to him. I opened my mouth and licked at his, hating the taste of cigarette smoke, but loving the real taste of him underneath it. My mind was working around Jake yelling and Saxon kissing, and I felt defeated and glad for Saxon's understanding.

We kissed until he was pressing into me, and I felt that he was hard. I was trying to kiss him and keep a cool head. I knew I didn't want to have sex, but I wanted . . . something. Something more than we'd done in France. Something better.

He got up and dragged me over to the bed with its rumpled, silky soft sheets. They also smelled like smoke and cologne and unwashed Saxon, which was, amazingly, not gross at all and actually pretty delicious. His hand moved to my hip and slid up my shirt, unhooking my bra and running over the soft skin of my breast, slightly flattened from lying on my back. I arched a little into his palm and he grunted appreciatively, pressing and squeezing and finally pulling my shirt completely over my head with one quick movement.

In all the times the same exact thing had happened with Jake, I had always been so ready for the next thing, I hadn't given much thought to how I looked or what he might be thinking. It was different with Saxon. I wondered if he thought I looked good and what he would do next and how quickly I should stop him if things went too far.

As usual with Saxon, it was just too much thinking. He was looking at my chest, breathing hard.

'You're beautiful.' His voice was hoarse.

'Thank you.' It felt formal.

He kissed my lips gently, then dipped his head down and licked one nipple. Without thinking, I grabbed him by his ears and yanked his head back.

'Ow!' he cried.

And I giggled.

He looked a little pissed off, then his mouth curved up and he laughed a little too.

'This is great for my boner, Blix.' He sighed and lay down next to me. 'I know you're a virgin, but you've done all this before, right?'

'Yes, Saxon. Just not with you.' I looked at him closely, then reached a hand out and brushed his hair back.

'Is it bad? With me?' His black eyes flicked down. I realized this was probably going to demolish his self-esteem. I felt bad, even if I had always thought he needed to be taken down a peg or two when it came to his sexual abilities.

'No!' I said. 'My head's just in a weird place right now.'

'I can help with that.' He ran his hand down my shoulder and to my elbow. I felt a rush of goosebumps. 'You think too much.'

'Only with you!' I insisted. 'It's like I'm on hyper-drive when you're around. I can't turn it off.'

'But you can turn it off with Jake?' He didn't say it with any rancor in his voice, but he seemed annoyed.

'It's because I know how he feels about me. And I know how I feel about him. And he's always protect-ing me. Even from myself. Which is annoying. But also makes me feel like I can push things with him.' I shivered again, this time from the cool air in the room. Saxon handed me my sweater. 'I guess I'm playing Jake's role with you,' I explained. 'I'm stopping you before things go too far.'

'That is so damn unfair,' Saxon muttered, lying on his back and staring at the ceiling while I pulled my sweater down over my head. 'So, why are you stopping me again? Because I don't want to upset you, Bren, but I have a confession: I'm not a virgin.' The sarcasm dripped off his last words.

'Exactly.' I adjusted my sweater. 'So having sex with me probably wouldn't be any kind of big deal for you.'

He rolled to his side and propped his head with one hand. 'Didn't say that.'

'But it wouldn't,' I pressed. 'And I don't know when a good stopping point would be.'

He narrowed his eyes at me. 'I would never force you, Brenna. I know I've been a dirtbag, but come on. I care about you. If you just want to kiss, that's fine. I mean, I kind of want to show off for you a little, but I'll take whatever. Gladly.'

'That sounds good.' I moved closer to him. He was so handsome. I pushed him back on the bed, off his side and onto his back. I straddled his hips gingerly.

'Wait, I thought we were being prudes?' He smiled and his teeth gleamed.

I pushed against his chest to get off. 'If you're not happy with it . . .' I started, but he caught my hips in his hands and pulled me back.

'Stop putting words in my mouth. You're dead wrong. One hundred percent of the time. I'm too complicated for you to try to understand.' He moved his hands up to my ribs, then up higher. 'You didn't put your bra back on.'

'No, I didn't.' I leaned over and kissed him on the mouth experimentally. He stayed perfectly still. I kissed his cheekbones, way too nice for a guy. I kissed the stubble breaking out over his wide jaw and his black eyebrows.

I kissed his mouth softly, then licked a little at it until he opened to me and put his hands on my hips. He moved his hand up under my sweater and he pressed at my breasts. Soon my sweater was off again, and this time, when his mouth dipped down to kiss me, I didn't back away. He sucked on my nipple, and I felt the familiar warm heat between my legs. He flipped me on my back and kissed down along my stomach, down to the top of my jeans. He flipped the button open and pulled the zipper down, his lips kissing a line down from my belly button to the top of my underwear.

'It's not Tuesday, Blix.' He grinned.

I sat up on my elbows and looked down. I was wearing Tuesday underwear. But they were neon pink and green with stars on them, so they were also super-cute.

'They're ironic underwear.' My body rioted.

'I like them.' Saxon fished his fingers under the scalloped waistband. I put a hand on his wrist.

'What time is it?' I asked.

He craned his neck and glanced at his alarm clock. 'Almost three.'

I sat up, pulled my sweater over my head, grabbed my bra, and put it on under. 'I have to go. Now. Come on.'

He groaned. 'Seriously? Now? C'mon, Bren. Ten more minutes, and you would have been mine for ever.'

I laughed, then kissed him again. He smiled. 'C'mon. Mom will be home soon, and I don't want to freak her out.'

'Gotcha.' He grabbed his coat and keys and put his boots on. 'If I'm going to have a chance at more action, I need to stay in your parents' good graces.'

'At least we're both clear about what this is all about,' I said evenly.

He smiled and took my shoulders, ran his hand down to my elbows and back up, then shook me a little. 'Joking. I mean, I want to get in your pants, but I like you.' I narrowed my eyes at him. 'I really do. Promise.'

'Let's go. I hate you when you're being sentimental.' We walked to the Charger and he took out his cigarettes.

'Smoke out the window, please. I don't want to smell like cigarettes and sex.'

'Why not?' Saxon asked, but he rolled the window down. 'If you're going to come to the dark side, why not come all the way?'

'This alliance is on my terms. No cigarette smoke.' I opened his glove compartment.

I watched him watch me. It was a kind of ballsy thing to do. If I was just some girl he liked. But if we were tenuously together, that changed things. I rifled around until I found a little container of Tic Tacs, orange of course, and ate some. He held his hand out and I put some in his palm.

'Thanks.' He started the car, but then he sat and looked at me for a long minute.

'What?' I felt a slow burn crawl over my skin.

'Nothing. I don't want to get too sentimental. I just like you. That's all.' He pulled out, and I watched him drive without worrying about if he noticed me looking or not. I was making an effort to stop thinking while I was with Saxon. In Paris every minute with Saxon had been a betrayal of Jake's trust. Back home, Saxon was that incredibly complicated guy again, and I was back to my old habit of thinking and double-thinking every move I made when he was around.

But I could break that habit. Or I could give it a decent try.

I fiddled with the radio stations, not finding anything I liked. He pointed his thumb to the backseat. 'There's a CD case there. Lots of good stuff.'

I unbuckled my seatbelt for a second to get it, nervous about his crazy driving. When I turned my head to make sure we were still on a road, I caught him checking out my butt in the rearview mirror. He smiled at me and shrugged.

'You don't expect me to look? It's a good view.'

I would have kicked him, but I didn't want to make an already precarious driving experience worse. I slid back into my seat, refastened the belt quickly and plopped the case in my lap. It was filled with burned CDs.

'What's good?' Some of them had song names scrawled on them, but most were just weird titles, like Saxon had made his own mixes and named them. I flipped through the discs. '*Unbelievable Orgasm Mix*,' I read. 'Is that a good one?'

'Doesn't the title speak for itself? But considering that's just wishful thinking at this point, why don't you spare me the torture?'

'*Driving in a Car with a Boy*,' I read.

'That one's great. A friend of my mom's, Nessa, recorded some of the tracks with her band. They do this kind of modern Celtic shit. I know, it sounds weird, but it's wild.'

'Sounds good.' When I popped it in, his bizarre explanation made sense. Her voice was sexy and infectious. And because Saxon was Saxon, I wondered if he had had a crush on this Nessa woman. Or if he had slept with her. 'I love it,' I said. And didn't mention my other musings.

'So, what are you doing Friday night?' he asked casually.

'Um, nothing.' My first Friday night back in the States should have been all about me and Jake. But that . . . wasn't going to be.

'Do you want to go on a date with me? I'll dress nice, pick you up. Take you wherever.'

'That sounds good.' I looked over at him, curious. 'What do you want to do?'

'How about dinner and a movie?' he suggested. 'I don't want to get too wild.'

'All right. I really want to go out for sushi. There's

a new place in Vernon. Thorsten said it's supposed to be really good.'

'Sounds like a plan.' He smiled around his cigarette. 'Since you picked the food, are we going to be all equitable and let me pick the movie?'

'All right.' I loved movies. Just going was great. And there wasn't really any genre I hated. Except slasher-type horror movies.

'There's a new zombie movie playing. I think it's supposed to be good.'

Why did he have to pick the only type of movie that would freak me out? I made a face.

'Chill, Blix. I'll be there if you need someone to protect you. Or someone to leave the theater and screw around in the backseat with.'

I laughed outright. 'I'll make it through the movie. Nothing could gross me out more than that backseat. It's probably got the DNA of half the girls in this county on it.' I glanced back and shuddered.

'Cruel,' he said. 'But potentially true. I'll be sure to spray it down with some Lysol before I invite you to climb back in.'

We were at my house. 'Invite me in.' His voice pleaded with me.

'No.' I shook my head. It was getting easier to relax with Saxon, but I needed to have a sanctuary of my own, and that's what my room functioned as. It was bad enough the ghost of Jake still loomed large. 'Uncle.'

'What?'

'I'm saying "uncle",' I said. He looked at me blankly. '"Uncle." I've had enough. Of you.'

He laughed again. 'You're a stone bitch. But I like you like that.'

I popped the passenger door open and he grabbed my hand and pulled me back. 'Goodbye, Brenna.' And before I knew it, I was in his lap, my mouth and his tangling hungrily. I finally pulled away and got out, shaky and uncertain.

Chapter 12

I didn't look back at his car when he pulled out of the driveway. I went to my room, and I had two immediate desires: I wanted a shower, and I wanted to call Jake. But I didn't do either. I headed up to the attic, which was above our garage, low-ceilinged and dimly lit. The boxes were all labeled. Mom and I moved around quite a bit when I was a kid, and a lot of our things had been lost. What we had, she treasured, and it was all carefully boxed and organized. It took a lot less time than I'd expected to find what I was looking for. It was in the box labeled 'Brenna's Art: Age 5 & 6.'

I found the book, the one I had loved so fiercely that I had colored all over it. The original pictures were muted, sketchy and incredible. My scribbles over the top were vibrant, harsh. And also beautiful. Together they made a complicated, beautiful mess. I put the box back and took the book downstairs.

Thorsten and Mom had used Christmas as an

excuse to spoil me again, and this time it had been in the form of software and a new printer, plus a huge pile of soft cotton T-shirts in my size. I also had a feeling there was a silk-screening press in my future. After my successful sale of T-shirts at local Folly concerts, Mom and Thorsten had been so impressed with my skills, they had upgraded and added to my equipment. That's just the kind of awesome people they are.

I scanned some of the pages and manipulated them on my laptop so they would make workable images. Then I fiddled with the contrast and repaired the low resolution. But there wasn't a lot I needed to do. My kindergarten self had all of the artistic imagination in an afternoon of scribbling that I now needed hours of focused work to achieve.

I ran a print-off of the final design and pressed it onto a T-shirt with the iron. The design was amazing. I had never been so impressed with anything I made before. I had got so into it, I didn't hear Mom come in. She was in the doorway when I finally sensed her presence and looked up.

'Mom!' I ran to her and gave her a hug.

'Hey, sweetie. I see you found your book.' She sniffed my hair. 'You smell like smoke.'

'I rode my bike a little far, and Saxon drove me back

here.' I obviously omitted any mention of the action in his messy bedroom.

'That was sweet of him,' Mom said carefully, looking at my shirt. 'This is incredible, honey.'

'Yeah. Too bad I made it when I was five.' We both studied it for a minute.

'Well, use it as inspiration for new things.' She ran her hands over the design. 'So where was Jake today?'

'He and I still aren't dating.' I swallowed hard as the ugliness and confusion of the day shook through me again. 'And we're not really talking right now.'

'Oh, Bren. I'm sorry.' She did sound sorry, but I knew it wasn't so much about the fact that I wasn't back with Jake as the fact that I might be hurting over it.

'Saxon invited me out on Friday night. I wanted to go to that new sushi place Thorsten told us about.' I glanced at her, interested to see her reaction.

'That sounds fun.' Her voice was guarded. 'Does Jake know?'

I wasn't positive why she was asking. I figured it was mostly curiosity. I was sure she wanted to know if I was following her 'date lots of guys' advice. 'I don't think Jake cares one way or the other,' I said, remembering our kiss in the greenhouse. Which was technically our second kiss in a Zinga's greenhouse.

That kiss was sharper in my mind than every deliciously intimate thing Saxon and I had done together, and I really didn't know why.

'It will work itself out, Bren,' Mom promised. It was a promise that made no sense, but I somehow trusted her simple words.

'Thanks, Mom.'

She left me in my room, my beautiful, comfortable room, and I worked like a fiend, printing and ironing. I took a long shower. I made some playlists. I did some extra homework. I ate dinner and watched TV. I didn't want to go to sleep. I didn't want Monday to come. Or, more pointedly, I didn't want Monday afternoon to come. I didn't want to see Jake, to have to deal with what we still had and didn't have any more.

Especially since what we'd had before was comparatively simple.

And so completely good.

Damn my longing for Saxon. If I had known how complicated this would all get . . . I still would have done it. No doubt. I needed to know. And I needed to be free. Even from the most amazing, understanding guy there was.

That night I lay in my bed and wished the phone would ring. I willed Jake to dial my number, to tell me that kiss had sparked something in him, that even though I'd screwed up he still wanted me.

I had done as much for him once, and it had sucked. I had accepted his massively unbalanced past. Thinking about the crazy things he had done had made me insane – imagining the other girls, wondering what it had been like and how I held up. Especially since I had nothing to compare it all to. And the better he was, the more adoring, the harder it was. Because it clouded my judgment and made me unsure.

There was always the feeling that I was being adored from my place on a really high pedestal. Had I willed my own fall? It seemed a little crazy, but so did everything right now. Maybe I wanted to even the field with Jake. Maybe I wanted to see if he was as tolerant as I had been. Was I testing him?

My mind raced. All I knew was that letting go of him was proving more and more difficult, and there wasn't much chance of it getting better when I was going to be seeing him every day.

My head hurt, and I felt flushed and achy. Early January bike rides to the middle of nowhere, New Jersey, will do that to your body. I had too much to think about, but sleep eventually wound itself around me and pulled me down into its inky depths.

The next morning, I woke up with less time than I'd

planned to have. I did my hair in hot rollers, something I rarely did. I also used a new technique with my eye make-up and put on a new shade of lipstick. I wore one of the new T-shirts I had designed, a red one with a deep V-neck, and tight, slim dark jeans with red Converses. I knew I looked hot. I wanted to. I didn't want to think about who I was looking hot for.

I ate my breakfast, grabbed my backpack and headed out the door. Mom wasn't there to join me most mornings now. Since she'd gone back to teaching, she left in the early morning and was gone for most of the day two or three times a week. I was so preoccupied as I stepped out of the garage that I almost smacked into Saxon.

'Saxon!' I cried. 'What are you doing here?'

'You forgot your bike. It's in my trunk. So I decided to do the right thing and bring it back. This morning. And force you to ride in with me.'

I had forgotten my bike! Where was my brain?

'I guess so.' I felt a little like my head wasn't fully attached to my shoulders. 'We should go. If you want.'

He gave me a long look, his brow knitted. 'OK.' He came around and opened my door. That Nessa Celtic girl was singing, her voice beautiful as an angel's. And grating on my worn nerves.

I flipped the stereo off. My head was killing me, and I saw little explosive points of bright light whenever I closed my eyes. I knew that was probably not a good thing.

'What the hell's up, Bren?' Saxon snapped as he peeled out of my driveway.

'I just don't want to face today.' I realized that Saxon had no idea how close Jake and I were for hours on end at Tech, and no concept of how awkward this would be. And I had no will to explain it all.

'Relax,' he said, and that was his big comforting speech. 'And turn the music back on. If I'm going to listen to a girl bitch, I'd like it to at least be in Gaelic.' His voice was irritated.

I wished I'd insisted on riding in. A few miles of hard cycling would have made me feel better, but we were already nearly there now, and I wasn't up for an argument with Saxon. Before I knew it, we were in the Frankford parking lot and the haunting Gaelic singing stopped when he switched off the engine.

I got out and went around to the trunk.

'What do you need?' He followed, close on my heels.

'My bike.' Jake had been picking me up for lunch at Tech, but he wouldn't be now. I needed to ride there again.

'You're not riding to Tech. It's freezing.' Saxon grabbed my wrist and held on tight.

'Actually, I am, but thanks for thinking you can tell me what to do,' I snapped and wrestled my wrist free of his grip. 'Pop the trunk.'

'Pop it yourself,' he said nonchalantly.

Without another thought, I swung my backpack around, fully intending to smash a dent in Saxon's trunk, even if I couldn't open it.

Before my backpack could make contact, he grabbed my arm and my bag swung down and smacked my hip.

'Ow,' I whined.

'Jesus, you're lucky you're so damn hot,' Saxon growled. He popped the trunk, and I got my bike out, glaring at him a little.

We walked to the nearest bike rack, and I locked it on, then we walked into school together. I had English first. We were still working on *Ethan Frome*. Great. Always nice to have an uplifting read – nothing like a doomed Puritan winter love triangle to lift my spirits.

I took my coat off and put it in my locker.

'Great shirt.' Saxon touched a finger between my breasts. I stared him down.

'I made it,' I bit out shortly.

'Obviously. It's brilliant and ironic. Blixen all over.'

I couldn't coax a smile, even though he completely deserved one for that.

'I'm done.' He held his hands up and shook his head as he walked backward down the hall. 'Maybe your bitchy mood will have evaporated a little by Government. God, I hope so.'

I watched as he walked away, his one rolled-up notebook jutting under his arm. I felt bad for being so weirdly cold to him, but I felt worse for myself. I slumped into English and sat in my usual seat behind Devon Conner, my newest friend at Frankford.

'Hey,' he said carefully.

I smiled a little. 'Hey, yourself.'

'Your hair looks different.' He pointed and made a circle with his finger. 'Curly.'

'You should never just make an observation like that.' My head pounded and it felt like Devon's face was blurry in front of my eyes. 'You should compliment or say nothing.'

'Your hair is pretty,' Devon amended, not a hint of flirtation in his voice. 'Did you finish *Frome*?'

'It's a novella, Devon. Please don't tell me you didn't read it.' I sighed. Devon was brilliant, but chronically lazy. He was always behind in his reading and, annoyingly, he was always freaking out because of it.

'I did. I just really hated it.' He held the book up and stared at it doubtfully. 'I mean, it's normal that I hated it, right? Can anyone like that book?'

'I liked it.' My voice was sullen. 'It's realistic.'

'What? Attempted suicide on a sled? Come on, Brenna. That's just crazy!'

'No, not the sledding stuff. Although that was probably ordinary back in the day in New England. What else are they supposed to do but be depressed and sled to death?'

Devon looked at me critically. 'You also said the love story in *Pride and Prejudice* was realistic,' he griped.

I shrugged. Devon got nervous. He had been an outcast since middle school, socially retarded by Saxon's heartless bullying when they were young. It was easy to make him feel like he had done something socially stupid and get him all antsy. My bad mood was driving him that way.

'Sorry, Devon.' I patted his shoulder. 'I had a crazy break.'

'Did something happen?' He looked much more nervous than interested.

'I went to Paris.' I rubbed my temples and spoke through the crush of a headache so intense it felt like my brain was in a vise. 'And I wound up messing things up with Jake. And I kind of got involved with Saxon.'

Now Devon shrugged. 'Well, that was probably inevitable, right?'

'What do you mean?'

'Saxon has been pursuing you since the day school started. And he had all that mystery going on. He must have seemed enticing. If he got shoved in your face so often, what else were you going to do?' Devon looked at me pointedly. 'You're human, after all. And he's Saxon.' He said it like the name 'Saxon' was synonymous with some intense, undeniable deity.

I was positive that he was saying it to be helpful, but it made me sound like a two-timing wandering-eyed slut. My eyes filled with tears.

'Are you crying?' he asked, with none of the panic or sympathy most guys would have shown. He looked confused.

'Yes, Devon!' I sniffled and wiped under my eyes before my make-up ran down my face. 'I'm human, remember? When I screw life up, I feel this emotion. It's called "sadness".'

'But I don't think you did. Mess things up, that is.' He looked thoughtful. 'I just think it would have been easier for you if you'd been with Saxon first.'

'Why?' I wailed.

'Because then you would have gotten him out of your system. But now you put Jake aside. Which was probably not a good thing.' He blinked hard.

'Maybe you're right.' I contemplated his idea.

'But maybe not.' He flipped the pages of his book distractedly. 'If you were with Saxon first, he would have burned you, and that would have messed up your perspective on dating, which seems like it would be a good lesson. But you got Jake first instead, and that taught you a better lesson.'

'I don't get it.' My brain wasn't working on its normal level, and piecing Devon's logic together was taxing it beyond its limited capacity.

'If you had the worst boyfriend ever first, you'd have really low standards when it came to guys. But you got a great boyfriend first. Now you have a really high standard for other boyfriends to live up to. So . . . that's good,' he concluded awkwardly.

I looked at gawky, socially weird Devon Conner and felt a rush of affection. I grabbed his hand and squeezed. 'You should write a column.'

'About what?' He blinked quickly, which he only did if he was incredibly nervous or happy.

'Relationships.' The advice he had given me was brilliant.

He snorted. 'Yeah. A social pariah would make a great relationship columnist.'

Dawes burst in, late as usual, hardly able to tear himself away from the poor German teacher who was too nice to just run away from his pervy old advances.

He squinted at us unhappily. 'So, let's start with a pop quiz.' He narrowed his eyes further. 'Twenty questions on *Frome*.'

We groaned because that was expected, but I was glad to have something else to focus on. Granted, Devon's words were totally accurate and great, but they also brought up a lot of problems.

Like, if Devon's theory made sense (and it did), why had I spent time rolling around Saxon's bed yesterday? Why not go home and wait to talk to Jake?

And if Jake was the one, why did I have so much fun with Saxon? There were elements of Saxon that I really connected with. We were both excellent students, we were both great athletes, we knew how to carry a conversation that was witty and funny and flirty all at once. Not that Jake didn't have these qualities – he just didn't have them enough to feel like he could compete with me. He was always a little in awe. And I hated that.

I thought back to my pedestal idea from yesterday. I had hated being there. It was too much pressure, and it felt temporary anyway, like I was just waiting for myself to screw it all up, to fall off. Maybe I had pushed it for that exact reason.

Suddenly Dawes was calling all quizzes forward, and I had to fold away the thoughts of Jake and Saxon and scribble in the last five answers on my quiz. I finished just as Devon was starting to wave his hand back at my seat with crazy panic.

By the time the period was over, I was not feeling any more ready to see Jake. And I had to face Saxon in Government. Luckily, there was a quiz in Government, too, so there wasn't much to do except keep my head down and avoid Saxon's looks. Which were getting more irritated by the minute. When the bell rang, he followed me into the hallway.

'What's up with you, Blix?' He grabbed me by the elbow. 'This is crazy. You're acting like an asshole.'

'Because I didn't chat with you during the quiz?' I shook off his grasp and moved away from him subtly so that he couldn't get a hold on me. 'You're the one acting like an asshole.'

He managed to grab me again anyway, pulled me to him, and I melted into the way he smelled and the way his body felt against mine. He was bad, just like me. Corrupted, loose-moraled. We were never going to be on anyone's pedestal.

I kissed him hard, and he kissed back.

He squeezed my butt possessively, and I loved and hated it at the same time. My head felt swimmy and overheated.

'Much better,' he murmured in my ear, then turned to leave for class and did that athletic boy jog that I loved.

I felt like there were actual winged insects in my stomach. It was not a good feeling.

'Um, Brenna?' It was Kelsie. Her eyes were wide. She had a great new haircut, a cute little bob. I wished I could pull something like that off. But Kelsie looked like a pixie with excellent bone structure. My face was pretty enough, but in that broad, Slavic way that I can thank my Eastern European potato farmer ancestors for.

'I love your haircut,' I gushed. Yes, I was deflecting.

'Thanks,' she smiled. She shook it a little. 'It's so easy to do now! I love that shirt. Please tell me you went on some incredible trip to Europe to get it, because if you tell me you made it I'm going to puke with jealousy.'

'I did go on a trip to Paris,' I said sheepishly. 'But I also made the shirt.'

'You better have brought me one!' she demanded.

I took the rolled-up shirt out of my bag and handed

it to her. 'Black, V-neck, small. I wouldn't forget you.'

She hugged me and we went into craft class. 'I'm so glad my best friend is so talented,' she sing-songed.

I felt a rush of happy warmth. Best friend? I would have wanted to call Kelsie that, but I wasn't sure she felt that way. We were at a weird juncture for really close friendship; both of us had boyfriends and busy lives outside of school, so we didn't make a lot of time for girl stuff. Which, considering my current dilemma, seemed incredibly stupid. Maybe some girl time would have kept me from all of this insanity.

'I'm glad you like it.' We sat down and took out the last thing we had been working on. I was doing copper plating, and Kelsie was weaving something incredible out of her macramé string. My macramé had ended up looking like an old knitted hat turned inside out.

'So.' She looked down at her string with careful focus. 'Was that Saxon Maclean I saw grabbing your butt after you two kissed?' I knew she was trying to be non-judgmental, but Saxon wasn't the kind of guy you didn't have an opinion about. And he and Kelsie had been on one date earlier that year. It hadn't panned out. Lucky Kelsie.

When she did lift her eyes to mine, the look she gave me was so reassuring and kind, I felt choked with self-pity. I wanted to pour my guts out to her, but didn't know where to start. She helped.

'What happened between you and Jake?' Her face was so calm and sweet, I just let loose.

I started on Christmas, and I told Kelsie the entire tale, scratching inane lines and squiggles in my copper plate while Kelsie wove a beautiful, complicated knot pattern in her macramé.

When I was finally done, my eyes were hot with tears, my voice was shaky, and my copper plate looked like almost everything I made in Crafts – uninspired crap.

'It would have been better if you'd dated Saxon first,' she said finally.

I was so surprised that she had echoed Devon's sentiments exactly that I just looked at her, my mouth hanging open.

'Because you would have seen him for what he really is and gotten over it,' she rushed. 'And you could have been happy with Jake because you would have known.'

'Devon said that if I had done that, I would have had the worst example of a boyfriend as my first, and that I would have held all the rest of them to this really low standard.' Which was really harsh towards Saxon. He had his real flaws, but I knew he cared about me and had a weird system of loyalty. Plus, I had met his mother. Lylee was, as far as I was concerned, the worst kind of parasite, totally self-absorbed and content with using people for whatever material and emotional need she might have. Saxon never had a chance with her as his mom.

'Wow.' Kelsie put her nearly complete, perfect creation aside and rested her chin on her hands, deep in thought. 'Devon is really smart.'

'I know.' Then I added my portion of the theory to the mix. 'Part of me feels a little like Jake kind of worshipped me, you know. Like he didn't see any flaws. So maybe . . .'

'You wanted to throw some flaws in his face?' Kelsie asked gently. 'But, Jesus, Bren, couldn't you have just been a little bitchier or just dumped him and not dated Saxon? I mean, there's not a single guy in the world he hates more.'

I nodded. I didn't add that there was probably no one he had loved more either. And I realized that Saxon's not telling Jake about their blood bond might have a lot to do with me. My head buzzed and my throat ached from unshed tears.

By the time the bell rang, Kelsie had made me promise to call if I needed and invited me out with her and her boyfriend Chris later in the week if I wanted.

Saxon was waiting outside the door when the bell rang. We walked to what was quickly becoming my saving-grace period: PE. I'd always hated it in middle school. There were so many rules and the team thing was intimidating. But since I had proven myself some kind of cross-country star, I could spend the entire period running. Every day. And I needed it.

'Ready to run, Gump?' Saxon put an arm around my shoulders.

'I need it.' I took a deep breath and closed my eyes.

He looked at me quizzically. 'OK. No comment there.'

'Why would you say that?' I growled.

'Why are you looking for a fight?' he growled back.

His black eyes flashed, his color was high, and he had never looked so good. Or so excited. Saxon really did seem to have a thing for confrontation. It did something for him that peace just didn't. He reached for me, and we kissed hungrily. Usually I'd be embarrassed to kiss like that so publicly, but Saxon had a way of negating all social norms. When we pulled away, he was breathing hard, his hands gripped my shoulders.

'God, I want you,' he said in a low voice.

'It doesn't hurt to want.'

He slid his hands down to my hips and kissed me

again. It was good despite our strangely public arena. The hall outside of the locker rooms was crawling with people.

'Enough.' I turned and walked away, leaving him standing alone and shocked. And I know he loved it. Much more than I did. He thought it was part of a game, a flirtation. But I knew that it was just my weirdly muddled feelings, and that made everything even more weirdly muddled.

I was glad to get out on the track. Coach Dunn just nodded to me as I started my set. I popped my earphones in and ran to what I had downloaded the night before, a classical mix. But I realized my mistake pretty quickly. I thought no lyrics would mean less thinking. But running always started my thinking juices flowing, and the swells and washes of the music just let me plug my exact feeling and worries in. So much for my attempt at mind trickery.

I ran faster and harder, like I could outrun what worried me. It just wore me out. My muscles burned and my head ached, but I pushed past the stars that whizzed in front of my eyes.

By the time I'd finished, Coach Dunn was happy, but I could barely breathe, and my stomach was churning. One more hour, and I would be at Tech. One more hour, and I would be sitting across from Jake for hours.

Running until sweat drips down your face isn't the best thing for make-up or hair. I spent a long time in the locker room repairing what damage I had done and possibly avoiding Saxon. When I came out, the hall was empty. Saxon was waiting.

'You look nice.' His voice was cold.

'I ruined my make-up running,' I explained. We started walking to the cafeteria. It would be the first time in months I had eaten at Frankford. Jake had been picking me up so we could eat lunch together at Tech. I liked his sweet, happy friends. I liked his hand on my thigh under the table. It wasn't going to be anymore.

'Why are you all dolled up, Blix?' Saxon asked.

'What do you mean?' I asked carefully.

'I know the answer.' His mouth screwed into a tight little knot. 'I just need to hear you say it. So I can come to grips with this bullshit.'

I stopped and looked right at him. 'I got dressed up because I knew this day would be super shitty. And I wanted to look nice for me.'

He snorted. 'Lying to yourself doesn't change the truth, Bren.'

'That is the truth!' I insisted. It was. Partially.

'Your misery is contagious,' he griped.

'Then get away from me,' I said, my teeth gritted.

'I wish I could,' he snarled.

We marched to the lunchroom, moodily selecting food and going to the table where Saxon reigned like some hot young lord. He turned it on for the rest of his entourage big time, and their jovial kindness extended to me, since he and I were linked. But I was in no mood, and after a growl or two, everyone gave me a wide berth.

Finally the bell rang. I jumped up and started out, Saxon hot on my heels. 'You don't have to walk me,' I said hurriedly. 'I'm going to be late if we talk. Where's my bike?' I demanded.

'Back of my car. I came out and moved it after first,' Saxon said. 'Get in. I'll drive you to Tech.'

'No!' I panicked. I had this hope, this crazy hope that I was clinging to hard and fast. I hoped Jake would be waiting for me outside the squat little Tech building, just like he had in that weird in-between time after we'd started flirting but before we'd become a couple. I wanted that possible moment all to myself.

'Get in.' His eyes were sharp.

'No!' I yelled, my panic made worse because I knew, I knew Jake wouldn't be there, waiting. What had I done? 'Leave me alone!'

'No.' He grabbed my arms and then pulled me to him. 'No way. I have to do this. Get in.'

So I got in, only because he was so determined that

I didn't know if I could sway him after all. And, in the end, I just needed to get there and get this over with.

We pulled up at Tech, I searched the parking lot with a wild twitch of my eyes, and my stomach clenched hard. I could feel the cold slosh of whatever I had shoved in my mouth for lunch.

Jake wasn't there.

He wasn't there.

Chapter 13

I started to climb out of the car, but Saxon grabbed my wrist. I twisted away from him, but he pulled harder and kissed me. For a second, I settled into the kiss and relaxed enough to breathe. Then Saxon ripped his mouth away, and said, 'Get out. I'll be here to pick you up. We both have practice after school.'

I was going to tell him no, but was too impatient to fight again. I ran into the school, down the dark, low hall and into class.

I had been wishing things would be just the way they had always been. I was a little scared that Jake might have switched tables or even classes, and I thought about how that would have broken my heart. But my heart felt pretty thoroughly smashed looking at him, sitting exactly where he always sat, refusing to look up when I banged into the room. Every other person looked, even our jolly teacher.

I walked nervously to our table, took out a sheet of

paper, and got sketching on the second part of the project we'd started before break. I was glad to have something to do. Jake sketched too. Silently.

He was there, sitting right across from me, but he wasn't there. Same shiny brown hair, overlong and sexily tousled. Same long lashes, same adorably crooked mouth, same faded T-shirt and jeans, same tanned, muscled arms. My body ached for him.

I sketched, but couldn't keep my mind from remembering the way he tasted, how his body had cradled mine so many times, the sound of his voice at night on the phone, the way he drove and smiled and moaned. I wanted to apologize, wanted to ask him about our kiss and what it meant to him, but nothing came out.

He never looked up. Not once. When the bell rang, he was out of his seat and out the door before I could even put my things away. My eyes filled with tears, but I blinked and swallowed hard.

I had done this to myself. I totally deserved this.

I was walking to my next class when I saw him, a little more like the old Jake. He was laughing softly. He looked relaxed. I wanted to approach him. That's when I saw that there was a reason he was so happy.

She had long bleach-blonde hair and green eyes. She was pretty, in an obvious-pretty way, I thought meanly. She was wearing one of those tiny baby-doll shirts that crimps up under your armpits and leaves a sliver of belly an inch wide hanging out. The shirt was pink and said 'Gucci Princess' in silver letters. Didn't he realize how ironic it was that she, a lower-middle-class farm girl, would be wearing a shirt proclaiming herself the autocratic ruler of a brand she'd never be able to afford to wear on a regular basis except in the form of T-shirts that were basically cheap billboards? My heart pounded, and I couldn't catch my breath.

She was tanned, really tanned, and when she reached up into her locker, I saw that her belly button was pierced and had some dangly silver thing, like a fishing lure, hanging off it. Ugh.

That was who he wanted to date? I wanted to look away, but it was like a car wreck – my eyes were glued. Then he looked over her head, right at me. His look was so completely pissed off it made my heart thump. He looked back down at her and smiled that delicious smile that I knew so well. Then he pulled her to him and kissed her, hard and long. When he pulled away, she squealed and giggled, and Jake looked at me again, his eyes triumphant.

And there, in the crush of the hallway, I held up my middle finger like a school kid, and marched to my class.

The girl next to me gave me a sympathetic look when I sat down.

'I'm sorry you and Jake broke up,' she said, not sounding very sorry.

I wasn't even sure of her name. 'Thanks,' I said, my manners too automatic. I wanted to give her the finger, too.

'But, you know, Nikki has had a thing for him for like, forever. So, maybe it was, like, fate,' she said sweetly and meanly.

'Hey, Kara?'

'Um, actually it's Krista.' The girl backed down a little, I assumed because of the fury radiating from my face.

'Fuck you. OK?' I glared at her an extra few seconds, then got to work.

Again, no one talked to me. I worked all period, not stopping for a second, trying to erase the image of Jake kissing Nicole, or whatever her name was, from my memory. He attracted such a *type*. I mean, what was he going to talk to her about? Where were they going to go on dates? I didn't think about those questions too much. Jake had a certain reputation for a reason, and I bet he'd start living up to it again really quickly.

By the time I left class, I was so pissed off I could barely see straight. Jake caught my eye in the hall and winked, a mean, snide little gesture that made me hate him all over again.

Maybe I had orchestrated this entire disaster. Maybe this was all completely my fault. But I hadn't rubbed his nose in it.

Yet.

I sure could start. I went into our project period class. Jake came in after a minute and sat next to me. He could have changed seats. It might have been a little weird, but he could have done it, and he didn't. Even at the peak of my hate, I still loved to be near him. And I loved the way he smelled.

I took all that love I had in me, all the love for the way his cologne clung to his skin, for how his long fingers held his pencil too tight, for how he frowned when he worked hard on something, and held it tight for a minute, then I dropped it hard and tried to leave it behind. Yet, despite my best efforts to distance myself from him, I was happy to smell that he was wearing the cologne I had given him.

Desperate to stop thinking about his smile and his cologne and how I'd messed it all up, I turned to the hulking lug who sat at the table near us. I batted my lashes at him. I had his almost immediate attention. Jake glared.

'Hey, Matt? Do you have an eraser I can borrow?'

I asked, and giggled. That's right: I giggled like a mad woman.

'Sure. Yeah.' He fumbled in his bag for an eraser.

Then I winked! I winked right at him, and Jake looked like he was having a hard time keeping that smug smile on his lips. 'Thanks, Matt. I owe you one!' I gushed, then went busily to work erasing things that didn't need erasing because I had just asked to borrow an eraser, and now Jake was watching me.

'I had an eraser. If you needed one,' Jake said coldly, not lifting his eyes to look at me.

It was the first thing he had said to me since he'd ordered me to leave Zinga's.

'I *did* need one. And *Matt* was happy to lend it to me,' I said very slowly. 'Thanks anyway, Jake.'

Jake scowled, then glanced at me from under his bunched brows. 'I like your shirt,' he muttered finally. Finally!

I felt a secret thrill of happiness that we were talking again. 'It's something I designed when I was five.' The one I wore today was the scene where the little girl in the fairy tale asked some sparrows for help defeating the witch. I loved her wooden clogs and the kerchief on her head. I had colored over them with pink marker when I was young, so it looked like she had a pink halo and glowing shoes. I kept the original babyish letters and scribbles, but also added typed 'interpretations'. I'd translated this one as saying, 'Even though she's a little girl, she's brave and kind. She knows that the sparrows are smart and will help her. She knows who to trust.' I wondered what I had originally intended it to say, but that's what I saw when I looked at the illustration now.

'Really?' Jake asked, his voice finally soft and low and sweet.

'Yeah. The picture is something colored and worked over when I was just a little girl.'

He laughed and shook his head, but didn't say anything.

'What?' I smiled a little to encourage him.

'Nothing.' He shook his head again, looking like he wanted to say something, but knew enough not to say it. That made me extra curious.

'Why did you laugh?' I refused to let the conversation drop.

He looked up at me, his eyes sharp. 'You just would have done something that amazing when you were five years old.' He shrugged. 'Typical Brenna,' he added sourly.

And everything nice he had implied was blown away with the bitter clang of his words.

'What the hell does that mean?' I asked, my voice

low enough to keep the teacher from coming over to investigate.

'That everything comes easy to you,' he accused, his gray eyes hot and angry.

'That's a load of crap. I work my ass off for what I have.' My fury was so fierce I felt a rush of pure hate.

Jake shrugged his handsome, muscled shoulders.

I don't think anything on earth could have made me more pissed off.

'What? You think I'm just lucky? Or you think I'm spoiled?'

He looked at me, shrugged again, and my blood boiled. 'Maybe a little bit of both.'

The teacher gave a general command to everyone to get back on task, and I did, but I was so mad I could feel myself shake. Is this what Jake had always thought of me? Had he ever respected anything I'd done, or did he just see me as some spoiled girl with a silver spoon in her mouth? Had he said it to make me angry? Why had it worked so well? How much truth was there to his words?

Jake didn't look up at me, though I couldn't believe it was possible that my furious glares didn't scorch his skin. I had never felt this kind of plain, drag-out hate. I hated Jake – for what he had said, for what he tried to make me feel. For what he wouldn't say.

When the bell finally rang, Jake kicked his chair back and strode out of the classroom. Nikki was waiting to play tonsil hockey with him right outside the doorway. I pushed past hard enough to jostle them both.

'Watch it!' Nikki cried. 'Bitch!'

Jake and I locked eyes for a long moment, then I turned and stormed out, into the cold parking lot.

I burst out of the doors, and too late remembered that my bike was in Saxon's trunk.

'Brenna!' Jake called. He had run out, no coat on, no sign of Nikki.

'What?' I snapped. 'I'm not apologizing for bumping into you. You two should get a room. Or a truck,' I said snidely. But it hurt, to remember that the truck had been the place we had held each other such an incredibly short time ago.

'I just wanted . . .' He shrugged. 'I don't know. I just didn't want to leave it. Like this.'

'Like what? Like two people who aren't dating anymore?' I asked. 'Because that's why you're wrapped around Nikki. Or whatever girl it is now.'

He stared at me and his mouth hung open. 'What?' he yelled. 'Are you serious? *You* dumped *me*, Bren. Or did you forget? You called me from across a fucking ocean to tell me that you were busy throwing yourself

296

at the worst guy you could find.' He pulled his cap off and ran a hand through his hair. 'How the hell did you think I'd feel about that?'

'I had reasons,' I said, desperate to explain.

'To break my fucking heart?' he asked, his voice cracking a little.

I wanted to run into his arms. I wanted to take the last week back and erase it.

'I wanted to come and talk to you about it,' I said quietly. 'Yesterday. I've been thinking a lot, and I think I know why I did it. And I'm sorry I hurt you, but I felt like I had to do it. So, if you want me to explain, maybe I could sometime, when you're not busy with what's her face.' My mom hated that expression: *what's her face.* It sounded petty and mean, and that's exactly how I felt about her.

'Bren, I don't know,' Jake said, the pain raw on his face. 'Maybe we can—'

And he stopped. I heard the roar of the engine that stopped him. His face lost its vulnerable pained look and hardened.

'Forget it.' He shook his head with disgust. 'Your ride's here, Bren.' Jake stalked back to the school, throwing the door open with a wild bang as he went back in.

It was completely unfair to hate Saxon as much as

I hated him at that moment, but I hated him anyway.

I got in and slammed the door hard.

'Great. I can see you're still in a good mood.' He skidded out of the parking lot.

'You wanted to do this, be with me. Did you think I was always nice?' I asked, my mind reeling. Jake said I had broken his heart.

'No, Bren, but I didn't think all of your evil would be directed my way,' he griped.

'Are you saying there's someone more deserving of my evil?' I cocked on eyebrow at him.

He grinned. 'Nope. I would like to argue that your rage would make more sense if you let me be a little worse and earn it.' He reached across the seat and put his hand on my thigh, then inched up. Under normal circumstances, I would have swatted his hand away, but I just settled back and looked at him expectantly.

Saxon pulled over immediately and took off his seatbelt. 'Get in the backseat and give me fifteen minutes. You won't regret it.' He was wickedly good looking, his eyes bright, an eager smile on his mouth.

I thought about Jake and Nikki slobbering over each other in the hallway. I thought about the look of disgust Jake gave me when he saw Saxon's car, how he had marched back into school, presumably to her, with an intention that I didn't want to consider. The white-hot rage roared through me again. I undid my seatbelt and climbed back.

Saxon followed. The road wasn't often used, but it wasn't exactly deserted.

'What's your big plan?' I felt a shred of nervousness.

'Just picking up where we left off.' His fingers flicked the button of my jeans and tugged down on the zipper. Just the sound made me feel a strange excitement, and I pressed my hips to him.

He kissed me, frenetic little biting kisses that made me feel happily irritated. It was dizzying to be this close to Saxon. Before, I had been unable to turn my brain off, but now I was so pissed off, I felt like I couldn't think straight. Then I just stopped thinking. I let the fury crash over me, and it was nicely mind-numbing. I kissed him back, pulled his mouth to mine eagerly and pushed my hips against him again. It felt bad, but I also wanted it – like a guilty pleasure.

His hands worked around my waist, his fingers pressing under the line of my underwear, before he snaked down, up and in with a movement so quick it made me catch my breath. He moved fast, his hands unlike Jake's. I didn't want to think about Jake at that moment, but my mind wouldn't let me stop the comparison. Saxon dipped in and out fast and moved immediately to the place that made me squirm. He kissed me hard and deep, matching his hand to his tongue somehow, and I felt that loopy slide just before the fall. It all happened so fast; suddenly I was crying out and shaking and then Saxon pulled away, grinned, and climbed back to the front seat.

I lay in the back, panting, my jeans still undone, my underwear strangely bunched.

'Bren, stop slacking,' Saxon said, his smile wide with triumph. 'We're gonna miss practise. Put your pants on.'

I zipped up and righted myself before climbing next to him, feeling a little woozy. What had just happened? When I was with Saxon, I felt like it was always a challenge, a clawing, drag-out fight. Even my orgasm felt like something he'd won, somehow.

He seemed completely happy about the whole thing. He even whistled. It wasn't until he looked over at me that his face fell.

'Bren, you're killing me. Didn't you come?' He was clearly irritated.

'I did.' I wanted to put the emphasis on the 'I', but that seemed kind of ridiculous.

'What's your deal, then?' he asked. 'That was nice of me. I did it for you.'

I took a deep breath, but I can't say if I chickened

out or not. How was I supposed to answer that?

'It was nice. That I came,' I said haltingly.

'I guess it's just weird to have all three of us here?' he said nastily. He had screeched into the parking lot.

'Jake?' I took a deep breath, but my head spun more. 'Fat chance. He's with someone else.'

'I can guarantee you, he doesn't want to be,' Saxon growled. He banged his fists on the steering wheel.

'How can you be so sure?' I was excited that he'd even given me that glimmer of hope. I had my theories, but I wanted to hear what Saxon had to say.

'Because I saw his fucking love-struck face, Brenna,' Saxon said. 'I saw the two of you. Why am I even bothering? Seriously, get the hell out of my car.' He elbowed his door open, got out, and slammed it so hard the whole car shook.

I pushed my door open and followed him into the school. 'I'm not apologizing about how I feel,' I said to his retreating back. 'And I'm not pretending, either. Not with you. Not for one second. That's the only good thing about whatever we're doing, and it's great!' My words rang out and bounced around in the cold air.

'What's that?' He turned to look at me closely. His black eyes bored into me.

'I feel no pressure to lie to you. I don't know if I've

ever been this honest before. Or this much of a bitch,' I added. I closed the space between us and looked right into his bright, black eyes. 'You've given me the freedom to just do what I want without caring.'

'Great.' Saxon shut his eyes, and I watched his dark lashes tangle together at the corners. He shook his head. 'I've unleashed a hot, sociopathic bitch.'

'You have.' I pulled his face down to mine and kissed him gently. 'Thanks for that.'

Then I left Saxon, went straight to the locker room, and hit the track, running hard. Too hard. I was worn out less than halfway through practise. I had to dredge into my reserves and push harder. When it was all over, I was so exhausted I slept on the ride home. Saxon didn't talk to me. He played his Celtic music loud, but it didn't wake me up.

'Invite me in,' he said when we were in my driveway and he'd shaken me awake.

Mom would be home soon. I tossed him a quick smile. 'No thanks. I got my orgasm.'

'I'm good for multiples,' he promised, his fingertips creeping up my thigh.

'Pop the trunk,' I returned, twisting his hand away.

Surprisingly, he did.

'Should I pick you up tomorrow?'

I wanted to say 'no', but I was taken a little aback by how nicely he had asked. 'OK. Meet me at the end of the road?'

He shook his head. 'Not quite a fully fledged rebel yet.'

'Nope.' I kissed him quickly. 'Bye.'

I know he wanted to say more, or do more, but I wasn't interested. Saxon was helping me unlock a part of myself that I had never known lurked evilly beneath the surface. I had a hard time caring about anyone but myself, and I had no patience for anything that irritated me in any way.

Breaking up with Jake had set an entire chain of events in motion. I was changing. I could feel myself stretching out and breaking through, and the new me was coming out with a harder shell, twice as fierce as the old me.

My mind felt lost and my head pounded. I was hot and uncomfortably achy, followed by waves of chilled shivers. I was falling apart, and I didn't know what to do to stop it.

I went inside my dark, cool house, flipped the heat on and headed to the bathroom, where I took a long shower, the hot water pouring over me in relaxing streams. I was falling asleep under the warm rush, so I got out and toweled off. I pulled on my pajamas and climbed into my bed. I hadn't eaten dinner, seen my mother or done my homework, but my body was so tired, I just fell into a deep, dreamless sleep.

Chapter 14

By the time Friday came, the last thing I wanted to do was go out anywhere, but Saxon had been persistently nice and Jake had been doing every single thing he could to throw his relationship with Nikki in my face. There was such buzzing nastiness between the two of us, it was starting to erase even the best memories, the ones I kept nestled close to my heart and only took out to sob over late at night.

But every once in a while, I'd catch Jake's eyes on me, just for one fleeting instant, and something so strong and amazing it was electric would shock between us and melt all the anger momentarily. Once Jake broke his pencil in half while we stared at each other, not saying a word, not sure what we were feeling. As if she could sense it, Nikki attached herself to him like a burr and didn't let go for the rest of the afternoon.

'C'mon, Blix.' Saxon wove his arm under my

backpack and around my waist in the hall. 'Zombies and sushi. They make sense together somehow, right?'

'All right.' I tried not to sigh, because I'd done enough to upset him this week, even if I hadn't meant it. Saxon had a worse reputation than he deserved, and it made me feel like a lowdown creep to put any blame on his shoulders. What Devon and Kelsie had said may have been partly right, but it was a skewed picture. No one knew Saxon the way I did. No one knew how good and kind he could be like I did.

'It's *zombies*. And *sushi*.' He squeezed me harder than was friendly. 'The face you're making kind of communicates *root canal*.'

I hip-checked him gently. 'I've never even had a cavity, so there's no way my face is saying *root canal*.'

'You're a freak of nature.' He leaned in and kissed my neck, and it felt good and foreign at the same time.

'Hey, guys.' It was Kelsie, her voice falsely bright. She cleared her throat and tucked a strand of her dark, shiny bob behind her ear. 'So, Folly's playing a gig. Kind of unexpected. They got space at The Grange, so they're on tonight, and we're trying to get the word out.' She tugged a flyer out of her badge-covered leather satchel. 'Think you can make it?'

She studied the grimy dirt whirls on the linoleum while Saxon scanned the flyer.

'If we do raw fish, but nix brain-eating mutants, we'll make it. Sound like a plan?' He ruffled my hair as I studied the neon green flyer. 'I know the idea of any monster that eats brains hurts the brainiac deep inside you, so don't act like this isn't an awesome favor on my part.'

I managed a quaky smile and nodded my agreement. He kissed my forehead, saluted Kelsie, and headed back down the hall, whistling. It was the whistle that tore at my heart.

Kelsie gave me a long look, licked her lips, twisted her silver rings on her fingers, and finally asked, 'OK, what's up? What is it, Bren? Don't you dare even utter the word "nothing", because I'm not an idiot. You look like you haven't slept in weeks. You're even paler than normal, which I didn't even think was humanly possible. Spill.'

I opened my mouth and shook my head. Nothing came out. She tugged on my wrist and pulled me through the doorway into the cluttered chaos of the craft room. She set my mangled project in front of me, and it all started to feel like a pattern: I would pour my heart out to Kelsie while I bungled through another art mess, and she would listen, nodding at all the right times, clicking her tongue with concern, all while producing some artistic masterpiece.

'I feel so completely confused.' I jabbed my finger on the bent corner of my new copper plate and winced. 'I know that it's all my fault, this whole thing with Jake and Saxon, but I can't figure out how to fix it. The thing is, I'm really happy to be able to have Saxon around. He's important to me. But I don't think I can be his girlfriend. Something feels off, and I don't know why. Because he's not a jerk. I know you and Devon think he's awful, but I swear he's been really nice to me. So why aren't I happy to just stay with him? Isn't that what I wanted? Isn't that why I kissed him in Paris and broke up with Jake?'

Kelsie wove her thread with quick, nimble fingers. 'Are you asking me? Because I don't have the answer to that one, Bren. All I know is that you're smart. If you broke it off with Jake you must have had a reason. But that doesn't mean you can't change your mind. Right?'

I groaned and bent the wire tool I was using to make designs in the copper. My head felt soupy, foggy, totally unfocused. 'I don't deserve Jake. He's with this girl Nikki now, and I think he's, like, *been* with her.' I hadn't told Kelsie about the condom-wrapper picture or the many sessions of tonsil hockey I witnessed. Her eyes went so wide, it looked like her eyeballs might pop out and roll across the floor. I took a deep breath and was comforted by the mingling smells of chalk, paint and clay. 'Maybe what they have is real. I mean, he's still with her. It's never been like that before with him. I mean, other than with me. It was always one-night stands. But they're all over each other.'

Kelsie picked at an errant string in her project and pursed her lips. 'What does Saxon have to say about the whole thing?'

I could feel my ears burn like they were on fire. 'Saxon says that Jake still loves me and always will. He says he can tell I'm still thinking about him, even when we're together.' I focused on Kelsie's hands, palms down on the craft table, and it took me a minute to look up into her face.

'Saxon said *that*?'

'Yes.' I felt humiliated and stupid and like every single decision I'd made in the last few weeks was so wrong, I should have been walking around like a social pariah. What had I done?

The soft slide of Kelsie's fingers covered my knuckles as she pulled my hand into hers. 'I'm sorry it's all so fucked up right now, Bren. But I think you just need to be really honest with yourself and stop beating yourself up. You're allowed to screw up. You're allowed to make big, colossal mistakes. Trust me. Jake and Saxon kind of have to understand that, right? Aren't they, like, the kings of screwing up? Big time?'

She was right. And she was so wrong. I didn't want to make big, colossal mistakes, and I didn't really feel like I should be allowed to. Because while I was thinking about what *I* wanted and what *I* needed, I was leaving disaster in my wake. Jake and Saxon, two people I cared about more than almost anyone else, were getting hurt, and it was stupid, heartless, immature and spineless of me. Every move I made, every path I chose seemed to cause more chaos, and I racked my brain but couldn't figure out what would make it all better, once and for all. I had never encountered a problem I couldn't find the solution to before. And I'd never imagined I'd be the cause of so much hurt. It sucked, and I wanted to fix it. Scratch that – I *needed* to fix it.

That point got driven home when I saw Saxon, an easy, happy smile stretched on his face as he fell into step by my side, ready to walk me to cross country. Running didn't help me figure anything out either, no matter how mercilessly I pushed myself. My lungs sucked air in and gasped it out like a bellows until I finally doubled over on the track, staggered to a patch of grass and threw up.

Coach Dunn jogged over and thumped me on the back. Saxon came flying down from the soccer field, ignoring his coach's yells and Coach Dunn's reassurance that she had it all under control.

'Overdo it, Blixen?' she barked.

I spit and grimaced at the sour taste in my mouth. Saxon yanked a pack of orange Tic Tacs out of his pocket and shook a few into his hand. He held them up to my lips, and I ate them awkwardly, trying not to lick his smoky-smelling palm.

'Thanks,' I groaned.

'Maclean, it's all good here,' Coach Dunn said roughly. When she looked at his face, her voice softened. 'She'll be fine.'

'Should I walk her to the nurse?' He rubbed a hand over his mouth and looked so worried, it shot through my heart like a shard of glass.

'No!' I shook my head. 'I just overdid it. I think I was a little dehydrated. Maybe I'll just sit on the bench for a while.'

Coach Dunn nodded, and Saxon narrowed his eyes at me, then pointed two fingers at his eyes and flipped them back at me. 'I'll be watching. You get back on that track, I'll throw you over my shoulder and carry you to the nurse no matter what anyone says.' He gave Coach Dunn a grudging nod and jogged back to his waiting team.

Coach Dunn put a hand on my shoulder.

'Maybe if I feel better, I'll just do a couple of slow

laps?' I looked up into her tanned face, desperate for her to tell me I didn't have to sit on the bench with only my guilt-heavy thoughts to keep me company.

She shook her head. 'That's just junk miles, Blixen. A waste of your time and your energy. You'll ruin your pace, you'll wear down your strength. If you're going to run, run with purpose, at full health.'

'Junk miles?' I mulled the term over as I watched Coach jog back to the track. That's exactly what I felt like I was doing, and not just on the track. I was just logging in slow, useless miles, not sure where I was going or why I was even running.

I watched Saxon tear across the soccer field, his feet so quick and sure, and my stomach heaved again. What was I doing? He was a good person. And I was using him. My clammy hands shook, and I wished as hard as I could for the irritating shriek of the bell that would end this period. I wished for the end of this miserable day. I wished for a solution, a trip back in time, a way to make the right decision without ruining everything for everyone I cared about.

My head pounded as I stared at the food during lunch. No matter what I looked at in the cafeteria, it made my stomach churn like a washing machine. Saxon kept adding things to my tray with determination, but I lifted them back off and shook my head.

'You look like you're about to pass out. Let me take you to the nurse.' He slid his hand under my hair and around the back of my neck, his fingers kneading the space between my neck and shoulder.

'I have a big project due in graphic design, and I can't get the shadowing right on this new program. I have to go in.' I swallowed hard and picked up a banana and a carton of milk.

Saxon chewed on the side of his lip. 'You doin' this project with Jake?' He worked way too hard at keeping the words even.

I paid for my lunch and kept a good yard in front of him. 'No, not with Jake. Not that it should make a difference to you.' I collapsed into the orange plastic chair and attempted to choke down some food. The milk was watery and lukewarm, and the banana was soft and bruised, overly sweet and squishy. The urge to vomit took over again. It was like the world was conspiring to keep me puking all day long.

'No difference to me?' He folded a spork in half and twisted its plastic neck violently. 'What's going on between you and me, exactly?'

I stood up and swayed like I was on a boat. 'I gotta go.'

I hit a solid wall of Saxon. 'Where?'

'Tech. I told you. I've got a project.' My empty

stomach and crushing headache made my reflexes sluggish. I tried to duck and weave, but he was way quicker.

'You aren't riding there.' It was an absolute command.

I had a foggy thought that Saxon should join the army. I had a second, clearer thought that he'd either become the youngest general ever or go completely AWOL.

I looked up into the swirled gold of his eyes and at the tight pinch of his mouth. I pressed one hand against his arm to turn him, and breathed easier when the current of air that wafted toward me didn't smell so deliciously like Saxon. 'I appreciate it. I do. But you don't have any business telling me what I can and can't do.'

'This isn't a pissing contest, Blix. You look like shit. Seriously.' He glanced at the lunch monitors, busy with a head-on double-tray goulash collision. 'Let's go. I'll drive you.'

I would have said no, just to avoid the question he'd asked and I'd dodged, but I did feel kind of shaky, and my pathetic lunch hadn't made up for all I'd chucked in cross country. We walked silently to the lot, avoiding the office and the two hall monitors busy grading papers. The silence deepened in the car until it felt like we were avalanched by it.

He didn't even look up when we pulled in at Tech. It was like his steering wheel suddenly held all the secrets of the universe and he couldn't tear his eyes away.

'Pop the trunk?' As small as I tried to curl my voice, it was still deafening.

'I'm coming to pick you up. We've got a date, remember?' He felt around for his cigarettes, then drummed his fingers hard on the dashboard.

I put my hand on his cheek. 'Saxon?'

I couldn't translate what I saw in his eyes.

'Yeah?'

'I'll have to get ready, you know. Get dressed. Do my hair. We can't just leave from school. And I want to double-check with my mom. I didn't remind her about it, and I never mentioned Folly at all.'

He nodded, popped the trunk, and crooked his finger. I leaned into him and he pressed his lips flat against mine, then pulled back. 'I'm still gonna pick you up. Maybe we should just stay in tonight? Movies on the couch at your place? I'll keep a foot of space between us at all times, scout's honor. Or we could go back to my place, and I promise you'll rest the whole time. Or at least you'll be lying down the whole time.' He tried to deliver a crooked grin, but it just looked like a smile that had come unhinged.

'We're going out. I'm dressing up. You can drive me home. I feel fine.' I ran my fingers through his thick hair and laid a quick kiss on the smooth patch of forehead I'd exposed.

'I'll see you after school.' He looked like he wanted to say something else, but I slammed the door and walked my bike to the rack before he got the chance.

Once I was inside the low, dark halls of Tech, I didn't know what to do or where to go. There was still fifteen minutes until the end of lunch, and I didn't think my stomach could take the smell of any more cafeteria food. My throat burned, so I headed for the water fountain, and once I'd drunk enough for three camels, I hit the bathroom. I was about to leave the stall when a cluster of girls barged in, laughing and chatting. I felt like it would be way too much effort to face them, so I peeked out through the crack in the stall door to wait them out.

And I saw Nikki.

She was holding her hand out to take an eyeliner from one of her friends, and she put even more on under her eyes.

'So, how are things going with Jake?' I recognized the speaker who had the biggest bag of make-up I'd ever seen as Krista, the girl I'd snapped at when she'd felt it necessary to share how wonderful Jake and Nikki's being together was.

Nikki stopped ringing her eyes and put a hip half on the sink. 'You know, just before New Year, I thought this was going to be amazing? But he's not like he was that summer we hooked up. I mean, he was so fun. Now he's, like, all about work, he's so serious. You know he won't even drink? Like, not even one beer.'

'You know how they do that.' Krista fluffed her hair, which was really nicely dyed with lots of bright red highlights. 'It's, like, one week they can drink anyone else under the table, and the next week, they're all AA and telling everyone about the evils of drinking. But Jake could never hold his liquor, remember? Wasn't he, like, totally drunk when you guys slept together that summer?'

'We were *all* really drunk.' Nikki giggled and applied a perfect coat of lipstick. 'And he doesn't hang out with anyone in our old crew. We went to a field party, and he kept looking at his watch, like some old man. It wasn't even on the right time. It was, like, six hours off. And I was, like, "Why don't you just use your cell phone like a normal person?" Weird.'

The watch! Jake was wearing the watch I gave him, and it was still set to Paris time. I felt dizzy again, but this time it was so completely twined with hope and happiness, I didn't care if I passed out on the grimy tiles of the bathroom floor!

Krista looked at Nikki in the mirror. 'But he's so hot. Like, amazingly hot.'

Nikki's pretty green eyes sparkled, and she blushed a pink so gorgeous it would have been a bestseller if they could have put it into a compact. 'I *know*. I thought I had no chance when that new girl sank her claws into him. But they're done. Like, *done*. He gets so pissed off if she ever comes up.'

I bit my bottom lip and eased back from the crack in case they felt my eyes on them.

'She's a freak.' Krista lifted her perfectly shaped eyebrows and batted her mascara-caked lashes for emphasis. 'I talked to her, like, one time and she bit my head off. Bitch, much?'

'Whatever she did to Jake, I hope she rots for it.' Nikki gave the mirror a glare so perfectly malicious, I was positive she could see me through the stall door and was just waiting for me to come out so she could rip out chunks of my hair and tear the earrings out of my lobes. The hair on my neck stood up, but the look left her face when she popped her lips and checked her cell phone. 'C'mon, K, we need to get back to lunch so I can see Jake before class.'

I didn't breathe until the door shut again, and then

the breath rode on the back of a sob. I could pretend that Nikki was an evil bitch all I wanted, but I'd be dead wrong. When I crept out of the stall and looked at myself in the mirror, it was impossible for me to meet my own eyes in my reflection. Nikki had slid in where she saw an opportunity. That opportunity would never have existed if I hadn't been such a life-wrecker.

The bell rang, and I ducked back into the stall to wipe my eyes in peace while the bathroom clogged with more girls applying cosmetics, elbowing for mirror room, and chatting at ear-splitting decibels about school, life, love.

By the time I'd waited for the last girl to clear out, I was a minute or two late to class, but Mr Giles waved me to my seat with an understanding nod when I murmured something vague about my time of the month.

I sat across from Jake and kept my eyes glued on my paper. He did, too. When the bell rang I packed up slowly and he rushed into the hall, away from me. It was our new pattern. I exited the classroom and tried hard to ignore Nikki's giggles and squeals, knowing she got louder when I was around in an attempt to lay total claim to her territory.

'She should just piss on his leg,' I muttered under

my breath to myself. Unlike at Frankford, I didn't have many friends other than Jake at Tech, and it made my walk through the halls long and lonely.

During our last period Matt, the big guy I'd borrowed the eraser from solely to drive Jake crazy, turned to me and said, 'Hey, I bet you're going to the Folly concert tonight at The Grange, right? Don't you design all their shirts?'

Jake looked up at us and glowered.

'I do make their shirts. And yeah, I am going. Are you?'

'Sure am.' He leaned his chair back and almost tipped it. He flushed when he let the front two legs drop, and Jake smiled meanly.

I glared at Jake. 'I think it will be really fun. So I guess I'll see you there?'

'Brenna!' Our teacher, Ms Flynn, waved me to the front of the room.

The boys looked down sheepishly as I went up to the teacher's desk, ready for a lecture about keeping on task.

'I love this design,' she said, pointing to my project specifications on her desk, not even mentioning my chattiness. 'Your project is amazing, but the shading is off. I'd like to enter this in the countywide Young Business Leaders Design Competition. Jake Kelly seems to have the best handle on the program. Have him take a look and show you how to clean up the shading. And can you ask Matt to come up and bring his portfolio? Thank you.'

Before I could protest or make up some stupid excuse, she was looking back at her grade book intently. I went back to my seat and delivered my message to Matt. He left, and I cleared my throat.

'Um, so, Ms Flynn said my shading is off on my project.'

Jake stared at me, his mouth a hard line. 'OK?'

This was so completely wrong. This whole scenario was all wrong.

I bit the inside of my cheek hard to keep from breaking down like a huge toddler. 'She said you get the program. She wanted me to ask you to help me.'

'Oh.' Jake put both hands behind his neck and took a long breath in, then released it in a whoosh. 'Of course. Um, pull your chair over.'

I pulled it over, very careful to avoid his chair, his portfolio, his leg, his arm, him.

Jake opened the program, and I was still functioning on high alert. But, weird as we were together, I loved my work in class, and soon I stopped worrying about not bumping his arm or touching his hand because I needed his help. I had done for the last week, but hadn't had the guts to ask him. Now that he was explaining it, I was excited to make my design better. If the entire world was screwed up and it was all my fault, the least I could do was rock my project and work out every single kink.

By the time he'd run me through it a couple of times, I felt like I could do it better, and I nudged him out of the way and applied all he'd taught me, with some variations.

'Perfect.' He turned his head to me, and the smile on his face was the sun stippling through the trees in the summer, your favorite song blaring on the radio with the windows down, the warm crush of someone you love holding you in his arms . . . perfect.

And then it disappeared and the temporary reprieve from all the insanity was over. The memories of all that had happened in the last few weeks bull-dozed over us, and Jake's relaxed posture stiffened visibly.

'Thanks. For your help.' The period was almost over, so I exited the program, once again careful not to touch him.

'So, you're going to the Folly concert tonight?' He arranged his books in an overly neat stack.

'Yeah. Are you going?' I had to lean across him a little to switch off the monitor, and I inhaled his cold, crisp smell that always reminded me of leaves falling off the trees in autumn. How does someone smell like a season?

'I planned on stopping in after work.' His gray eyes cut over to me. 'I guess you'll be getting a ride from Saxon?'

'I guess you'll be giving a ride to Nikki?' I shot back.

'Nik drives herself.' His voice was hollow.

Of all the crazy things I'd seen and heard and thought, for some reason that one cut me deep, just the idea of him with an independent, older girl. Someone who could do things I couldn't, driving being the least of it. It made no sense, I had no right, but that didn't stop me feeling it.

I took a big, shuddery breath, tears so close I could taste them in the back of my nose and throat. Jake's eyes went from cold shale-in-the-winter gray to oldest-softest-Henley gray, and, just when I was sure I'd ooze into a puddle of sadness on the floor, the bell I'd waited for all day miraculously screamed the end of the period.

This time I broke the pattern – I grabbed my things and ran, promising myself the longest, gulpingest, most horrifically sobful cry-fest as soon as I got home and stepped into the shower. I just had to hold it together for a half an hour, tops. No problem.

I was already down the long hallway and could see the dim winter light through the dirty window squares in the metal front door that I was inches away from exploding through, when I felt a warm hand on my shoulder.

'Brenna?'

The brakes locked and squealed on all the thoughts rushing through my head, and only one thing propelled full force through the windshield of my sanity.

Jake Kelly.

I held my eyebrows high on my forehead and puckered my mouth as small as I could to keep the tears at bay as I turned around.

'You left your sketchbook.' He backed up and held out my black book, his arms stretched to maintain maximum distance between our bodies.

I held my hands out and grabbed the book on two corners so that not even one finger would brush his.

'I'm sorry . . .' he said.

'Thank you,' I said at the same time, then we both tangled and clumsily bumped words for half a minute until finally he said, 'Be quiet, Bren.'

I clapped my jaw shut.

'You ripped me up.' There was no malice or accusation in his words, and that made it feel like I had swallowed a bear trap. It was just us in the hall with his words stacked between us, naked, strong. 'I'm probably still not really over you and everything that happened. But I've been doing things, saying things that I hoped would hurt you, and that's dick. That's a sad-sack excuse for the way I acted, though. You'll always be someone I care about and admire. So, I'm sorry. If I hurt you, if I made you upset, I'm honestly sorry, Brenna.'

Wait! This was *my* speech, sucked from under me and pouring out from Jake's mouth so beautifully, it made my knees buckle.

There was suddenly nothing to say that he hadn't already said better.

'I'm sorry,' I tried weakly, embarrassed as soon as I said the woefully inadequate words.

He nodded, already walking backward, his hands in his pockets, his hat so low over his eyes, I didn't know if he could see me. He had delivered his message, and there was nothing left to say. He turned on his heel and left me, an inch away from the doors that I didn't blow through fast enough to avoid the bomb he dropped on me.

I walked outside in a daze, and Saxon was waiting. He put his arm around me and pulled me close.

'You look like hell. Tonight is officially canceled.' He led me to the car.

I molded my body to the leather seat and prepared to let the tears fall, but there wasn't even the prickly promise of a sob-fest. I felt lighter, freer.

'I want to go,' I announced, feeling sure, strong and hopeful. Scarily, newly hopeful. 'If you don't want to pick me up, tell me, and I'll find another ride.'

'If you're dead set on being an idiot, let me at least have the privilege of driving your Royal Craziness.' He flicked the car stereo on, and we listened to the Celtic girl wail and plead in her faraway voice.

He dropped me off, and I told him I'd text if my mother said no, otherwise he could pick me up at seven. Mom wasn't even home; I had to text her, and she gave a quick permission with a warning to be careful and an encouragement to have fun. I took a long, hot shower, but there were no tears to puff up my eyes or make my throat hoarse. There was only the curious echo of Jake's words.

I spent a long time getting ready, using the extra time to put on more make-up and try out cuter outfits, each tighter and more daring than the last. By the time Saxon knocked on my door I was in a short, tight black skirt, a black-and-red Folly shirt, black boots, and make-up that was smoky, sexy, dark and alluring when I'd really only aimed to be cute, pretty, made-up sweet.

'Holy shit.' Saxon took my hand and spun me around, then glanced at the empty house. 'Seriously, let's hit your bedroom. Now.'

I laughed, feeling powerful with all my eyeliner and mascara. 'No! We're going on a date.'

He was wearing a tight black T-shirt and dark jeans with black boots. Simple, understated, and sexy as hell. I could smell the sharp cling of his aftershave and that amazing under smell that was spicy, male and all Saxon.

I went to the closet to grab my coat and he came up too close behind me. When I spun around, I was in his arms.

'I don't want to go out,' he said, his mouth at my throat. I backed away. 'Don't. You smell so good. You look so freaking good. Be with me tonight.' When Saxon pleaded my entire body yanked and pulled toward him like an eager puppy on a leash.

'No.' I stepped away from him. 'We're going out.'

He blocked my path to the front door and escape. 'You don't want to be here with me alone.' His dark eyes went all black, and his words were just bare facts laid out uncomfortably in front of both of us.

'I want to go out.' I put a hand on his chest, and he

took my fingers and squeezed them over his steadily beating heart. 'With you, Saxon.'

He closed his eyes and leaned his forehead on mine. 'You want to go out with me. You don't want to *be* with me.' His voice was sandpaper on metal.

'I want to be with you, but I want to go out. With you.' I squeezed his hand, but he squeezed back so tight and so hard it startled me.

His eyes were clear and black as pitch: deep, hot, molten black. 'Don't talk circles around me, Blix.' He set his mouth in a tight line. 'You like me too much to tell me the truth, don't you? Oh my fucking God, I've moved into the damn friend zone.'

'What are you talking about?' I squeaked, because he was saying things that I knew were true but wasn't ready to face yet.

He shook his head and tossed his inky hair out of his eyes. The look on his face was a mix of stricken sadness and idiotic amusement. 'Nothing.' He cupped a hand under my chin and kissed me on the lips, full and soft and punctuated with the slightest moan. 'Let's get this over with, right?'

Before I could say anything, he yanked my hand, pulling me toward his car in the chilly light.

Chapter 15

Saxon cranked up the stereo and grunted at every attempt at conversation I made. By the time we got to the adorable little stone-fronted sushi restaurant, I'd come to the sinking realization that I wasn't going to be able to enjoy my raw fish.

Saxon wound around the front of the car and opened my door, marched up the steps next to me, grabbed the door to the restaurant and swung it open for me, ducking to avoid the tinkling silver tubes of the wind chime that hung too low in the doorway. He strode to the hostess stand, leaned close and spoke low to the girl with the stack of menus, and whatever he said made her giggle and blush. We were led to a cozy corner table in a low-lit, paper-screened side room, but I couldn't enjoy the quiet elegance. Saxon crossed his arms and scowled at me, but smiled sweetly at the waitress, and ordered tons of the most expensive foods on the menu. He cracked the chopsticks apart and grabbed all the pieces he wanted without asking me if I cared. Not that it was a huge deal, but he ate all the unagi rolls, which were my favorite. He also hogged the wasabi.

'Is something wrong?' I watched him wolf down the food and never make eye contact with me.

'Nope.' He took a long gulp out of his water glass and made a face like he'd chugged rotten milk. 'Maybe.' He folded his hands on the shiny dark wood table and leaned towards me. He waited for me to lean towards him and said, 'I'd kill someone for a bottle of sake. I don't think the waitress will serve me, though.' He leaned back and smirked. 'Not with you here, anyway.'

'What are you talking about?' I snapped back in my chair and shook my head. 'I don't look *that* young, and you definitely don't look twenty-one, so forget that.'

'I didn't think she'd serve me because I look twenty-one.' He ran a hand through his black hair, and he flashed me the wolfish smile that I hadn't seen in a while. 'I have other ways of convincing girls to give me what I want.' I bet his mouth was watering as he anticipated whatever my face might give away: shock, hurt, unhappiness maybe? Knowing exactly what he was thinking, I kept my slack-jawed, narrow-eyed, trembling-chinned facial tics under control and offered him a blank stare. His lips went sulky, but then he leaned over and added, 'Well, some girls. Not the cock-teases. *You* know what I mean. Right, Blix?'

There were a hundred barbed, nasty things I could say to him, but it would have been a waste of breath. I stood up and dropped my share for dinner on the table. 'I need to use the bathroom. I'll wait in the lobby for you.'

The side of his mouth twitched, and he scooped the money up and shoved it back at me. 'This is a date. I don't want your money.'

I grabbed the bills, smoothed them out and slammed them back on the table. 'You call this a date? This is a mess, and I *insist* on paying my share.'

'You're taking responsibility for your messes now? Refreshing.' He cocked an eyebrow at me.

'Is there something you want to say to me, Saxon? Because if there is, just say it.' I could hear the dare snapping in my voice.

He stood up so fast he almost knocked his chair onto the floor. 'I will, then.' He rushed at me and jabbed his index finger against my breastbone. 'I've made a fool of myself over you for weeks, and shame the fuck on me, because you were never into this, were you? *Were you?*'

All the air sucked out of my lungs and left me tight

and twisted in front of him. 'I'm sorry,' I stuttered. His face was so close to mine, I could see his pupils, deeper black than the midnight of his irises. 'I've been so screwed up, Saxon. I haven't been fair to you. Or myself. Or anyone.' I couldn't bring myself to utter Jake's name, even though he was the one I'd screwed over the worst. 'I was so stupid. I just wasn't sure about so much, so much was confusing . . .'

'I get it,' he bit out, sifting his words through his teeth. He tightened his hands on the back of the chair with a frustrated groan. 'So I was just someone to waste time with for you, too? Don't look all stricken. I've been that for other girls before. I just didn't expect it from you. That's all.'

'That's not true! You're so important to me. How could you think you're not? That's the reason why this has been so insane!' I put my hand on his forearm and he snatched it back like he'd been burned. 'The fact that I care about you is what started this all!'

'Important to you?' he sneered, brushing past me. 'Important for what? A ride now and then? Someone to run over and check on you when Jake wasn't paying you any attention?' He was about to walk away from me.

The room felt like it was tilting wildly. 'That's not what you are to me.' I reached out and grabbed on to the table. 'Saxon, listen to me. You mean so much to me. Believe me when I tell you that. Please, believe me.'

He whirled around. 'Believe you? Why? Because you've been so honest up to now? If you want me to believe I mean so much to you, why don't you prove it?' His lips curled back and he bared his teeth at me.

'How?' I reached out for him a second time, and he grabbed my hand hard.

'Come back to my place. Be with me. Just me. Just *us*.' His eyes were dark and wild, and I could see that he knew exactly what he was asking me.

My heart hammered hard in my chest, and part of me wondered what it would be like. I knew I could trust him. I knew he'd care about me enough to make it special. I also knew in the pit of my heart that it would be a huge mistake, and one that would be impossible to take back. I knew my own heart, and I told him the honest truth.

'I can't do that, Saxon. Not with you, not with anyone.' My knees shook so hard, I swear they knocked together.

'Why not? Because of him? You never wanted me, did you?' he snarled, his hold on my wrist tightening from rough grab to full, blood-stopping tourniquet.

First I felt a white-hot blast of fury, and I knew that

if I opened my mouth, I would spew acid words right into his arrogant face. But two deep breaths and the desperate bite of his hand on my wrist dissolved the jagged edges of my anger and melted it into something softer. Something sadder.

In the middle of this pretty paper room, under the low glow of the creamy lamps, I could see that Saxon was fueled by a twisted kind of love. I put my hand on his, on the hand that had bound itself so fiercely around my wrist, and loosened his fingers one by one.

'That's not how it works. That's not good enough for either one of us.' My voice stayed soft but firm. We squared off, our eyes locked.

'Coward,' he accused, his voice raw as gravel on new skin.

'Not at all.' I raised a hand to his cheek, but he shied away from my touch. 'I'd be a coward if I slept with you to try to get an answer or make things easier. I won't do that for either one of our sakes.' I took the bills off the table and folded them into my pocket. 'You pay. I'm sorry I bitched about our date. It was really sweet of you to take me out.'

'Brenna.'

No one had ever said my name like that before; like a plea, like the endnote of an argument, like it was the most hopeless, sorriest of all the words there were to say.

'I *care* about you. I do. But some things are mine to give, and could never, ever be yours or anyone else's on demand. And it will never be up for discussion. Does that make sense?' This time, when I reached for his face, he didn't back away. He closed his black eyes and his eyelashes tangled together. He nuzzled his jaw against my hand.

When he finally spoke, he seemed calmer. Or maybe defeated. 'You think too much, you know that? Brainiac.' He brought my palm to his lips and kissed it, then tucked a strand of hair behind my ear like it was his to move. I didn't even attempt to stop him. 'Go to the bathroom. Or whatever. Let me take care of the bill and see if I can get the waitress's number. Maybe she can steal me some sake for later.' He tried to waggle his eyebrows with sexy bravado, but I didn't miss the bleak look that shaded his eyes. I did ignore it, and his face communicated his thanks for that.

I stared at my reflection in the bathroom mirror, too pale and with purple circles under my bloodshot eyes. I wasn't completely happy with what I saw, but at least I could look myself in the eye again.

Saxon was waiting in the lobby, hands in his coat pocket, toothpick dangling out of the side of his mouth. He made a move to take his hands out of his pockets, then reconsidered and left them in. He nodded at me. 'C'mon. We have a concert to get to.'

'Saxon?' I took a few steps toward him and he took an equal amount of steps back, maintaining an exact distance between us. 'We could see the zombies. If you wanted. I don't mind.'

He smiled the unhappiest smile I'd ever seen. 'Don't you ever get tired of being all mature and level-headed? You make the rest of us look like even bigger fuck-ups in comparison.'

'Mature? Level-headed?' I held my hands up. 'What are you talking about? I made the biggest mess. Ever! And . . . I know I hurt you.'

The smile got wider and infinitesimally sadder. 'Don't give yourself so much credit. Plus I don't want your pity date to ruin the zombie awesomeness. Another time, another girl who doesn't mind brain decimation.'

'Another girl?' I felt relieved and disappointed at the same time.

'You didn't think you'd be the last, did you?' He took two steps toward me and bumped the toe of his boot to the toe of my shoe. 'Come on. Now! Party time. Let's go.' He held his elbow out to me, and I linked my arm through it. His smile was smaller, but it had a tiny sprinkle of happiness. Or, at least, not as much sadness.

Everything had gone completely wrong, but somehow it had snapped back into the strange, unspoken, uneasy place that we had been at back on the first day we met, and I was happy to be there again.

By the time we pulled up at The Grange, cars had already choked the gravel driveway and people were milling around the doors and inside the rickety wooden building. The back of Saxon's hand brushed mine, but he pulled it away without a glance in my direction and waved back at a few girls from the women's soccer team who called him over. For a second he looked torn.

'Go.' I waved my hand toward the girls.

'I'm here with you.' He bumped his shoulder against mine. 'You're a pain in the ass, but I'm not going to just ditch you.'

'It's cool.' I pointed to the table where Kelsie was busy hocking shirts. 'There's Kelsie. I'm going to say hi. You go talk to your friends.'

He squinted at me for a minute, then nodded. 'Good thing I hedged my bets, eh, Blix?' He tossed a glance toward the girls' soccer team, now gathered in full force and cat-calling to him. 'Not exactly what I wanted, but you know what they say about getting what you want.'

'That you should want what you have instead?' I guessed.

'No! That's ridiculous advice. Jesus, who told you that? Never mind, don't even answer that. Just forget you ever heard it. They – and by "they" I am referring to those who know what the hell they're talking about – say that you can't always get what you want. But if you try sometimes . . .' He held his hand out for me to finish.

'You just might get what you need?'

He shucked me under the chin and gave me his best cocky smile. 'There's hope for you yet.'

He walked away from me with a determined swagger and didn't look back. I know because I watched the whole long beeline he made to his adoring fans.

I wanted to say hi to Kelsie, but she was flooded with people and looked super busy. I wasn't sure if Devon was planning on coming. He'd said his mom had unofficially grounded him when she got a call saying he'd failed to turn in two major history assignments.

It was way too cold to have worn this ridiculous short skirt, and I shivered a little in the biting wind. I was already feeling dead tired, and being out in the frigid air didn't help at all. If I'd had my license,

I would have happily driven myself home. Since I'd taken a ride from Saxon and we'd made our awkward peace, I wasn't about to hunt him down and ask him to take me home early. I made my way inside and saw a few people from school I knew, but before I could make my way to them, Nikki blocked my path.

'Hey there, Brenna.' Her eyes looked glassy, and I noticed the sharp smell of alcohol on her breath. She had three friends giggling behind her, including Krista. Not one of them looked remotely sober.

'Um, hey, Nikki.' I attempted to brush past her, because I could feel that she was looking for a fight, and I wasn't interested in that at all.

'Jake's here, but he isn't interested in seeing *you*.' She poked a finger out, and I think she was aiming for the center of my chest, but she weaved and hit my shoulder instead.

'OK. Look, I have someone I have to go see. I'll be going. Now.' I realized that I had been backed into one of the darker corners of the little low building. Shit. Backed into a corner and facing down four angry, drunk, and possibly high girls wasn't my idea of a good time. 'What do you want me to say, Nikki? You two are together. Fantastic. Jake and I haven't talked outside of school in weeks, so you don't have anything to worry about.'

'Then whysee wearin' the stupid fuckin' watch you gave 'im, huh?' she slurred. She blinked fast, and I saw a tear slide out of the corner of each eye. 'You don't deserve someone like Jake! So whysee still into you? You're a bitch and a liar! You better leave him the hell alone!' She lunged forward, and I took one step back into the corner, reaching along the wall in the hope there was a door to a bathroom or outside or something, anything I could duck into.

'She's not worth it!'

'Forget her! She's nothing but a useless bitch!'

'If Jake doesn't know how lucky he is to have you, screw him!'

Her friends were all pulling her back, but she was still straining forward, determined to get at me. I really didn't want to see what the outcome of being jumped by four girls half in the bag was, but I clenched my fists and got ready to fight my way out of this corner I'd somehow gotten backed into.

Suddenly, from out of nowhere, Kelsie yanked two of the girls back and all I heard was a set of quick yelps before they went flying. In an instant she grabbed Krista by the red-tinted hair and snarled, 'Get the hell away from her!'

Kelsie usually came across as a really gentle, sweet girl without a mean bone in her body. Watching her lash out at these girls made my jaw drop; suddenly all that hippie calm gave way to an intense rage. The first two had backed off, but Krista was about to get into it when Jake appeared and threw himself in front of Kelsie.

Krista wound up landing a weak punch on his chest, and I sank against the wall with relief. If she had used her full strength and landed the punch on Kelsie, it would have smashed right into my friend's face. Jake yanked Krista up by the shoulder.

'Shambles is waiting outside. Tell him Nikki will be out in a minute.'

'I'm not leaving!' Krista snapped, her arms flailing.

'You're drunk and high. I swear to God, I will call your father and have him come down if you don't go now.' Jake's face was cold and serious. Krista stopped wailing and jerking around and stomped to the door. Jake looked at Nikki, and I cowered at the pure disgust in his eyes. 'Seriously, Nik? What's with you lately?'

'Like you give a shit!' she screamed. 'You haven't paid any attention to me in weeks! I know you're still talking to that slut!'

'Calm down.' Jake took her by the elbow. 'You need to go home. Let Shambles take you. He'll drop you to get your car tomorrow.'

'Why not *you*?' Her angry screech ended in a

hiccup. 'I spend more time with him than you, and you're supposed to be my boyfriend! Why are you with me if you don't even want to be?' The tears that coursed out of her eyes made her make-up run in murky black rivers down her cheeks. 'You still love her, don't you? Don't you? Just admit it, you liar!'

Jake's eyes locked on mine across the few feet that separated us. The electric shock that went through the air was so intense, I was surprised no one else around us reacted. My heart warmed and swelled, and I wondered if he felt it, too. Then he tore his eyes off me and looked back at Nikki.

'You're drunk, Nik. And this isn't the time or place to talk about this. I'll call you tomorrow, when you're in your right mind. OK?' He spoke to her firmly but gently, and as much as I hated being the voyeur in the corner, it was fascinating.

When Jake and I dated, he usually deferred to me. He was the one who messed up, and I was the one who had all the right answers. It was amazing how many different versions of us there were and, in a strange way, I was glad to see this other side of Jake, even if it did tear at my heart to watch him curl an arm around Nikki and walk her out into the parking lot.

Kelsie snuggled next to me. 'You OK, girl? You look kind of beat.'

I wiped my suddenly damp eyes with my knuckles and let out a shaky laugh. 'Kel, it's been the world's longest freaking night. I'm glad I'm here and all, but you don't know how I'm lusting for my bed.'

'Did you come with Saxon?' She craned her neck and looked around for his dark head.

'I did. We're, um, not together anymore. I mean, as much as we were, we're not. After tonight.' My tongue felt tied in a fat knot.

'Oh.' She smiled a smile that was all sweet sympathy. 'Are you happy about it?'

I nodded weakly. 'I mean, *happy* might not be the right word. I'm just . . . I guess, at peace with all the stupid mistakes I made. And I know there's that old saying about how much you learn from your mistakes and all that, but seriously, it just sucks. It sucks being wrong and stupid and screwing everything up for everyone.' I leaned my cheek against her shiny, smooth hair.

She patted my side. 'You're being hard on yourself, Bren. You know, all you can do is the best you can do. You're going to screw up sometimes. But the people who really love you will hang in there. Like me.' She kissed my cheek, and I felt like I could relax for the first time all night.

The band came on stage, and I tried to put all the

craziness of the night behind me. Kelsie and I screamed along with all the songs, danced until we were buckled over from laughing, and acted like the happy young fools we were. Saxon came in with three soccer girls who looked like they might scratch each other's eyes out over him, and they were all strong, gorgeous and determined. That scenario was probably Saxon's wet dream. He joked and grinned a lot, but once in a while I caught him looking at me with no trace of a smile on his face.

By the time the last song played, I could hardly keep my eyes open. 'I hate to ask you,' I said loudly in his ear, "cos I can see how much fun you're going to have, but could you give me a ride home? I don't mind if you need to, uh, bring a friend along.' I glanced at the three girls, and their six glaring eyeballs and six aggressively crossed arms and three anxiously tapping feet. 'Or three.'

Saxon's smile died on his lips. He put his mouth close to my ear. 'Really? You don't care?'

I shook my head, and when he pulled away, I was startled at the twist of his mouth.

'Saxon, I thought you . . . I didn't mean . . . please!' I thought we were settled, I thought it was all OK between us, but his look made me feel like maybe we weren't.

He cupped a hand over my mouth. 'Stop!' He gave me a half-smile. 'You open your mouth and make things worse. Drop it. I appreciate your open-mindedness. Really.' He pointed to the spot on the floor where I stood. 'Wait. Right here. OK?'

I nodded and watched Saxon corral his three competitive, gorgeous admirers and followed them with my eyes until I lost the four of them in the crowd. Folly played an encore, then a second, but Saxon didn't come back, and I decided to snake through the wild fans and find Kelsie. I'd just text Saxon and let him know I'd gotten home without him. It would be less awkward that way, anyway.

Just as I was leaving my assigned spot, I felt his hand on my arm, and couldn't have imagined a better feeling. Saxon would take me home, and I could go to bed and let this whole day wash away. My eyes felt hot and heavy, and all the smoke in the room coupled with my and Kelsie's sing-along made my throat a burning, clawed mess. When I turned to tell him I was ready, I saw that it wasn't Saxon.

'Jake!' I felt myself blush. 'Sorry, I thought you were . . . someone else.'

There was no way to talk without getting close, so we leaned into each other for necessity's sake. And I may have breathed in the smell of him, just a little, just to remember, but it was mostly because the air was so stuffy, and he smelled like a clean, cold breeze. 'Saxon sent me.' His voice rumbled close to my ear. 'He said to tell you something came up. He asked if I'd mind giving you a lift.'

Our eyes hooked, and I tucked the moment of closeness next to my heart even though it scorched me like a hot coal.

'It's fine, Jake. I was going to see if I could get a ride back with whoever brought Kelsie. You know, since we live right around the corner from each other.' I wanted to go with him so badly, I knew it was a stupid idea that would only shake an excruciating dash of salt on a gaping wound.

'She's waiting for the band to finish up. You look kind of tired. Let me take you.' His voice was reasonable, adult. The same voice he'd used with Nikki, but without the disappointment and blame.

'Um, OK.' I ignored the warm anticipation that gurgled through me at the thought of Jake and me in his truck alone together. I tried to remind myself that we were completely broken up, and he had a girl-friend he cared about. I tried to ignore the flash of his watch, and I begged my heart to slow its pounding beat when I saw that it was still set on Paris time. For me.

I wanted to take his hand, but it was a tremendously stupid idea. Plus, his hands were tucked into the pockets of his jacket. I found Kelsie and said goodbye, pointedly ignoring her wildly raised eyebrows as she glanced at Jake.

We walked to his truck in silence, and he opened the door for me, pausing longer than he needed when he went to shut it. He got behind the wheel and pulled out. Minutes ticked by and I couldn't think of anything to say. I had this twisting, aching feeling that I was wasting a chance, a miracle opportunity.

And then I thought of Saxon. And how he was surprised that I was OK with him and the soccer stalkers. How he was disappointed that I was OK with it all.

I thought of how he told me to wait, making me think he'd be right back.

But he decided not to come back for me. He got Jake instead.

Just like he promised in Paris. He paired us back up.

But it was all wishful thinking. Way too much had happened, and there was no hope for us. Well, no hope for us as a couple. But I decided that if I had made my weird version of peace with Saxon, I could do it with Jake, too.

'I'm so sorry about Nikki tonight.' Jake spoke just a

second before I had screwed up enough courage to tell him that I wanted to mend our tattered relationship back to the friend level at least. 'She was out of line, and she shouldn't have gotten her friends to gang up on you. She's paranoid that we're still, you know, into each other.' He adjusted his baseball cap with one hand, pulling it low over his eyes.

I tried to laugh it off, like that was the craziest thing I'd ever heard, even though I was looking at the watch that Nikki was smart enough to notice. 'That's crazy! I mean, you know, we haven't even talked. In a while.' I meant it to sound like a fact to support our good behavior, but I couldn't keep the regret out of my voice.

'I told her that. She sees what she wants.' He cleared his throat. 'Anyway, she didn't hurt you or anything, right?'

'No.' I felt a little prick to my pride. 'I could have defended myself, Jake. It's just . . . I heard her in the girls' bathroom earlier today, and I know she cares about you. I mean, she was talking about you and me, and she was kind of upset. I could tell she wasn't, um, herself tonight.'

'As long as you're OK.' Jake's voice was low and rough. 'So, other than all the craziness tonight, have you been OK?'

'I've been great.' I nodded as if that was the honest truth, and I hadn't spent the last few weeks feeling like my heart was broken in my chest. 'And you've been good?' My voice came out in a high, trembling squeak.

He cleared his throat again. 'I've been all right. A lot of work, you know?'

'How is work?' I clung to anything that would keep us talking.

'Lots of hours. All the college kids went back to school when winter break ended, so I got a full schedule again.'

I wondered if he was staying warm enough. I wondered how he was sleeping. How he was eating. I wondered why I was wondering all of this, considering he wasn't my boyfriend anymore.

'I think you—' I began.

'I've missed—' Jake said at the same time.

'Wait, what were you—' I asked.

'What did you say?' he asked.

We both stopped talking, and he opened and closed his hands on the steering wheel. 'Bren, say what you were going to say. Please.'

'I think you work too much,' I said, my voice soft and quiet because I knew I had no business butting into his life anymore. My hands were sweaty in my lap. 'Not that it's any of my business. What were you going to say?'

He stared straight ahead, fiddled with the heat vents and finally said, 'I wanted to say that I've missed . . . you.'

My ears burned, my eyes bulged, and suddenly I couldn't swallow. My heart skipped two beats, my skin was on fire. He missed me? *Jake Kelly missed me!* I had screwed everything up completely and thoroughly, he had a new girlfriend, I'd dated Saxon, and he still missed me.

'Aren't you pissed off at me?' I gulped while I waited for his answer.

He gave a quiet laugh. 'Yeah. Of course. I've never, ever been so mad at anyone in my life, Bren. But I can't help missing you. I've never had anyone in my life like you. I've been trying to tell you for the last few days . . .'

I strained in my seat, the belt cutting tight against the side of my neck, against my attempt to push closer and hear him say what I wanted so badly to hear.

'. . . that I want to be friends. Not just in that cheesy way people say it when they don't mean it. I want to talk to you sometimes. I don't want us to spend every day in class avoiding each other.' He looked over at me and offered a small smile. 'OK?'

It was so much more than I deserved, but I still felt deflated. 'Of course. I was hoping we could be, um, friends again.' I leaned back into the hard springs of the seat. 'What about Nikki?'

'Nik will be cool.' Jake spoke with total certainty.

I would have been perfectly content to have this stilted, awkward conversation last the whole night, but we were pulling into my driveway. Jake cut the engine, and I sat for a long second.

'Thank you. For the ride. I was so tired, but I didn't think Saxon was ready to leave. It's just been kind of a long day, and it's so nice to finally be home.' I clamped my mouth shut to stop the blabber that bumped stupidly out of my mouth.

'You're welcome. Anytime. And I mean that.'

The air in the cab of the truck was cold and metal-heavy. I put my hand on the door handle, but Jake had already gotten out and was headed to my side of the truck. My heart jack-hammered in my chest. I watched him through the streaked, mud-splattered glass of the front windshield, and with every step he took closer to me, my body felt more like it was about to seize up with nerves.

By the time he opened the door, I wasn't positive I could trust my shaky legs, but I managed to step out, so close I could smell the green mint on his breath, see the prickly stubble on his jaw that my fingers itched to touch and the flicker of his pulse beating in his neck. It looked fast. Maybe as fast as mine? Everything in that second was happening too quickly for me to be sure of anything.

For one split second, it felt like we were right back in my driveway at Christmas, back when I hadn't spoiled the magic, back when things were easy and the pull of his love was so strong, I could sleep with it wrapped tight around me, snug as a blanket all night.

He reached for me, and for one second I swear the stars swirled in the sky and the moon glowed brighter. He crushed me to him, and I knew that I hadn't imagined his heartbeat was wild, because I could feel it pounding through his chest and setting mine to its exact rhythm. I dug my fingers into the stiff fabric of the back of his jacket and closed my eyes as tight as I always did just before I blew out the candles on my birthday cake every year. *I wish, I wish, I wish . . .*

But it didn't come true.

Jake's arms snapped away from me and he nodded one short, brisk nod. 'Better get inside. It's freezing out here.'

He got back into the truck and slammed the door shut so hard the whole thing rocked a little.

I shivered in the driveway for two shuddery

breaths before I sprinted into the house, closing the door with a quiet click just before the first of a thousand regretful tears poured out in a silent stream. The last thing I heard before I went to wash my face and wish my parents a good night was the sound of Jake's truck pulling slowly out of the driveway and away from me.

Chapter 16

The weekend went by in a blur. Mom had a ton to do at school, and I had a few projects of my own. I kept staring at my phone, willing it to ring, but it never did. I spent a lot of time fiddling with the thermostat, adding layers to my flannel pajamas, and making cocoa so hot it burned my tongue and left the tip all raised and bumpy. I didn't know if it was my general lack of sleep, the sudden cold snap that frosted all the windows, or the empty, gut-wrenching cramp in the pit of my stomach every time I thought of my ride home with Jake and all that was still so wrong between the two of us, but I couldn't get warm.

Monday morning, I woke up after sleeping like the dead for twelve straight hours and anticipated feeling a little better, but my head felt stuffy and I couldn't focus. Saxon tried to talk to me on the ride into school and kept asking if I felt OK. I told him I was just tired.

I couldn't remember what the teachers said. Every muscle in my body ached.

Saxon looked over at me during class with a worried expression and revived his threat about carrying me to the nurse, but I convinced him I was just a little tired. I could barely run at track. Coach made me sit out again. I was coughing a little, and there was a pain in my chest. I wanted to cough it out, but it just wasn't working. I never got sick, so I figured it was just stress and residual exhaustion from jet lag.

Tuesday and Wednesday were pretty much the same. I just couldn't produce many details about the days. My throat squeezed closed and my tongue expanded like a fat piece of sandpaper in my mouth. Saxon hung close by and tried to force me to go to the nurse, but I didn't want to miss seeing Jake. Even if he was going to be wrapped around Nikki, I needed to see him. It was like a horrible addiction. He did manage to disentangle himself long enough to hold me by the arm and tell me I looked terrible. I remember his face looked swimmy, but so handsome it made my eyeballs ache. I think I told him that I was fine, not to worry, but I couldn't be sure.

By the time I got home that night, Mom was there, fussing and worrying over me. I could hardly keep my eyes open to talk to her. I felt like I wanted to throw up, but I couldn't remember when I had last eaten. I heaved a little, drank some cold water from the bathroom tap and went to bed. A hacking cough kept me up for a lot of the night, but in and out of consciousness, I dreamed – confusing, boy-filled dreams.

When I woke up the next day, my room was too bright. I squinted against the light and felt the stress of being late. But this was really late! I jumped up and stared at the clock. It was after ten! I felt shaky on my feet, and a little nauseous.

I ran to the bathroom, and heard Mom call to me from the kitchen. I skidded out and looked at her, blinking the sleep out of my eyes.

'Your alarm went off for fifteen minutes, Bren. You didn't even open your eyes.' She frowned.

'I never sleep through my alarm.' My speech was slurred with sleepiness.

'I know.' Mom pursed her lips. 'I think we should go see Dr Hrabachuck.'

'No,' I said woozily. 'I feel fine.'

'You don't look fine, Brenna. Saxon and Jake both called me. You haven't been yourself in school. You look worn out. Maybe it's just exhaustion, but I'd like to have it checked out.' She frowned at me. 'Go back to bed, sweetheart. I'm calling to make an appointment.'

Saxon called? Jake called? I felt a swell of happiness

through my aching weariness. I wanted to argue with Mom, go to Tech and see what I was addicted to seeing, but I went back to my room and crashed, suddenly overwhelmed by the full weight of my tired body. Mom came in a while later and put her hand on my head, then murmured something. I heard her call Thorsten outside my bedroom door.

Then Fa was there, carrying me out to the car and buckling me into the seat. I remember being at Dr Hrabachuck's office. I remember his bushy moustache and his white teeth when he smiled. Later, Mom told me I fainted. She told me while she was crying and holding my hand, which I patted while I told her it would be OK.

It wound up that I had pneumonia. It had probably started as the flu, but I never got it checked out and it spread into my lungs. Mom blamed herself. She had been busy organizing things for spring semester classes, and she hadn't been home to see me, so she never realized how crappy I was feeling. For my mom to miss something like a major illness was pretty weird, but we hadn't been spending as much time together lately.

Dr Hrabachuck put me on strict bed rest, lots of fluids, antibiotics and painkillers. I spent a lot of time coughing and even more time sleeping. I was mostly bored and tired. Mom had given instructions to the few people she thought might call not to. She told them I needed my rest. I knew this because Kelsie sent me a message on Facebook, which became my only window on the outside world after four abysmal days in bed.

Hey, Bren!
How are you? Your mom told me that I'm not allowed to call, but I've been freaking out. Pneumonia! You really do it up when you get sick! Saxon has been really worried. It's kind of weird, but also really cute. Maybe he's not such a jerk-off after all. He's been picking up your homework for you. I think your mother is going to let him drop it off Sunday afternoon if you're feeling better. There's a few celeb magazines in there from me and a really good romance novel. I thought you needed something interesting and not by some dead Russian to read. Call me when your mom lets you! Miss you!
Hugs and Kisses,
Kelsie

Today was Sunday. I was feeling much better, but also kind of gross and skanky. I got out of bed and my legs actually wobbled under me. I made my way to the shower and turned it on. Mom was at the bathroom door in a minute.

'What are you doing?' she cried.

'I can smell myself, Mom.' I put a hand on the wall to steady myself. 'I'm just going to take a shower.'

She looked worried. 'Are you sure you feel strong enough?' Her blue-gray eyes were nervous.

'I feel great, Mom. I mean, I'm a little weak, but mostly good.' And I did honestly feel good, finally. My head was clear, and I had stopped trying to hack my lungs out of my chest.

'OK.' She looked worried. 'I'll be right down the hall, and I'll listen out for you if you need me, sweetie.'

She left, and I stripped down and stepped into the good hot water. I hopped back out after a second to grab a toothbrush. My body felt weirdly weak, and my stomach was caved in. As soon as I smelled the mint of the toothpaste, my stomach started to rumble. I was hungry! That had to be a good sign.

I pulled on a comfy pair of yoga pants and a long-sleeved T-shirt. I combed my hair back and put on some lip-gloss. Then I took a look in the mirror. I looked like a pale, hollow-cheeked version of myself, with dark circles under my eyes and pale lips, shiny from my raspberry lip-gloss.

I ventured out to the kitchen and was greeted by Thorsten's bear hug. 'Brenna! It's so good to see you up!'

'Fa,' I squeaked, my voice crushed by his arms. 'I'm glad to be up, too.'

'You look hungry. Come have an apple tart with me.' He pointed to the distinctive box.

'Zinga's?' I tried to keep my voice casual.

'Jake brought them over on Friday.' Thorsten grinned. 'I think he was trying to sneak in to see you. But you know Mom. She told him that you weren't having any visitors. Then she gave him the "laser eyes".'

I groaned. 'No she didn't.' That was what Thorsten and I called Mom's angry stare, the one that cowed rowdy students and made grown men shake in their boots.

He chuckled. 'You know she did. It's OK, Brenna. He's a big boy. He can deal with it. Do you want some tea?'

'That would be nice, Fa.' I sat down to eat my tart and wound up wolfing it down so fast I nearly choked. So, Jake had come to see me. I wondered if he mentioned the visit to Nikki.

Just then the doorbell rang. Thorsten looked up, surprised, but it was Mom who shot past like a bullet and answered it.

'Thank you, Saxon.' I could see her reach for something through the four inches she'd opened the door before she tried to slam it in his face. 'She's not up for visitors yet.'

'Mom!' I called in a panic. I couldn't imagine the entire day lying in bed alone again. I was starved of conversation, a friendly face. I couldn't stand that Saxon was on the other side of the door, and I might not see him. 'I'm up. Please, can he come in? I feel really good!'

Mom peeked at me from her post by the front door and pursed her lips uncertainly.

'Please?' I begged. 'I'll get back in bed. I won't exert myself. Please?'

'All right,' Mom said, but she didn't look happy. Saxon followed her in, a pile of books in his hands. I couldn't remember ever seeing him carry even one book. He looked like a wild animal that someone had let in the house because it promised it would be on its best behavior.

'Maybe I could make Brenna a tray of food so she can eat while she relaxes,' Saxon offered, his face angelic.

Mom clucked her tongue appreciatively and walked me to bed, calling orders over her shoulder to Thorsten. She got my pillows arranged so I could sit up, and smoothed my covers. I asked if she would open my curtains and crack the window, and she did that, too.

'Tell Saxon to close the window if you get too cold,' she fussed. 'And he can't stay long, honey. You're supposed to be resting.'

'I know, Mom. But I feel really good. I promise.'

'Yeah, well, you thought you felt good enough to go to school this week and you were practically dying of pneumonia.' Mom crossed her arms. 'I don't know if I can trust you to make your own decisions anymore.'

I didn't roll my eyes at her, but it took a real effort. Then I saw Saxon come in with a breakfast-in-bed tray that we'd only ever used for Mother's Day. Mom gave one last worried look and left.

'What the hell is wrong with you?' Saxon asked quietly as he set the tray down over my legs. He put a napkin on my lap and pulled my desk chair next to my bed so he could sit near me.

'I'm recovering from pneumonia.' I took a sip of sweet, milky tea.

'You know that's not what I'm talking about. Why would you have kept going to school when you were so sick? Why wouldn't you go to the nurse? Are you an idiot?' He reached out and picked up my cup of hot tea when he noticed me wriggling to get into a better position to eat.

'I don't know, Saxon.' I took a big, hungry bite of my second tart. 'I just felt crazy. I was sick, so I guess I just wasn't thinking straight.'

His mouth was pressed in a tight line.

'What? Geez, between you and my mother, I'm going to die of guilt before the fluid in my lungs does me in.' I ducked my head to see his face, and he looked up, defeat in his expression.

'That was crazy, Bren. Like big-time crazy, going to school like that,' he said in a low voice. Like he was admitting something.

'OK?' I pushed the food away. 'What are you getting at, Saxon? Just spit it out.'

'I'm saying that you weren't going in every day so you could keep up in Government. And you weren't going to see me, much as it hurts my ego to say it.' He got up and fiddled with my things, opening drawers and poking through my underwear, flipping up jewelry-box lids, pawing through books – just to use up nervous energy.

I knew where he was going, but I wanted him to come out and say it. Both because my saying it would illuminate my desperation (and I had been feeling pathetic enough lately) and because if he said it, it meant he was worried about it. And if he was worried about it, it meant there was a chance it might all work out.

Which would hurt Saxon deep down even though we'd agreed to just be friends. My heart ached.

'What do you think I was going in for?' I blew on my hot tea, keeping my eyes on the gently rippling liquid.

He fished his fingers in a small glass bowl on my bookshelf and held Jake's gold posey ring looped loosely around the tip of his index finger.

'I promised I'd fix it for you when we got back.' He leaned on my desk with one hip and threw the ring up in the air. He caught it with a quick flash of his hand, then did it again.

'I told you that was a stupid idea.' My heart dropped like an iron weight in my stomach. 'I know you got him to drive me home from the Folly concert, but we're just friends. He's with Nikki now. I can respect what he wants.'

Saxon stopped fidgeting completely and the room suddenly felt too still. 'When we were first back, and you called and came to my house, I thought we might end up together, even though I knew it was a long shot. And even though it was kind of a disaster, and has pretty much been a disaster every time I got together with you, I kept holding out hope that it would work. The other night, when we went out for sushi, and we were at your house, before, I knew that whatever pull he has on you, it's his thing. I don't have that. I can't make you feel that way about me.' His eyes were completely black and flat. They looked resigned.

'You've been amazing. I really care about you. I've loved spending time with you, Saxon, and don't be pissed off when I tell you that I've loved being your friend. I feel like I know myself better now, since I've been with you.' I glanced up, but his eyes were too dark and pained to look into. I wanted him to know how much he meant to me, but I realized there was still just one thing he wanted to hear. And it broke my heart that there was no way I could say it. There was no way I could lie to him or myself anymore. 'I've loved every minute of being with you.'

'Yeah, I've been a good teacher, right?' He broke his stillness, and threw and caught the ring. 'Letting you see just a little of the dark side. Just enough to make you realize it's something you want to stay far away from.'

'You aren't on the dark side.' I rolled my eyes for him to see, just so he would think that I thought he was being melodramatic. 'I like you the way you are. And I don't regret any of it.'

'You're doing that thing where you stick your chin up. I know what it means, Bren.' He took my hand and slid the ring back on. I had lost a few pounds being sick, so it was loose on my finger. 'You're trying to convince yourself of something when you know you're full of crap.'

There was a light knock on my half-open door. I sat up, expecting Mom, and saw Jake instead. My heart hammered.

'Hey, Bren.' His eyes were red-rimmed and darted nervously around the room, failing to focus on anything. He held a bouquet of flowers in his hand, pink and green and white. It was the brightest, freshest thing I had seen in days. 'If you don't want me here, I'll leave.' He looked at Saxon and nodded. The two of them eyed each other warily, but it didn't seem like there was any anger between them.

'I was just leaving.' Saxon got up.

'Don't go.' I grabbed his wrist, and he looked down at my hand, then traced Jake's posey ring with the tip of his index finger. The air in the room already crackled with tension.

He kissed my hand, leaned down, and said quietly enough that Jake couldn't hear, 'The look on your face when he walks into the room? That's love, Bren. I can't compete with that no matter how many times I jerk you off in my car. I know why I worked for you. I'm glad it lasted while it did.' He kissed my cheek.

I grabbed his arm. I knew there was no way to make it right, but I felt the heavy lead of a guilty conscience on my shoulders. I hated that the way I acted brought Saxon pain. I wished I could take it all back. He was giving me a mocking look that tried to trick me into thinking he didn't care. 'You're being a self-obsessed ass,' I hissed. 'Stop being so melodramatic. Please stay.'

He kissed my cheek again, then turned and left.

And I was alone with Jake.

As much as it hurt when I saw the disappointment in Saxon's eyes, I knew that every single thing he said was true. I *did* love Jake. I loved Jake Kelly, and if he was coming to tell me that there was a way for us to be together again, there wasn't one fiber in my body that would be capable of resisting him.

I sat up straighter and tried to move the tray on my lap. I wasn't necessarily looking for him to swoop in and help me, but I did want to see how he'd react and if things would still be cool between us.

He hurried over, grabbed the tray and lifted the whole heavy thing with an ease that reflected regular hard physical work. He put it down gently while I watched his muscles flex. He pointed to the chair uncertainly.

I nodded. 'Sit down.' I reached over and ran my hands over the petals of the flowers, some of them already scattered lightly over my bedspread. 'Are the flowers for me?'

He picked them up and placed them on my lap. 'Of course.' He stared at them without really seeing them.

'Thank you.' I pulled them up to smell them.

'You're welcome.' His voice was robotic. He sat and folded his hands awkwardly, seeming unsure what to do with them. 'You were really sick,' he informed me, his voice shaky.

'No.' I shook my head. 'I mean, I had pneumonia, but there weren't any complications or anything. I'm fine.' If he was here because he thought I was at death's door, then I didn't want it. It would be like having someone love you because he was under a love spell; you could never trust a contrived love like that.

'You look really bad.' He hung his head.

'Thanks a lot, Jake,' I teased, trying to figure out exactly why he was back in my room and how long it could possibly last.

'You know what I mean.' He looked up at me, his gray eyes stark and wild, his face so angry, I dropped the bouquet in surprise. 'I wasn't even around. If something had happened—'

'That's because we broke up,' I interrupted as if

I was explaining some kind of complicated secret.

'Yeah, about that . . .' He very slowly took my hand and ran his thumb over the posey ring Saxon had slid on. 'You wanted to tell me why. That day you came to see me at Zinga's.'

'You didn't want to hear.' I stared at my hand in his and my heart fluttered. 'When I came and saw you, you told me to get lost.' I furrowed my brow. 'Now you want to know?'

'I was so damn mad at you, Brenna.' He stroked my hand with quick, soft touches. 'And I still am. Kind of. Then you had to go and almost die. Like Kate Winslet in *Sense and Sensibility.*'

I smiled at his obvious attempt to butter me up, even if he was claiming to be pissed off at me. 'Marianne Dashwood,' I corrected. 'Kate Winslet just played her in the movie.'

'Whatever,' he said good-naturedly. It was a huge relief to hear Jake's voice with all the sweetness I was used to. 'Anyway, you didn't come to school, then Saxon called and told me, and I was freaking out.'

What? 'Saxon told you?' I asked. 'Why?'

'I was really pissed off to hear from him at first, but he explained everything.' Jake's gray eyes were calm, like we both knew perfectly well what he was talking about and that it was all good.

369

'What did Saxon explain?' My voice sounded far away and tinny in my ears.

'How you were still into me from the beginning,' Jake said with a shrug. 'How you regretted everything. How you would be glad to get back together with me.' He licked his lips nervously. 'And I knew it was what I wanted. I didn't want to date some random girl. I want you. It's always been you, Brenna.'

That moment was a little golden gift, and everything sane and rational in me screamed that I should scoop it up and accept what Jake was offering.

But something about this was off. There was something I just couldn't get a handle on. My just-recovered brain muddled confusedly through the words Jake had just spoken. Not the final ones that were kind of melting my heart in the background; the earlier ones, where he wiped the slate clean so easily it made my stomach clench.

'Jake, why did you take Saxon at his word?' I pulled my hand free of his.

He sat up straighter, his now-empty hands resting on his lap. 'Why would he lie?'

'Why wouldn't he?'

'So what he told me wasn't the truth?' Jake asked, confused and just at the edge of hurt again.

And I wanted to apply the emergency brakes again

and stop this train wreck that I was about to create. But what was the point of going through all of this heartache if I was right back where I started at the end of it all?

'It was Saxon's version of the truth,' I explained. 'And it was part of a deal he made with me.'

'What kind of deal?' Jake demanded.

I didn't like his tone. I knew I had hurt him, but part of the reason I did what I did was because I wanted to be able to care about Saxon on my own terms, without Jake's anger. And maybe I'd taken it way too far, but I didn't regret getting to know Saxon better. I felt stronger for having been with Saxon, even if being together as a couple wasn't right for us in the end. 'An exchange. He felt like he'd helped ruin our relationship, so he decided to help fix it. I told him I didn't think it would work.'

Jake looked up at me, his eyes wide with realization. 'But it did work, didn't it?' he said slowly. 'I was so happy to hear him say what I wanted to hear, I never really thought about whether it was true. Or just more lies.' His face hardened a little and he stood up. 'Sorry, Bren, but I can't hear any more lies from you.'

If I hadn't been recovering from pneumonia, I would have been on my feet and staring him down in a fury. As it was, I had to make do with sitting and waving my arms around like a deranged angry woman. 'I never lied,' I said fiercely. 'You say you want the truth, but it seems to be the only thing you don't want to listen to!'

That stopped him in his tracks. He came back and sat down. 'All right. What's the truth?'

I had no idea where to start. What was the truth?

'The truth is that you put me on a pedestal.'

He frowned. 'You say it like that was a bad thing.'

'It was.' I twisted the gold ring on my finger.

'For me to love you? For me to realize how amazing you are?' He shook his head. 'Sorry if I fucked up by telling you that you're important to me, Bren,' he added sarcastically.

'Loving me and idealizing me aren't the same,' I said quietly.

'I didn't idealize you,' he said, too quickly. He hadn't even bothered to think about it.

'Yes, you did. You knew what I had done. Or hadn't done. I guess that was pretty ideal in your mind. The virginal, pure girlfriend. But you thought that meant I would never mess up or make a wrong move.'

'Well, you're smart – a lot smarter than me. When did thinking that become such an awful thing?' he demanded.

'That's another thing.' I swallowed hard. 'You put yourself down; it's a habit, I know, but it says something about what you really think of me.'

'What do you mean?' He stared at me.

'If you're such an idiot and I'm with you, what does that say about me?' I challenged. 'Not much, right?'

'But that's not how I mean it—' His eyebrows crashed low over his eyes.

'I know,' I interrupted. 'But it's only because you haven't really thought about it. I always knew I'd mess up at some point. And it kind of felt like the longer we went with you telling me how terrible you were and how great I was, the more it would suck when we both faced the fact that that's not true. And you being a loser and me being perfect are two huge lies. And each one is equally terrible in its own way.'

He didn't say anything for a while, which was totally to his credit. He was thinking. Granted, he was thinking for a just few minutes about things I'd been obsessing over for months, but it was the first step.

When he finally opened his mouth, he snapped it closed again. I wanted to hear what he had to say, wanted to know if it had made any difference to him.

'What is true, Brenna?' he asked finally, his voice a little cracked.

'What's true is that I thought about you *every day*.

And I missed you so much it made me ache. And I wanted to see the pictures you posted. And I hated missing school because it meant not seeing you, so I went even when I had pneumonia.' I took a deep breath. 'And what's also true is that I tried really hard to make something work with Saxon. I really tried,' I added for emphasis. I could feel myself radiating a shameful red.

'Why didn't it work?' Jake asked. 'He's smart. I mean, he's like a genius. And he's loyal, in a weird way. And he's good-looking, I guess. I mean, I know girls find him attractive. Or whatever.' He shook his head. 'It's pretty weird to be sitting in your room defending fucking Saxon of all people.'

'He is a genius.' I chose my words carefully. 'He's loyal, and it is weird. And I am attracted to him. He's also caring and tries hard to do the right thing, whatever that means. To him.' I looked at Jake closely. 'But he isn't you. And that makes all the difference.'

'Why?' Jake's voice sounded hopeful.

'Because it's *you* I want. I'm not giving you a specific reason, because I honestly can't. I just want you.' I shrugged, but my shoulders felt really heavy. It hadn't been that long since we had been intertwined, our lives expanding and contracting in the same rhythm. Then we were apart, and I felt scattered, but I didn't know for sure that Jake felt that way. I realized that his whole visit might have been fueled mostly by guilt.

But then he was leaning forward, his eyes bright. 'You want *me*? You're sure?'

I thought about all we'd been through and all everyone had said and all I'd wanted and missed and done. That all made a difference, but in the end, there was only one truth.

'Yes,' I said. 'I want you. I'm sure.'

Jake moved slowly next to me on the bed, then gathered me gently in his arms and crushed me, suddenly, against his body and held tight. 'Jesus Christ, Brenna,' he said roughly. 'This has been a crazy fucking few weeks.'

I put my arms around him and grabbed tight, balling my fists around his shirt in an effort to pull him closer to me. 'You smell so good,' I choked out, breathing him in hard. 'You feel so good.'

'I take it you missed me?' he asked, smiling his adorably sweet smile – and all for me.

I smiled back, but there was already a nagging fear in my too-busy brain. Jake and I were back together, back where we both needed to be, but this wasn't going to just snap back to what it had been; and I knew I didn't want that anyway. The truth was, we had both done things to inspire jealousy in each other, just because we wanted to. This relationship was not the same beast it had been when we started dating, and I wasn't sure what that meant for us.

Because I loved being Jake's girlfriend, but I also loved being free. I loved doing my own thing. I couldn't just go back to the way it was.

I also couldn't just dump Jake and then expect him to come back with open arms. There had to be a middle ground.

But in that moment, Jake's eyes were looking at me hungrily. 'I missed you so much. You have no idea.' He kissed me, just a warm dry kiss at first, then a set of small, teasing kisses, then deep, insistent kissing that opened me up the way only Jake ever had.

I knew now that it wasn't what he did physically, because I had done it with someone else. It was his elemental taste, the way his tongue felt on mine, the sound of his voice when we pulled apart and he said my name. Every piece of it made me feel filled up and warm and *home*.

Which didn't necessarily make sense. There was very little that Jake and I actually had in common. All I knew was that when I was with Jake, I felt calm. I felt at peace. I felt the exact way I'd felt the second I walked through the door of my home after being in another country. Paris was exotic and gorgeous and amazing, but there was only one place that would ever smell like home for me.

We must have been suspiciously quiet, because Mom made a lot of noise walking down the hallway and poked her head in.

'Sorry, Jake.' Mom flashed the laser eyes. 'Brenna's had a long day. She needs her rest.'

Jake answered, 'Yes, Mrs Blixen.'

He stood awkwardly, and Mom relented a little, sighing. 'Five minutes.'

She left and he grabbed my face hard and kissed me. 'I would tell you I'd come over, but your mother will be in and out a million times tonight,' he whispered. 'Can we talk on the phone?'

'Yes!' I felt giddy despite my trepidation.

He walked to the door, and looped back to grab the bangles off my desk. 'I need these.' He grinned and continued out backward while I laughed, my relief intense and wonderful.

I heard him say goodbye to Mom and Thorsten, heard the door close behind him and felt a warm pulsing in my lowest regions. I wanted him back in this room, in my bed. I didn't want to waste a minute. I was already plotting weekends and dates with him, getting all worked up about the things I hadn't realized were so wonderful a few weeks before.

And then I remembered that Saxon was probably feeling like shit. I grabbed my cell and dialed his number.

He picked up fairly quickly. 'Blix. It all worked out?' His voice was lazy.

'Jake and I are back together,' I said as calmly as I could, and waited with my eyes closed and my lips pressed together.

'Well, I'll bow out gracefully then.' His words sounded perfectly casual.

'That's not what I want,' I rushed. 'I want to be . . . don't make me say it, Saxon.'

'You're lucky you stopped short,' he chuckled. 'No girl has ever uttered those words to me. Let's go back to rival soul mates, all right?'

'Sounds good.' And I realized that it wouldn't work in a way that would leave either one of us completely satisfied. It never would, and there was no point in trying.

'You know how to make one big-ass production, Blix. Pneumonia? Next time tone down on the melodrama. Jake would have come back to you without all the theatrics.'

'Hardy har har,' I griped, but I let out a silent sigh of relief that we were joking a little again. 'What are you doing for the rest of the day?'

'Nikki Devine is going to need some comfort and want some revenge. I'd say my bed will probably be full. Don't fret over me, Brenna.'

'Saxon,' I begged. 'That sounds like a shitty idea.'

'You had your chance.' His voice slid into sexy mode. 'Don't try to deny the other fine ladies a piece of me. It isn't fair.'

I laughed a little, more to make things seem normal than because I actually found anything funny about his plans. 'Goodbye, Saxon.'

'Until we meet again, Blix.'

The connection clicked off, and finally, peacefully, I drifted into the first contented sleep I'd had in weeks. I know I dreamed, and I know they were crazy, but I was completely happy when I woke up later and couldn't remember a thing.

Chapter 17

There was a new clawing need in my heart for Jake. Things had always been intense between us, but now that I'd almost lost him, I clung to every chance we had to see each other. Mom was absolutely against him visiting for the rest of the week, but by Wednesday, I couldn't stand it anymore and begged her to let me go back to school.

'I'm fine,' I pleaded. 'My appetite is back. I haven't had a fever, haven't coughed at all. I'm going to die of boredom if I have to stay home another day. Also, I'm falling behind in school. Please, Mom. Please?'

'Fine.' She narrowed her eyes at me. 'But you are not riding to school on that bike, I don't care if it's seventy degrees tomorrow. So forget that.'

'Do you want me to take the bus?' I held my breath, but didn't go so far as to dare to hope.

I hated to use it against her, but her guilt over my sickness and break-up with Jake all bubbled to the surface and made her relent. 'Jake can drive you for now.' She sighed and left me to do a private dance of happiness.

No one had ever been happier to wake up at the crack of dawn and get ready for school than I was that first morning back. Only a week had passed, but it felt like a month. I dressed, packed my backpack, ate breakfast and brushed my teeth, all the while humming happily. When I heard the gravel crunch on the driveway, I practically flew out the door and into Jake's waiting arms.

He pushed his face into my hair and squeezed me so tight I gasped.

'Where's Mom?' He checked the windows, looking for her telltale curtain flutter.

'She had to leave early to prep for her classes.' I felt like I couldn't get close enough to him. I jumped up and wrapped my legs around his waist. His hands cupped my butt and he nuzzled my neck.

'Let's skip.' His eyes drank in my face. 'I've wanted time, just the two of us. Things still feel so weird, Bren. I just need a day with you.'

'I can't.' I let my feet drop back down to earth. 'I can't miss today. I'll fall too far behind in my classes. But maybe . . .'

He looked at me with eager interest.

'Um, maybe I could tell Mom that I was spending the night at Kelsie's this weekend?' My heart hammered at the very thought of that lie. 'But if you think your dad would find out or if you have work . . .'

Jake's jaw hung open like it had come unhinged. 'You want to stay the night? With me?'

I nodded.

He kissed me hard then whooped.

'You tell me what to do and I'm there. Don't worry about my dad, don't worry about work.'

We ran to the truck together, and our secret hummed through me all day.

Especially when I walked up to Sanotoni's room. It felt like I was wearing a neon sign advertising the fact that Jake and I were about to spend a romantic night together behind my parents' backs and despite the fact that I had been Saxon's kind-of girlfriend just a little while before. Saxon hugged me wordlessly when I walked into Government, which helped my guilt peak even more sharply.

'Hey.' I held onto him for a second longer than I needed. 'It's good to be back.'

'It's good to have you back, you know, and not looking like the first victim of the zombie apocalypse.' He pulled back and narrowed his eyes at me. 'You look like you're up to no good.'

My face flushed. 'No, I'm not. I don't know why you'd say that. I'm not.' I stopped talking with a snap of my jaw.

He studied my face. 'What would have you so flustered?' he wondered out loud. 'It's not drugs. It's not rock 'n' roll. That only leaves one option.'

My face flamed so hot, I was sure my hair would catch on fire. 'It's not that,' I hissed.

There was a flash of something painful in Saxon's eyes, but it was gone so fast, I could have imagined it. 'Well, maybe not sex. But I'm willing to bet my favorite bong and my best pair of handcuffs that it's sex-ish. Am I right?'

'Stop,' I begged in a whisper.

'You don't have to be such a prude, Bren. Especially around me.' His voice was hard and sharp as a knife's blade, but he backed off and we spent the period doing completely mundane work. It would have been totally fine, except for the glint of something raw and wild in his eyes once or twice when I caught him stealing a look at me.

I was relieved to get to Crafts and away from Saxon's knowing, judging eyes. Kelsie was more than happy to help when I asked her about Friday.

'Of course.' She paused in her weaving for a minute and looked me in the eye. 'You do realize that you two are, like, meant to be? It was making me seriously depressed when you weren't together.'

'It doesn't feel real yet.' I slashed at the copper with a sharp tool and made odd, jagged lines that didn't look nearly as cool as I thought they would. 'We talk every night, and I'm so happy every time, but sometimes I wake up, and I'm not sure what's happened. Like I wonder if it's all still messed up.'

Kelsie's fingers flew over the white string. 'It all happened so damn fast. One week you two were practically married, the next you were in Paris and then with Saxon, and then you were sick. Now everything's all right.' She plucked at her project. 'You guys really need this night, just the two of you, just to reconnect and sort through things.'

I brushed my finger over the sharp edge of my copper sheet. 'I know. I feel a little weird lying about the whole night. What if we get caught?'

'You won't.' Kelsie winked at me. 'It's airtight. Anyway, you're lying for a really good cause, so you just need to stop worrying about everything. OK?' She nudged me with her foot under the table. 'OK?'

I nodded. 'OK.'

'Something else bothering you?'

I watched her deft fingers as she made the string into something gorgeous. 'It's Saxon. It's . . .'

'Weird?' She raised her eyebrows.

'That's a fairly massive understatement.' I twisted my hands together. 'I know I brought this all on myself. I know that. It's just, why the hell did I do it?'

Kelsie shrugged and laughed at the same time. 'Because you were faced with two incredibly tempting guys and you're a red-blooded woman?'

I wrinkled my nose at her. 'If you're ever around when my red-blooded woman-ness rears its very stupid head, please smack some serious sense into me.'

She crossed her heart. 'Promise, sweetie.'

I managed to dodge Saxon during cross country and text Jake to pick me up for lunch, which seemed the safer option until we made it into the cafeteria and Jake steered me away from our regular table and over into the corner.

'Why are we eating here?' I dropped my bag and looked over to where our usual group chatted and joked.

Well, our usual group plus a few extras.

Nikki glared daggers in my direction.

'C'mon.' Jake took my hand and led me to the lunch line.

I felt tears prick at my eyes. Jake turned to ask if I wanted mashed potatoes, and almost dropped the tray on the floor. 'What's the matter?' he asked, his face close to mine. 'Do you feel sick again?'

I shook my head and swallowed a few times until I got my bearings and could speak without blubbering. 'I just messed so much up, Jake. I screwed it all up.'

'What?' He moved out of the line and pushed my hair back from my face. 'What's screwed up? You and me, we're good. We're fine.'

'You can't even sit with your friends because of me.' I waved a hand toward the lunchroom. 'And Saxon and you? I just made that a crazy mess.' I couldn't stop the tears and didn't bother to try. 'What was I thinking?'

Jake hugged me tight and kissed my hair. 'I have no clue, Bren. But it's done, OK? It's in the past. The only person I want to eat lunch with is you. Saxon will deal the same way he always has. And you need to stop getting all worked up and eat. You could have died, and you don't have your strength back yet.'

I gave a weak laugh. 'I was in no danger of dying, Jake. Have you been talking to my mother?'

'C'mon. No more crying. You love open-faced turkey day. I'll sweet-talk the lunch ladies and get you extra cranberry sauce. All right?' He wiped his rough thumbs under my eyes.

'You're so good to me.' I felt the tears well up again.

'I know it. Just keep it in mind the next time you think about breaking up.' He smiled and kissed my nose. 'C'mon, before all the mashed potatoes are gone.'

We got our lunch, and I tried to ignore Nikki's dirty looks from across the lunchroom and focus on Jake's smile and sweet jokes.

Friday came fast, and, despite all of my angst, Mom OKed a sleepover at Kelsie's with a slightly distracted 'of course' after extracting a promise that I keep my cell on and grilling me about my general health. I told her I would take the bus right to Kelsie's on Friday.

'Do you want me to pick you up on Saturday, sweetie?' Mom asked.

'I think Kelsie's mom will be OK with dropping me off. It's right down the road.' I felt my heart hammer as I waited for Mom to see through my ruse.

'Great. I'll be at the college for a few hours in the afternoon. My freshmen are handing in their first big paper this Thursday and Friday, and I want to have a good chunk graded over the weekend.' She sighed, and I patted her hand.

'The grading will be over before you know it.' Secretly, my mind eased. Mom was totally focused when it came to grading, so I could relax about her checking in on me too much.

'I know. It's just these kids are raised text messaging.

Their spelling is abysmal.' She gave me a quick hug. 'Please promise me you'll never spell the word "before" with the numeral four.' She shuddered.

'I promise I will never, ever spell with numerals. Even when I text.'

'You are my silver lining, sweetheart.' Mom patted my butt, and I hurried to my room to give Jake the good news.

I spent Friday a bundle of raw nerves, especially since it seemed like Saxon could see right through me and read every nervous thought jangling in my head. By the time the school day was done and I got into Jake's truck, I felt too keyed up to sit back and relax.

Jake's good mood was a stark contrast to my nervous worry. He'd smiled blithely through the entire afternoon, and didn't even give Nikki a second glance when she'd stopped him in the hall to invite him to some bonfire. On the ride to his house, he whistled along to every song on the radio, and he ran to get my door with a frantic excitement that reminded me of a puppy.

I could have gotten bogged down in worry and unease, but with Jake so happy, I decided to let myself fall into the happiness, too. We'd had so much drama and craziness, it was nice to just relax. He wrapped his arms around me and kissed me soundly. I wrapped my arms and legs around him and he lifted me up and carried me into his house, both of us laughing hysterically. He put me down on the dining-room table and put one finger up, indicating that I should wait a minute to see what he had planned for me.

'Look at this.' He opened the fridge, and there was a tray of lasagne that could have fed a small army.

'What's that?' My lips curved up in response to his proud smile.

'A friend of mine gave me her mom's lasagne recipe. I got all the stuff to make it and cooked it last night. We just have to put it in the oven, and it will be ready for dinner.' He held the tray out proudly. 'I grated cheese for this. Like, a lot of cheese.'

I got up, took the tray out of his hands, and set it on the table next to us. I wound my arms around his neck and just looked at him for a long minute.

'I love you, Jake.' I had said those words before, but I wanted him to understand how much I meant them, with every breath I took and every beat of my heart.

'It's just a lasagne.' He was trying to joke, but I could see the worry that clouded his eyes.

'I'm really sorry for everything. Honestly, I screwed up big time.' I kissed him softly. He kissed back hungrily, and soon I was pressed against the kitchen counter, and Jake's hands were everywhere at once.

He finally pulled back, panting. 'I'm going to put that lasagne in the oven. You wait for me in my room, OK? I'll be five seconds.'

I kissed him, grabbed my backpack, and headed down to his sterile little room. My hands brushed over the bangles on his desk, and I felt a smile tug at my lips. I turned to the bed and I felt a little clutch of panic.

The last time I'd seen that bed, it was in a picture Jake had posted. With a condom wrapper on it.

I knew everything had been washed and changed since then, but it still felt alien and dirty, somehow.

Jake skidded down the hall and burst through the door, then stopped and saw me staring at the bed. He looked back and forth between me and the bed. 'Bren? Is something wrong?'

'Uh, it's just . . . you know, the last time? It was you and . . .' I couldn't finish the sentence.

Jake pulled me into his arms and kissed my lips. 'She didn't mean anything, OK? It was stupid. The only reason I did it was to make you jealous, and it was still a dumbass move. Do you believe me?'

I leaned my head on his chest and nodded. He scooped me up and dropped me on the bed with a bounce, then climbed on top of me and boxed me in with his arms as I giggled and squirmed.

'This is our space. This is our night. We both did things that were dumb, but let's forget them for a while.' I stopped giggling and he lowered his mouth to mine, kissing me softly. 'I've been waiting to get you alone since the minute I left you in your driveway before you went to Paris. I missed you so damn much.'

I pushed my mouth back up, close to his and we kissed and held each other first sweetly, then with a more powerful need. Soon we were surrounded by discarded items of clothing and toppled pillows, our hands and mouths grabbing greedily at that feeling we had both needed from each other for the time we'd been apart. When we were finally satisfied but before it went farther than we wanted to go, Jake kissed my shoulder, pulled his shirt on, righted his pants, and pointed down the hall.

'I can smell the lasagne, so it must be done. You hungry?' His hair was tousled, his eyes were hooded and heavy-looking, and I wanted to crawl into his arms and never come back out again.

'Starving. I'll be out in a minute.'

Jake whistled down the hall and into the kitchen, and I called my mother to check in. She asked how the night was going and complained about her students' inability to follow very clear instructions, then we exchanged goodnights and clicked off. I let out a sigh of relief and headed to the bathroom. I searched for a brush, but only managed to find a comb, so I did the best I could to my wild hair and headed out to the dining room.

Jake had the lasagne on the table, which was set with plates bordered with olive, orange, and gold tulips, mismatched plastic cups, and paper napkins from Dunkin Donuts.

'Dinner is served,' he announced solemnly. I sat across from him and watched as he shoveled an enormous amount of layered pasta onto the plate.

I took a bite and closed my eyes. 'This is amazing. I had no idea you were such an awesome cook, Jake.'

'I was thinking about shaking up my weekly dinner menu a little. But maybe I have to make a little less next time. I think this lasagne will last a whole month.' He motioned to the enormous dish in the center of the table.

We laughed and joked through dinner, and I helped him portion the leftovers to freeze for later. We washed up the dishes side by side at the sink and had a soap-sud fight that left us breathless and necessitated getting out the mop.

'I should invite you over more often,' Jake commented as I sopped up the last of the water. 'Awesome dinner and a spick-and-span kitchen?'

'The dinner was all you. And I only mopped because I feel bad about how totally soaked you got. I didn't want to be a sore winner.'

I shrieked when he came at me, his fingers bent to tickle my sides.

When we were done in the kitchen, it was still only eight o'clock.

'Wow.' Jake stretched and yawned a huge fake yawn. 'I'm ready for bed.'

I felt a sudden flurry of nerves. 'Um, you want to go to bed?'

He started down the hall backward and crooked his finger at me. 'Yep. C'mon. It's chilly. I need you to warm me up.'

I swallowed hard. 'What if your father comes home soon?'

'Pool and darts tonight. He'll be in after midnight, and he'll go straight to bed. C'mon.' He was at the door of his room now. He crooked his finger again, and I followed like I was connected by a string.

He shut the door and we tumbled back on his bed in his dim room.

'What do you usually do on Friday nights when we don't go out?' I ran my fingers through his hair.

'I wait for you to call me. Or I play video games.' He looked at me and smiled. 'Wanna play?'

'OK. But I don't want you to be a big baby if you lose.' I sat up, cross-legged, and waited while he flipped on his PS3 and opened a dresser drawer full of games. He took out one and held it front forward, his face serious.

'This is *LittleBigPlanet*. Have you ever played this game?' I shook my head. He sat down on the edge of the bed. 'This game is the most amazing game in the world. This game will change your life. Are you ready to play this game? Brenna, stop laughing. Are you ready?'

I straightened my mouth and tried to be as serious as I could. 'OK.'

He turned on the TV, put the game in, set up the remotes, and explained the directions. Which weren't all that specific, since the point of the game was basically to create worlds that you could play in. Our Sackpeople flipped and whirled through cities and around fantastic gardens of our own creation. We engaged in friendly battles, met other Sackpeople, and explored the graphics and world possibilities. Jake and I made an amazing team: he was careful and thoughtful, I was experimental and fearless, and our world grew and expanded like an amazing Wonderland. We got so sucked into the game, I had no clue at all how much time had gone by, but I couldn't contemplate stopping. Before we knew it, we heard the roar of an engine outside, and Jake's father was home. I froze, and my Sackgirl's menacing high kick fell short of Jake's Sackboy's karate slash.

'No worries.' Jake rubbed a hand on my arm. 'He's not even going to stop in here.'

I heard his father put his keys down in the kitchen, then listened with dread as his heavy boot-steps echoed down the hall, closer and closer to Jake's door. I was positive he'd stop and poke his head in, especially since the light from the television must have been visible under the door, but he didn't. The master bedroom door opened and snapped shut.

I let out a huge breath I didn't even realize I'd been holding in.

Jake put an arm around me. 'He wouldn't care if he knew. I swear.'

I felt a hot prickle when I realized that Jake was saying it because he was positive about it. Because he'd had other girls over and his father hadn't cared.

Jake put the controls away, flipped the TV off, and put an arm around me again, but I brushed it off. 'Don't be so worried,' he crooned in my ear.

'I'm not.'

'What's wrong?' He put a hand on my chin and rubbed it gently with his fingers. 'Brenna? Tell me.'

'Was she here? Did she stay over?' It was stupid to ask. We were trying to forget that it had all happened, not keep dragging it out over and over. Especially since I was the one who broke up with Jake and fooled around with Saxon.

'Do you want me to answer that? Really?' Jake's voice was hard with frustration.

'I guess you already answered.' I looked around his cramped, bland room, so foreign in the dark. It was weird to think that this was the exact place Jake had sat when we had our marathon phone conversations. I decided to focus on those thoughts and how generally good the night had been instead of pointing fingers. Especially when I really had no business pointing out anyone else's mess-ups. 'It really doesn't matter. I'm ready to go to sleep now.' I smiled.

Jake's return smile was cautious. 'Do you need to wash your face and all that?'

I nodded and grabbed my overnight bag, feeling weird and shy suddenly. 'OK, I'm going.'

'OK.' He laughed and fell back on the bed. 'I'll be right here.'

I changed in the bathroom and spent a long time washing my face and brushing my teeth. I sneaked back in the room and found Jake dozing. I poked him awake, and he stumbled across the hall. I snuggled under the covers while he was getting ready, and his pillow felt uncomfortable under my head, but smelled perfectly familiar, just like Jake.

He opened the door softly and closed it behind him. He pulled off his shirt and let his jeans drop, then yanked off his socks, balled them all up and threw them in the hamper in the corner of his room. He stood for a long minute, so handsome in just his boxers, in front of the bed, then slid in next to me. His body was long and warm next to mine, and I rolled into his arms, where I fitted snug and tight as a key in a lock.

He looked down at my face in the dim glow from the streetlights that shone in through his window. 'I love how you look when you have no make-up on.'

'What? I spend a lot of time putting make-up on when I know I'm going to see you! I won't do it any more if you're going to be so unappreciative.' I leaned up and kissed his chin.

'You look great no matter what, but I love you without make-up on. You look so beautiful, and I guess I feel like I get to see you in a way no other guy gets to.' He pressed his mouth to mine.

'I love you so much,' I whispered when he pulled away.

'I love you.' His arms clamped around me tight. 'More than anything in the world. Don't forget that.

I know I tried to be all cool with it, but it broke my heart when I thought I'd lost you.'

I held him tighter. 'I'm so sorry. I never wanted to hurt you.'

He held me close and whispered, 'Forget it. It's just you and me, no problems, doing this thing together. We'll be unstoppable.' His voice dropped off sleepily. A few minutes later, he was snoring softly, and I was still locked safe and sure in his arms.

Chapter 18

After that night, life went back to something like the normal it had been before Jake and I broke up, but it wasn't exactly the same. For one thing, my cross-country glories meant that our team kept going and going, and the season stretched out all the way to States. Once Mom gave her OK for me to run again, I was as fast as ever. I had been a little nervous that with no craziness to worry about, no stresses to work out on the track, I'd just stop running. But that didn't happen. In fact, I ran faster, the buzzing in my head gone and replaced with calm focus.

Jake made every big meet with my parents. He and Mom had come to an uneasy truce.

'Bren, don't you think that dating a little more would be a good thing?' she had asked the night before I went back to school.

I'd said it before, and I would say it again: my mother was the best mother on earth, but she was no dummy. She had seen most of the whole sordid thing unfold right in front of her eyes, and she was dead set on milking the momentum of it.

'I will,' I said honestly. 'If I meet someone great, I will hang out with him. I promise. But, Mom, I have to say this: Jake is awesome. It sounds like the biggest teenage cliché, but you don't understand what he's like.'

Mom sighed a long, tortured sigh. 'Jake is a great guy, but that doesn't mean you two have to be joined at the hip to be happy.'

'I hardly see him,' I protested. 'We only see each other for a few hours in school, and he works a lot. Also, I have cross country, and I've been seeing Kelsie more.' Kelsie and Chris had decided to spend more time with friends, since they'd been practically living together and getting on each other's nerves. I was glad that she reached out to me. 'I'm not exactly weeping every minute I'm not with him.' Although I didn't admit that I did get sad without him. Especially once in a while when the panic of our breakup rushed over me.

'I just want you to keep your options open,' Mom said, and then she said a few more things that were basically along the same line of the first statement, and I listened respectfully, but as soon as we were done talking, I gave her a kiss, and when she left my room, I called Jake. I did not tell him what Mom and I had talked about. Because things with Jake were still a work in progress, which I liked, but had to be careful with.

Like I had to balance what 'freedoms' I wanted with what might hurt his feelings. Hence, no direct hanging out with Saxon. Who had, since our last meeting at my sick bed, been in and out of the pants of half a dozen girls, at least that could be confirmed. But that didn't really creep me out; what was weird was the kinds of girls he was picking: brains, cross-country runners, artistic girls, all types that in some form or another I liked, respected and felt a definite connection with. He only ever commented on it once, in Government.

We were viciously trying to capture more blue states in a geeky bid to control Sanotoni's US map. I said something random, and he laughed. That wasn't that out of the ordinary; I had a fair ability to crack Saxon up.

He looked leaner, a new set of tattoos peeked out from under the sleeves of his Blondie T-shirt, and his hair was cut in a low mohawk. He'd also acquired a lip ring, which he moved incessantly with his tongue. Now he was laughing, and the silver hoop around his bottom lip gleamed. 'You're damn funny, Blix.'

'I'm glad I can amuse you.' I rolled my eyes at him, but I actually meant it.

'It's not as easy as you'd think,' he confessed. 'I know I have a short attention span, but that's only because I'm hard to amuse, not easy. You're the only girl I've ever met who kept my interest.' He grinned, a tight, angry slash of his mouth. 'But you and Jake deserve each other. Don't you?'

I looked busily down at my paper. 'I'm not answering that,' I said quietly. The good mood was gone and we were back to business.

Other than Saxon, Jake and I tried to spend more time with other people, friends and in groups. My T-shirts, the fairy-tale ones, sold as quickly as the ones I had made for Folly, and without an awesome group of musicians to push them. Kelsie encouraged me to take them to some local art fairs, and I was doing really well selling them and meeting fantastically cool people.

Like the guy who made knee-high leather boots by hand. Apparently Steven Tyler from Aerosmith had three pairs. I met a lady who made bark baskets based on an ancient Native American template. I also met jewelers, instrument makers, weavers and wood carvers. It was like this whole other community within a community.

And Jake was mostly cool with it. 'I want you to do your thing,' he said, as he glared at the young drum maker's apprentice with dreads and a big smile for me and Kelsie. 'I trust you.'

And that was the truth. If nothing else, Jake knew I was honest. Even if I couldn't tell him right away, Jake knew I'd always eventually come clean. Even if my compulsion to always tell the truth had so much more to do with my inability to deal with any bottled-up emotions than a truly good spirit.

Not that that was easy. We had found a spare, quiet afternoon to just be together in his little boring room. Jake and I had lounged around kissing and laughing. But then we got to talking, and I made him tell me. Everything. I came clean too, because I thought it was important to do it. Even if it sucked. Which it did.

Apparently the condom wrapper on the bed hadn't been a prop. Nikki hadn't been anyone he particularly cared about, but that hadn't stopped him from sleeping with her and easing into a casual dating relationship. Which added one more intimacy to his already overlong list.

And even though he'd slept with Nikki, he had no problem being incredibly pissed off that Saxon and I had fooled around. The talking turned into arguing.

Mainly about why my few sessions fooling around with Saxon carried more weight than his sex with Nikki.

'But you *liked* him,' he argued, his face rigid with anger.

'But you *screwed* her,' I said coldly.

We stared each other down until Jake nodded. 'Fine. Can we call a truce?'

'I don't know. Can we?'

'I want to.' He pulled me back into his arms and kissed me soundly. 'Are we done driving each other crazy for a while?'

'I think so,' I said. And that was the truth, too.

And it was the truth that it felt good to be back with him. I loved to hear the rumble of his truck, which now pulled right into my driveway. I didn't want Mom and Thorsten not knowing, and they were surprisingly cool with it. Mostly because February and March were so cold they made your stomach clench when the wind blew, and the thought of me in Jake's always-warm truck was comforting to them.

It was on the way to school one random day in March that Jake brought up the one thing I hadn't imagined him having any interest in.

'So I have junior prom this year.' He flipped radio stations.

'Oh yeah? Do you have a hot date?' I snuggled next to him.

He laughed. 'Maybe. Maybe not. My girlfriend is smoking, but she's this wild liberated woman. I'll ask her, but she might shoot me down.'

'Don't you think a wild, liberated woman might want a poufy dress and some body glitter and a corsage?' I was already getting a little rush just imagining it all.

'Are you saying you'll go with me?' Jake asked.

I leaned over and kissed his neck, smooth and hot-skinned and perfect. 'Of course I'll go with you. You'll dance with me, right?'

He blushed a little. I loved it. As I salivated over his reddened skin, he looked straight ahead wildly. 'I want to. But my spine is pretty much soldered directly to my hips, Bren. I'm not really good at dancing.'

'I'll teach you,' I promised. Not that I was world class, but I had a few moves. And the point of a prom was dancing. 'And I'm not going to be able to go to the shore or anything after prom.'

He laughed again. 'Do you really think I was expecting to weasel your virginity away on prom night? Do I look like that much of an uninspired jackass?'

'Don't ask,' I teased. 'You can go back out with your

friends after you drop me, or Mom can give me a ride home.'

He shook his head. 'I know you try to be all fair-minded, but give me some credit. I'm not going to split after prom without you, and I'm sure as hell not asking Mom to come pick you up.' He shivered. 'That just gave me a chill. Like, an actual chill down my spine.'

'What? The idea of leaving me after prom?'

'No, the image of the evil shooting from your mother's eyes when she finds out that someone is ditching her little girl.' He raised his eyebrows at me. 'I have no defense against that kind of pure angry woman power.'

'You have no defense against *any* woman power.' I grinned.

'Hey,' Jake said as Frankford came into view. 'Today started out pretty awesome. Let's skip, I'll take you to the new Christian Bale movie so you can squeal over him and then I'll take you back to my place and you can calm my bruised ego. Eh? Eh?' His gray eyes were crinkled up with his smile.

Who could say no to that? My heart felt big and warm and blooming. 'Let's do it.'

Christian Bale was delicious. Almost as delicious as the mozzarella and tomato sub with extra oil and vinegar I ate after. Then we went back to Jake's house.

We'd been taking it reasonably slow since we got back together. Part of the whole reconciliation thing involved me getting over the fact that Jake's wrongs would just have to be more extreme than mine. I was furious that he slept with another girl, but we were completely broken up at the time. I had gone as far as I'd gone with anyone with Saxon. I didn't love it, but I understood that making peace meant I had to let it go as best I could.

But the giddiness of the whole afternoon made us even giddier in bed. Jake stripped down to his boxers. 'C'mon. Skivvies time,' he added, shaking his hips in what I know he thought was an alluring way, but it made me laugh so hard, I almost couldn't breathe.

'I hate that word,' I gasped out when he finally stopped gyrating in front of me.

Winded, he fell on the bed next to a fully clothed me. 'What word?' he panted.

'Skivvies. Doesn't it just sound kind of gross?'

'Yeah,' he said. 'I think it was an old-fashioned word for men's underwear.'

'Well, that makes sense then. There's nothing grosser than men's underwear.'

'Do you want me to take them off?' Jake asked, grabbing at his waistband.

'No!' I laughed again.

Not that we hadn't been naked before, but it was always a gradual kind of thing.

'Come under the covers with me,' he coaxed. 'I'm freezing.'

'You're the moron who just took off all of your clothes,' I pointed out.

'So I'm dumb and cold. Take some pity on me.' He wriggled under the covers like a little kid. 'I'll beg,' he said agreeably. I don't think he had any idea how adorable he was, his handsome, clean-shaven face, his shiny brown hair and smoothly muscled arms and chest.

'You love begging.' I giggled.

'Only to you, baby. C'mon, Bren. I sat through that traumatically crappy movie.'

'It was a good movie!' I protested.

'I fell asleep twice, and mostly all I could think about was this itch on my a—'

And he stopped because I had taken my shirt off.

'New bra?' he croaked a little.

It was. Pink polka dots, very scantily cut with just a little lace. The underwear matched. Once I was down to them, Jake was sitting up straight.

'Wow. I'm really glad I picked today to seduce you back to my house,' he said in a low voice, and pulled me down onto the bed next to him. Then his mouth was on mine, and I felt the scrape of his watchstrap, the watch I'd bought him, as he slid his hand up my stomach and cupped my breast. 'Brenna,' he breathed, his mouth moving down along my collarbone and to the tops of my breasts, pushed up and out by my excellent bra. Then my excellent bra was off and on the floor, and Jake's hands and mouth were everywhere it had been.

He kissed down my ribs and along the line of my stomach, then concentrated on my belly button, and my hips. He stopped kissing me for a minute and lifted his head.

'Do you mind if I go further?' he asked, his voice quiet in the cool of his room.

I wasn't sure. Jake's fingers played at the lacy waist of my underwear, carefully tracing a finger under the elastic band. He waited patiently.

'I don't know.' Part of me wanted it so much I was squirming for him to continue; another part of me shied away from something that intimate.

'Then I won't.' He said it evenly, in that sweet Jake voice that he always used with me when we were fooling around. He wasn't about to force anything. We kissed and touched until I was warm and exhausted.

He took a long piece of my hair and held it out.

'You have great hair.' He put it to his nose and inhaled.

'Yeah? I was thinking of dyeing it. Black.' I looked at him from the corner of my eye.

He smiled and shook his head.

'What, you don't have anything to say?' I taunted.

'No way. If I say what I think, you'll have black hair tomorrow just to spite me.'

'So you think I'd look ugly with black hair?' I hooted.

'I didn't say that. Stop putting words in my mouth!' he ordered. 'I'm just saying, if I say, *Don't do it, Brenna,* you'll do it just to show me you can.'

'I don't do things like that.'

'That's exactly how you do things.' He ran his hand over my hair. 'I like that about you. That you'll take a challenge to the extreme.'

'Rebel, rebel,' I muttered, remembering Saxon's descriptions of me.

'So, about prom,' Jake said, his voice a little nervous again. 'I bought the tickets already, but I have to pick a corsage. Right? So when you know what color dress you're wearing, let me know and I'll go get something. That matches.' It sounded like he was asking me.

'OK.' I kissed his nose and wiggled with excitement. 'I will. Where are you getting your tux?'

He looked confused. 'Do I have to wear a tux?' he asked.

'No,' I said. 'But most people do. Do you want to wear a suit?'

'I don't know if my old suit will fit,' he said, and I didn't have to see it to know that it would be a short, gawky, poorly cut polyester mess.

'Maybe, if you don't want to rent a tux, you can go and buy a new suit.' I was desperate to keep him from what I was positive was his awful mess of a suit.

'Don't you want to see my suit?' he asked, his mouth curved into a smile.

'No, I don't.' I grimaced.

He jumped up anyway and left his room. He came back with a suit in a crinkly plastic bag. I got up and looked while he pulled the bag away.

You could tell on sight that it was an expensive suit. It was chocolate brown, three buttons, and a fabric so fine and soft it looked like it had to be made with silk. But I didn't know for sure.

Jake pulled the pants on. They were a perfect fit. He put the jacket on, no shirt underneath, and he looked amazing. Just like that. His body was suit-perfect. And the suit was great on him – much better than any boring black tux. He would look awesome. I had underestimated Jake's judgment again.

'Wow.' I smoothed my hands over the lapels and along the arms. 'I really like it.'

'It was my grandpa's. Apparently he was pretty loaded. Anyway, I'm supposed to be the spitting image of him. I guess. No one has any pictures or anything.'

'Your mom's father?' I felt a little weird knowing what I did about his father when he was in the dark.

'No. My dad's. That's what she said, anyway, Mom. It's weird, though, because my dad is supposed to look just like his father, too. And I know that must seem weird, because I don't look anything like him.' He looked down at his body in its suit. 'And there's no way he would have fitted this suit.'

I felt a cold quake in my stomach. Jake's mother had told him things about his real father without him realizing it. Maybe she'd planned to tell him all along. I was sure she never thought she'd get cancer and die young. She probably thought she'd have plenty of time to tell him everything. There was no way to know what she had planned.

'Bren? You OK?' He was next to me in a second. Since my run-in with pneumonia Jake had been as insane about my health as Mom.

'I'm fine.' I smiled a forced smile. 'I'm just shocked that a suit that old can still look so great. I'll get a dress that goes with it, and we can go shopping for a good dress shirt and a tie. And socks.' I shuddered a little to think of Jake dressed to the nines with white tube socks on. 'And shoes,' I added, when the mental image of his boots finished everything off.

'I'm glad you like it.' He wriggled out of the jacket. 'I knew you'd think it was some crappy department-store suit.' He laughed. 'I know how you think.'

I didn't have anything to say to that one. Thank God he didn't know, not really.

Later that night, I talked to Mom about the prom.

'Mom, Jake is going to his junior prom, and he invited me.' I was careful to keep my voice even, like it was no big deal one way or another.

If Mom felt any trepidation about prom or Jake or anything else, it all left her head when she imagined prom-dress shopping.

'Oh, Bren!' Her eyes sparkled, and I could see the wheels in her head turning as she planned it all out. 'Let's go next weekend! We'll try Lord & Taylor first. They always have a good selection. If not, we'll go to Neiman Marcus. Oh, this is going to be so fun!'

I was glad Mom was so excited. So excited, she didn't really pester me for many details. Other than what Jake would wear. When I told her about his great suit, she grabbed onto the idea, excited about the 'classic' look of a good suit. I left my mom to toy over the intricacies of prom-dress buying and claimed I had homework to do.

Which I had. But more importantly, I had to call the only person I could talk to about Jake.

'Hey, Blix. I'm about to go seduce the field hockey center from Sparta High. She's a little mean, but very, *very* sexy. Like an Amazon.' Saxon filled me in on things I didn't care to hear because he wanted me to be jealous and to know that he was getting on with his life without me. I knew I kind of deserved it, so I put up with it and tried not to react in any way that would encourage him to tell me more.

'Good luck with that,' I said absently. 'Can I talk to you for a minute about Jake?'

'What is it?' His voice dropped that uber-sexy drone he'd been using on me as soon as I mentioned Jake's name.

'He invited me to prom. He's going to wear a suit. It fits him perfectly, and his mom told him it would because it was his father's father's, and he's the spitting image, but it didn't make sense to Jake since he looks nothing like the man he thinks is his dad. And I had to sit and listen to the whole thing, and I don't think it's right . . .' I trailed off from my long-winded ramble because I really didn't know what else to say, and I wanted to know what Saxon's take on the whole thing would be.

'Just keep your mouth shut,' he snapped.

I bristled. I didn't expect him to be sweet and understanding, but he didn't have to be an asshole, either.

'I don't think it's right.' I squeezed the phone tight.

'What? That Jake has a really good suit and a few questions?' he snarled. 'Look, he has an OK thing going. I'm not going to pretend it's super fantastic for him, but it's not shit. And knowing the truth would be illuminating the shit.'

'I think he needs to know,' I pressed, my palms suddenly sweaty. 'I don't like keeping it from him.'

'Is this about Jake, Brenna? Or is it about you?' Saxon asked, his voice rough. 'Because it sounds like it has to do with your goody-goody conscience. I'm sure you made some inane promise to never lie again, but you made a promise to me first, and I expect you to keep it.'

'I will.' I'd promised Saxon that I wouldn't tell Jake that he and Saxon had the same father, and I wouldn't. 'Do you have any intention of telling him?'

'No. And now, I have a girl to try to get into my infamous backseat. So this conversation is over.'

He clicked off, and I was left in the quiet of my bedroom. I pulled out my schoolbooks and tried to get to work on my homework, but this was nagging at me, and I couldn't shake it.

Chapter 19

I suddenly felt tense with Jake, and I had this terrible fear that I would just blurt the truth out. I imagined every possible reaction from him. I imagined him furious at me for keeping it from him. I imagined him getting emotional, being elated, shrugging it off. But mostly, I imagined his anger. Because that seemed the most likely.

I was able to put it out of my mind when I went shopping with my mother, mostly because Mom was such a focused shopper, it was hard not to concentrate when she was in charge.

She swept into the formal section of Lord & Taylor like she owned it, and began picking up dresses – basically anything my size that was remotely pretty – then hustled me into the carpeted, big-mirrored dressing room and started pushing things at me.

I went in and out of the dressing room in dresses that were clinging and billowy, turquoise and ruby, sequined and embroidered, beautiful and . . . not so much.

Mom was ruthless and quick, ordering me in and out of things with such incredible speed, I actually felt like I was getting a workout.

Finally I tried on *the* one. I knew it the minute I shimmied into it. It was icy blue, with silver embroidery on the fitted bodice. It had a sweetheart neckline and a big, ballroom-style tulle skirt. It felt like it floated around me. It was big and kind of over-the-top, but I loved it, and Mom did, too.

'That's it,' she said decisively. 'Do you love it? I can tell from your face what you're going to say.'

'I love it.' I sighed, and I felt that dreamy happiness that only a really fabulous, completely extravagant princess-style ball gown can create in a girl.

'You can use your silver heels from Paris.' Mom took one more long look, then hurried me out of it, and helped me hang up the discards as she chattered. 'We're not going to find anything sexier here. But I'd like to look at some jewelry, too. Since it's strapless, you'll have a lot of open neck space. And we want something pretty for your hair. What are you thinking of doing to it?'

Mom and I chatted all the way to Cinnabon, where we got deliciously gooey buns and ate them giddily.

We were having such a good time I took a chance on talking to her about my Jake dilemma. Not with any actual details, of course. Mom had an ironclad memory, and I was never sure when something I said to her would come back to bite me in the ass.

'Mom, I have a problem.' I took another sticky bite of cinnamon bun.

She took a sip of her soda, wiped the sugar off her fingers and looked right at me. 'What is it, Bren?'

'I have a friend. And I know a big secret about him. One that could be really important. But it's not really my business to tell it. Only, I don't like keeping this secret from him. And the reason I can't tell . . .' And then it got too convoluted.

'Tell me, Bren.' Her voice was wise as an oracle's.

'The man Jake lives with isn't his real father, but he doesn't know it. His mother was pregnant with another guy's baby, and she married Jake's stepdad without telling him.' I took a deep breath. 'And Jake's real dad is also Saxon's.'

Mom was less surprised than I expected. 'They have the exact same frame.' She nodded. 'And their facial shape is the same. If it wasn't for their coloring, everyone would realize that they're related.'

It dawned on me that my mother was trained to see the lines and patterns that connected everything. I had never really noticed it because I was so close to the two of them.

'So Saxon is the one who told me, and their father told him. But Jake's been in the dark all this time. And he knows things are weird, but he can't figure it out. And I don't think his stepdad knows.'

'I doubt that, sweetie.' Mom took a long sip. 'Just because Jake's stepfather doesn't say anything doesn't mean he doesn't know. Lylee mentioned Jake's mother when we were in France. Apparently they all had reputations for being pretty wild, and they were both very young mothers. There was probably a lot more going on than anyone realizes.'

'Oh.' It was all I could think to say. I'd been thinking of this from the perspective of a friend or girlfriend. But I hadn't really wrapped my head around it as the problem of a son or daughter. Once that dawned on me, I realized that there was going to be more to the entire situation because parents always kept their kids in the dark about certain things in order to protect them. That's all there is to it.

By the time Mom and I were home that night, I didn't feel like calling Jake or Saxon. I unzipped the bag that hung on the back of my closet door, a long white bag that held my blue dress. I pressed my face to the soft tulle of the skirt and sighed. Like a girl. Long and contented. I was thrilled that I could appreciate small happinesses. Like the most incredible dress in the world.

My phone rang, and it took me a minute to fumble it out of my purse, so by the time I had it in my hand, there was no time to check and see who was calling.

'Hey, Bren!' It was Kelsie.

'Hey! I just got the most beautiful dress for Jake's prom. Please come over later and love it with me.' I pressed my face against it again.

'Omigod!' she squealed. 'Tell me what it looks like.'

Then Kelsie and I spent a good fifteen minutes talking about my fabulous dress, right down to the tiny crystal flower centers.

'I have to see it,' she said finally. 'Listen, it's so weird you got that dress, because I was calling about prom; Chris has this good friend whose date ditched him and he's, like, heartbroken. Anyway, he's had this little crush on you, and I was wondering if you might be willing to go with him? Please?'

'Um, when is it?' I felt a little nervous. Kelsie had a big heart. A big, big heart, and she tended to see people in their best light. Like a really creepy, moody guy could be, in Kelsie's eyes, a misunderstood sweetie. It was refreshing and admirable. Unless you

are the crushed-on blind date of said psycho/
sweetheart. 'And do I know this guy?'

'It's Nate. From the Folly show. Remember Nate?
And it's in three weeks.'

I did remember Nate, and I sighed with relief as I
called up the memory of him. A genuinely nice guy
with a lot of tattoos and facial metal. And, since Tech's
prom was in two weeks, I could go as long as Mom
said yes. Which she would, no question, since it was
technically 'dating other guys'. I grinned to myself
when I imagined her jaw drop over Nate's neck
tattoos.

'I'll ask Mom, but I'm almost sure it's a go. Can you
hang out later?' I know it was selfish and shallow, but
I wanted her to see my dress.

'Yes!' she cried. 'If your mom's cool with it, I can
come over Sunday.'

'Perfect.' Jake worked all day Sunday at Zinga's. I
would still get to see him after his short shift on
Saturday.

I went to find Mom when I got off of the phone and
ask about the other prom. She was practically bursting
with maternal pride.

'Two proms? That's wonderful, sweetie. It will be
so much fun for you!' She pursed her lips.

'What is it?' I asked.

'It's just . . . the dress.' She took a deep breath and sighed.

And I felt my heart sink a little. It was kind of a *ta-da* dress. Not really one I'd want to wear twice in two weeks. Or, more to the point, not one I'd want to wear in front of my friends and another guy and also for Jake.

'It would be crazy to buy another one,' I insisted, stifling Mom's eager, wide-eyed suggestion-to-be. 'Maybe I have something in my closet,' I suggested, though super-formal wear wasn't really something I had in abundance.

'Oh, I do!' Mom cried. 'I have something perfect! Come on.' She pulled me up to her room.

Mom and Thorsten's room was huge and airy. There was just the big white bed, two blond pine dressers and a big matching armoire that had their TV in it. Some of Mom's black and white pictures were hanging in silver frames. Most of them featured me.

She led me to the walk-in closet she and Thorsten shared; or, more appropriately, the big walk-in closet that she dominated. Thorsten had about a foot of space for his whole wardrobe, and Mom's stuff popped out everywhere else. She pawed through hangers, holding things out now and then and rubbing them appreciatively before she moved to the next thing. Mom was a little bit of a fashion fanatic, so she had a ton of great stuff. Finally she gave a happy shriek and pulled something out.

'Look, Bren. What do you think?'

It was perfect. It was a Mandarin style dress, form-fitting red silk with butterfly closures at the neck. It looked like it would fit.

'I love it.'

Before I knew it, Mom had stripped me down like I was six years old and had the dress wiggled over my head. It fell in a whoosh of fabric that rubbed against my skin like flower petals. She spun me round so that I was facing the mirror on the back of her door, and I took my own breath away.

The dress for Jake's prom was pure princess loveliness, but this dress was hot siren sexiness.

'You look incredible.' Mom gave me a quick, hard hug. 'I have the perfect black pearldrop earrings. I love it.'

Mom decided that the waist needed to be taken in a little, so she pinned me and then got me out of the dress and shooed me away so she could sew.

When I got back to my room, I caught my phone on the last ring.

'Hello,' I gasped.

Jake laughed, and I felt a low, sweet heat in my stomach. 'Hey, Bren. Were you running?'

'When I heard the phone.' I unzipped the bag over my dress and trailed my fingers over the tulle. 'Mom and I got a killer dress for the prom.'

'I can't wait to see you in it. What's the color?'

'Blue. Light blue.' Then I imagined a horrible fake blue-rose wrist corsage. 'That doesn't mean you have to get me a blue flower, you know.'

He laughed again. 'Don't worry. Nothing tacky, I promise.'

And I felt a tiny smidgen of guilt when I worried that he wouldn't know for sure if something was tacky or not.

'So, about prom . . .'

'Yeah?' I could hear him attempting to keep it cool, be calm, not jump to conclusions, but the remnants of the past few months still had our nerves scraped raw.

'Frankford's is a week after Tech's, and Nate, from Folly, his date just cancelled on him. Kelsie told him I didn't have a date . . .' I was not about to ask permission. But I was also letting him know. Getting the balance perfect wasn't easy, but I was working on it.

'Do you think seeing this wannabe rocker in a tux will make you fall in love? Or lust?' Jake's voice

was mostly joking, but there was a sliver of serious-
ness in it.

'Absolutely not. He's not remotely my type.
Though it *is* kind of sexy that he's in a band.'

'Did I ever tell you I played the flutophone when I
was in third grade? My music teacher said I had real
potential.'

'You never told me you rocked a plastic recorder!
Why did you give it up?' I inwardly cringed at the
memory of my entire class whistling shrilly on our toy
instruments. How had our music teachers been able to
stand it? Not to mention our parents.

'After I mastered "Mary Had a Little Lamb",
nothing else really inspired me. I think it was a mistake to put "Three Blind Mice" after "Mary".'

I laughed. 'So you traded your rock-star aspirations
and became a motocross freak?'

'Music didn't have enough danger for me.' Jake
chuckled. 'I might have to shake this Nate character
down before you go out with him. You're ridiculously
hot in everyday clothes. I don't really want to think
what you're going to do to this poor guy when you're
all dressed up.'

'No shakedowns. Nate's a nice guy, and I don't
want you freaking him out,' I warned. 'And you know
you can trust me.'

Jake didn't hesitate for a single beat. 'I know that.'

'Thank you.' I didn't have to say it, but I liked him to know that I did appreciate his willingness to trust me, even after I'd screwed up.

'No problem. So, can I see you tomorrow night? Or do you have a meet or a practise or something?'

I was technically part of the spring track team, but since distance was my thing, I didn't really shine, so it was easier to wriggle out of things like practise.

'I can get off. Do you have something particular in mind?' I fell back on my bed and listened for his voice.

'Nope.' I could hear his smile through the phone. 'Just a lot of you.'

'Sounds good.' I felt like I had to clamp my mouth shut to keep from blurting out the truth about his father. I just hated this last thing between us, especially since it was also a thing between me and Saxon. Again. 'Maybe we can go pick up a shirt and tie and shoes,' I suggested.

'And socks. I know you're picturing my big white tube socks.'

'You would look like a fool.' I was all serious now. He thought it was hilarious, but I really, really didn't.

'Bren, who the hell would be looking at my socks?' he asked, and he sounded serious, but I couldn't be sure.

'Jake, you can't have a fantastic suit and then ruin it like that.' I tried to stay calm.

'God, you get so serious about fashion. I better step up my wardrobe if I want to keep in your good graces.' I could hear for sure that he was kidding now.

I tried to put the issue of Jake's father out of my mind. He wasn't here, he wasn't part of Jake's life, and Jake didn't need him. So what was the point of getting all crazy about it? By the time we said goodnight, I was resolved to leave it alone, just like I had been leaving it alone without any problem all these months.

Chapter 20

The next two weeks flew by, and before I knew it, it was prom night. Mom had scheduled a hair appointment in the middle of the day on Friday. Tech had given us a half day, anyway. There was no point in trying to keep everyone around after lunch on the day of prom, so they just gave in and sanctioned the skips.

Mom and her stylist, Darlene, discussed my do over my head while I got a pedicure, which I had never had before and was heaven. Darlene desperately wanted to give me highlights, but my mother put her foot down and said no. They did agree on lots of curls and twists and they argued happily over hairpins. I also had my make-up done, and it looked good, like my version of sexy but heightened. By the time Mom and Darlene had finished their cappuccinos we barely had time to get back to the house and get the dress on.

I checked my reflection in the mirror under the

sun visor in Mom's car. I looked really beautiful. I imagined all of the girls in all of the schools across the country doing the same thing on prom night – looking at their reflections and seeing a more beautiful version of their everyday selves. Maybe that was why there was so much sex on prom night. Maybe it was just the byproduct of the heightened vision of ourselves that we got.

Before I could sort out the American teenage sexual motivation, we were home and Mom was hurrying me in. I almost had a heart attack when I heard tires crunch in the driveway since I was far from ready, but it was Thorsten. He'd left work early to see me off. And he'd picked me up a new memory card for my camera. Who could ask for a better dad?

Mom shooed him away and put the dress over my head, then slid the heels onto my feet, careful to maneuver around my French pedicure. She tweaked and pressed and pinched and then I was done.

And she was teary-eyed.

'Oh, Brenna.' She held my hands and pulled away to look at me. 'You look so beautiful.'

Then Thorsten came in and started snapping pictures until I heard the crunch of gravel again and knew that it was Jake. I felt my heart beat fast and my breath came quick.

Jake!

Mom and Thorsten went to get the door, and I peeked out of my room. He looked amazing. He looked like he should wear a suit every day. It fitted perfectly, and the brown was a great color on him. I had picked him an ivory dress shirt and a blue tie. He had new socks and new shoes, good Kenneth Cole shoes that were expensive, but Jake didn't even bat an eyelash. He'd promised he would put himself completely in my hands when it came to fashion.

Which was a smart move on Jake's part.

Mom was going wild, pulling at his jacket and oohing and aahing over the hand-stitched mother-of-pearl buttons and the real silk lining. Jake laughed good-naturedly.

I put on a last spray of perfume and some more lipstick, then double checked my reflection. I looked like I could have been at a ball for the French aristocracy, pre-Revolution. I took a deep breath and stepped out of my room.

'Holy shit.' Jake's mouth swung open. Mom and Thorsten looked at him in surprise. 'Sorry. Excuse me.' Jake turned bright red. 'But, seriously, wow. She looks amazing,' he said softly to them.

Which was sneaky and smart. Because Mom and Thorsten forgot that Jake just swore and got all teary over me. Then they placed us in front of the fireplace and took pictures, and moved us outside, in front of the azalea bushes, and snapped more.

'You look so beautiful,' Jake said softly against my ear.

'You look pretty great yourself.' I squeezed his hand. He smiled, then held up a cardboard box.

'Your corsage.'

And if I had to describe why Jake was so completely, unexpectedly perfect, I could have done it shallowly by explaining what was perfect about the corsage. It was a cream orchid with just a hint of bluish purple inside of it, just enough to echo my dress color. It was a wrist corsage, but he had asked that the florist put a ribbon over the rubber bracelet piece that holds it on your wrist. So when he slid it on, he could tie it and it looked gorgeous and old-fashioned and simple. And absolutely perfect.

I could have been easily talked into skipping the whole prom and just making out in his truck for a few hours, but Jake had no such deviant thoughts, at least that he was letting me know about. I kissed Mom and Thorsten, and we waved as Jake's truck pulled out.

'I'm excited. This is going to be a good night. I like your necklace,' he added.

It was the silver 'B' he'd given me for my birthday that fall. I replaced the black ribbon with one that matched my dress, and it looked great. And I had on my poesy ring, the one I didn't take off anymore.

'I'm excited, too.' I wasn't about to admit just how willing I had been, seconds before, to ditch the whole prom thing and just make out with him.

The place was a good half an hour away. Sussex County didn't offer many upscale venues, so we had to go to nearby rich Bergen to find a really nice banqueting hall. It was well worth the drive. The place was old and stately and gorgeous.

Jake pulled in and came around to open my door. He helped me out and then kissed me.

He put a hand on his chest and shook his head. 'I swear to God, you look so beautiful it makes my heart hurt.'

'Thank you.' I smiled and blushed, and smoothed my hands over my skirt. 'I'm glad you like it.'

'I love it.' He pulled me to him. 'I love you.'

His mouth moved over mine hungrily, and I felt his hands tighten at my waist like he was willing himself to keep them right there and not go roving. I smiled a little, realizing that he was just as eager to roll around in the truck as I was. Finally he pulled away, his mouth smudged with lipstick. I found a tissue in my purse and blotted his lips, then repaired my own in his rearview mirror.

'Ready?' I asked.

'Hell, yeah.' He folded his hand in mine. 'Let's go.'

The coolest thing about prom is seeing people you see a thousand times at school in their everyday clothes, but all decked out in their fanciest dresses and tuxes, dancing and going crazy. It's like an alternate reality that lasts just one night.

I didn't know the kids at Tech as well, but I knew enough people from hanging out with Jake that I was comfortable there. Jake was obviously really proud and wouldn't let go of my arm when we walked around and talked to everyone.

My heart jumped a little when I saw Nikki glaring from across the room. She was wearing a tight black halter dress. She looked really sexy and really pissed off. For a minute, I was nervous that Saxon had come to prom with her, but that thought passed pretty quickly. He told me that he and Nikki only hooked up once or twice after the breakup, before they both got bored and moved on. She was here now with some guy I vaguely remembered from a motocross race Jake had been in.

'Hey, Jake.' She made an attempt to brush past me. Jake pulled me next to him before she could.

'Hi, Nikki.' He was careful to keep his voice polite but uninterested. 'You know Brenna. My girlfriend,' he said pointedly.

'A bunch of us are going to the shore after prom. Wanna come?' She pushed her considerable cleavage toward him. She was completely ignoring the fact that I was there.

'No thanks,' he said and started to maneuver me away. 'Sorry,' he said in my ear.

And I tried to hold it together, because tonight was already great and Nikki was just a blip, and I had started everything when I broke up with Jake and threw myself into Saxon's arms, so I had no just cause to feel what I did.

But I felt it. My entire body went shaky.

Jake noticed, grabbed my hand in his, and led me outside, where there was a quaint garden, some fountains, koi-filled ponds, and the requisite gazebo decked with fairy lights.

'Are you all right?' He smoothed his hands over my arms.

I nodded and blinked back tears.

'Really?' He cupped my chin and looked into my eyes.

'It's just skanky to think that you . . . had sex with her.' I said it, even though I knew it was going to tear

435

through some of the night's romance.

'I wish I hadn't,' he said adamantly. He took his hands off my face and stuck them in his pockets. 'I wish you hadn't broken up with me.'

Maybe he wasn't blaming me, but maybe he was. I wasn't sure, and it didn't really matter after all.

'But it was different.' I felt like I should just stop talking about it, but I couldn't.

'I know.' His mouth was hard. 'You didn't have sex with Saxon.'

'No.' I shook my head. 'It's different because I cared about Saxon. I wouldn't have risked anything between you and me with someone I didn't care about.'

'You say that like what you did is better than what I did.' His eyes were a little angry.

'I guess I think it is. I wouldn't have done anything with Saxon unless I cared about him. I wouldn't just jump into bed with someone I didn't even have feelings for.'

Jake shook his head. 'Do you hear what you're saying, Bren? You cared about him. Probably care about him. Trust me, it's easiest if I just don't think about it too much. Sure, I had sex. And I regret it, I really do. But I can't care about anyone else. Sex with someone you don't care about is nothing. Literally less than nothing. But just having feelings for someone else, even if you never hold their hand, that's something.'

It was what Saxon had told me. That even if we never acted on it, just feeling what we did was an act of cheating because I wasn't being honest about my feelings with Jake.

Jake grabbed my hand and yanked me along the little stone path, over the bridge, up into the gazebo, away from the crowds, and sat me down on one of the little benches. 'What you did, it really broke my heart.' His voice was scratchy. 'And I understand why you did it. And at that time, I wanted you to understand how bad you hurt me, so I hurt you the only way I could.' He ran a hand through his hair in a gesture of frustration. 'I couldn't connect with someone like you and Saxon connected. I slept with Nikki because I couldn't open up to any other girl. I couldn't force myself to feel anything about another girl like I feel about you. There's only you, Brenna. I've been with so many girls and have never felt even a little bit of what I feel for you. So I'm sorry, but that's the only way I had to show what I felt. I don't expect you to completely understand.'

I did understand, as well as any virgin could. Because I had felt that lack of anything real when I had been physical with Saxon, but we hadn't pushed it that far. We hadn't actually had sex. Jake had. Again.

But he had been honest, and he had explained it to me the best way he knew how. So I tried to explain to him what I had done, the best way I could.

'What I felt for Saxon,' I said, then stopped. 'What I *feel* for Saxon is a kind of attraction, but it isn't love, Jake. I love you. And I do care about him. He is someone who I feel connected to. But I couldn't love him. Not even when I tried. It was always you. I never loved anyone the way I love you.'

He kissed me, and I could feel the relief like a sigh from his mouth. 'I love you, Brenna.' He kissed me again. 'And I'm glad we talked. But this is prom. It's supposed to be fun. So, let's go dance, all right?'

I followed him in because I wanted to repair the night and because he was excited and because I wanted to apologize and be apologized to. Those thoughts were all swirling around in my head, so I wasn't thinking too much about Jake being excited to dance.

But he did dance, and I was shocked at how good he was at it. I always had a feeling he might be a little bit of a natural, but he'd said he was too nervous to try. Something in him was completely, adorably unleashed, and he danced really well.

I hadn't danced like this since that night in Paris, and I thought for a minute about how odd it was that I was wearing the same silver heels again, this time to dance with Jake. But I didn't think about it too much. We danced to the fast songs, Jake drawing a cheering crowd around us. He had to take off his coat and roll up his shirtsleeves. I could feel the pins loosening from my hair and knew my professional make-up was probably a little runny, but we both kept dancing through the set, right until the first slow song. Jake didn't miss a beat.

I was in his arms and he was dancing me around the room with ten times more style than the other awkwardly swaying couples.

'Jake!' I cried. 'Where did you learn to dance like that?'

'È un segreto,' he said, pulling me in to kiss him.

'Italian? Dancing? What's going on? Are you trying to seduce me?' I asked, pulling away.

'Sì, amore mio.' He smiled. 'I learned to dance from the only person I could ask, other than you.'

I shook my head, unable to fathom who he could have asked.

'I asked Saxon, Bren.' He looked at me closely.

Jake always managed to shock me, but this was way beyond. I stopped cold on the dance floor, creating a sudden traffic jam, but I didn't care.

'What? Saxon? Why Saxon?' I felt nervous, though there was no real reason to feel that way.

'Do you remember the day I tried on my suit?' He gathered me back into his arms and moved me out of the way of the oncoming dancers.

'Yes,' I said, my voice soft. The day I wanted to tell him about his father. How could I forget it?

'And you knew about my dad. I could see it on your face.'

I stopped again, and now the other couples were starting to mutter with annoyance. It was just bad dance-floor etiquette on my part. Jake led me out of the ballroom, to the now-full gardens where our classmates were in various stages of full-on grinding and face-sucking. Jake led me to a more secluded section.

'I wanted to tell you,' I rushed. 'I really did. But I didn't think it was my right. It was Saxon who told me the whole thing. I didn't know what to do about it, Jake. I'm so sorry.'

He took my hands in his and kissed my knuckles. 'Don't be sorry. I get it. I get all of it. The truth is, I've known for a long time.'

'Why didn't you say anything?' I was blown away. Totally and completely at a loss. He'd known? All along?

He shrugged. 'How do you talk about something you're not even supposed to know? Also, who do I talk to about it? Saxon can't handle it. My real dad bailed, my mom is dead, and my stepdad probably already feels like he got dealt a pretty shitty hand, so why rub it in, you know?'

'You could have told me,' I said, not really sure if I wanted to hear why he hadn't told me.

'I thought about it. But when I thought about your situation, I figured you'd be the last person who I could tell about it. Once I knew about your real dad, it helped me let go.'

'Of what?' I moved closer to him on the little bench.

'Of this idea I had that there was someone out there who really loved me. God, that sounds so fucking sappy. But my mom, whatever crap Saxon says, my mom loved me. She was just kind of irresponsible. And my stepdad stepped up, but he can't love me, and I really don't blame him. So I had this idea that my real father would give a shit about me. Which makes no sense, since he never even bothered to admit I existed.'

'So you want to meet him?' I put an arm around his waist. He put his arm around my shoulder, and I leaned my head on his chest.

'I did. Then I met you. And I realized that everyone gets dealt a hand, and mine has been parentally shitty. But I think that maybe my crappy family luck got balanced out, since I got you.' He kissed my forehead.

I don't think anything anyone had ever said to me made me feel more loved in my entire life. 'You think I'm what you got because your mom died?' I could feel the tears in my throat.

'No. I mean, I don't think she had to die for me to get you. That would be insane. I'm saying that being with you helps me see that I don't need to have perfect parents. No one gets it all.' His fingers trailed up and down my shoulder and arm.

Then I thought about my great parents and Jake. And even Saxon. I felt a jarring sucker punch of guilt.

It was like Jake knew what I was thinking. 'Even you, Bren. Your real dad left you high and dry. But he made room for Thorsten, right? And who could be a better dad than he is?'

'That's true.' I craned my neck to look at Jake.

'And I want to tell you about the other girls, but don't get pissed off, OK?' I nodded wordlessly, and he took a deep breath. 'They didn't mean anything because they were just holding a place until you were there. But I didn't have much, as far as affection went. So a body to sleep next to and someone to hold for a little bit was a big deal for me.'

I realized how he must have gone virtually untouched. No mother to hug or hold or be near. A stepfather who was at best only resigned to his unfair fate as provider. Jake had been completely alone and those girls had offered him some comfort the only way he could get it.

I put both my arms around him, trying to make up for all of his lost opportunities. 'I'm here. I'll be with you.'

'I'm hoping you will.' He left a trail of kisses along my forehead.

'When did you figure it all out?' I squeezed him tighter.

He laughed a little. 'Saxon tried to tell me a couple of times when we were younger. Once he got out this huge-ass hunting knife.' He pulled his hand out and splayed his fingers out wide, pointing to the skin between his thumb and index finger. There was a long silvery scar there. 'He sliced our hands up and said we were blood brothers one night when we were just kids. His dad, our dad, I guess, had just left – not that he'd been around much before – and Saxon was kind of a basket case. Anyway, we fell asleep and I went through his wallet. The picture of the three of them was in there. I knew because my mom had a picture of him, too. She showed me it before she died. So I knew.'

'Are you mad? Or upset?' I looked at his face, but, as usual, it was serene and happy.

'No way. I'm lucky.' He pulled me up and kissed me hard.

'Does Saxon know? That you know?' I whispered.

'No. But it makes it all easier. For me to get a grasp on. I mean, he's my brother, right? So I can hate him and love him at the same time.' He rubbed his hand on my back in soothing little circles.

'I think he'd be happy if he knew you knew,' I said carefully.

Jake shrugged. 'I'll wait for him to tell me. Saxon's got a lot of hang-ups. And now that you and I are back together, it's gotta kill him a little.'

'I don't want to come between you and Saxon.' I sat up and looked Jake in the eye. 'You're brothers.'

He laughed, that soft, low sound that I loved. 'Bren, blood or not, you've been the best family I've ever had.'

I felt a lump in my throat. 'But I screwed up, big time.'

'Well, I can't really fault you.' He gave me an unreadable smile. 'I mean, you have good taste. And these genes must be irresistible to you.'

I laughed a little. 'Does it make it weirder for you? That Saxon's your brother and he and I—'

'I don't love it,' Jake cut in. 'But it makes it easier for me to understand what the hell you saw in his loser ass.' He paused. 'I'm guessing it's whatever you see in my loser ass.'

And we both laughed, and I finally felt good, light and happy. We went back inside and danced more and ate, and when Jake nudged me out way before the last dance, I was happy to follow. He had one of my mixes in the CD player in his truck, and it wasn't long before he found somewhere to park. I unbuckled my seatbelt and slid over to his side, kissing him excitedly.

'You look really beautiful tonight,' he said between kisses. 'Like Cinderella at the ball. No other girl looked half as pretty as you.'

'You look very hot yourself.' My fingers pried at his already loosened tie. I pulled it over his head and worked his buttons undone. I put my hands on the hot skin of his chest, then right over his beating heart. I laid my hair-sprayed, stiffly curled head over that pounding heart. The heart that I protected.

He kissed my sticky hair, moved lower and kissed my forehead, kissed my cheeks, my mouth, my neck. My big blue dress seemed to fill the entire interior of the cab.

'I love this dress. I love that you wore something so pretty just to come out and dance with me.' He batted away some of the never-ending length of tulle.

'I love you.' My voice was thick with the emotion

I felt. I loved him so much, my heart bucked in my chest.

Jake laid me down on the long, narrow bench seat and kissed every inch of skin that wasn't covered with shimmering blue fabric. Since that didn't include much of the top half, Jake moved down to the bottom section and kissed my ankles, bound in the silver straps of my shoes. He kissed along my calves, smooth from my extra vigilant pre-prom shave. He kissed up to my knees, which were strangely ticklish, then his head moved up farther, and I couldn't see anything but misty swaths of blue tulle. He pulled his lips off my inner thigh and said, 'Are you OK?'

I could feel the blood hammering in my head, and I had to swallow hard before I answered. 'Yes.' It was high-pitched and didn't sound exactly like my voice.

'If you don't want it . . . just tell me. OK?' His voice was low and quiet.

Maybe it was all the cloth between us, but I didn't feel nearly as nervous this time when Jake pulled my underwear down my hips, then over my knees, then around my shoes. His mouth was right at the inside of my thigh, right where the skin was soft and smooth and rarely ever touched. Then he kissed just a fraction higher. I sucked my breath in and felt my hips buck on their own, anticipating what was coming next. I bit my lip a little to contain all of the excitement that was bubbling in me.

'Are you OK?' he repeated, his voice calm and reassuring, a voice I could trust no matter what.

I told him I was, because as nervous as this made me, I was more curious about it, and I knew if there was one person on this earth I would be comfortable exploring my curiosity with, it was Jake Kelly.

'I've never done this,' Jake confessed suddenly, his face still obscured by all my dress.

'Never, um, gone down on a girl?' I felt my face pink just from saying it.

'Yes,' he said into the fabric. 'I wanted . . . I wanted my first time to be with you.'

'That's what I want, too.' I bit my bottom lip again as he rubbed his face against the inside of my leg, his breath hot on my thigh.

Then we stopped talking and his mouth was up higher than my inner thigh, and he kissed me where it seemed impossible that anyone would kiss and it felt incredibly better than I could have imagined, just his lips and me in this entire world. Everything we had ever done before had been just as perfect as I had imagined, but this was a different kind of excellent. I loved the way his mouth felt on me, warm and wet and insistent. His tongue drew along my skin and I wanted to scream out how good it felt. Then he licked quickly and I felt myself sinking into an oblivion that was only Jake's mouth and my body, laid out in front of him and waiting for him to do whatever he was going to do next. My mind went fuzzy. For a minute the reality of the cool night and the cab of the truck and Jake Kelly and his mouth all rushed back and I almost snapped out of it, but his tongue moved slowly and my mind blurred.

My hands dug at the leather of his truck seat. His hands were around my thighs, his fingers pressed into my skin. I could feel his hair brush against my leg as his mouth opened and pressed against me. There wasn't enough air for me to breathe, and once the air rushed back, I couldn't pull it into my lungs fast enough. Jake's kisses became rushed and needy, and after a minute or two it was just complete and total bliss. My body shook from it, and I half sat up, my teeth set against how good it felt.

I cried out in the space of the truck, alone, just me and Jake, the two of us happy and loved and loving, and I didn't know if it was possible that life could feel better. Ever. When I finally came back to reality, I was in Jake's arms. We sat together, silent and contented in the long, cool night until it was time for me to go back home, to go back to whatever normal life would be like after we had been so close.

Chapter 21

One week later, I was scheduled for another hair appointment. I thought it was crazy, but Mom said that since we didn't spend anything on the second prom dress, it was a deal. Only my mother would come up with that kind of insane logic and manage to trick me into believing it all the way to the salon.

In reality, I loved the time she and I spent together. It was fun to have her fuss over me and gossip with Darlene like we were all grown women. This time my toenails were bright red, to match my dress, and so were my fingernails. It seemed a shame since my French polishes were barely chipped, but Mom just rolled her eyes when I made that point.

This time Darlene went in the complete opposite direction with my hair. She pulled the flat iron through it until it was pin straight and so shiny it shone like glass. I was going to argue that I could have straightened it at home, but when Darlene finished, I realized that I could never have worked the wonders she did. She concocted some kind of magic mixture of creams and gels and brushes, and she had done it all with half an eye on my head, chatting ninety miles an hour to my mother.

When she was done, I was slack-jawed with shock. She combed a really deep side parting, and it made my whole face look different. Then she took out a red silk flower Mom brought and fixed it to a bobby pin that she slid in and reinforced with other pins so that it would hold for the entire night just over my ear. My make-up was smoky and sultry. It was all very prom-appropriate.

Back home, it felt a little like déjà vu. Mom got me into my dress and zipped me up, and I stepped into the same magic silver heels. Thorsten came in to snap pictures, and finally, I heard the crunch of tires in the driveway that sent my heart skipping.

Jake!

Jake was coming to see me off. He was glad I was going, in that resigned, he's-a-great-boyfriend-so-he's-not-going-to-worry-at-least-to-my-face way. When he got out of the truck, I was already outside to meet him. He whistled low and long.

'Holy hell, Bren.' He stood next to the truck, immobile. 'You look damn fine.'

I ran up to him as well as I could in my column of a dress. 'Do you like it? It was Mom's.'

'Damn you look hot!' He picked me up around the waist and spun me around easily. 'Now, I know this is only your second prom and all, so keep in mind, the way we ended our prom night was very unusual. That's not normally what happens.' He raised his eyebrows sternly.

'I know that,' I scoffed. 'It usually ends with sex on the beach, right?'

He swatted my butt affectionately. 'You're lucky you're cute.' He wrapped an arm around my waist and walked me in. 'So who's this guy again?'

'His name is Nate, and he's very nice.' I purposely failed to mention the 'little crush' part of the date.

'Is he single?' Jake's voice got a little low and mean.

'Yes,' I admitted. 'But he knows I'm with you.'

'I'm going to stare him down,' he warned. 'No contact, 'cos I'm not a psycho, but I am going to do a little eyeball intimidation.'

'No you're not.' I shook a warning finger at him. 'Or I'll dirty dance with him all night to spite your overprotective ass.'

'All right.' He sighed and pulled me aside for a few hurried kisses before we made it to the front door.

Thorsten and Mom said hello to Jake, and the atmosphere in the room was slightly uncomfortable. Mom's idea of me 'dating other guys' didn't involve Jake showing up beforehand. But I wanted him to see my dress and my hair. It was exciting, and I didn't like for him to miss it. After a minute of chatting with my parents, I told Mom that I wanted to show Jake some of the pictures I'd put together from Paris.

'OK.' She didn't really attempt to disguise her reluctance. 'Just remember, they'll be here soon. You don't want to hold the group up.'

'We'll be fast, Mom,' I promised, dragging Jake to my room.

Once we were in, he groaned a little. 'She hates me again?'

'She's always hated you to some degree. But she loves you now, too. It's complicated,' I said cheerfully. 'Look.' It was a big leather scrapbook. I had filled it with black pages and did all of the pictures in black and white with a white border around them. Then I had put them in with little tabs, just like old-fashioned photograph albums.

Jake sat next to me and we opened the book. It started with Jake's first group of pictures, plus the ones he'd taken but hadn't put up before I called him to break up.

'They look really good.' He traced a finger along the edges.

We looked at his pictures of me in all the places that he made me go that last day before Paris. Then there were some of the pictures I'd snapped when we landed: a coffee shop at the airport, some road signs in French with the countryside a blur behind them, the view from my dorm window, fresh bread stacked in the window of a baker's, a stray cat in front of a fancy iron grate.

Then there were Jake's angry pictures, including two of Nikki. Those two hurt the most, for me. She looked very posed, doing her pouty/kissy/seductive look. She was in Jake's room. In his room. That stung hard, but I didn't like to ignore things just because they kind of sucked. I had learned it was better to just face them, air them in the open.

But it still hurt to see them.

'Why would you have put those in?' Jake's voice was a little sharp.

'Because that's what happened when I was gone.' I glared at him. 'We're not pretending it didn't happen, so why not have the documented evidence?'

He flipped the page and there were pictures of Saxon, his tattooed back, him standing in front of my window before we went out.

We looked through the whole thing quietly, then he closed the book and we sat together for a long minute.

'When you broke up with me, I listened to *Ethan Frome*,' he said quietly.

'The recording I made for you?' What could make the most depressing book in the world even more depressing? Probably listening to a recording of your ex-girlfriend read it while she's getting it on with your brother. Geez, Jake really embraced the Wharton.

He nodded.

'Why would you have wanted to hear my voice then? You didn't even want to talk to me on the phone.' I twined my hand with his.

'I never didn't want to hear your voice.' He rubbed my hand with his thumb. 'And I did want to talk to you on the phone. But I felt bad that we'd split up, and I didn't want to give in to you until I'd had time to think it all through. You're *really* easy to give in to. Especially for me.'

'Did you like the book?'

'Yeah, I did.' He picked my hand up and examined the bright red polish on my fingernails. 'I mean, I felt bad for Ethan Frome. Like, what else was he supposed to do when he saw Mattie? I felt like I knew what he was feeling when he first saw her, because that's what I felt like the minute I first saw you.'

'Really?' I was surprised. We had never really talked about it too much.

'Oh yeah. Probably even more than Ethan felt, because I had seen a lot of good-looking girls, but when I saw you, it was like I knew you were something special.' He rubbed his neck self-consciously. 'And all my stupid decisions, those could have been my Zeena, you know. I thought about what it would have been like to not have the option to be with you.' He smiled at me, a slow, seductive smile that made me feel like shimmying out of my silk dress and into his arms. 'That was the minute I knew I'd never let you go completely. I thought you might need your own time to figure stuff out, but in the end, if I had any say in it, we'd be together.'

'So you don't want us to run our sled into a tree?' I attempted to be funny to keep my hammering heart from beating right out of my chest.

He laughed. 'No way. No sledding tragedies for us. And I'm glad you were smart enough to take me back.'

I laughed and grabbed him, and the two of us were wrapped around each other when Mom knocked, frowning a little.

'Kelsie and her friends are here.' She trained her laser eyes on Jake.

Jake pulled away from me reluctantly. 'Let's go,' he said with a strained smile, set on getting back in Mom's good graces despite the ultimate impossibility of it.

When we got to the kitchen, Kelsie squealed and made me turn around. She looked like an angel. Her dress was gathered ivory with sparkly beading all over it. She had curled her hair and done her own make-up, and she looked gorgeous. Her date, Chris, looked really handsome too. Nate came up to me with a plastic box. It had a red rose on a rubbery wrist band. I held my hand out so he could put it on my wrist, then kissed him on the cheek, pointedly ignoring Jake's withering glares. Nate looked nervous. Mom and Thorsten snapped pictures all the way to the door.

Jake walked out with our group and kissed me despite Mom's narrowed eyes. 'Have fun. Be careful.' He squeezed my hand tight.

'Don't worry.' I kissed him again. 'I'll call you when I get home.'

'I'll be up. You know that. No matter how late,' he added, as if he were always up late. Jake was one of those people who would go to bed before nine and wake up by six every day by choice.

We climbed into Chris's Volvo and waved goodbye. Nate smiled at me nervously. We chatted about Folly and school and people we mutually knew on the way there. Frankford's prom was held at a hall, not the same one as Tech's, but they were all kind of strangely familiar after you'd been to one.

We filed in and did the formal picture thing.

'Thanks for coming with me,' Nate said when he had his arms awkwardly around me. We smiled at the photographer, a bored-looking middle-aged lady.

'No problem.' We stepped down and went to our assigned table. 'It's fun to go to prom.'

'Well, it's really cool that you came with me.' He cleared his throat. 'And you look really pretty.'

'Thanks, Nate.' I smiled as reassuringly as I could. 'You look really nice. I like your tux.'

'Um, I can't really do the fast dance stuff, unless it's like moshing, but if you want to slow dance, we could do that.' He was cute in a metal-faced, neck-tattooed way.

We went out onto the dance floor and he put his hands at my hips, so I put mine at his neck and decided to have fun dancing like it was our eighth-grade dinner dance.

'So, is Saxon going to, like, beat my ass?' Nate's eyes made a nervous check of the room. Presumably for a sneak attack from Saxon.

I looked at him questioningly. 'Saxon isn't my

boyfriend, Nate. Jake is. The guy who was at my house.'

'Oh.' Nate's eyebrows pushed together for a minute. 'Just, ah, Saxon said that he was going to beat my ass. I don't really know him, so I figured it was because he found out you and I were, like, going. Even though it's not, you know, a date or anything.' There were a few beads of sweat on Nate's forehead.

I sighed. Between Jake glaring at him at my house and Saxon telling everyone that he was going to 'beat his ass', it would be no wonder if poor Nate was right at the edge of a heart attack.

'I don't know. I mean, about Saxon.' I looked him right in the eye and said firmly, 'Just ignore him. He tends to talk a lot. A lot more than he should, in fact.'

As if on cue, Saxon appeared next to Nate. 'Beat it, Nate. Or I really will beat your ass.'

'Excuse me.' We stopped dancing and Nate looked like he might faint. I glared at Saxon. 'I'm dancing this dance with Nate. I'd tell you to ask me again later, but I have a feeling that I'm not going to want to dance with you at all tonight.'

Saxon's eyes were black as pitch and sparkling with fury. 'Finish your damn dance, Nate. But she's not gonna give it up for you anyway. If you want a sure thing, I'll hook you up with Tara Jordan. She's

459

technically my date, but she's a little tipsy, so she'd be happy to be your date instead.'

'Saxon!' I cried.

But Nate's face looked eager. I rolled my eyes at him. 'It's cool, Brenna. Do you want to dance with Saxon?' He was already looking around for Tara. So much for sweet Nate.

'Whatever.' He was gone like a gundog on the scent.

Saxon grabbed me and pulled me close. 'C'mon, Blix, don't be pissed off. It was agony watching you march around with that goon. I had to cut in before I forked my own eyes out.' He spun me around and dipped me low. 'You look fucking hot.'

'Thanks,' I said flatly. I didn't return the compliment. I knew he already knew how good he looked. He was wearing all black: black suit, black shirt, black socks and shoes. The only break in the outfit was a red tie. Like he knew I'd be wearing a red dress. Everything he wore fitted perfectly and was expensive looking. He knew how to dress, that was for sure. I needed to get my mind off how good he looked quickly. 'So how did it work out with the Amazon?'

'What?' He looked totally confused.

'The girl. From the field hockey team?' I reminded him.

'Oh, her.' He smiled a smug smile. 'If you're asking if I screwed her, then yeah. And she's as athletic in bed as she is on the field.'

'Great. That's exactly what I wanted to know.' He tried to pull me closer, but I kept a little distance between us. 'Thanks.'

'But we're not an item.' He spun me neatly, and the momentum threw me right into his arms, nice and snug. 'Neither are Tara and I. So if you still want some action, my car's in the lot.'

'Just stop.' I stopped dancing and he pulled me back into his arms.

'Stop what?' He wrapped an arm around my waist.

'Stop this.' I pulled away from him. We were in the middle of the dance floor with two feet between us and couples moving awkwardly to avoid bumping into us.

'What do you want?' he asked, his black eyes bright.

'I want to be able to come to a prom and not be harassed by you.' When I saw the look of disgust on his face, I grabbed his hand. 'Really? You want to know what I want? I want to talk to you without all of this bullshit between us. I want to be able to have you as a friend.'

'Not fucking possible.' He stalked off the dance floor.

I followed him, because, as always, nothing felt finished with Saxon. 'Wait.'

'Why?' He threw his hands up. 'You can't imagine how sick I am of all of this, Brenna. All of this is just bullshit.'

'All of what? Prom?'

'You know exactly what I mean.' He closed the gap between us, stuck his face next to mine, and spoke low, for my ears alone. 'Not *prom*. My whole *fucking life*. It's bullshit.'

'Well, whose fault is that?' I pushed at his chest. 'You want what you can't have. You take whatever is the easiest thing you can reach. You let Jake go, you won't accept friendship with me; what do you expect?'

I had followed him all the way out to the foyer. He pulled me into an empty dining room, dark and quiet compared to the wild, music-filled ballroom.

'I have fucked things up beyond repair.' He pronounced each word deliberately and turned his back to me.

'What? What have you fucked up?' I put a hand on his shoulder and turned him toward me.

'You and me.' He ran a hand over the short, shiny hair of his mohawk.

'I'm here, right? I'm talking to you. I'm with you. I'll be your friend, if you want.'

'I do. And more.' He looked at me, his eyes begging.

'Well, learn to settle,' I snapped. 'That's all that bothers you in life? The one girl you were never compatible with doesn't want to be your girlfriend?'

'There's Jake, too.' He slumped into a chair.

'Jake's an understanding guy. Didn't you tell me that?' I sat in the chair next to his. 'I know you gave him dance lessons.'

He looked up in surprise. 'He told me that he'd kill me if I mentioned it.'

'Yeah, probably because he was embarrassed that he learned to dance from a dude.' I raised my eyebrows, waiting for him to answer back.

Saxon smiled, a tiny one at first, then wide across his entire face. 'How did he do?'

'He tore it up. A regular Fred Astaire.' I sighed and got a warm feeling low in my gut when I thought back on that night. 'We had a great time.'

'Yeah, well, he's pretty light on his feet for a guy,' Saxon said wryly. He shook a cigarette from the pack in his pocket and lit it.

'You're not allowed to smoke in here.' I pointed to the prominently displayed 'no smoking' sign in the room.

'I don't give a shit.' He blew a long lungful of smoke into the air.

463

'So, why would Jake have asked you for help if he didn't feel something other than hate for you?' I waved the smoke from his cigarette away from my face.

'All right.' He blew smoke out in a long stream. 'But when he finds out that I lied about us being brothers, he's going to hate my guts. I guarantee it. That's not the kind of shit you just get over, trust me, Blix.'

I grabbed his smoking hand, took his cigarette, and put it in my mouth. I lifted his hand, and pointed to the place where the long silver scar was, the same as Jake's. I took a drag and blew the smoke out. 'Tell me how you got this.'

He looked at me, shock robbing him of any ability to speak for a few long seconds. He finally sputtered, 'How the hell did you know I had this scar?'

I shrugged. 'Do you want me to tell you how you got it?'

'No one knows that. Unless Jake told you. But why would that old shit come up?' He took his cigarette back. 'You smoke like a fucking nerd.'

I grinned at him. 'I *am* a nerd. And Jake *did* tell me.'

'Why?' Saxon asked, and the look on his face was more anxiety than hope.

'Do you want to know? Or do you want things to just suck? Forever? Because as much as you bitch about being unhappy, you sure seem to do everything you can to stay that way.' I watched him take another drag.

'You're such a bitch, Brenna.' He pointed his cigarette at me. 'But you're damn sexy. That makes your incessant bitching easier to take.'

'And you're shitty company. I'm going back to the dance. You know, the big prom, full of people? People who are at least pretending to be happy and dancing and having fun. That sounds preferable to being here, in this smoky-ass room listening to you whine about how awful your life is.' I turned to leave, but Saxon grabbed my hand.

He pulled my wrist up to his lips and kissed it. 'Tell me what you know about my scar.'

'I know that you and Jake became blood brothers.' I leaned close to him. 'Because you wanted him to know that he was your brother, even if you didn't really have the guts to tell him. But it worked.'

'What do you mean?' He narrowed his eyes at me.

I shook my head at his dense inability to see the truth. 'He figured it out. He knows. He's always known.'

'Jesus Christ, isn't there anything you two haven't fucking blabbed to each other about?' he snapped. He crushed his cigarette onto a china plate on the table and stalked out.

465

I watched Saxon leave and felt a strange chill settle over my skin. I walked back into the midst of the big, happy gathering, but my heart wasn't in the dance. That changed when I saw Kelsie, who pulled me onto the dance floor, and made me forget Saxon's drama for a little while. We danced until we glistened with sweat and had to go to the bathrooms to put damp paper towels on our faces. I checked the hallways and the room Saxon had pulled me into, but he wasn't around. Before I could worry too much, the DJ played something that made Kelsie drag me back onto the dance floor, and we didn't stop for a second until the DJ took a break for dinner.

The meal was nice enough, but I couldn't really enjoy it, since I kept craning my neck, trying to catch a glance of Saxon's dark hair and all-black ensemble. I checked every table where any girl he'd chased in the last few weeks sat. It was an insanely long list, and I'm sure I forgot more than a few, but he was nowhere to be seen.

After dinner and a few more songs, I needed a break.

'Kelsie, I'm going to take a walk outside. Get some fresh air.' I put my lips close to her ear so she could hear me.

'Do you want company?' She fixed the flower in my hair absent-mindedly.

I did, but I could see her eyeing the dance floor. The lights had been dimmed, a slow song was playing, and Chris looked dapper in his tux.

'No thanks. I'll be back in a few minutes. I just need to cool off. Then more dancing?'

'Definitely!' She squeezed my arm, kissed my cheek, and floated across the dance floor and into Chris's waiting arms.

I went out into the open courtyard to breathe in some fresh air. I headed to the gazebo; this place had one just like the last place, complete with twinkling lights.

I climbed the springy wooden stairs and sat on one of the benches when I heard a scuffling noise beneath me. I leaned over the side and saw Saxon sitting in the mulch, a silver flask in his hand.

'Hey, beautiful,' he slurred. 'Woss going on?'

'Saxon, you're drunk.' I leaned over farther and he smiled a huge, dopey grin.

'You look pretty up there. Like some fiery goddess. Come on down, baby.' He waved at me clumsily. 'I got more here for you.'

I walked back down the steps, around to the back of the gazebo and squatted down in front of him. The smell of liquor coming off him was so strong it stung my eyes when he breathed out.

'Wanna sip?' he offered, waving the flask under my nose.

'No.' I took the flask out of his hand. 'I don't think you can drive. Did you drive?' He didn't answer. I shook his shoulder. 'Saxon, how did you get here?' I asked loudly, as if increased volume might push through his liquor-soaked brain.

'My fucking bike.' He laughed to himself. 'How d'ya think, Blix?'

'Well, can someone come and get you? Can someone come and drive you home?'

'Lylee is screwing her way across the Mediterranean,' he said slowly. 'And any friend I had, I screwed his girl. And girls don't count as friends. Oh, 'cept you, right, *buddy*?'

'Right.' I got a lump in my throat when I thought about the sad truth of Saxon's social life.

'Sit by me, Blix.' He patted the mulch next to him. 'Sit by your big fuck-up friend for a minute.'

I sat down next to him and put one arm around him. He leaned on my shoulder, then nestled his head against me and breathed in, a long, hard breath. 'You smell so fucking good.'

'You need to get out of here.' I was a little worried. I hadn't dealt with many drunk people, but Saxon seemed really far gone. I didn't know if he might have alcohol poisoning, and I wasn't sure how I was going to get him home. I didn't want to involve any more adults than we had to. It would suck if Saxon got suspended or in bigger trouble because of this. It might be all the excuse he needed to just up and quit everything.

I felt a warm, wet splotch on my collarbone and realized he was drooling happily, having fallen into a noisy sleep. What if he threw up and choked on it? I pulled my cell phone out and dialed quickly.

'Hey, baby,' Jake said. 'You're home early.'

'Jake, I'm at prom. But I need you. Can you come? Please?'

'Are you OK?' I heard him pick up his keys.

'I'm OK. I'm at the Lakeside. In Short Hills. Can you meet me behind the gazebo in the garden?'

'Yeah. I'll be there in fifteen minutes. Call right back if you need anything at all.'

Chapter 22

The sky got darker and quiet, and the only sound was the distant din of the music and cheering from the prom and the gentle snores from Saxon's half-open mouth. I adjusted him slightly because my arm was cramping and my shoulder ached. His head flopped loosely against me. Was he OK? I felt my throat tighten. Maybe I should slap him awake or get him some coffee.

I tried to nudge him up, but he didn't respond to my shakes and shoves. Then I heard the sound of footsteps running across the path.

Jake was there, looking confused. 'Bren?'

'He's really drunk.' My voice was thick with tears. I felt some of my worry subside at Jake's entrance. 'I didn't know what to do.'

Jake eased me up by the hand, letting Saxon slump over. He held me close for a minute. 'You did the right thing.' He kissed me. 'I'm here. I'll help him.'

'I don't think he can sleep alone.' I glanced at him, all loose-limbed and drooling. 'I don't know if he's all right.'

Jake crouched next to him. He slapped at his face a few times and Saxon's eyes slitted open. 'Piss off, brother,' Saxon croaked.

'Not a chance, asshole,' Jake said and smiled, then looked at me. 'I'm going to take him home, but I want to take you first. Can you get me someone to help move him to the truck?'

'Let me help,' I pleaded. 'I can carry half his weight. And I don't really want anyone else to know. I think he kind of wanted to get caught.'

Jake snorted. 'Sounds like Saxon.'

I heard Kelsie then. 'Brenna! There you are! What's going on?'

'Saxon got a little too drunk.' I waved my hand toward him. 'We're trying to get him out of here before any of the monitors notice, and he gets in serious trouble.'

Kelsie glanced down with her eyebrows drawn. 'Do you guys need help?'

'Thanks. I think Bren and I have it. I'm going to drop Bren at home if that's cool,' Jake answered.

'No problem,' Kelsie said. She made her way to my side and kissed me. 'Be good. Call me when you get a chance, OK?' She eyed the two guys with me uncertainly, and I promised to call, letting her know with a look that I'd fill her in on the whole story later.

Jake and I half carried, half dragged Saxon to Jake's truck and buckled him in, then cracked the window so the cold night air would blow on his face.

I sat in the middle, right next to Jake. He pulled onto the highway and put his arm around me. 'This was a nice surprise.' He kissed my hair.

'Are you being serious?' I asked, not sure if he was.

'Well, a drunk brother sucks, but it's nice to see you, especially the way you look tonight. I'm going to come out and say it: I was worried about you and that dress and all those drooling guys checking you out.' He leaned over and kissed my temple.

'Is he going to be OK, Jake?' I looked over, and Saxon's head flopped forward heavily, like he was a huge, punk ragdoll.

'No worries, Bren. I'm going to crash at Saxon's with him tonight. I'll drop him at his house, then drop you home, then I'll go back to him,' Jake promised.

'Should we chance leaving Saxon alone?' I asked nervously.

'It's only like ten minutes tops. So, other than Saxon pickling his liver, how was prom?'

'It was all right.' I shrugged and sighed. 'Nate

ditched me to try and skank Saxon's date. Saxon whined to me the whole night. Though we did dance a little.'

'Not a top-class prom experience like you had with Jake Kelly, huh?' He squeezed my shoulder gently.

'No.' I leaned against him. The middle seat only had a lap belt, so I didn't usually sit so close to him. But it was nice. 'I think Saxon is drunk because I kind of told him that you knew about the brother thing.'

Jake sighed, a long, tortured sound. 'Jesus, Bren. Can't you leave anything alone? I told you that he couldn't handle it,' he muttered, but he didn't sound very annoyed. Not really. I hoped.

'Are you pissed off at me?' I smoothed my hand over his leg.

'No. I knew you weren't going to be able to leave it all alone. It's fine, Bren. There just isn't any turning back at this point.' He kissed my hair. 'But I know you probably had our best interests at heart. Or whatever. You're a damn crazy woman.'

'Thanks,' I griped. We pulled into Saxon's dark driveway and got out of the truck. Jake and I each took one shoulder and dragged him into the house, through the fancy foyer and pretentious living room, down the long hall to his room. Which was immaculate. I didn't know if it was his doing or

473

Carmella's, but it was a vast improvement on the last time I had seen it.

We got the sheets back and hauled Saxon onto the bed. We turned him on his side. I took off his shoes and wrestled him out of his jacket and tie, then put the covers up around him and flopped next to Jake on the couch.

'Prom won't be over for a couple of hours.' He ran a finger along my cheek. 'Do you want to hang out here till you're due back?'

It was strange to be with Jake in Saxon's bedroom, but the night had been so weird in general, this just felt like one more insanity to add to a long list. I nestled into Jake's arms in the dim quiet of Saxon's room.

'I'm happy to stay here.'

Jake's mouth found mine quickly and definitively. 'I love you, Brenna. Whatever happens, know that.' He kissed my neck, flicking the woven butterfly clasps open with sure fingers.

His words made my spine stiffen. 'What's going to happen?' I asked, pulling away.

He pressed his lips to the jutting bones around my collar, exposed by the gaping red fabric. 'Nothing is,' he said, then moved his mouth lower. 'I just said it to say it.'

'You don't say anything just to say it.' I pulled his head back up. 'What did you mean by that?'

'Nothing, Bren.' But I knew he was trying too hard to move his hands and lips in a way that would make me forget or not pay any more attention.

'Tell me.' I pulled at his face, forcing him to look up at me.

'Nothing,' he repeated. 'Like I said, it was just something to say.'

'Jake!' He stopped, but he didn't lift his eyes to mine. 'Tell me.'

'Next year is senior year for me,' he said finally, his voice low.

'I know that.' I hadn't really thought about it much, mostly because it would mean that after next year Jake would move on while I stayed behind, still looking at one more year of school while he was free to do whatever he wanted.

Part of me really hoped he did something incredible, something that would prove to every person who had ever doubted that Jake Kelly would ever amount to anything that he could go beyond everyone's expectations. But a bigger part of me wanted, selfishly, Jake's presence and calming love all the time, all through my own senior year. I wanted him to put his life on hold and wait for me to catch up, and I also wanted him to wait for me to tell him what his next step should be.

Because I didn't trust that he could possibly know what to do next without me there to tell him. Not that I thought he was stupid. I just looked out for him in a way he couldn't even do for himself. He'd been taught how to survive from circumstances, but that didn't mean he could truly make good decisions for himself. He needed someone with perspective. Someone who believed in him. Who cared about him. He needed me. Or at least, I wanted him to.

'It's not like I have this incredibly bright future, Bren,' Jake said. 'I know no one expects much out of me. I see the way your mother looks at me.' His voice was hushed in the darkness.

'My mother is a fanatic about me. She looks down on everyone.' I felt panicked, and I wanted to convince him that whatever he was thinking wasn't really what he needed to be thinking. I wanted to talk him out of whatever it was he was planning, because I was so scared to let him go.

'I'm not an idiot, Brenna.' Jake wrapped his hand around mine. 'I haven't had many adults take an interest in me. I appreciate your mom's honesty. I really do. I don't have much going for me now, and she's upfront enough to realize it and call me out.'

'That's not true, Jake!' I cried, because I wanted badly for it to be not true, despite how I really felt.

'I'm not on your level, Bren.' He smiled, and it was so sad, it made my throat catch. 'I'm not ready to travel the world and go to college and make something of myself. I know I can stay right where I am and be fairly successful, in Sussex County, by Sussex County standards. But it's not really about money or financial success. I know that. If I want to keep you, I have to think about moving on.'

My eyes filled with tears. 'No you don't,' I said, my voice jumbled in panic. 'That's stupid, Jake. This is all based on what? A few looks from my mother? This is insane!'

'Bren,' Jake said gently. 'You know what I'm talking about. It's like you inviting me to Italy. I want it. I think. But it's so out of the realm of my reality. At least I thought it was.' He held his hands up then lowered them. Like he wanted to make his point, but he wasn't positive how to do it. I waited patiently for him to stitch his ideas together.

'You know, I went to the library and got the tapes and I learned some Italian. Like, I have a grasp on a foreign language. Then I got this image of myself as *that guy*, that guy who gets the tapes from the local library and learns it all, then goes back home to his dad's shitty lake house every night and does nothing about it. I'm not going to rot here, a guy with a whole lot of potential but no opportunities! I've seen that play out, and it's just depressing.'

'Then don't be. But that doesn't mean you have to leave! You can stay here and prove everyone wrong!' I put my hands on his cheeks and kissed him softly, then pulled away.

'I'm not planning anything just yet. But, after next year, I'm gone, Bren. I have to be. For you. If I want to keep you.' He moved a hand over my cheek. 'And I love you more than anything in this world, so I'll do it, even if it rips my heart out.'

'What if I'm not waiting for you when you come back?' I laid the ultimatum out, desperate. It was my last-ditch effort to convince him that he was a total psycho and his plan was pure bullshit. If I could, I would have dumped him just as a scare tactic. But I was way too chickenshit to try that again.

His hands shook a little, and when he looked up, his eyes were wild with pain. 'Then you were ready for better than me. I'm trying to prepare myself for that, because I think it's a real possibility. What's the chance that I'll get the opportunity to date you past high school?'

I hated that he was asking me that question, and I hated my own gut reaction to the idea of us dating past high school. No matter what I wanted, yearned for, the reality was just a logical fact, and I knew that the chances of staying happy with your high-school boyfriend were slim to none. But, despite the logic, I loved him so much, I wanted to defy the odds. With him.

'Why are you saying this?' I asked, my eyes singed hot and dry and my throat scratchy. 'Why are you bringing this up now?'

He let out a long breath, then put his head in his hands. When he looked up at me, his eyes were serious, too serious. He was going to tell me something I didn't want to hear at all.

'My father . . . my real father contacted me a few weeks ago,' Jake said slowly.

It took a full minute for the words to sink in. 'When?' I asked. I searched my mental database, scanning for a day when Jake had seemed particularly hurt or down or up or . . . anything. But I couldn't remember a single thing that seemed out of the ordinary.

'It was the beginning of the month,' Jake said. 'I got a letter, and there was a phone number. He wants me to call, to talk to him.'

'Have you called him?' I tried to shake the shock that grabbed me hard by the throat. He didn't tell me? Why did he keep it from me? Why would he have gone through something like that on his own?

'Not yet. His letter . . . it was a lot to take in.' He couldn't meet my eyes, and it was easy for me to see why. He was ashamed. 'He pretty much told me that he felt bad for never contacting me, that his family has a lot of money, and that he wants to give me a push in the world. Like, he wants to help me make something of myself.'

Make something of himself? Like Jake wasn't good enough exactly as he was? And where the hell had his father been for the last seventeen years of Jake's life? Hadn't Jake considered all of these things?

'Do you want his help?' I asked, careful to conceal the hurt in my voice.

'I've never had an offer like this.' Jake shrugged a little. 'I sort of want to tell him to fuck himself, you know?' I did know. That was the first thing I had expected Jake to tell his father. 'But I also feel like I want to take what he's holding out. How often do you get that kind of opportunity? And it might bring me to your level.'

I shook my head. 'Stop that! My level? Come on, this is stupid! You don't have to sell out to your scumbag father to be good enough for me! You're perfect the way you are. And you're a hard worker. Whatever you want, you can get it on your own.'

This time, when he laughed, it was bitter-sounding. 'Babe, it's just not that easy.'

'Why not?' I challenged. 'I believe in you. I know you can do whatever you want.'

'Damn it!' He ran his hands through his hair. He stood up and paced Saxon's enormous room. 'Yeah, I could do it! I guess. If I work my ass off and never catch a break and eat everyone's shit! I can take twice as long as I have to get what I want. Christ, I'm tired of busting my ass for every damn thing, and I've hardly started doing it yet! I'm seventeen years old, and I'm fucking tired! I don't want to look at my whole life doing the same damn thing. I want something to come fucking easy for once. Can't you understand that?'

'Nothing comes easy,' I countered.

He looked at me and bit his tongue. Because he was a gentleman. But I knew exactly what he was thinking: I had never had to face real hardship. I had never had to make the choice to bust my ass just to keep myself in clothes and food and a couple of luxuries. I had never once shown up anywhere and had anyone look down their nose at me. I had never had to think, *I'm not good enough to sit with this person. I'm not smart enough for this person.* I had lived a charmed life in so many ways. He hadn't.

'Everything comes easy to some people.' He didn't meet my eyes. He wasn't going to say it, wasn't going to call me out. 'I've never been one of those people, but I might be ready to be there.'

'You'll change,' I said weakly, feeling like a coward. If Jake felt like this was some kind of golden opportunity, I should be happy for him. Right?

'I need to do that anyway.' He grabbed my hand and rubbed it soothingly. 'I'll still be me. I'll still be Jake.'

I shook my head. 'How can you say that? How do I know that for sure? It's a big gamble, right?'

'Maybe.' He leaned over and kissed me softly. 'I have nothing to lose. I feel like I might have to take it.'

We sat in the cold quiet of Saxon's room.

'If this isn't happening until next year, why did you bring it up?' I knew I was fishing for some more news I didn't want.

He leaned his head back on the couch and looked up at the ceiling.

'You're going to get that place at the workshop in Ireland this summer.'

'Maybe. There are probably a lot of applicants.' But I had a good feeling that I would get it. Was that just another aspect of my charmed life? That I could just expect good things to land in my lap?

'You're going to get it,' he repeated, looking up at Saxon's ceiling. 'And I'm going to pick fucking fruit at Zinga's like some damn migrant worker.'

'You work hard, Jake. It's honest work,' I argued.

'My dad invited me to go see him. At his family's place.' He looked at me out of the corner of his eye. 'They're in New York. I was thinking of going.'

'How's your . . . stepdad going to take this?' I asked.

Jake shrugged. 'I know you have a hard time believing this, Bren, but he'll probably be relieved not to have to worry about me all of the time.'

'He cares about you,' I countered.

He shook his head. 'He feels responsible for me. If he knew my father was around, I think he'd want me to go with him. At least for a while.'

'I think you're wrong.' I felt petulant and uneasy.

He shrugged again. 'I might be.' But his tone of voice said that he didn't think he was.

'This sucks.' I twisted my hands in my lap.

'It's not perfect,' Jake said, then sat up. 'But I've never had a chance like this before.'

'I know.' I hung my head. 'I'm being a bitch not telling you to just go for it.'

'You're not.' He grabbed my hands and kissed them. 'I know you want to protect me. But my father isn't going to change what we have. I know you probably think I'm crazy, but what I feel for you is real. It isn't going away, no matter what happens with my dad. I love you so much, Brenna. I love you more than anything.'

'I love you, too, Jake. I love you no matter what.'

And, right there, I knew that if I was going to lose Jake, he was already gone. There was nothing I could do but let this all play out and trust that fate would bring the best. In the bright moonlight, with Saxon snoring lightly behind us, while I was wearing this red silk dress that had made Jake's eyes widen with want, I pulled Jake's mouth onto mine and tried to imprint the taste and smell and feel of him. Just in case fate really did the unfathomable and tore him away. I wanted a solid memory of Jake Kelly, *my* Jake Kelly, uncorrupted, full of love for me, pining, wanting, just about to burst out of his shell, but not quite there. Yet.

Acknowledgements

First and foremost, I want to thank my strong, smart, fierce mother. Her maniacal faith in my ability to do absolutely anything is sometimes overwhelming and always encouraging, especially when I start and I get the urge to curl into fetal position and eat massive amounts of comfort pudding. I give her all the love and respect in the world.

And thanks to my baby sister, Katie, who never pulled a single punch in her young mean life. Especially the day she ripped that 'Do you want to be a writer?' leaflet from an Avon novel back when we were in high school, raised her perfect eyebrow, and stuffed the page in my hand with a single fateful remark: 'You could write a better book than this, so you should.'

I want to thank my brothers Jack and Zachary for supporting me even if they act like books will burn them if they hold them for too long. Thank you to my 'baby' sisters Jessica, Jillian, and Jamie, who make me laugh and remind me of what it was like to grow up in NJ. Thanks to my dad, who constantly calls and updates me on any book/writing/publishing news he hears on NPR. I'd like to thank my grandparents for calling me and nagging me to get my work out there or just generally encouraging me so I could make some money and stop mooching off them. But also, of course, because they love me and think I'm a decent writer. Thank you to all my family who have cheered me on and believed in me, no matter how obnoxiously lost in my own fictional world I've been. I want to thank those friends who inspired the friendships in this book and still warm my cockles: Ronan, Jessie, Kimmy, Liz, Jesse, Aaron, Ellen, Lou, Fran, Frank, Chloe, Elisa, Lauren, Biffy, Holly, Jen K . . .

An unimaginably huge debt of thanks goes out to the long line of teachers who loved and nourished my voracious little reader-mind: Mr. Post, Mrs Schroth, Mr Flynn, Mrs White, Ms Mattil, Ms Hassenplug, Mr Bauer. Every single one of you swept me up in reading and inspired me to write more – or less, if I was being too longwinded. Thank you for your red pens, your passion for words and your patience with my sometimes irritating exuberance.

I could not have done this without my incredible friend, Alexa Offenhauer. She untangled my crazy sentences, updated my 90s era fashion nightmares, and rooted for the book with her entire, brilliant heart from day one. A ginormous thanks also goes out to the hugely talented YA authors Caryn Caldwell and Angie Stanton for being so sweet but firm as critiquers, and lovely and inspiring as writers, loooong email exchangers, and friends. We need one-on-one drinks together pronto, ladies! Tamar Goetke for reluctantly embracing her inner teen and being my meanest beta, and who shames me by reading and proofing my work while managing to be the most amazing mommy/wife/daughter/friend and make delicious treats to fortify me. Thank you to Brittany Hansen for her uncontrolled squeals of girlish delight. I tucked them in my head for ear cleanings and to give me happy courage when I just wanted to sink into a bottomless pit and stop this writing madness. I want to thank Courtney Kelsch for understanding more than anyone this particular romance in this particular place and reminding me of why it's an important story to tell (while also reminding me not to mix my verb tenses). Thank you to Elisa Keller for being my woman-to-go-to when I need to know where apostrophes go or do not go in area landmarks, and for diving headfirst into the quirky romance of my bungling teens-in-love. I want to thank the friends I've met or connected with in a new way since my books came out. So many people popped up to help me, support me, offer me a good laugh, and make me feel generally amazing, and I appreciate every comment, encouraging word and hilarious video link! Thank you to Dr Holly Kuzmiak-Ngiam for always having a sweetie-pie comment at the ready and kindly offering to help me make spreadsheets to organize my insanity. I can't thank the online book blogging community enough! So many people said so many nice things and helped spread the word just because they love books and reading. Thank you to the other YA indie writers who are busy and brilliant and hard-working, but still took time to email me, befriend me, and assure me that I'm part of one of the most amazing groups of creative people out there!

Unbelievable thanks to my editors, Carmen McCullough and Julia Bruce who combed every last line of the Brenna books and kept me on my toes. Your diligence and dedication are very much appreciated! Huge thanks to the lovely Lauren Abramo, who helped me through every single detail with such patience and grace . . . I am bowled over by her constant good cheer and professionalism. To the awesome cover designer, Rachel Lawston, who truly made the series pop with your incredible interpretation of the gang, an overwhelmed thank you! Seeing my characters through someone else's artistic vision is an incredibly gorgeous thing!

Last, but never least, thank you to my girl, Amelia, who I hope grows up crazier and more amazing than any girl I could imagine in any book . . . but not too fast. And a big, wet, sloppy thank you to my husband, Frank, my love, my best friend and the coolest guy I've ever known. His awesomeness has inspired some great fictional romance.

And a huge thank you to my readers! I love hearing from you! I love knowing you have songs that go along with my books and that you've already cast the Brenna Blixen movies! I hope Brenna, Jake and Saxon meant as much to you as they do to me. Anytime you want to drop a line, send me an email at lizreinhardtwrites@gmail.com.

Love to you all!

Turn up the heat with Liz Reinhardt . . .

DOUBLE CLUTCH

The First Brenna Blixen Novel

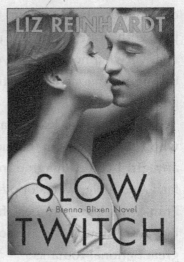

SLOW TWITCH

A Brenna Blixen Novel

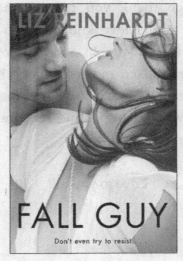

FALL GUY

Don't even try to resist . . .